the geometry of love

I Gareth,

Diolch am dy

gef nogaeth –

mwynha! . . . . . .

Cariad,

J e
x

Dedicated to:
My dearest friend, Amanda

Thanks to:
Jeremy, Norman, Beverly, Roger and Kim for all their talent, patience and hard work

the geometry of love

jane blank

y Lolfa

Cover illustration: Beverly-Jên
Cover design: Y Lolfa

ISBN: 9781847710390

Printed on acid-free and partly recycled paper
and published and bound in Wales by
Y Lolfa Cyf., Talybont, Ceredigion SY24 5AP
e-mail ylolfa@ylolfa.com
website www.ylolfa.com
tel (01970) 832 304
fax 832 782

CONSEQUENCES

MUSIC WAS PLAYING: THAT cor-anglais pipe weaving 'figures-of-eight' in the air; music to charm snakes. The food cartons were still on the table, and in the corner the television played silently to itself, running close-ups of weeping women's faces; men pointing guns and moving emphatic lips.

He had changed. Now he was wearing his real clothes: the white cheese cloth top; the loose trousers. Both suited his muscular body. As he danced I could not take my eyes off him. It was the even quality of his skin; the fact of it stretched tight over muscle and bone.

He made me pant. Breathing was hardly possible, my stomach too excited, guts tense as a fist around a fish. Each time he lifted his eyes to catch mine I felt my muscles contract, small flicks that made me shift on the chair.

He stopped dancing for a moment and smiled that Marlon Brando smile he had; came towards me. I closed my eyes, felt his fingers lightly on my neck, in my hair. With a downward stroke he took the elastic band from me and the hair dropped, settled itself. He stood back very slowly, and watched.

I got up, moving in slow motion like a figure in a dream and shook out my hair, eased down my dress, first one strap, then the other.

Breasts. I held them, one each in the palm of my hands, squeezing gently, rhythmically. I undid the bow at one side of the bikini bottoms and they hung open; then the other side and the flap at the front fell away. I reached behind and pulled them from between my legs, I didn't want to spoil his view.

But even as I turned and made my way down the corridor towards their bedroom, his eyes on my backside, there was a hard place in the back of my mind. A knot, no bigger than an acorn or a nutmeg kernel that would not dissolve.

No!

I watched him from the bed, light from the open doorway finding only half his face; the other was a black half-mask. This eye looked at me, its white shining in the gloom; watched me, was hidden as he pulled off his shirt without undoing the buttons. He stood motionless again. In moving he had shifted the shaft of light which was now across his belly, his chest, his neck and mouth. Now both his eyes were hidden. His breath came deep, raising the hard, convex belly covered in dark hair. I watched it rise from his trouser line in a dense fan, beautifully symmetrical. A thick line joined this hair with that on his chest. I had never had a man before, only boys.

As he slid his hands the length of his body to ease down the trousers, I turned away. Just for a moment the shriek of protest again, an owl's cry in the night.

No!

I turned and crawled away from him across the bed, heard his moving, felt the mattress shudder to his weight. But he took my ankles in his hands, the fingers meeting all the way around them, and pulled hard. My elbows buckled and I was dragged on my front, the sheets rucking up under me, all the length of the bed.

I buried my face in the musty covers, hardly breathing, and opened my legs.

At last there was light instead of darkness beyond the square of window. Only light, no other point of reference, as this room was twelve storeys up.

He took me by the hand to the bathroom and washed me, taking particular care between the legs, working to a lather as I sat on the bidet. He soaped me again and again, rinsing with warm water from the glass jug. I sat quietly, legs open, head back, hands holding tight the bidet's rim. When he'd finished he took a towel and bunched it between my legs, pressing, pressing.

Afterwards I bent to clean my teeth, and he stood leaning against me, looking at my face in the mirror. I cleaned meticulously, showing him everything. Moisture seeped from me. Only in the tiny acorn-place did I care.

We went back to the bedroom. I lay back on the bed and opened myself for him again, but he carried on dressing. As each part of his body was covered it was as if another light went out in me. He left the room, returned with my clothes. Tears were on my cheeks. He took my hands, pulled me up, and I stood like a rag doll, swaying slightly as he bent to fit my pants, pushing apart my thighs to place the double triangle of material, kneeling by me to tie up first one side, then the other. I lifted up my arms as he pulled my dress on and brushed and brushed my hair, oil from his stroking hand smoothing down the dry strands.

But I couldn't eat what he made for me, the smell of last night's takeaway was sickening. The television, left on from the previous night, played different sorts of pictures now, the bright colours of morning: things to sell, a chat show, a children's programme. I turned it off. He ate a peach; I watched.

I couldn't speak. He asked me questions in his strange English, and I replied with a nod, a shake. It was as if to speak would break something.

He took the car keys and we left the flat. Only then did I think of Miranda.

CHAPTER ONE

KNOWING MIRANDA BEGAN WITH my mother. I'd heard about her long before I saw her, as Mum taught in the school I went to, and Miranda was in her class and a year older than me, which was a lot then.

Mum was sitting at her desk one day, with all the children lined up to give in their homework and Miranda's ("A big girl, all teeth, tossing back her hair") turn came. "And where's your homework, Miranda?" says my mother.

"My Mummy says…"

"Don't you Mummy ME!" and the begging note from her mother is crumpled up and lands twenty five yards away (so the story goes) in the bin.

"There was a gasp from the class," says my mother, "but she brought her finished work in to me the following morning."

Miranda was no bully, well not in the common way. In the beginning she was in the fourth year, me the third, and I had always known of her, since my first week as a new kid in the school. She was a natural V.I.P in the way some children are. Not that she was popular. You just noticed her. There was always some rumour about her, always someone whispering behind their hand after she'd passed. And she was never picked on, even though she was usually alone. She looked like a girl in a boarding school story, tossing her long, wiry hair when she walked and looking neither to left or right as she strode the corridors, the only person in the whole of Upper School to wear the optional blazer.

On the day that was to change my life, she called to me out of the music room window: "Sue Jones, wait for me, I want to tell you something."

'Oh no!' I panicked, 'weird Miranda!'

Even the teachers talked about her. They said 'Miraaanda' and rolled their eyeballs. Just the gesture was enough.

I buttoned my coat up fast and tried to make it down the steps before she'd call me again.

"Hey, you're Mrs Jones's daughter. I'm in her class. Are you walking home?"

"Yeeeeess," I called up, guardedly.

"I don't live within walking distance. I should go to High Bridge actually but Mummy sent me to Silverhill Church Of England School and then to Abbeymoor."

"Oh," I said. We were attracting a lot of unwelcome attention by now with her shouting down from the window. Actually, anything Miranda did attracted attention; if you had any sense you'd give her a wide berth.

"Where do you live then?" she bawled down.

"Abbeymoor Road," I replied in a stage whisper.

"Is it a detached house?"

"Yes."

"Oh, I go past there." No she didn't, it was miles out of her way! She didn't even go out through this gate. "Wait on, I'm coming down," she said, and her head disappeared inside. Sandra and Louise were coming down the steps, staring at me. "Wa'n't that Miranda?" Louise asked. I nodded my head grimly. "Didn't know you knew 'er," Sandra said, looking impressed. Any hope I'd had of escaping before Miranda could come down vanished as she appeared in the doorway, waving energetically and smiling her wide smile. Sandra and Louise took one look and scarpered.

"Toodle-oo," she called after them.

"Are they your friends?" she said. I nodded. "I don't see you round with them much. You're usually on your own. Anyway I live on Abbeymoor Road too, at the bottom, by Steelers Rest," she said. "We could walk home regularly if you like." I didn't answer. It wasn't that I wanted to insult her or anything. I was just too dismayed to speak.

"Does your mum give you a lift?" she said, looking curiously at me from around her hair.

"Sometimes. Not today," I said. "She's part time." I was moving fast, but she was easily keeping up with me.

We walked on, Miranda talking excitedly and asking questions, which I answered in monosyllables. We walked down past the smallish detached houses, each one different from its neighbour; past the big converted mill, past the strange, smoke-blackened semis, past the flats and to the main road. We crossed onto the traffic island.

As we stood there, engines snarling in front and behind us, and the bigger lorries throwing our hair about, Miranda reached for my arm and tucked it in hers. I pretended not to notice until we got across the road. Here cherry trees were a partial screen from the traffic. Here too, each house was different from its neighbour, though many had a mock Tudor feel. I managed to get my hand away from her grip by pretending to sneeze.

"What does your father do?" she asked as we walked on.

"He's a doctor," I said.

"What sort? Is he a GP?"

"No. He's an eminent Neurologist."

"Oooooh! Where does he work?" she said, stopping and staring.

"Victoria Hospital."

She had come to a halt and was swinging her bag, legs open, arcing her bag through them, forward and back like a swing boat in a fair.

"My father's a choreographer. He's married to an Algerian woman, and they live in Paris," she said, exaggeratedly casual, looking down at her feet, then quickly glancing at me, probably looking for a big reaction. I tried not to oblige.

"Do you see him often?" I asked casually, picking a bit of fluff off my coat.

"No."

"Oh. I'm sorry. Would you like to see more of him?"

"Of course I would, don't be daft!" She hoisted her bag onto her shoulder again and started off. I had to jog to keep up with her until she arrived at my gate and loitered, fingers on the latch, one eye on the front door. It was unnerving to think that she now knew exactly where I lived.

"I mean, it's not your fault for being so thoughtless, but how would you like it?" she said.

"I don't know. How do I know what it's like?"

"You can use your imagination, can't you? My dad left my mum when I was three." I was out of my depth. Divorce was quite rare in our school then and gave any children who'd suffered it huge kudos. In Miranda's case, not only was there separation but also abandonment and her father a glamorous Frenchman as well! She was suddenly interesting to me, like a character in a novel,

"And you haven't seen him since?" I asked.

"No."

She was looking down, scuffing up a bit of moss with her boot. I couldn't see her face. "Um, have you got any brothers or sisters?"

I asked at last.

"No," she said. "Well, yes. I've got half siblings you know. Half Algerians."

"Oh. I've got a younger sister and a big brother."

"I know." She still hadn't looked up.

"Anyway, how did you know where I lived?" She didn't answer, just smiled slightly under her hair and moved her hand again to the latch.

"Well, I'd better be going, now," I said quickly. "I've got my cello lesson at half past, and I could do with a drink or to eat something before I get going."

It was strange: here I was, me, who tried to keep her head down, hide her ugly face behind her hair, talking quite fluently with notorious Miranda. I was keeping my end up, I was talking back. And yet there was something unhealthy about her. It wasn't just the direct way she spoke. More the closeness she kept to you – finding opportunities to touch me and my things; standing too close, putting her hand on my gate.

By now she'd peeled quite a lot of moss off with her boot, and it was lying upside down in soily lumps on the drive. "My bag's heavy," she said, looking at me intently.

"I expect you get a lot of homework in the fourth year."

"Yes. Especially in the top sets. I'm in set two."

"Oh, right," (I was in set three).

"It's the best one to be in actually, because you're still a high flier but you don't get the pressure."

"Yeah, I suppose so. We have a real laugh in our class. Some of the boys are really good fun," I said.

"You have to get yourself organised in set two, particularly now it's O level year. Nobody does any CSEs in set two."

"No they don't in set three either."

"I'm doing ten O levels," she said.

"So am I."

"How do you know? You don't know yet. I don't expect you've even picked your options." She had an adult way of questioning: keeping her face very still, looking you straight in the eye. I hated it.

"Well," I said defensively, "I haven't filled in the forms but I know what I'm doing."

"I'm into languages. I've got a natural capacity for them, probably because my father's French."

"Can your mother speak French?" I asked.

"Oh yes. She's a natural linguist."

"Mum speaks Welsh."

"Does she! I thought she had a strange way of speaking. It's a funny accent, Welsh."

"It sounds a bit like Pakistani actually. At least it does when people who can't speak it try to say things," I laughed.

"It's not that thick though, is it? When we stopped in Wales once they were speaking it so thick that I couldn't understand a word of it. They can switch it off though, and speak so that you can understand them."

"Are you sure they weren't speaking Welsh, Miranda?"

"Yes. I couldn't understand them, their accents were that thick!"

"No." Suddenly it was me with all the answers, I liked it; "were they speaking a different language?"

"They might as well have been!"

"That's not an accent, they were speaking Welsh! It's a separate language." There was a pause in which we each looked at the other, straight on, for the first time. She was taller and broader than me, the effect enhanced by all the hair.

"Oh. Well you'd better be getting in then, I'll see you," she said coldly. She was humiliated, picked up her bag and set her mouth in the self-conscious way you do when you're embarrassed. Then she turned and walked away; her steps bigger than they needed to be, swinging her hair deliberately from side to side.

"Hang on a minute!" I shouted after her. I hated people leaving like that, hated feeling guilty. "Er, do you want to come in for a bit, put your bag down?"

"Yeah, okay," she said. The teeth, overwhelming in a sudden big smile as she turned and came back towards me, made me nervous, made me realise my mistake. Okay, she was half French and in the fourth year with divorced parents, but she was still the legendary 'Weird Miranda'.

What would Mum say when she came home? Miranda'd be all over her, poking into everything, saying stupid things: there'd be a spy in the house.

"Hang on, maybe it'd be better some other time … 'cause of my cello lesson," I said, quickly.

"Yes, good idea," she smiled. "There's a bus due now anyway. Yeah I'll come round tomorrow or Thursday when you're free, and we can spend a couple of hours then. I'll bring my viola. We can get another violinist and form an official quartet." She paused. I stood, dumb. "We could meet regularly, at your house. Your Mum teaches tomorrow."

I shook myself. "I think so."

"She does. She has us."

"Oh, right."

"Maybe we can get a lift home?" she said.

"Yes. Well, I've got to go. See you." I turned away in horror and made for the front door, the nearest. As the heavy porch door clunked shut I had a horrible feeling, a physical feeling almost, of dread. No one had ever singled me out before: I was a middle child, had never had a boyfriend and had never been any girl's best friend. For the first time I felt I had come suddenly into focus, like an ant under a magnifying glass; like a wolf in a gun's sights.

"…and there they were," said my mother, "all lined up. I had them lined up properly every lesson by my desk to give their homework in. Anyway, here comes Madam, blinking her eyelids at me and tossing her hair around.

'I haven't brought it, Mrs Jones and my mummy says…'

'Don't you mummy me!' I said, and I got the note, screwed it into a ball and threw it half way across the room, bang into the bin. 'Cor, you ain't 'alf got a temper, and a bloody good aim as well,' said Arabella Tolstoy, a great big fat girl. I sorted her out."

"Who, Arabella Tolstoy?" I asked.

"No, Miranda," said my mother. "There was a gasp from the line, but she brought her completed work in next day."

"What was in the note, Mum?"

"I don't know! Some poor excuse. They need to learn. I don't mess about with them, oh no. Her bloody mother's useless. Never comes to Parents' Meetings. Sometimes the girl doesn't even have the money for her materials."

"But I thought she was well off! She always looks like a girls'-school girl!"

"Oh no. Her mother's on her own. Father left them. No, she's subsidised for all types of thing. Very poor her home life is." She bashed the mixture around emphatically.

"Can I have a go?" I said, looking to change the subject in case my mother, fired by teacher-zeal decided to re-run the whole incident again. We were preparing for the quartet rehearsal Miranda had organised, and my mother was stirring the hell out of some cake mixture.

"Well all right, but don't break my bowl. It was my mother's."

I swirled the mixture round vigorously for a bit, it was harder work than it looked. Meanwhile Mum was sifting icing sugar and coca powder into a smaller bowl. However grim and embarrassing this practice was going to be, at least I was going to get a cake out of it.

"How is it that you've got friends with that Miranda Dupont anyway?" she said after a while. For some reason my mum always called my friends by their full names, Christian and surname, even if she hadn't taught them. If she really didn't approve she preceded their names with 'that'.

"Aren't you pleased, Mum? I thought you'd like her. She works like a maniac and always wears her blazer."

"She's an odd girl, very odd. For goodness sake, give it to me." She snatched the bowl and spoon back and started beating it around again. It was already done, but she had to have the last word.

"I thought you'd like me being friends with her, Mum."

Though that wasn't strictly true. I had an instinct that my parents wouldn't trust her but couldn't really put my finger on a reason. Maybe it was the fact that she was some sort of loose cannon. I'd seen teachers smirking behind her back, and Mum had said they made fun of her, but I think in a strange way they were more wary of her than of the other kids. She seemed immune to their sarcasm and actually sought them out, looking intensely at them when they spoke to her and talking to them in her precocious way. In the few weeks I'd known her she'd taken to walking me home, even though it was well out of her way, talking with unnatural enthusiasm about her school work and various teachers. The only time she'd missed meeting me outside the third year entrance at lunchtimes was when she was busy bothering a teacher, showing them the extra research she'd done in the library or making them go through every bit of work again especially for her. For a teacher, giving Miranda attention, even negative attention, was looking for trouble.

"She's intense," said my mother, slamming the oven door closed, "far too intense. You give her a wide berth."

But I couldn't do that, it was already too late.

CHAPTER TWO

S HE HAD ENTERED THE house that first time with an air of triumph. Weeks had passed in which I'd found one reason after another not to bring her home, but she told everyone – that we were friends, that she was coming to my house. She questioned me constantly about my family, my mother in particular and, though I tried to give nothing away, there was no detail she didn't remember. It would all come back to me in something she said a few days later. She even passed the nuggets she gleaned from me to my mother, who started coming home and asking awkward questions. What had I told her? How did I come to be her friend? "You mustn't go telling everyone our business you know, Sue. I'm a teacher. They can't know all our business."

I knew! But she kept seeking me out. If she saw me in the distance she'd shout across and come, bearing down on me, the other kids I'd been with scattering, to whisper wide-eyed in corners. I had even fewer friends now, although some of her status seemed to rub off on me. It was rarer, for instance, for anyone to try and kick open the lockless toilet door when I was in there. Despite all this I had been holding my own, until the offerings started.

I'd known at once when Mum came home and told us about the gifts that some 'grateful pupil' had started to leave in her room. There was never a note, just my mother's name printed out by one of those click machines we all used.

They were good things too, things she'd like; small, compact presents that could be easily smuggled in. When Mum talked about her mystery fan I felt cold. A cliché, I know, but it was literally true. There was something truly chilling about the fact that the handbag mirror matched Mum's bag perfectly; the set of tea towels our kitchen; even the travel slippers were the right size. The level of intent behind it, the sick, obsessive research! Mum was amused and flattered but not surprised. I think she thought of it as her right as the super-teacher she'd always known she was.

But it was not until things started to arrive on our porch step that I plucked up the courage to tackle Miranda about it.

"It's you, isn't it? I know it is. Why are you leaving Mum these things, it's creepy!"

We were round the back of the school by the tennis courts. There was an unspoken understanding that we didn't meet in school itself. It wasn't that we were ashamed, more that we got too bothered, attracted too much attention. If we'd been in the same year it would have been all right. If my Mum wasn't in the school. If I wasn't the lonely oddball. If Miranda wasn't Miranda.

She looked at me, eyes half closed behind her hair, and smiled.

"Come on, it's you doing it."

"I can't think what you mean," she'd said with the same, sly smile.

"The dog barked, and I nearly caught you at it! That's so creepy, Miranda. It's sick. Think how Mum'd feel if she thought someone was prowling around the house whilst we were still in bed!"

"How doesn't she know?" I stayed silent. "You keep the things!"

"I have to. They're in a bag under my bed. I'm terrified Mum's going to find them and think I've been shoplifting or something. How've you got the money anyway?"

But she wouldn't be drawn. As the bell went for the end of

lunch she said simply, "It's very frustrating, you know. To know all about someone, be really close to them and never be able to tell them. Never even be let into their house. You're jealous."

"What! What the hell d'you mean?"

"Of me and Mrs Jones."

"What're you talking about – she's my mother. I can see her anytime I want. She's my mother, for God's sake!"

"But you don't appreciate her."

I was looking at her then as you'd look at somebody insane. Only then did I realise quite how far gone she was – quite how far she'd be prepared to go.

So I gave in. She was coming round. She'd organised it all – the other violinist, the time, music from the library. She'd even sorted out the refreshments – a flattering voice to my mother about how light her sponges were (she'd know, of course, being in her class for cookery) and about how *her* mother didn't bake at all.

She entered our house that first time with the whites of her eyes blazing. She had on a heather-coloured tweed suit, court shoes and American Tan tights. Her long, wild hair was brushed within an inch of its life and she pressed the bell precisely thirty eight seconds after the appointed time.

I felt edgey, worse than when Mum came into my room to 'clean' (why did that have to involve looking in my special jewellery box and the ballet case where I kept my secret writing?). Miranda was the prowler who noticed everything. Without touching it, without turning her head, she scanned it all, weighed its value, came to conclusions about us.

For my Dad she played the 'A' student: engaging him on the biological and chemical front and talking passionately about her music. I looked on stunned. The rather gormless first violin boy she'd found looked bemused, and Dad was impressed as she outlined her grand plans for the quartet.

In the interval, Mum served coffee and cake to her loud delight, and I watched her handling the antique tea set my mother inexplicably had out to show her. She held an exquisite cup in her delicate fingers, stroking it absent-mindedly as she tilted her head, first to one side, then the other as she listened to my mother speaking about her collecting passion. Obediently she held it up to the light to peer, long-sightedly at the mark beneath, admiring the opaque delicacy.

When she'd gone I felt my chest release again and as I turned from the door, the vision of her jaunty, receding back still in my mind, Mum said, "Well, I wish *you* girls would take an interest in my lovely things. Really, I don't know what's going to happen to all the family heirlooms when I'm gone."

But at least the first step had been taken and Mum, disappointed, reported that the mysterious gift fairy came no more.

This, then, was how it started. She would find me, come home with me, set up meetings, but we never went to her house. I think at that stage I still felt hopeful that it would all fizzle out if I could only be polite but vague. Anyway, it wasn't me she was coming to see, it was my mum, so what would be the point of going to her place? Slowly, though, she changed my life.

I'd had friends before. I know I'd looked like a loner, but I did have friends. Well, at least one friend for wherever I went: an orchestra friend, a ballet friend; always at least one girl from school. Nothing could have prepared me for Miranda, though. She was 100% committed, to me.

Usually week nights were telly, homework and practising the 'cello and piano. Friday nights orchestra; Saturday mornings orchestra then round to the friend's or round town. Sunday mornings piano lesson, and Sunday afternoons feeling ill from eating too much Sunday dinner and miserable because another week was on the horizon and I hadn't done any of my homework yet.

But Miranda was no respecter of routine. Any night, every night, she would be waiting to walk me home, waiting by my mother's car. She was like a lover to me: seeking me out at lunch time; looking in my sandwich box; loitering in the corridor between lessons. She didn't care if she herself was late. "I just smile at them and apologise profusely," she chimed when I asked her. "And of course, I'm bright, and I always hand in immaculate homework, especially for your mother."

"Why did you particularly fix on my mother, if you don't mind me asking?" I'd said to her once.

"Why?" She'd thought for a moment,

"I think it was because she was tough. She wasn't frightened of me, just because my mum's on her own and I'm odd and I didn't have any friends."

"You mean she was nasty to you, so you fixed on her. That's well weird."

"Not really that. She just wouldn't have any nonsense. I liked it."

"Yeah well, don't expect me to understand you!" But I did in a way. Maybe Mum had taken her seriously. Maybe she hadn't been put off by Miranda being a weirdo and had managed to treat her like a normal girl.

That period was a quiet time between us, a waiting game. We hadn't really got going yet, pre the shimmering sixteen rubicon where everything was going to happen. I was kept in the house to do my homework and ferried about like an heiress from place to place, always under escort. School had improved. Kids in my year stopped calling me 'Anne of Green Gables' (the red hair) and fourth years said 'hello' in the corridors. Even teachers were more interested, for instance asking me what I wanted when I knocked on the staffroom door at lunchtime, even on the days when Mum wasn't in, instead of opening it with a 'Go away.' Maybe they talked about us.

However, I still wasn't getting any further with Peter, the first violinist from our quartet, who I'd been developing a crush on. Miranda said we should mate up because we looked alike, and either couples should be wildly opposite extremes like Blacks with Whites or Scandinavians with Italians where you made gorgeous hybrid babies or, if that wasn't possible, you should breed to type. Whatever you did, don't get someone insipid with mousy hair and grey eyes. That way the whole world would get more and more boring until, in the end, everyone would be a non-descript sepia. Miranda was doing Genetics this term in Biology and had taken it to heart. So much so that now when you asked her what she wanted to be, instead of British ambassador to the Congo she wanted to crack the human genome. However, I think it was her thinking he looked like me that started putting me off Peter, and anyway I'd been moved to set one in English, and Tom Booker'd started talking to me.

Tom and I got together really over the 'Scottish play'. I always volunteered to be Lady Macbeth, but most of the boys were too scared to read. They pretended it was beneath their manhood, but Tom Booker's manhood was so secure he didn't care. He read Macbeth with a strong Sheffield accent and pronounced all the strange words syllable by syllable without a second's hesitation.

He was effortlessly bright but super-cool with it, training for the Territorials and going dancing in the Northern Soul clubs. He had older brothers who sneaked him in, and they travelled to Manchester and even Newcastle chasing the best scene. None of the rest of us would have been allowed anywhere near the big clubs so this mixture of cool and brainy was irresistible. His best friend was the only black lad in our year, an association which was good for both their images. He also managed to pull the best girls, and when I asked him why he always came to talk to me and caught up with me on the way home he said, "Cause you're a laugh and you've got brains an' all. Yer one of the lads," which wasn't what I wanted to hear.

But somewhere out there, *my* Mr Rochester was riding towards me. Standing on some cliff edge, Heathcliff threw back his mane of black curls and howled my name. Somewhere, across a crowded ballroom, Darcy searched for me, as though he would never be free. But for now I didn't even have a Knightley to give me dry advice whilst secretly ogling my tits.

Day merged into week; term into year. Sometimes it was hot, and I took my fat legs out to redden them a bit; sometimes it was Autumn and the wind blew down from the moors beyond the school and I could stand it no longer; I took the dog as protection against murderers and my mother's questions and made off through the dark. Then words would drive my feet. Gelert the Corgi cross would tear off, frantic with delight, and I could feel my own thick auburn hair (curly and foul since the disastrous perm) whipping around my face. I could feel the fat on my legs clenching and turning to shapely muscle with each step.

Trees formed strange concentric rings around the orange street lamps; sometimes the moon shone, cold and knowing, veiled and unveiled by clouds of dark grey that were beaten across the navy sky.

My darling had to be dark. He had to have flashing teeth and eyes. His hair had to be real curls, a bit of the gypsy perhaps. Actually, probably a lot of the gypsy, but academic too. A drop out, but only because he wanted to be. He'd be lean and passionate but a one woman man, and I'd be she.

Getting home from these trips my face stung, and I knew my skin was glowing and I was beautiful at last. I'd mumble something vague to get Mum off the trail and head for the bedroom where, in the dim light of my bedside lamp, I'd write and write: poems of love; steamy melodramas where the heroine always bore an uncanny resemblance to myself. It was on one of those evening escapades that I found myself at Miranda's for the first time.

I looked forward to her coming around now, and, strangely enough, the more she came to my house, the less she seemed to obsess on my mother.

Apart, that is, from the time when I'd come upstairs from making us a snack to find her sitting on my parents' bed, all my mothers shoe collection scattered across the floor. Some frenzy must have driven her, in the ten minutes I was downstairs, to violate my mother's private cupboard. She even had one on, a size four silver sandal on her size seven foot, and she was laughing, the big, white teeth prominent in her open mouth. In her hand she held a white plastic boot from Mum's Glam Rock phase. I'd been furious with her, and she seemed to toe the line a bit after that. I'd called her the 'wicked step-sister' for weeks.

But tonight there was no Miranda, and these days there wasn't really anyone else anymore. Through the double glazing of my room the traffic kept a constant crescendo and diminuendo effect.

There were unknown people behind those black windscreens whose faces I'd never see. Somewhere out there Tom Booker had decided whether or not he was going to bother to do his homework, or, more likely, finished it effortlessly because he had something to look forward to, something else to do tonight, I thought bitterly. Maybe even now he'd be at the bus terminus in his leather coat: I decided I'd take the dog for a walk.

"No Mum, I've done it all. I didn't have much to do. No I won't. I don't, just in case she goes in front of cars. No I know she hasn't. Yes I have. No I won't. Bye."

Out at last.

I looked good at dusk, especially with back-combed hair, and I'd put some blusher on and lip gloss, and my eczema wasn't too bad at the moment. I was sure I looked stunning. The dog was manic and pulled me up the hill, making a regular, rhythmic choking sound, but the bus terminus wasn't far now. I stopped for a moment to throw my hair forward so I could flick it back and look all gypsy and Kate Bush. Tom definitely wasn't there. I felt the expectation leak away. What now?

I went up the side street and behind the old library, letting the dog off the lead. She shot off, and then dropped into a trot, her hairy back legs like a pair of plus-fours, claws tapping.

A light rain was falling and we passed no one on the streets, not even many cars. Those that did pass loomed, grumbled, swished, the echo of their wheels remaining for a moment, and were gone. We moved together down the hill and into town, the houses getting smaller and older. From many there was not even any light leaking past the curtains. Although I never said the words, even in my mind, I think my legs knew where I was going. Even the dog seemed to know the route, disappearing down drives for a moment then reappearing, over-taking and careering off again down some dim alley.

Each time we came to a cross-roads she stopped and looked back for me; one gesture enough to send her off again with a clatter of claws. When we were about to rejoin the main road I called her and put her lead back on. It was suddenly light, cars passing regularly here.

Now I could see Miranda's house across the road, in darkness except for the hall light. I was sure she must be in. The dog pulled me up the steps and waited, looking eager. There was no bell, you just had to hammer on the glass. No answer. I tried again. It was raining harder now, and I wished I'd brought the money for the bus home. Suddenly Gelert, who'd lost interest and taken to sniffing in the flower beds, perked up, scraping her nails against the glass. The door to the kitchen was open, a dark figure moving towards us. It called out, I answered. The door opened a little, and the dog thrust her way in, tail corkscrewing, body flexible with welcome.

"Are you on your own?"

"What's new?" she said. I was amazed that she didn't even register surprise at seeing me. She took me by the hand; she'd been crying. "Tie the dog to the bottom of the stairs."

"Why?" I asked. She took the lead from my hand and looped it round the stair post, leading the way into the kitchen. I followed. She climbed up onto a breakfast bar stool and nudged me toward the other one. Then she pointed. On the floor were three small lumps. One was moving. I got off my chair.

"Don't," she said.

"What's wrong? What's the matter with them?"

"My mum's put poison down. It paralyses them." One mouse

was moving slowly away from us across the lino. It seemed to be dragging its back end.

"Listen, you can hear the squeaking."

"I can't hear anything," I said.

"Listen," she cried. "Two are still alive, just listen!" I went back to my stool and faintly, almost as high but not so loud as a bat's squeak, I heard the sound.

"How long have they been like this?"

"I've been watching them for nearly an hour. It's awful."

"Where's your mum?"

"Staying the night with Brian." She started to cry again, huge tears but no sound.

"For God's sake, how can you stand it!" I got up to put the overhead fluorescent on. The one that was trying to get away had stopped crawling and lay twisted, panting. I went a bit closer; there was blood on its mouth, a thin trail coming from under the tail. "Bloody hell, Miranda, why haven't you killed them?"

"I can't kill something that's still alive."

"For God's sake." Now I was up I could see that one of the others was still alive. It was quivering, blood matting its tail fur. It was from this mouse that most of the squeaking was coming. "We've got to do something. Why didn't your mum put a trap down, just chop their heads off?"

"She's squeamish."

"Oh great, and because of that these've got to die in agony!" The dog whined impatiently. "Get me a spade," I said.

"What spade?"

"Any spade!"

"I haven't got a spade," she said.

"Well I'm not going to put up with it."

"How are you going to kill them?"

"I'm going to bash their brains in."

"That's disgusting!"

"And you can clean it up," I said. I started looking in cupboards and drawers. There were lots of knives. I picked up a skewer and some fondue forks. The bodies seemed so small. "You can't stab them with that!" she cried. The logistics were just ridiculous. There must be some good way of killing them: something quick that wouldn't leave half their bodies smeared on the floor. I found the rolling pin, "No!" she shrieked. I was feeling desperate. The first mouse, frightened I suppose by all the activity, had started trying to move again, but this time all it could manage was a pathetic sideways scrabbling with its front paws. This was getting beyond a joke.

"Why don't you just go away?" I asked. She didn't answer. "You're making it worse, Miranda."

"How can you kill them?" she said.

"I'm not. Your bloody mother's killed them. I'm just putting them out of their misery." She didn't answer me, just sat, bare toes twisting around and around the foot-rest of the stool. I'd never seen her vulnerable like this before; never dared talk to her like this. I found a metal palette knife. "My mother's crepes knife, it's French!"

"What does it matter what nationality it is!" I crouched down on my haunches, feet flat on the floor, flat knife poised just over the mouse's head. I could see my arm coming down with the knife as if it were a slow motion wildlife shot; the goose landing, slowing wing beats, splat. It was as if I was remembering something I'd seen already rather than imagining it, but I could not even let myself think about the contact at the end. The dog, Miranda, even the mice, had gone deadly quiet.

"I can't do it," I said, but I stayed there, arm poised, unable to give up. The mouse had stopped moving. For one lovely moment I thought it had died. Then it started to pant, struggling to lift up its head. "Sue, come away," she said, "you're not up to it."

"Right," I said, "I'm going to drown it." I fetched the washing up bowl.

"Not in that, for God's sake!"

"What else can I do?"

"Why are you getting so involved?"

"How can I not? Nobody else is doing anything," I said.

"You can't use the washing up bowl, it's not hygienic."

"Who the sod cares!" The dog started to whine in the hall. "For God's sake!" I shouted, "someone's got to do something."

"There's a bucket outside," she said quietly.

I opened the back door, with difficulty as it was swollen and damp. The yard was dark and mossy, the cliff behind keeping out the sun. There was an old metal bucket with leaves and slime in it by the backdoor. "Have we got gloves?" I shouted through.

"Gardening gloves?" she said.

"Anything."

She came out into the yard, shuddering to pass the dying mice in her bare feet. The door to the outhouse hung off its hinges when she opened it. She fetched me some suede gloves and tip-toed back in. Now I had everything I needed, and there was no getting out of it. I went into the house, put a piece of kitchen roll onto my right hand and bent down over the mouse that was still alive. With my left hand I tried to pick it up gently by the tail. It was impossible as my fingers didn't reach to the tips of the gloves.

"I don't want to pick it up by the body, it's haemorrhaging. I'll hurt it."

I had a brain wave. "Can you pass me some cardboard, torn off a cereal packet or something?" She gave me a piece of Shreddies box, and I slid it under the mouse to make a stretcher, then tipped it carefully onto my hand. I think by now the creature was past caring, but the act had developed a momentum of its own. I carried the body, occasionally quivering as some spasm ran through it, outside. It started kicking feebly again. The cold air I suppose. I bent over the bucket. I couldn't just tip it in, it might start swimming; that'd be horrific. On the other hand, I didn't want to cause any more stress by dangling it by the tail.

"Is he dead?"

"Give me a chance!" I shouted in. I thought for a moment and then bent the sides of the board up to make a sort of boat and lowered it in horizontally, gloves and all. It might have died of shock as it entered the cold water. At any rate, there was no kicking. I held it under for five minutes by my watch until the water really hurt my hands and then brought it out. All the blood was gone from the soggy body, but it looked all bone under the wet fur, as if it'd been dead for weeks. "Where shall I put the bodies?" She came out with two plastic bags,

"Can't we bury them?" I said. "It seems awfully undignified." She looked at the body and started crying again, huge double-strength tears. "Mum wouldn't like it. She's a bit squeamish." I managed to button my mouth, took the open bag and slid the body and cardboard in. Putting the bag down I went back in and studied the other body. Definitely dead. "I need more cardboard." She brought me some and, with the remaining glove, I pushed the body onto its stretcher, then into the bag where it landed on the other mouse. I wondered if they were related.

After that I could imagine her at home. Not only that; my feet had found a way to her house, and I began to go often. Something had changed between us.

Sometimes now the quartet even met there. Her mother was hardly ever in, but her Granny would have made a cake for us, or scones. Miranda would answer the door in her tweed suit, sometimes even keeping the matching hat on through the rehearsal. Gradually, though, her style began to change. She let go of the Miss Moneypenny look, even moving differently, one action lingering into another, so that she gave the impression of sensuousness, sheer enjoyment of herself. That was the term she found Marcus.

CHAPTER THREE

ALTHOUGH NATURALLY A CONSERVATIVE, being fascinated by money, rules and tradition, she'd got involved with the resident school Communist through the debating society. He was a born eccentric, as wise and pompous as a Judge of fifty. He too was only in the fifth year but was even more notorious than Miranda. He knew everything about everything and took on any teacher and won (except for the Games staff whom he stayed well clear of). She was, literally, all over him at every opportunity: smoothing back the thin curls from his receding hairline and warming his tiny white fingers under her skirt at break time.

The quartet rehearsals had got a bit erratic recently and Miranda no longer took the detour every day to walk me home. I think the crush on Mrs Jones was over. I hoped I wasn't as well.

But I kept myself busy. In Summer other kids went to the Lido, but it was 'a rough sort' down by the park and I wasn't allowed to go. In bad weather, I watched the world through the double glazing, imagining the wind from the moors, watching the distant lights of the multi-storey flats by the railway station.

I read and read. It was always novels, mostly nineteenth century or perhaps biographies of the Brontes: Gaskell's or modern ones with no detail spared in terms of Emily coughing in the night, each heave bringing her closer to the graveyard under the sash windows of that small house. There was plenty of suggestive detail about Branwell and lots of pictures. Sometimes I read Social History such as 'Eyam: Plague Village' or about the lives of children down the mines or Slavery. The occasional family outing took in the plague village itself or perhaps the Bronte parsonage where it was shocking to see Charlotte's tiny shoes and how close together the bedrooms were; how impossible it must have been not to hear as each sister coughed herself to death. Sometimes Gelert and I walked on the moors where the granite outcrops gave us bleak views of Wuthering Heights country, black-soiled and full of grandeur, where almost every crag held an Iron Age Fort or Neolithic circle.

Gelert was not exactly Emily Bronte's 'Keeper', but there was always the possibility of bumping into Tom Booker to keep me from total despair and boredom. I practised, went back and forth to cello and piano lessons and orchestra and did the minimum homework I could get away with.

Miranda was flourishing. And me? Well, I'd changed my style as well. Gone was the prissy 'Pollyanna' of the lower school. Thanks to a huge pair of seventies glasses, Indian prints, thigh length socks and a perm, the fourth year me was now a retro hippie. I knew I looked ugly, but at least it looked like I'd done it on purpose.

But my role as redundant friend came suddenly to an end one morning. I'd been off school with one of my many bouts of illness. Nothing exciting like TB or pneumonia, but just enough to label me as boring and sickly.

I read and re-read the note Miranda'd put through my front door. She'd recorded the time, 8.02 am and marked it 'urgent', but I knew that anyway. Why else would she have stayed on the bus all the way to my stop and then have had to walk the rest of the way to school? Where had she been until the bell at twenty-to-nine? Nothing scribbled about the note. She'd used her best Quink pen for it and written it on a flat surface. No mention of me having been away from school. Hadn't she noticed?

'See me, My love. Terribly urgent. I'm suffering under the weight of this knowledge I must impart. Meet me by the big oak lunchtime.' Mira x

I wasn't about to miss out on this.

The main doors were open as I came in late with my cello later that morning, having waited for a lift from Dad after persuading him that I wasn't going to die if I ventured outside. The familiar foxy smell greeted me, coming from the damp, king-size mat just inside the corridor. It had been raining but wasn't now, just grey, clammy, 'nothing' weather. I banged my cello through the swing doors. Three tough girls from another set, so far below that I got vertigo even to think of it, were warming their bums on the giant radiator. It was lesson time, but this was nowhere on the way to anywhere but the girls' toilets, where the door was always open, wafting out sweet vapours, so no staff ever came here. The thick girls hated anyone who was in the orchestra. In a way I knew what they meant. There are few instruments that you don't look a prat playing, and the cello wasn't one of them. They thought the orchestra was a way of getting out of lessons legally, which it was actually. When you were in the top sets though, missing lessons had limited charm as you had to catch up afterwards. 'Come to think of it,' I was thinking as I came in, 'that was probably why the council *did* bus poor kids into this area, to create a snake pit underneath the posh kids' feet so they kept working.' It scared the death out of me, looking down.

Usually I had ways of avoiding them, but I was out of my routine today. One of the girls (she was in the fourth year, but I didn't know her) was chewing. As I passed her she hacked up. It landed on the mat. I was about to say something really cutting like,

"Your aim's about as good as your O levels're going to be," when I realised that she probably wouldn't exactly smart at an insult like that. Meanwhile, my feet had continued walking and I was nearly round the corner. To tell the truth, I hadn't got time for this. I had to track Miranda down and find out what was going on. I'd seen so little of her lately. I'd gone up an orchestra on Friday night, and we had our breaks at a different time. She didn't go much anyway anymore. There was another strange thing too, when I came to think about it: she didn't wear her blazer anymore in school; in fact, she looked completely different.

"You're Mrs Jones' daughter." I stopped and did a rewind, ending up opposite the radiator, and waited.

"Yeah," said her friend. I recognised her as the one who'd been trying to bully my sister in Drama.

"You think you're fucking great, you do." She seemed to be waiting for an answer. "Well?" she said at last.

"I thought it was a rhetorical question," I answered.

"You think you're well 'ard, you do."

"You're weird, you are," said the friend. I put my cello down on the floor.

"She goes round with that weird girl. That witchy one."

"She's well sick. She cops off wi' weirdo Marcus. The one that's always up on 't stage for summat." There had been a rumour going round that Miranda had had sex. But I couldn't believe it, as she would have told me about it.

"You look like a weird wolf, you do. Ergh, look at 'er!" I looked down, ten to nine, nearly time for the bell.

I picked up my cello and leaned my chin on it. Then I gave them a show I hoped they'd never forget, my 'Old Hag' face. I'd done it by accident last Autumn and nearly scared my sister to death.

She thought I was possessed, but really it was just coincidence, that white rose head swinging into the room, and then the sash window suddenly hurtling down and decapitating it. I'd learned it for third hag in the Scottish play last year. I gave them a good dose, letting a bit of white froth come into the corner of my mouth and dribble onto my chin. The breathing (Darth Vader mated with a wolf snarl), was particularly good.

"Shit!" one of them shouted. I breathed my horrible breath into her face, hoping I still smelt of the streptococcal sore throat I had been off school with.

"You're fechin' mad, you are!" said the other one, sliding along the wall towards the corner,

"Trace, wait on!" shouted her friend in a strangled voice, shoving my cello out of her way as she ran. I only just caught it and managed to hitch it onto my shoulder, much the safest way to carry it when the bell went. The leader had left her bag behind which I kicked under the radiator so it wouldn't get trodden on in the stampede for break.

I wondered how I could wangle going to find Miranda. She didn't hang around Music much anymore, not since she'd had the row with the teacher about CND, and I didn't really want to go in the fifth-year classroom with my cello, just in case they took the piss out of me. I had lugged it to the penultimate flight of stairs but had to stop because of the bell. I pressed my back against the wall, holding the cello case before me like a shield. No one banged into me. Not many kids I knew came down here, it was mainly lower school. Kids were getting trendier, though. At least a third were wearing their shirts out of their trousers or skirts. Many had their ties really fat, and even some second and third years had Kickers. It was depressing really.

Finally the rush slowed to a trickle, and I set off up the last flight, pushing my back against the music room door. There was a horrible sound coming out of there, clarinets. Two fat sisters, teacher's pets, were playing chamber music. The music teacher was unreasonably pleased to see me, a big smile spreading on his baby face. The sisters looked up as I staggered in. The really fat one was one of Miranda's few other friends, and I didn't know what Miranda saw in her.

I plonked down the cello case and started to unpack it, did up the bow; fetched out the spike and twanged across the strings, in tune as usual. Just as well, as I never had figured out how to tune it, and I didn't want to show myself up in front of them. Miranda's other friend was Mr Dipnall's particular favourite; I think they were probably having an affair. She could hardly cross her legs they were so fat. I'd watched her calves grow over the four years I'd been in the school; now they were so wide that they didn't go in at the ankle at all but joined continuously on, fat hanging down in an arc behind her leg when she sat down and shaking with every step she took in her square, high-heeled shoes. It was now or never.

"Mr Dipnall, I've just got to give a message to Miranda Dupont from Miss Birchrood; she told me on the stairs."

"Fine, Susan. Don't be too long, though. We're already into assembly time."

Fifth-year form rooms were on the second floor. I climbed the wide stairs and passed along the empty corridor, glancing into each room. The windows were at shoulder level. A couple of teachers glanced back at me but I was one of the good ones so they didn't suspect anything.

I saw her before she saw me. Her class were the only ones without everyone at a desk. She was perched on the corner of hers, one shapely leg in its big boot swinging back and forth, the other flexed against the ground. She didn't even look up even as I opened the door; she had her back to it and her mind on the thin, manic boy standing between her legs. Mr Taylor looked up from the register. I had to go right up to him to make him hear over the noise, "I need to see Miranda. We need to sort out the programme for the concert." I thought on the spur of the moment that it was probably better not to take the name of a teacher in vain, my mother said they talked about us in the staff room. He nodded and went back to the register. A couple of fifth years were looking at me in amusement; I wished the bloody perm would grow out! Mr Taylor looked up, surprised; paused for a moment, "Miranda!"

"Yes, Dear," she called.

He smiled. "Friend!"

She turned and saw me, came down the aisle between the desks all fluttery arm movements; smiled at Mr Taylor, grabbed my hand (I wished she wouldn't do that!) and closed the door on the noise. "How can he stand it so loud?" I said.

"Oh, he likes it. He knows he can stop it any time he wants."

"I know that. But why does he have it in the first place?"

"Maybe he just likes to show that he can stop it anytime he likes."

There were two types of teacher in our school: those with noisy classrooms and those with silence. Those with noisy classrooms were known to be failures, but Mr Taylor was the exception. He had the top band Maths groups. Miranda said his lessons were good fun, but I'd never had him. I had Mr Sayers, who ruled by sweat. He wore fawn or mustard-coloured nylon shirts, and if anyone was messing about, he'd come up behind them and put his arms each side of them. The smell! You had to hold your breath just to live. Very effective if you didn't want kids messing about in your lesson. Not brilliant if someone wanted help, though, and lots of people did in set three.

"What's the matter, anyway?" I said. We'd come to a dark little mini corridor leading off to the music rooms. No one went there, as it was a cul-de sac, and even if Mr Dipnall did see us, he wouldn't mind.

"I'm in love," she said, expansively.

"I know," I said. She paused and suddenly I knew what was coming. "I've had sex." I gave myself the satisfaction of a minimal reaction.

"I've lost my virginity," she tried again, but I held on tight, pushing my fringe off my glasses and behind the ears. "Well, almost. We were disturbed by my mother."

"No! Oh my God!" I just couldn't help myself reacting. In a flash, the vision of my own mother's shocked face in a doorway hit me.

"It was awful. I didn't know she was coming home. We were in her bed."

"No!"

"Yes, it was awful!" But she was smiling; I would've died. How could she?

"Her face, though!"

"How could you?" She didn't answer, just smiled at me.

"Well, what did you want to tell me?" I bluffed, looking her in the eye.

"Well? I mean, I've come all the way up here for nothing!" I sounded like my mother.

"I just wanted you to know," she said. Then, putting her hand on my arm, condescending. "Your time'll come."

"Sod off, Miranda. You sound like a Jehovah's Witness! I don't want my mum there on my first time, thank you very much. Put me off for life. Ugch!" She wasn't listening to me, or at any rate, she wasn't looking. She was hanging over the banisters, head to one side, seeing how far her long hair would hang. I waited a bit, but she stayed there adding a flexing movement, stretching her back tendons by bending the other leg at the knee, fancying herself.

"Right, I'm off." I sounded peevish even to myself. Before she could react and try to persuade me otherwise, I was off down the stairs. I would have liked to take two at a time just for effect, but I wasn't very good with heights.

I waited outside the girls' toilets until I was sure she had gone, and went back. Somehow I knew for sure, without knowing why, that everything would be different between us now. When I arrived, the 'musicians' were already at the coda of some ghastly version of Handel's Water Music arranged for schools' orchestras in a Rumba style. All the cello had to do was repeated tonic-chord quavers. The fat sisters played the tune, and Mr Dipnall busked all the rest of the parts on an electric organ over a synthesiser beat.

"I can't understand where all the rest of the musicians have got to this morning," he said sadly as we were packing away; I managed not to comment.

I dragged myself to History, where Miss Holmes was giving out letters for a trip to the local ancient industrial hamlet. This must have been the third visit at least to the bloody place since starting school, age four. Okay, cholera epidemics and lead makeup poisoning had something about them, but who wanted to know about the bloody manufacture of pig iron, what ever the hell that was! All the boys loved her, though. She was their perfect woman: dinky slim legs, wide white smile and dead straight silky blonde hair. My only hope was the ugly duckling story: one day I'd be that revamped duckling, and she'd be PAST IT. I stared at her little fingers on the register as she cradled it with one hand, fingers each side of the spine. Her delicate nails had a flawless sheen of clear polish and were perfectly shaped, you could tell she didn't play a stringed instrument.

"Are you all right, Susan?" she smiled, inclining her head. Most of the class to the front of me turned round. "Yes," I grunted. I had thought it was the school girls, not the teachers, who were supposed to be the sexy ones: ankle socks; games skirts; gymslips etc. No one I knew would have been seen dead in any of that. That's what the women staff wore on non-uniform day, embarrassing! The only one I knew who'd been into that sort of thing was Miranda when she'd been younger. But as far as I could see now, proper grown women were better-looking than adolescent girls. They had shapely faces, were slimmer, and they smelt better. Their clothes suited them too, and their hair always looked the same.

School continued awful the rest of the day. I had slimy Mr Robinson in the library, who didn't teach us anything. All you did was copy, literally copy, straight out of a book. My sister said he used to pinch her bum, but he didn't do anything to me, which I suppose in itself was a sort of insult. Then it was Geology in the demountables. The bloke always wore out-door pursuit clothes, though he wasn't a Games teacher or anything. He lived opposite Tescos, yet he was always in his hiking boots and a fleece lined lumber-jack shirt, with shoulder-length hair resting on his collar and a beard to keep him warm in hostile conditions. All we ever did was look at lumps of rock and identify them from a book.

I made a quick exit on the bell. There was no way I was going to go through all that again with Miranda. No one was walking my way, and I wasn't walking anyone else's. Not even the big oak tree looked very green today. It looked dusty. A wall had been built around it, and a car park put on top. There must have been loads of trees here before the school. I treated myself to a short glance over the field where we did cross-country running, or rather where Miss Macdonald, the lesbian Games teacher, hoped we were cross-country running. That was one of the only decent bits of Games actually: getting on your duffel coat and having a brisk, bracing walk across the moor, coming back to a warm shower and school dinner.

"I'll slipperrr yewehe !" Her catch phrase was always delivered in her Glaswegian accent. It sounded tamer than it was actually, because the 'slipper' wasn't something your Granddad would wear, but a rubber-soled plimsoll. I only came near it once. That was because I hadn't fancied the thought of taking a running jump off a spring board, landing on my head on a four foot high 'horse' and ricocheting off, hoping somehow to land on my feet. I'd politely declined the offer, even though she'd volunteered to 'put a hand under your back'. What good would that have been to me on my way through the air to the Games mat? I'd escaped anyway, just. Thinking about it, it could only have been either that I was such a lost cause in Games that I wasn't worth beating, or that my Mum worked as a teacher in the school, or that I wasn't the right type of kid to beat: Kids from Abbymoor Road never got hit.

By now I was past the nice green bit looking out to a wild horizon, and well into suburbia. I was Bourgeois; this was 'suburbia'. Marcus was right, and he was who she wanted now. He'd called my house, 'Jacobethan' with a mocking smile. 'Not even the nerve to be post modern.' Skinny, posing bastard!

I opened the porch door which clanged shut, and the front door that opened with a vacuum-like sucking noise. It shut with a deep swish, and me and my sunken heart were home.

CHAPTER FOUR

I'D COME IN THE front way to avoid Mum. I opened the door to the lounge where Dad was and shouted "Hi, Dad, I'm home!" to the top of his head. He was playing some Debussy, quite smooth and slick but too loud as usual, (he played everything as if it were Beethoven or Rachmaninov). He'd obviously been in there a while as the pipe smoke had layered itself like nougat, escaping past me into the hall in wisps. It was safe to clock in with Dad, because he'd never give you the Spanish Inquisition. It was unlikely that he'd even stop playing. The piano stopped. "Hello, Susie, you're home."

"Hi, Dad." The piano continued.

I went on up to my room and closed the door. It was the smell that was the best thing about my room; just itself. Though I did burn the odd joss stick and smoke an occasional herbal cigarette, I didn't really like leaving those smells there. It smelt mostly of my pillow, and the smell from the studio-couch; a sort of straw smell. I threw myself face down on the bed, which creaked in its comforting way, and felt better immediately.

Through the floor came the fast tap of my mother's feet, hooves which crossed and recrossed the kitchen hundreds of times a day; doing her little circuit from corner to fridge to bin to sink to table to drawer. She had a certain speed which never varied, though the gap between sounds changed. That was when I tensed up: was she crossing to the hall door to shout up; or, even worse, to come up? In between the taps she was rolling, spreading, stirring. Sometimes she chopped, or she was filling the kettle or a saucepan, different sounds. She was always there, and the sounds were always the same: Dad's piano; Mum's step.

I was hungry, but snacking wasn't allowed, and anyway I'd just get hassle if I braved going into the kitchen. I felt slightly demented. Tea wouldn't be until six; I'd got loads of homework, and there was nothing on telly. I didn't even have my 'cello lesson to go to. Thank God at least I'd done my piano practice before school, so there wasn't that to do as well.

How could she? Without even telling me she was going to! I went to the sink and looked at myself in the mirror. Bad move I knew, especially in this mood, but I was drawn to it just as Sleeping Beauty to her spinning wheel. I clicked on the fluorescent light with a sense of doom. It shone straight down, shadows pulling on my face. I could see just what I would be at forty. I leaned over the sink, feeling it slide into its familiar position, digging into the abdomen. Everything was falling into place. Pressing the insides of my arms against the glass, I started on my face; fingering like a chimp does, stopping to test. However, it was not insects I was looking for but eczema, hidden in the creases, in all the places where other people my age had spots. I was very short-sighted, so I took my glasses off for this, and I could see in this light as though through a magnifying glass.

At first it took an expert eye. But I knew where to look, and when the eye couldn't see them, I found the rough patches with my hand. It had been a couple of days since I'd done this, so they were all just perfect: dry and scaly but closed. I rubbed at the edges first. Soon they started to come away and redden. I moved further in. Sometimes there was a scab just below the surface that I could worry with the end of my nail. I searched the crease in my chin, easing up the outside of the scab as soon as all the dead skin on top was rubbed away. Clear yellow plasma came to the corner. I scraped away a bit more. The yellow dried quickly, glue like, in irregular beads, very satisfying to pick off and roll on the finger tips. It tasted salty. I did it until the bright, thin blood appeared as if from nowhere at the surface of the under-scab skin. It hurt, so I pressed it down with a cotton wool ball soaked in the special clear stuff Dad'd bought me and moved on to the next patch. I finished when my back hurt, and I could feel the stinging all over my face. This was when I turned off the light and rinsed my face in water as cold as I could bear. Again and again I rinsed, then patted it dry with the towel; I didn't dare look.

There was no way I wanted to be seen for at least another twenty minutes until the red had subsided a bit. When it'd dried off, I could put a bit of talc on it to disguise it, shake my shaggy hair across my face. I propped my back against the wall with a pillow behind it and dragged my school bag up onto the bed. I might as well get on with homework, as I wasn't allowed out to friends' houses or anything during the week.

Physics. Unbelievable. There was no substance to it. It wasn't even like maths; lots of columns of satisfying sums where you could get out your ruler and then give them a big tick in red pen. You just had to get it. It was pulleys this week, and I didn't have a clue. You had to answer three questions, that was bloody it! I put it back in my bag.

History: The Chartists. We did trade union and social history because Sheffield was a left-wing council. 'The Socialist Republic of South Yorkshire.' I felt quite proud of that actually. Everyone on our road put up Conservative posters before an election. Embarrassing. The Chartists weren't very interesting really, dates and principles. I liked slum conditions and accidents in the mills, Smallpox, that sort of thing. We had to write out a list of Chartist grievances and Government objections to the movement.

I liked looking at the two sides. There was never any hope for the Chartists.

I'd just finished this when Mum called upstairs. I quickly sorted out my face as best I could and then combed my hair over it as some sort of camouflage.

I kept it there during the meal. Last time I'd been picking Dad had said,

"Tell, me, Susie: these lesions, does anything come out of them? Any sort of puss, fluid?" For God's sake, Dad!

"Er, yes, sort of transparent yellow stuff." The trials of having a medic as a parent! Luckily tonight they seemed more interested in talking to my little sister about the trampoline club.

I cleared the plates and went back to my room. Mum never made us do anything during the week. Our work was homework and practising our instruments. I pushed aside the bead curtains and got the Physics out again. Not a bloody clue! I could ask Dad but he'd go on and on. First he'd try and find something interesting to say about it; then he'd want to see it when it'd been marked; then he'd think of a few more interesting things I could do to further explore it, thanks Dad! In a moment of desperation I drew the pulley in action and made three calculations involving long division in quite an ingenious way. The finished article looked unlikely, and I'd forgotten to use a ruler but, sod it. Mum was going again on her kitchen treadmill, and from the other room came the sound of the telly rising up through plaster, floorboards, carpet. 'Nationwide' signature tune. It was only six o' clock. The wind was fiddling at the window, creating a vacuum, releasing it. I turned off the light and went to sit looking out.

It was getting dark. Already gloomy on the street, the sky was grey and red, trees black where they touched it against the skyline. Out there, in his house by the park, was Tom, having effortlessly dealt with his Physics (he was in set two); he probably had a couple of mates round and was playing Dungeons and Dragons. Or maybe he was on the streets patrolling his territory, or down in the tennis club by Miranda's, thrashing his thick friends at Space Invaders? But he was beyond my reach in every way.

A fine rain was falling. I couldn't even go to Miranda's with the dog, she'd probably be devising the new Derbyshire version of the Kamasutra with Marcus. It wasn't an attractive thought. Not just that I was prying and it made me feel like some twerp with no life. The picture wasn't very pretty either. Miranda was all right, but Marcus was a weasel. If I knew Miranda, the bed clothes would be stale, her hair greasy at the roots, and the rake-thin Marcus would be bouncing around on her with his veiny skin all white.

The back door slammed in the kitchen, and I heard the thump of my brother's rugby kit hitting the floor in the utility room. Everything in the house seemed to relax when Huw came in. He filled everywhere with noise, with himself. You could smell him home. Where ever he was you could hear him too: showering with the radio on; spraying himself with Brut; playing Genesis and Pink Floyd albums in his room; the slap of the metal strings as he played his electric guitar with the amp switched off. His low voice blended with Mum's in the kitchen; the sound of the washing machine door slamming and then the cycle beginning. Soon there'd be a smell of food as he had his tea reheated, plus maybe a pork pie on the side.

'A man needs meat,' my mother said. He charmed my parents senseless. He was naturally academic, though not especially good at any one subject; a good all-round athlete, with a particular propensity for Rugby (unfortunately my Welsh parents had to make do with League up here) and musical too. He played the violin like a dream with his big, red fingers, and led the county youth orchestra. He was Nazi blond too, like my father as a boy, stocky and muscular, though you could tell even then he would eventually be fat. My mother fed him like he was a heavy-weight boxer; the sooner he escaped to university, the better, before he went to seed. No parents could have had a son more wholesome. Only I knew his secret vice.

I could hear him on the stairs. He didn't seem able to take one step at a time but always two; three as a challenge on special occasions. I anticipated a trip to the loo and, yes! There he went, not bothering to close the door as usual. You could hear the difference between him and my Dad: Dad's was muted (well, he closed the door) and came in bursts, ending in a trickle, followed by the sound of paper unfurling from the roll, the flush and the tap in the next door bathroom. Huw's was Niagara, with no let up. He stopped once, towards the end, burst forth again and then, more often than not, dipped with a final flourish, and left. You thought twice about accepting a sandwich from Huw.

Today he didn't pound back across the landing after visiting his favourite loo but knocked on my door and flung it open. I was unprepared. He threw himself on the bed, propped his head on his hand and started fiddling with my Physics homework, turning the book upside down and looking from different angles with a puzzled expression on his face. I snatched it off him and put it on the window sill. "What do you want?" I said.

"What're you doing at the weekend?"

"Why?"

"Well, there's a party going off at Steve's house, and I thought you might like to come. Bring your friend. Miranda is it?"

"I can't."

"Why?"

"Well, she can't, she's busy. Anyway, she's going out with

someone, they've had sex and everything. You don't fancy her, do you?" He looked interested. "She's too young for me. Gary likes her, though. But I'll tell him someone's already got her. She looks lonely to me." He was sitting up now, swinging the light-pull back and forth.

"Lonely? Miranda! She has a brilliant time. What makes you say that?"

"Oh, she just seems sad, like she's always smiling too wide, acting too big or something. I don't know, she's your friend."

"Huw, supper!" shouted my mother

"Coming! Christ, you can hear everything up here, Sis," he said.

"Don't call me Sis."

"Soz." Why did boys always have to abbreviate everything, anyway?

"I suppose I'm not invited anymore, then. To the party? You know, if Miranda can't come?"

"No," he said, "course you are. Jan fancies you."

"Jan! Why?"

"How do I know! Anyway, you can come with me if you like, but you'll have to make your own way home; I'm staying over." He left, leaving the door open. Slowly I closed it. Jan! He was gorgeous. A bit dippy, but really sexy in a 'Tom Brown's School Days' sort of way. He always looked ruffled: tie open showing his neck, shirt hanging out; brown eyes and wide smile. Me! I couldn't believe my luck. He must be nearly seventeen at least. Maybe he'd fallen in love with me when we played that game of Mouse Trap last term, when he was waiting for Huw to get out of the bath. Turned out it was Huw's first shave (only bum fluff, really).

What was I going to wear? Something to accentuate the positive. There'd been a really good article in *Just Seventeen*, 'How to be a Siren with Spots'. Okay I didn't have spots as such, but I did have a lot of other things and the theory was the same: play up the good bits and disguise the crap.

I took a long, slow look in the mirror. Bad. Red skin, okay, but it'd be dark and there was always hypo-allergenic makeup. Nice lips: right, liner and loads of gloss. Nice almondy eyes: mascara and eyeliner. I'd leave my glasses off: after all I didn't have to see him, just get off with him. Hair? A disaster, unless I could back comb it and make it look wild and sexy. Legs? Short but curvy; good bum, flat tum (tight trousers then with over-long legs and high boots). Perky tits, something clingy.

I crossed to the window and looked out. The rain had put a lovely varnish on the road and pavement. They gleamed. I wondered whether perhaps Miranda wasn't busy breaking her mother's bed springs, but was alone in her lonely house after all. What would she say when she found out I was going to lose it too. Without her, and to Jan!

She'd be in her house alone tonight – no tea made; nobody to care whether she did her homework or not. What *was* she like when she was all alone? A smaller person, maybe? I had a vision of the big hair dropping and settling, as if being in public were like a huge hair drier blowing up from below, making her fly-away mane stand out all manic. What else? Maybe there was no Marcus tonight; no mother to cook her tea. There was never a father concerned about her complexion. Maybe it wasn't so great to be Miranda?

Rain beat against the glass, and the soft voices of Huw, Mum and Dad came comfortingly through the floorboards. I grabbed my best pen and my lockable diary (an essential precaution with my mother about) and wrote Miranda's story, something I often did when I was stuck in the house on my own and couldn't face the homework or family.

'After school she let herself into the silent house; into the darkening hall. The door eased closed, sealing out as it did the sound of the traffic. Her hair drooped as soon as she was alone, as though a fan had been turned off suddenly. It hung, limp and desolate on her shoulders. Her whole profile was narrower as she turned, her back against the door's light. The walk was different too. Is it true for everyone? Does everyone put on a public walk when they go out? She did turn and walk back up the hall differently from if she had been watched. There was a straightness about it, a seriousness. Climbing the stairs, she held on to the handrail like a woman of fifty, banged her hip on the post as she turned the corner to go into the bathroom. There she sat on the toilet, legs, as usual, wide apart to wee. It came out in a huge, horse-like rush, stopping suddenly and completely, seemingly in mid flow. Strangely, as she was alone, she kicked the door closed with her foot. Leaning right forward, she wiped front-to-back with a thick pile of folded paper. How wasteful she is! Never folds over and re-uses; never flicks over to the other side. Before she flushes, she peers into the mirror on the medicine cabinet above the cistern, screws her mouth sideways to make her cheek taut, looking for spots. There aren't any, well, none that a long-sighted searcher could find. She pushes the end of her nose to one side. This is a sure place, the enlarged pores never disappoint and sure enough, the promised maggot comes spiralling out. She washes her hands on the Imperial Leather.

She enters her room in the empty house. The carpet is pale pink: deep, luxurious, and dirty. She puts on a record; actually it is there already: Donna Summer. She replaces the coffee-coloured, transparent plastic lid of her record player. Needle catches vinyl with a gritty sound. She puts on scrunch socks over her smoky grey tights.'

Did she put on her exercise sweat pants now, the plastic ones? I'm guessing that she didn't, that those went on when she was expecting visitors. Is that so unfair? Now I am in her room seeing her when I'm not there; spying on her. Is that sick? Instead of raiding my wardrobe for all the Femme Fatale gear I can muster, I drag my imagination away from Jan and the party. I wrestle it down, fix the restraining harness firmly to it, and pick up my pen again:

'And now she sits at her desk, the large one made of oak, in the room that is not a proper teenager's room. A room with a faded flower design on the duvet cover and walls covered with dining room paper: metallic, textured. On cold nights she wraps the tartan car blanket, which is folded neatly on the chair, around her legs. Not even considering the sweat pants then, she pulls on her powder blue towelling bath robe, which is two sizes too small, and sits on the fake leather chair. Her work is neat and stored with immaculate precision, though she disguises the fact by throwing magazines or scarves over it before I go round. She opens the black plush box and takes out an ink pen which is weighted, cool and smooth to the touch, and with her left hand she opens her collected Hopkins poems and reads. She lets it close again, puts her pen down into one of the ridges in the table, lifts her stack of files at one corner and fetches out a wedge of lined A4. She picks up pen, props open her book with the hard back edition of the Oxford Encyclopaedia of Quotations, and begins to read, occasionally making notes in careful writing with a slender white hand.'

My back was hurting where I'd been leaning too long on the window sill. Sucking in my cheeks (both sets) in order to improve the profile, I took a quick look in the mirror. Not bad! That warm cream feeling after I'd had the good news was still with me, though with a wobbly core to it somewhere. For instance, was he going to demand I had sex with him on this first date? Jan's face materialised briefly in my mind's eye; the way he looked coming in from cross-country on a Thursday afternoon, when all the six formers had half day Games. Some walked in, having obviously just been round the block for a fag; others heaved in red and panting, their shirts sticking to them. He'd come round the corner like he was just starting out, fringe down over one eye; legs mud-splattered and golden brown. He reminded me of a public school boy in a film. He didn't go in for designer sports gear, though he was on the schools' cross country team; just old trainers, grubby tennis shorts and his white school shirt. I think it was the white shirt that did it for me.

I lay back on my bed and closed my eyes. Where was I? Miranda. She was leaving me. She was leaving me for Marcus, and I couldn't compete with the thrill of it, the danger, the sheer invasive physicality. As I grew to need her, she grew away from me. To get to me had been her ambition for so long; now she had me, and she was moving on. At first there'd been no cracks in her armour, but slowly she'd begun to seem more human. Like a magic painting she'd revealed herself as time had painted brush after brush of water over us. Knowing she was lonely, knowing she was fallible, though, should just have made her seem less awe inspiring, shouldn't it? Instead she became like a heroine in a story.

Her loneliness gave her a poignancy; her desire to conceal it and not play the victim an epic quality.

All right, it was only fair. Miranda's turn to speak. I did this sometimes, let her speak, pretended I was her, living in her life. What did she think of me, then?

'She's gone, back with her dog to Munchkin land.' (The door clunks shut. She climbs the stairs heavily, bumping her knee ... goes for a wee). 'It's creepy in the house alone. I can almost see the spectre of an intruder rounding the corner, his face looking up, oblong and flat as he starts on the bottom steps. I'm looking down into his black eyes. A really good piss, knickers right off so I can really open my legs, give it my all. Bearing down. "Bear down Mrs Dupont!" said the midwife (one of my mother's legends).Give it a good wipe (none of this faffing about with folded paper) a good regular swipe and then wash hands, Imperial Leather, something to hang onto apart from slime. Have a deco to see if there's any zits. Nope. Bound to be a couple in the nose sump; yes! Bingo! Granny said the other day, "My darling, why have you such bad skin. I used to be a hat model. I had beautiful skin. Your mother has beautiful skin. All the women in the family are famed for their complexion." (Famed?!) "Even your father: sallow yes, but not a blemish." She was holding my jaw in her hand, moving my face from side to side and making a little clucking sound, as if she were trying to bond with a small animal. "You, you have holes in your face!"

"Alright, Granny!" I'd pulled away. Who wants their acne investigated and discussed in a loud old lady's voice at family tea?

"It is worse this side. Very bad here. Do you lie on your right?"

"No, Granny, I don't. Let's talk about piles or something

instead, shall we?" That'd hurt her. I'm sorry, but I'm not going into it anymore. Anyway, I am lopsided, spot wise. The window and the light in the bathroom are on the left in the mirror, on the right of the person squeezing, so, spots on that side get left alone and heal up, right? At least I haven't got eczema, though. Poor Sue, it's disgusting!'

But the sound of the dishes being done downstairs cut across it all. Not too bad, actually. I was pleased with it, and I'd given her a chance to criticise me back.

'Miranda works on (I continued) lifting the pages with her right hand, writing with her left. Sometimes the finger tips spread out under the page, elbow placed on the desk as though she were a delicate female Atlas, holding up the world. Sometimes she plays with her hair; not a restless twining of it around her fingers. She gathers it low at the back of her neck, makes a tube of it in the palm of her hand and runs her hand slowly down it. It is like the enclosing, downward motion done around a cat's tail. After six such strokings the flyaway hair starts to lie flat: all the follicles lying the same way, and light begins to bounce off it, quietly glossy. She has long calves like a Negro, long Achilles heel and thin ankles. She is big for a British girl, and her stubby eyelashes turn up. Slim toes explore the carpet pile. They are dancer's toes, moving independently of one another. Even the skin, pale though it is, is dry, as if it grew pre-talced. Even after winter, when most people's feet appear from their shoes pallid, damp and shrivelled like fish adapted to life in underground caves, Miranda's feet were pure porcelain.'

I wasn't allowed to go around the house in bare feet. Dad always shouted, "Put your slippers on." The danger of a percussive injury and gangrene setting in I suppose. Hooray for a medical background!

'She goes into the small kitchen. Nobody home again. It's not very light. The window and the glass in the door look onto a yard with an out-house. Behind that, the tall, weathered red brick wall and a cliff.'

It's not really a fitted kitchen, and there's nowhere to sit more than two at a time. Family meals sometimes do happen at the big table in the dining room, when Granny comes. Then the lace table cloth and the coloured under-cloth are removed, and the best cutlery is set on polished wood. It's a bit crunchy underfoot as no one really takes charge in this house. Sometimes Miranda fetches a dust-pan and brush, but the crumbs always live in peace in the corners.

'She opens a tin of beans and puts a piece of Fletcher's sliced white under the grill, does both sides while the cheese is sliced, strong cheddar for preference. Then a load of cheese, piled in the middle and back under the grill till it blisters, burning slightly around the edges. The beans meanwhile are bubbling furiously in a small, wonky, aluminium pan which is sitting on the gas claws. She manhandles the toast onto a white Pyrex plate with an ugly pattern of faint blue flowers and pours the beans on top, careful to cover every little bit of the crust with a bean or juice. Meanwhile the tea is made in a porcelain cup with a rose motif: weak, a good splash of milk. She perches on the stool by the breakfast bar, the toes of her left foot curling over the bottom rung. Not even a clock's ticking sounds out, though the air is alive with the smell of charcoal, fat and bean sauce. She still eats daintily even though there is no one to see. But there is a certain tension in hearing your every bite sound out, each slurp accentuating the silence. She picks up her plate and mug and goes upstairs. Yes, it's still quiet, but it's not the same quiet in a bedroom as it is in a lonely kitchen. She climbs into bed and pulls the duvet over bare legs; a little shiver of pleasure runs from shoulder to buttock with the warmth. The clock radio flashes green, a stopped number some seven hours back: school, the gym and swimming away. Beans on toast in bed is not ideal, especially with long hair, but she's got a big mouth, steady hands and a flexible back from all that dancing.'

I was bored with all this: lonely, abandoned Miranda; Miranda having the time of her life with some sixteen year old mad professor more like! There was only one way to find out. Her mother answered the phone. "Oh hello, Sue. I'll get her for you now." (That was one theory down the drain then.)

"Hello, Petal."

"Were you in bed?"

"Yes! How did you know?"

"I thought you might be with Marcus tonight."

"No, he's at a Socialist Worker meeting. Come round."

"I can't, remember. It's a week day."

"Oh yes. Why won't they let you out, don't you do your homework or something?"

"Course I do my homework! Actually, I'd probably get it done even better if they'd let me go out somewhere; there'd be something to aim for."

"Yes, I agree." There was a pause.

"You haven't actually had sex then?" I said.

"Well no. It's not that easy finding anywhere."

"No, quite. Anyway, I better go. Miranda?"

"Yeah."

"Do you fancy my brother?"

"Huw?"

"Yes."

"Well, he's quite dishy in a Gestapo sort of way, but he's a bit too clean-cut for me. They're all like something out of Brideshead Revisited, him and his friends."

"Yes, I know. If he wasn't my brother I think I'd fancy him, though. He's just so confident."

"Yeah, well, he's got it all, hasn't 'e. See you then, Susie."

"See you." Well, there went all my theories down the drain, but at least I'd guessed the bed bit right. Miranda's mother liked to keep it cool in the house, and the only way to keep warm was to get into bed. Miranda said it was for health reasons, but I reckoned it was to save money. But now, at last, I had something of my own: Jan.

CHAPTER FIVE

MY PARENTS HAD AGREED to the party, with certain foolproof conditions such as, 'You must be back by midnight and I mean *in the house* by midnight!' Obviously my mother didn't believe you could have sex if the pubs were still open. I couldn't stop thinking about Jan. I couldn't stop thinking about Tom Booker either, but that was nothing new. I just couldn't imagine a time when Tom hadn't been the picture in my mind. He came round loads, always bringing some mute friend with him as a chaperone in case people thought he was going out with someone as uncool as me. Of all the beautiful girls he went out with, not one was any less than drop dead gorgeous, inarticulate and dumb (in the American sense of the word). I knew he was attracted to me from the way he smiled at me, the way it made me feel, he just didn't realise it yet. Anyway, back to Jan.

Where Tom Booker was Barry Hines, Jan was pure EM Forster. He was a South Yorkshire Youth cricket champion, the white gear looking as if it had been made just for him. He rubbed the ball on his trousers with a faraway look, brown eyes squinting a little as a lock of hair fell over his left eye. Then he'd crucify the batsman with a fast ball that seemed to surprise even himself. He probably lacked the self-confidence to make a top doctor like Huw (who had 'the necessary authority and drive', according to Dad, and an endless ability to charm the women patients; my own analysis), but he was going to be something great, if only he could get over his vagueness. Like me and Miranda, he was good at English, but apparently great at sciences too, so it would have been a waste going on with English at A level. I could imagine him as a vet actually, leave Huw to charm and bully the people. Jan's strong, gentle hands would hold an injured kestrel as well as pull a dead calf from a cow. It was the time of James Herriot, and, although the actor wasn't very sexy, I got off on the whole thought of it.

I'd gone through the panic stage of thinking about the party and had reached a strange, calm state, like being on the top of Ayers rock: clear and airy with a good view. I even knew what I was going to wear.

The four weeks to the party passed quickly, my dull routine punctuated by visits from Tom Booker or glimpses of Jan: through the Biology lab. window dissecting a rat with loving care, his white coat all undone; far in front of me in the corridor surrounded by friends; looking up from his lunch as us fifth years passed in the queue; smiling at me with his wonderful dog-brown eyes. Just a second of him as he passed was enough to tingle me everywhere. Was this love?

The only major news, apart from me being in love, was Miranda's break up with Marcus. Marcus and Miranda had been reading *Aristotle's Poetics* for English, and apparently they were one another's other half. Marcus felt they would be lulled into a fake sense of security by finding one another so early in their lives. It would be good for their 'art' (Miranda's dancing; his political and philosophical writing) if they could suffer a bit more, alone.

I listened in silence as Miranda sobbed the unlikely tale down the phone, my mind full of pictures of the ill-matched pair. Now I could have her back.

The break-up liberated yet another Miranda. Somewhere between the mother's bursting in and Aristotle's spoiling it all, they'd lost their virginity, and, although she was strangely reticent about the details, it changed her. Gone was Thatcher's 'power dressing' Miranda, and 'love child, Politbureau' Miranda. Here was Miranda the teenage vamp. She wanted everything, every ounce of experience, every moment of adulation, and she got everything she wanted. After Marcus, she wept for a week wrapped in her blue dressing gown, eating chicken soup (she believed in doing things properly). Then she gave me her tie-dye padded waistcoat and her back copies of 'Socialist Worker' and began stage three. There was nothing I could do but stand back and watch with a heady mixture of envy and amazement.

However, now Miranda wasn't the only one with a life. On the night of the party Huw waited for me by the front door, and after I'd 'done a twirl' for my mum and dad to see the party outfit, we left together. "Looking good, Sis," he said. I knew it. I was in one of Mum's black and white 'Mod' dresses. I'd recently got into the B52s, and my mother's collection of genuine 60s clothes was the envy of loads of the girls in my school. I'd started wearing them instead of hippie stuff to school discos. They showed off my slimness better. We took a bus to the University 'shabby chic' area of town. This was Marcus country, but there'd be no way he'd be at this sort of party. This was more your Young Conservative lot, but I couldn't afford to be picky.

When we arrived the party was already heaving, with someone running around on the roof flicking beer at people as they arrived at the front door. The open sash windows of the lovely old house had bums hanging over them as people perched on the sills. Huw patted me fraternally on the shoulder as we climbed up the steps. In Sheffield, the really posh people had massive, shabby mansions. It wasn't cool to be too prissy. Mum had our house 'just so'; that showed she was uncertain of her social position, Marcus had told me. These people, though, had nothing to prove. Even Huw's aggressive desire to do well at everything and my 'ennui' was a sign of our shaky foundations. I was only first generation Bourgeoisie after all. The gilt furniture with which our house abounded was the final proof. Now Marcus, however, was the real thing: money and education for generations. He'd only gone to a state school because his family were so left wing and right on.

"Yes," I'd argued lamely back, "my parents could have sent us privately, but Dad admired the academic rigour of Abbymoor School and the range of Science subjects and languages offered at A level." It hadn't sounded very convincing, even to me.

I found myself on my own. As I wandered through, clutching the plastic bag of Coke and Dandelion and Burdock Mum had made me bring, a couple of people I recognised said things and grinned. Huw had disappeared before explaining how I was going to get off with Jan.

I stood in the kitchen for a bit. The parents had obviously had a hand in the whole party, judging by the remains of home-made pizzas, black olives, quiche and fresh fruit pavlova. The fruit salad had hardly been touched. There seemed to be a different type of music coming from every room. Snatches of Hendrix, Joy Division, Pink Floyd, Genesis, Meat Loaf, Motor Head, The Cure and The Beatles drifted into the kitchen each time the door opened and closed on someone. It seemed, from the volume of distressed traffic passing through the kitchen, that the garage was a good place to be sick. An outside loo perhaps?

I stood in my figure-hugging black and white mini dress and white plastic knee-high boots (also my mother's, though a bit small) for nearly an hour; there were two more to go before the taxi would come and collect me. No sign of Jan. Not a breath, not a whisper. No Huw either. I'd set myself up by the bar thinking that 'bar maid' was a good cover for 'abandoned,' and anyway, many of the lads were too pissed to pour their own drinks. There was no chart music: no Adam Ant, Heaven Seventeen or Human League, and all the girls at this party looked like hippies. There was certainly no one else dressed in plastic boots with silver buckles.

An acquaintance of Huw's, a gormless, lanky boy who'd come to Abbymoor from public school to do Science A levels, returned to the bar for his fourth San Miguel (the huge amounts of parentally-sponsored drink were holding up extremely well). I'd had a few dribbles from the white wine boxes when I'd first come in but soon lost heart. He leaned on the 'bar', his reddish eyes constantly flickering on my legs, which endeared him to me. He told me how he was a Physics genius but was anti-social. "In what way?" I asked.

"Human Social Intercourse." His eyes didn't even flicker when he said it, and would I like to go upstairs with him?

"Sure," I said, for some reason in an American accent. It looked like Jan wasn't here, and there was no way I was going home without achieving at least a grope after going to all this trouble. I'd already made up my mind that I was only giving tops tonight. It had been a hard decision when I had been considering Jan, but I found there was no temptation to change my plans with this 'Ben' character. As we searched for a place to ourselves I let him open the doors to the bedrooms. I didn't want to catch Huw with his bum in the air.

Eventually we found a room. It seemed to be a walk-in airing cupboard with rush matting on the floor. I thought I'd take a tip Miranda had given me and start with the dos and don'ts -:

a) I don't give oral sex

b) no love bites and

c) I don't go all the way on a first date.

He looked bemused. Downstairs was for snogging, but up here was for the serious couples; there was no way I was going home tonight without something to tell.

It started off unpleasantly. Ben was a smoker and had a tongue like an old slipper. Okay, I wasn't exactly a snog-virgin (there'd been my cousin in Blackpool and that first time in the Guides' disco), but I wasn't about to have my tonsils coated in nicotine.

So, his foul mouth was out of the equation, down below was out of bounds, only tops left. In order to get my bra undone I had to heave him off me. God, he had no idea of the logistics of the thing! I remembered reading an article about how sex was better for older people. I'd been pretty sceptical at the time (all those wrinkly thirty-somethings), but it almost made sense now when you came to look at it. It was like a ballet routine. A sort of 'Pas de Deux' where each partner knew the other's moves: the weight of their body, what they liked. It was proving impossible with the dress (should have considered this when I was thinking what to wear). The delay was proving costly as Ben had his hands down his trousers and was rearranging something. In a minute it would be out through his flies, and we'd be onto a whole different ball game.

I pushed him off and got to my feet (I've always been able to think quick in a crisis) and slowly, oh so very wiggly, eased down my mini dress. A compromise might be me stripped, him clothed, I might be able to control it more. He groaned with delight and reached inside his trousers again, but I wasn't having any of it. Pulling open my front fastening bra I let him have a good ogle. Dropping to my knees and grabbing the offending hand, I put it safely on my tit instead. This was nice. I knelt, he sat with his long thin legs straight out in front of him and kneaded me gently with both hands. So this was what it was all about! I wondered how it was going to end. The nails were digging in now, over long (did he play the guitar?) and not too clean. Anyway I was getting cold and, with the dress down and the bra pulled right open, I wasn't keen on someone bursting in on us. I peeled his fingers off me and nibbled them with little kisses, but his other hand strayed back to his trousers. I wasn't falling for that. "I've got to go now, Baby," (where *was* that American accent coming from!). He reached for me again, and this time I shoved him away. He looked up at me with his face bloated with desire, eyes dazed, as though he were a new-born mouse, all blind and hopeless, deserted by its mother and ready for the drowning bucket. I quite liked him.

By this time I'd got the bra done and the dress up. I crouched down in front of him for him to do up the zip. Before he did he kissed me gently on the back, placed his hand, just once, flat on my spine and then eased up the material. That, despite all the tit kneading and nipple pinching, was the most erotic of all. I felt a shiver move down from where he'd touched, into my belly and right inside. I turned around and kissed him, just once, and stood up quickly. He adjusted his trousers, and I put out my hand to help him up, then opened the door. What had been only bass line gathered tune and harmony, individual voices coming clear of the muddle of sound. He squeezed my hand just once as it held open the door, and we went downstairs. He was a lot taller than me, and I was aware of him looming over me as we came down into the hall. "My taxi'll be waiting," I said.

"When's it for?"

"About five minutes time."

"I'll wait with you."

"No, it's okay."

"I'd like to." He looked earnestly into my eyes.

"No, really. I'm happier not. I'll just wait outside."

"Can I call you?" he asked.

"No," I said. Miranda was right. You should say what you mean with men.

"Oh." His face looked suddenly crumpled and lumpy with disappointment. I turned my back quickly on the party and, closing the front door, stood on the steps in the night air. Everything tingled. Blood warmed from the tips of my toes to the roots of my hair. I'd done it! The first date, and entirely without Miranda!

Behind the opaque glass of the door behind me a shadow waited; I could feel it. Playing hard to get didn't come naturally, but I supposed I'd learn with practice. I walked down the grand drive and onto the dimly lit avenue, not too dangerous, even though the taxi was at least another fifteen minutes away. The 'Black Panther' was about somewhere in South Yorkshire, but I wasn't worried; they said he only killed prostitutes.

Well, Jan had missed it. Missed me, I mean. I wondered too how Tom Booker had fared tonight. Probably clubbing; out winning Northern Soul albums for his dancing, making girls meet him in their dreams. But most of all, where was Miranda? I couldn't wait not to tell her; for her to happen to phone me, and for it all to drip, everso slowly, everso casually into our conversation. Yes!

The taxi driver arrived, a silent man with the radio down low. I wondered if he could tell that I'd nearly done it. We drove back through Fullwood, past the dark mansions, and home.

Huw was up waiting for me. As I came into the kitchen he looked at me quizzically,

"I've sent Mum to bed. She was into waiting for you, but I thought you could probably do without the Spanish Inquisition tonight."

"Thanks," I said.

"How did it go, anyway?"

"I thought I was doing without the Inquisition!"

He laughed.

"Anyway," I said, "I've got a few questions of my own, like, where the sod was Jan?"

"Ah, Jan." He finished his toastie. "He didn't turn up."

"I know that, Huw. Why?"

"Who knows, with Jan. Maybe cleaning out his terrapins or something."

"That's a shit excuse!"

"Anyway, you seemed to be doing OK without him."

"How do you know!"

"I saw you."

"No!"

"Well, go upstairs, whatever."

"I'm not going out with him; he's too wet."

"He's all right."

"Go to bed, you two!" Mum's voice. We looked at one another and winced, had she heard?

"Anyway, why are you home?" I stage whispered as I tiptoed towards the hall.

"Imogen wasn't there. Night, Sis."

I went up first, poking my head round Mum and Dad's door before they had a chance to come in to me. "Good party, Susie?"

"Great, thanks, Dad."

"Get to bed now, Sue, you've got piano in the morning," said my mother. Did she know? I didn't need to be asked twice. Getting undressed in the semi-dark of my street-lit room, I relived the strip. It seemed even more exciting in retrospect. I kept seeing myself as it were from his angle, curvy, slim; giving it, taking it away again. I felt my body up, watched my hands in the long mirror.

In bed I stretched ecstatically under the bed clothes. Again there was that same feeling of warm blood in all the extremities. Whenever I closed my eyes I replayed a part of the performance, usually seeing myself from his perspective. God I was gorgeous! I fell asleep curled in embryo position as usual, on my left side, my right hand cradling my tit.

Next morning I was just writing my diary (code of course) when the phone went,

"Susie, it's Miranda." Bloody hell, did she have some sixth sense or something!

"Darling," she said through sobs, "you've got to, you've just got to read *Roots*. It's the most heartbreaking book. Oh, God, I wish I was black!"

"Miranda, you've never read *Roots*?"

"No, no. You've just got to. You'll be blown away."

"I have read it! Ages ago. There was a series. Where the hell've you been all your life, Miranda? It was major popular."

"Oh, well, I've only just discovered it. Earl gave it me."

"Earl?"

"My new lover. He's gorgeous. So noble. So exotic."

"Where's he from?"

"Doncaster."

I laughed. "Anyway, I thought you were in mourning for Marcus," I said suspiciously.

"Life must go on, you know. I've grieved for him but there comes a time when you just have to move on."

"Really," I said. "Anyway, long time no see."

"Yes, I've been so busy! Sixth form life is a whole different ball game. What've you been up to?"

"Oh, just copping off with a few people."

"What! Who?" She spluttered. "Where?"

"Ah, haa!" (God it was great!) "Oh well, must go. I don't want your demanding work schedule to suffer."

"Sod off! You haven't lost it, have you?"

"Er, no. But I had a good try."

"Nooo! Do tell, reveal all, immediately."

"No way! You'll have to wait for this one. Shall I see if I can stay over yours after the Rotary Club gig?"

"Can't do, sorry. I've told Gran I'm with you. I'm actually staying the night at Earl's. His mum knows and everything, and she's okay about it. Are you still there?"

"I suppose so," I said. Even now she had to be a step ahead! My news had been neutralised.

"Shall I come round early then instead?" I said, limply.

"Do. By the way, Petal, I've got a surprise for you."

"What?" I know I sounded churlish.

"Well... all right then I'll tell. I've invited Tom Booker and Luke to play with us at the gig."

"No!"

"Oh yes. Doesn't your best mate look after you, hey? Next Saturday everyone's coming round to mine, and we'll go on from there. Toodle oo!" And that was it.

Well, I would have to give up on Jan now anyway, as he'd never go out with me when he knew I'd got off with his friend, and I didn't really want to repeat the airing cupboard episode with wacky Ben, so that was probably the end of that chapter in my adventures. But Tom Booker... that was something, and if anyone could get us together, it would be Miranda.

CHAPTER SIX

PERHAPS I SHOULD HAVE smelt a rat as soon as she opened the door to me wearing some orange plastic 'plus fours' and a halter-neck top. As well as sex, she had taken up exercising in a big way, being particularly fond of the weights. I was looking forward to being in the sixth form myself. You got to pick only the three subjects you liked and had loads of time off from school. Like Miranda, I would have 'hobbies,' as she'd taken to calling her dates. My train of thought was suddenly interrupted as I saw Miranda's expression. Have you ever read Blyton's *The Magic Faraway Tree?* Moonface? Well, you can imagine it then. Her face glowed, big, round and zealous.

"What's up?" I said, suspicious. "Byron's here," she simpered. "We've been experimenting."

"Oh God!"

"Well are you coming in then?"

"Yes, I suppose so. Where is he?"

"In the bedroom of course," she replied, cheerily.

"What're you doing with him? He's a creep! How do you know him anyway? What's happened with Earl?" All this came out as an unpleasant hiss.

"Oh it just didn't work out. He was a prude. Can you imagine that?" she said, rolling her eyes. I had nothing really to say; I'd never even had a chance to meet him.

"What are you wearing those for anyway?" I said as she removed the gown. She was topless, the exercise pants elasticated at the waist.

"They make me sweat," she said.

"What do you want to do that for?"

"You lose weight, ninny."

"But why are you wearing them now? They'll be here in half an hour!"

"I can't take them off, they reek."

"Well why don't you have a bath or something?"

"There's no time. There's no hot water."

I left my cello in a downstairs room and followed her up. Music was playing in her room, Hot Chocolate. As she pushed open her door I saw the boy from school, Byron Saltfisch, lounging on her bed and rolling a large bottle of cooking oil to and fro. He appeared not to be wearing anything except Miranda's towelling bathrobe without the cord.

"Sue Jones, Dearest!" he exclaimed, coming toward me and giving me a lovey hug. "You're just in time to help us with an experiment. We can't agree, you see."

"What experiment's that then?" I replied, turning on Miranda. "What is it makes me think it's something rude?" She laughed. Both of them were looking at me expectantly. I had two options here: comply, or get out. An ironing board in the corner of the room, with Miranda's study lamp angled over it, caught my eye.

"Is that something to do with it?"

"Yes," said Byron. "We reckoned we could get more of a purchase on you if we could move all round. It'd blow your mind."

"I don't want it blowing." I looked at Miranda, who was by now wearing nothing but the sweatpants. "What exactly've you been doing?"

"We...ll," she said, "we've been experimenting to see

how quickly it takes men and women to come, given various stimulation. It takes me much longer to come, for instance, than him." She gestured toward Byron with her thumb.

"But of course I can do it more. I'm up to my fifth."

"Oh." They were both looking at me. Byron had removed the bathrobe and was standing naked: skinny, brown and very hairless, apart from the weedy strands around his measly cock.

"We thought, if we could use two pairs of hands for stimulation, then we could speed it up," said Miranda, already picking up her alarm clock. "The quickest I've done it is three minutes."

"That was pretty good," said Byron.

It was make or break. If I left now, that was my chance of Tom Booker out the window. I didn't have a hope in hell of getting an orgasm at all in these circumstances. It was hard enough on my own, trying to follow the instructions from *Our Bodies Ourselves* at the same time as vibrating away a million times a minute. It gave you Tennis Elbow.

Tom Booker and cystitis, or leaving with my dignity intact?

"OK, I'll do it," I said.

"Brilliant! Come on, Babe," said Byron, going to pull my jumper off over my head.

"I'll do that! For God's sake, give me a bit of space, will you!"

"Okay, okay, keep yer'air on, why don't you!" Miranda gave me a leg up onto the ironing board and I lowered myself down. It wobbled dangerously. The clock ticked, loudly. For a couple of minutes I lay prone whilst they greased up their hands and made other preparations I couldn't see.

"I hope this isn't going to give me a urinary tract infection!" (Remember, I was a doctor's daughter).

"You'll be all right," chirruped back Miranda. First she set to on the breasts, pressing down on them with the flat of her hands and rotating them, one clockwise, the other anti. Byron was on duty at the bottom half, concentrating hard, like someone rubbing at a persistent mark on the kitchen floor. It wasn't so much friction as pressure, the same spot, like a pneumatic drill. I was the tarmac. It was made worse by the talking that was going on over the top of me; in fact the whole thing reminded me of being on the theatre trolley when I was about to have my tonsils out.

Now and again Miranda stopped to assess my reaction, her face expectant at first, but each time looking a little more exasperated. "Aren't you feeling anything, then?"

"Yeah, a bit, but you're going too fast, you're too rough."

"There's nothing wrong with what I'm doing. You must be a mutant or something."

"Just be a bit gentle, can't you."

"For God's sake, Byron, go easy will you," snapped Miranda.

"Yeah, please, I'm getting friction burns."

"Just stop talking! Concentrate!" The ironing board didn't help. Neither did the fact that they'd put it right under the overhead light. The whole effect was pure 'A & E'.

"Why does it have to be me anyway? Why can't one of you two do it?"

"We've done it."

"Not with me here you haven't."

"Will you just lie back and concentrate for God's sake!" But there was nothing doing. It occurred to me that faking it would save a lot of time and me at least a lot of discomfort. The logistics were a problem, though; I was worried to move much, in case I fell off.

Just then the doorbell rang. All activity ceased for a moment.

Miranda wrapped an ornate silk number around herself whilst I saw to my horror that Byron was planning a further determined effort. "Get me up, will you!"

"You don't have to. I'll get the door."

"Miranda, I'm not lying here like this when Tom Booker walks in!"

"Okay, just get her up, then." Byron heaved me to my feet and held the board steady whilst I lowered myself down. One year younger than me, he had joined the school in the third year, when all the groups were already made. There was no way that those friendships, having already congealed, could ever have been altered; yet someone, his parents I suppose, expected a little chink to appear in someone's gang that he could fit into. If he hadn't been so weird that would've been impossible. As it was, he was his own personal gang of one, and he hung around with other alien children who made a sort of high status non-clique on the periphery of everyday school. Byron was high camp, an up-market 'Adam Ant,' and having recently read the fictional memoirs of Lord Byron, I knew how apt his name was. He wore shirts with frills and high black boots, but whereas other kids' New Romantic gear was the watered down version from Dolcis or Chelsea Girl, everything he had looked expensive. The shirt looked real linen, pure musketeer; the boots gleamed; the steel sole caps clicked in the corridor when he walked by. Who knows how Miranda, two years his senior, had got hold of him, but they belonged together in that fascinating parentless world that I could only visit. Both had divorced parents who were always out, and he lived with his Dad in a penthouse by the park.

I shoved my clothes on and waited on the landing for Tom Booker to come up, nursing an unpleasant burning sensation. No-one ever said Tommy; always his full name. I'd got my wrap-around skirt on, just managed to tuck the clingy top in (long sleeves because of the eczema).

'Booksy.' He did sometimes get called that by his mates. He'd be wearing that long, brown leather coat, undone. No one else in the whole school had anything like it, but he didn't get the piss taken out of him. Standing at the top of the stairs, I could see him coming up two at a time. He was looking and smiling at me already, big mouth in a freckled face. Freckles! How was it he could get away with them and still look gorgeous?

"Susie!" He called enthusiastically (as I said, he really liked me, but he didn't know it yet). For a moment there was a hanging feeling, the top part of my body seemed to be leaning toward him, hypnotised by him smiling that smile, right into me. He had on the jumper he always wore, that I dreamed about him in. That tight lamb's wool one, so soft, stretching across his chest which was as broad and shapely as a man's.

"Hey, Booksy!" The strident voice of bloody Byron Saltfisch butting in, androgynous bastard! "Salty! Wha' you doing here, mate?" Saltfisch pushed past from behind me and they wrestled shoulders for a couple of seconds. Byron hadn't a hope in hell, so he cheated and pulled away, leaving Tom to stagger backwards, laughing. Luke was on the stairs by this time.

"Hey, Lukey! How'se it going!" Saltfisch again. He slapped Luke on the shoulder. I stood there like a spare part while they did their adolescent male jostling-greeting thing.

"Make us a bit of room." Miranda. Three sets of male eyes gazed on her as she climbed the stairs. Although at this time her backside had not yet taken on its true proportions, she had a riveting swing and huge hips. Mysteriously the kimono had come completely open, and as she ascended we were looking past the wide, slow smile of Miranda at her tits (not particularly big, but bouncy and with huge nipples); belly, sweat pants and calves. With each step she clenched her toes luxuriously into the stair carpet. Saltfisch laughed. Luke stared with his mouth hanging open, and Tom called out, "Hey, M'anda, what you done with yer togs?" I loved him! Miranda chuckled, but she wriggled the robe back up round her as she reached the top step. They were too young for her, really. She wasn't even trying.

"Are we going or aren't we?" I said. Miranda raised an eyebrow in my direction and squeezed between Saltfisch and Tom Booker, throwing, "Get the instruments ready, will you Dearie, "over her shoulder to me as she went into her bedroom. Tom was smiling at me again, that same toe-curling liquid green smile. He had me sussed. I felt the blush start in the little hollow at the base of my throat. "Hey, let's go," I said. "You're not coming are you, Saltfisch?"

"Na. Not really my scene."

"It's not really anyone's 'scene'. It's a favour."

"Yeah, yeah, for the grandmother, I know. I wouldn't be seen dead."

"What am I playing, Sue?" Tom Booker was standing near me on the stairs, looking down at me. He always smelt so gorgeous. Not of anything in particular, just himself.

I pulled myself together, pushed past Saltfisch and down the stairs, calling back up, "You have the bodhran; Luke can've the tambor. I'll get them now." Christ, what was I on? Saltfisch'd tell Tom Booker, and that'd be the end of us, before we even got going! He could have had anyone in our year or the years below, but he kept hanging out with me. He kept calling for me, him and Luke at the door, any night of the week. He'd leave the girlfriend character outside, sometimes for nearly an hour, sometimes in the rain, while we had a laugh. God knows what we talked about, why he wanted to talk to me. Even though he was from the houses down by Furnace Park, he was in one of the top sets. He'd got brains, and I loved it when he used them on me. His dad had been in the SAS, and we had some wicked arguments about CND. Now I'd be just another stupid slag, a character in one of Byron Saltfisch's sordid sex stories, but not even with the street cred of the girlfriend with the cucumber. At least she'd been able to come, over and over again for hours apparently (faker, the stupid ponce couldn't even tell). I should've faked it. Damn Miranda! Sod it, why couldn't I just say no?

"For God's sake, come on; there'll be no point going in a minute!" I yelled upstairs.

"Coming, Dearest!" answered Miranda from her boudoir.

"She's coming!" shouted Saltfisch, giggling obscenely.

"Right, well I'm going. Catch me up!" I flung up the stairwell at them before I went, picked up my cello in its soft case and slammed out of the door.

I couldn't believe I'd been so stupid. He was bound to tell, and if he didn't, Miranda (despite being threatened copiously) would allude to it so obviously, so filled with her own self importance, that it would all come puking out anyway. Sod it, I wasn't pretty enough to go out with him anyway. Where could we have gone? Not the Northern Soul clubs, no way. I'd never have fitted in with the girls there. I didn't dress right, talk right. I was from the wrong side of town and, though I'd read all about Mellors, he'd not had to put up with his mates taking the piss out of him. Anyway, I wasn't exactly the lady of the manor. What was it Marcus had said? Bourgeois?

Gloom, doom, I had it all as I crossed the main road by the park. A white van slowed down for the couple of plumbers inside to shout something obscene ("Hey, Girly. Can I be your 'cello?")

perhaps, I didn't catch it properly. I was impressed, actually, as it took a pretty exceptional man to even know that it was a cello, let alone think up something rude to shout out as he drove by at thirty miles an hour!

I heard my name being called: Miranda with her guitar was running down the hill by the bus stop and laughing, her long hair flying away behind her, wrap-around skirt coming open to reveal long brown legs and looking like an opening shot for a French film. Tom Booker and Luke were walking together behind her carrying the instruments, and Saltfisch nowhere to be seen, thank God. I waited for them before crossing. No use letting her see how I felt; it'd be all such a big thing, with her crying, and all in front of Tom.

She arrived breathless and laughing behind me, just as the lights were changing for us to cross. "Hey, hasty, why didn't you wait for me?"

I used the crossing to move ahead without answering. I could feel her tugging at my cello where I had it slung by a strap over my shoulder. This was just too much! Stopping dead I turned round, only to look right into Tom Booker's face. "I thought you needed some help, Sue, that thing looks heavy."

"Oh, thanks. Yeah, thanks a lot, but it's okay, I'm used to it." Three smiling faces looking at me: him in front; next to him Luke, and Miranda in her tall clog sandals, eyes and forehead taller even than Tom. I felt close to tears. "Come on then," I said. "We're nearly there now. Let's just get it done."

I couldn't hack those 'Love Story' looks with him; no more. Why hadn't I just said no, just gone away again as soon as I saw her in the plastic pants; saw bloody Saltfisch?

We were past the railings now and up the wide steps of the Victorian semi where the Rotary Club had its meetings. Miranda pushed past me to ring the bell.

Through the window I could see row after row of old people
sitting waiting. They seemed to be all dressed up. Before she'd
even had time to touch the bell the door opened, and a handsome
old man with a Canadian accent told us we were late and gestured
to us to go through. I was first through the archway, and a vigorous
round of applause broke out. I bowed. Miranda was poking me up
the backside with her guitar, so I went forward to the piano and
started unpacking my cello. The applause continued, to include
the two boys, who came to stand beside me. The bodhran was
nowhere to be seen. Instead, Luke was carrying a triangle and
Tom was holding a tambourine. God only knows how they'd got
talked into this.

Miranda crossed in front of the piano and did a little bow to
the audience who clapped furiously again. Miraculously, her
skirt was now done up perfectly decently and she'd got an alice
band from somewhere which held her hair back from her face,
framing it and making her look almost innocent. She slid her
guitar out of its case, smiling and talking to the audience as she
went. I could see the kind face of Miranda's grandmother in the
front row, beaming.

"We're the concert group from Abbeymoor School, delighted
to be here by special invitation of the President of the Rotary
Club. Luke will play the triangle," he grinned companionably,
"with Tom Booker on the tambourine; Sue Jones on 'cello and
piano, and myself on guitar and piano." There was more loud
applause. "We intend to play for you today a selection of old
and new pieces, both classical and popular. Some of them we'd
like you to join in with." There was a murmur of pleasure in the
audience and some sporadic clapping. It was a nice piano and I
was beginning to enjoy myself, although the irony of my position

was not lost on me. Less than an hour ago I had been lying on an ironing board with my pants down. Now I was part of a clean-cut group of nice young people doing a charity concert. It was pure Von Trapp family singers.

'I am sixteen, going on seventeen,' I hummed quietly to myself.

Tom was sitting on the corner of a table, looking utterly comfortable with himself. Luke standing beside him looking around, equally relaxed. What on earth were they doing here? How would they explain this to their cool friends?

Miranda sat on a chair and produced a tiny footstool from an ethnic-type rucksack that I hadn't seen before. She put one bare brown foot on it.

"The first piece we're going to play for you is Scarborough Fair, immortalised by the indomitable Paul Simon and Art Garfunkel, Sue's favourite song." It wasn't actually. I preferred Edelweiss, but I let it go.

She gave us the opening chords, and we sang together, just guitar and two voices, me doing the Simon, her with the glory. I have to admit, it sounded pretty good. My voice was clear but unexceptional, whilst hers was folksy, breathy, the sort of voice you could stand to hear for hours. I was aware only of Tom watching me as I sang, and I tried not to open my mouth too wide in case he saw my fillings. As I stood behind Miranda, leaning on her chair as we'd planned, she kept looking up through her hair, eyes half closed, and what was meant to be an entrancing smile. I think she was half modelling us on ancient footage of Sonny and Cher. A thunderous round of applause followed our performance, and Miranda took my hand and kissed it, perhaps rather OTT for the Rotary Club? I bowed. Tom was clapping and Luke was doing the thumbs up.

"For our next item we intend to use the whole troop." ('Troop'? I caught Tom smiling). "This is another traditional song that some of you, born and brought up in Sheffield might know: 'On Ilkley Moor Bar Tat'." Someone in the audience groaned. "We'd like you to join in, clap along, sing, tap your feet, anything you like. You can even change the words if you like, I know the naughty kids do that in assembly."

What was she on? I spread the first chord on the piano with a flourish. Miranda was on the recorder for this one, leaving me and the boys to sing and play the piano, triangle and tambourine at the same time. This didn't bode well. However, we'd played this one a bit in school, and with each verse we got more and more old folks to join in. We seemed to be speeding up too, which helped. Luke was on the triangle. Every time we got to the chorus and he had his 'on the first beat' bit we got faster, so that by the end it was a breathless gallop to the finish. We even had one loud old man singing 'thou art fat' which speeded up to 'the fart' by the end. All through it Tom kept looking at me, grinning. This must have been the weirdest date he'd ever been on, if indeed he even realised he was on one.

Next was a bit for recorder and piano and then me on the 'cello with Miranda accompanying. She had Tom turning the music, reaching past her, brushing up against her, even though the bits that I'd been doing on the piano earlier had been much more complicated and I hadn't asked for help. Luke stood by me, but I didn't trust him and turned my own. I put my all into it, and I have to admit it was pretty good. Even the dodgy high bits sounded all right, apart from the fact that Miranda had no idea how to accompany a stringed instrument and kept drowning me out.

"Now for our penultimate number, chosen by the boys," said

Miranda, swivelling round on the stool to face the audience. "This is where my colleagues, Luke and Tom, come into their own. If you should feel like clicking your fingers or tapping your feet to this one, go right ahead."

One lady on the front row looked a little alarmed at this, but on the whole there was a look of anticipation, with people sitting up straighter in their seats and adjusting their bra straps or cuff-links.

"Right," Miranda hissed at me as she came round the side of the piano, "contingency plans, all right?"

"What contingency plans?"

"If it all falls apart, you and me'll just come in with 'You're the one that I want', right?"

"No it's not all right, I don't know the words!"

"Just go 'Bop bop shawaddy waddy' or something, okay?" She glided off. Luke and Tom were now in front of the piano, Luke smiling nervously and holding a pair of maracas. I'd heard Tom singing in assembly when we were in junior school, and it wasn't too good; well I liked it, but it wasn't for public consumption. It was a real boy's voice: hearty, sincere, but a bit flat. When he was concentrating, he always reminded me of Dick in the Famous Five, that straight piece of fringe hanging down over his left eye. Miranda was on the piano again, and I had a home-composed bit of pizzicato on the cello. Although I hadn't played it before, it was pretty much all open strings, and after a wince-worthy beginning in which only Tom could be heard, and I had to put all my energy into not catching Miranda's eye to prevent us from launching into the Grease number, Luke seemed to take off. Singing low and deep and bang on tune, he held the room in his hands. I'd never heard him sing before. He wasn't naff on the maracas either. After a while Tom stopped singing altogether, just snapped his fingers and moved his hips a little. One old lady was clapping off the beat, and several were clicking their fingers. Nearly everyone on the front row had their feet going. Luke finished us off with three firm shakes of the maracas and bowed. There was massive applause, and Tom turned round to gesture Miranda and me to our feet. When the applause seemed to be struggling a little, Miranda clapped her hands in the air.

"Ladies and Gentlemen. Thanks so much to Luke for his wonderful rendition of that fine calypso tune." A renewed burst of applause.

"Now it's time for our last piece." A perceptible murmur of disappointment.

"It's one that you'll all be familiar with and which was supposedly composed by Henry the Eighth himself. It is of course (pause),… the famous 'Greensleeves'! Sue and I will play it for you on a variety of instruments." More applause as we got settled, Miranda back at the piano. The first time through was the two of us singing with the piano, me picking out a couple of phrases in harmony. Then, as Miranda hummed the transition passage, I picked up my cello, and we played an instrumental version, the cello playing the tune. It was all hush in the room, the sound magnified by the wood floor and bare walls. Last time through was Miranda singing and playing the piano with me doing some simple harmony we'd worked out on the 'cello. We held the last note especially long for effect, and the claps rang out. The old man who'd let us in had got to his feet, and Miranda came from behind the piano and took my hand. I looked round at Luke and Tom who were bowing. Then Miranda was between them, bringing them up to the front, and I felt his hand holding mine. Despite all the excitement it was perfectly dry, and he was holding me firmly, like he wasn't ashamed to be seen with me in front of everybody. I had my cello and bow in the other hand, spike in the floor as we bowed together several more times, Miranda's hair sweeping the ground.

The Canadian man in his blazer came forward to shake hands with the boys and to kiss Miranda and me rather gratuitously on the cheeks.

He made a short speech and presented Miranda and Tom with an envelope each. More clapping. Isn't it odd how the natural authority of some people just shines through? How did he know not to pick Luke and me? I felt a bit guilty about our shoddy show and the fact that we'd dragged along Luke and Tom without telling the club there would be four of us. Book tokens in the envelopes, bound to be. How were we going to share those out then?

Miranda was by now surrounded by old lady friends of her grandmother's, and as I packed away my cello an elderly couple, waiting by the piano in a queue to go down the centre aisle for tea, were looking in her direction. "Fine young lady. It's nice to see them getting on so well together, doing something useful for a change."

"Lovely young people."

"I like a group, not all this couples business all the time. They get so intense so young. It's much healthier going round in a group, all together, getting on with something."

"Hobbies. Walking, Scouts, that type of thing."

Tom was coming toward me through the crowd. I smiled, then went back to putting my music together. "Sue, great spread."

"Yeah, Miranda says. Loads of home-made cakes."

"Scones, clotted cream."

"Lashings of ginger beer!"

"You what?"

"Ah, nothing. Just what the Famous Five characters were always saying."

"What?"

"I don't think Enid Blyton was a boy's sort of thing."

"Anyway, lets 've a scowne, I'm starving." Everyone in Sheffield seemed to say 'scowne' like that. I said it 'scon'. That was normal in my family but I kept getting the piss taken out of me for being posh.

"Luke wanted you to have this." He gave me one of the envelopes. "You did more for the gig, you should have it."

"A fiver book token!"

"It's mad trying to share a token. They didn't know me and Luke were coming, and you love reading."

"Thanks, Tom." If I looked up he was going to be smiling at me. If he looked me right in the eye I was sure he'd see the video playing there, of me being vivisected on by Byron.

"Shall we go and get something to eat then? Where's Luke?" I asked quickly. Maybe Luke was more important than I'd ever imagined. A modern Miss Bates who acted as a chaperone, made the lovers feel easier. Didn't she act as a foil too, rather like a pretty girl chooses a plain one for a best friend, to accentuate the difference?

"He's giving a maracas demo to some old ladies in the other room."

"This I have to see!" I said. He laughed. We shoved my cello under the piano for safe keeping and went next door.

This room had the same lovely big windows, ceiling to floor, through which the mellow evening light was falling. It lit up a huge table, dressed in a white linen cloth and loaded with food. The room smelled of clean old people and baking, light catching the tiny cut-glass bowls people were using for trifle. We honed in on the table where delicate ham sandwiches perched on fine china.

Being a veggie, I avoided these and went for the vol-aux-vents, filled with mushrooms and wine sauce. Tom was still wearing his leather coat which seemed rather incongruous in the pastel room, and he, like me, was trying hard to be polite and not to pile his plate too high. Despite the fact that we were just about the last in, there was hardly a dent in the feast.

Miranda was positioned with her back to the window, where the light made a dark halo of her hair. In two long fingers she held a chicken's wing, giving her big smile to the statuesque old gentleman in the navy blazer. By now I'd done my duty on the savouries. "What about the scones? Come on, you first," I said to Tom. He piled up an enormous amount of home-made gooseberry jam on his and a dollop of yellowy cream, whilst I went for the strawberry with whole berries.

"Where's Luke? He's not been kidnapped, has he?" I asked again.

"Can't imagine any of the old girls wanting 'im, can you?" he said. I kept my gaze on Tom as, whenever I looked round, I kept catching someone's eye and I did not want a disruption of our tete-a-tete. "We'll have to go in a bit. We're meeting Tim Bree in the Leadmill nine o'clock."

"Yeah, me too."

"You're going down the Leadmill?" he asked, surprised.

"No. I mean I've got to go. ... I'm out tonight..."

"Wher're you – ?"

"Luke! There he is. Luke!" I called. Narrow escape. To be honest, I had no idea where the Leadmill was. It had live bands, but people like The Cure, not exactly Miranda dancing music, which had to be all soul vocals and beat. Luke's face came toward us through the crowd, the two of them looking so pleased to see one another it was almost touching. "Well, come on then," he said to Luke, hand on his shoulder. "We've gor a bws t'catch. See ya, Sue." That smile again! I think it was the fact of it being half hidden under the fringe that made him so cute. "See ya," I said, as cool as I could.

On his way out he went to Miranda, still by the window and shook her hand. The old gentleman shook his and Luke's, something was said and he laughed and made a mock salute. I'd forgotten Tom had been in the Cadets. Him going was like someone'd turned the dimmer switch down in the room. I wanted to cry.

I felt a small dry hand in mine. Miranda's Granny, hair in a bun, blue dress picking out the colour in her eyes. "Thank you so much, luv. It's been a lovely concert. It's so good to see you having fun with those boys. I think it calms Miranda down, having you about." I managed to say nothing.

"Come and call with her for tea one day. I'll make my lemon cake that you all love so much."

"Thanks, Granny," I said.

Miranda strode up, biting on a huge strawberry. She held the leaf between her teeth for a bit, just like Ermintrude from *The Magic Roundabout*.

"We better go, Gran. I've got a friend coming round tonight. I'm making supper."

"When's Jean and Brian home then, luv?"

"Oh, first thing tomorrow, I think."

"You won't be lonely?" She looked worried, "I've offered and offered for her to come to me, you know."

"Yes, I know," I said.

"Are you going to keep her some company tonight?"

"Erm, well I thought I'd…"

"Yes, of course. Sue's staying, aren't you, Petal? We're off now, Granny. I'll give you a phone when Mum gets back." She turned to face the room. "We're going now, thank you all everso much for the welcome. See you soon, I hope."

"Bye," I waved and, picking up our instruments on the way out, we left the Rotary Club. "That was a lucky escape," I said as I balanced dangerously on one of the collapsible seats at the bus stop.

"Yes, I thought 'On Ilkley Moor' was going astray for sure."

"No, I didn't mean that! Your Gran, I think she might suspect."

"What?"

"That you're having sex."

"Oh, that. She knows."

"What!"

"Well, at least she knows I'm not a virgin."

"Miranda! How?"

"Well, after my Mum caught me that time with Marcus, the next time I went to Granny's. She told me not to jump the gun and that the cart never belonged before the horse."

"Oh hell!"

"And then she told me some tale about a cousin of hers who could play the piano and speak fluent French but had had to marry a stoker and died in childbirth. Apparently she had to give it up."

"What?"

"The piano," she said.

"God. Sounds like DH Lawrence or something. What did you say?"

"Well I just said, What a shame, and that people didn't have to get married these days no matter how enthusiastic they were."

"What did she say to that?"

"She just stroked my face and did the tea."

"You're so lucky. My Mum"d've gone mental."

"Takes too much energy."

"Miranda, I'd probably be able to come and stay, keep you a bit of company if you want. I could phone Mum."

"You can if you like, but St John's coming over. You can meet him, 'my new beau'," she said, putting on her Blanche Dubois accent and Vivien Leigh smile.

"Never mind," I said. Again I felt that funny feeling you get just before you cry. A sensation of something dry and hard rising up through your innards and into your throat. I fought it down, tried not to think about myself sitting alone in my bedroom whilst Miranda cooked for and petted her new lover and Tom Booker danced for a Leadmill full of stunning girls. Instead we talked about school for a bit until my bus came, and she waved me off. I hadn't even tackled her about Byron and St John on the go at the same time. For Miranda, obsessive in everything she did, sex had replaced the crush on my mother; sex had replaced her Marxism; sex was the new thing. I mounted the steps of the bus with a numb heart and saw her waving all the time until it rounded the corner, and I was out of sight.

CHAPTER SEVEN

MIRANDA THE PANDER HAD got us together, and I was now convinced more than ever that Tom was really keen, but what had come out of it? By even a nerd's standards it had been a hopeless date. And even Ben didn't call. Anyway, water under the bridge, or rather underwear in the airing cupboard. I'd done quite well out of the incident, actually. The warm blood in the extremities effect lasted for several weeks, whenever I thought about it. It was also quite impressive to Sandra and Louise, who hadn't yet been out with anyone older than the fifth year. Sandra really fancied Huw, and was impressed that I'd been invited to an upper sixth party in the first place. I didn't tell either of them the gory details, but threw in casually to the conversation things like, "I didn't realise how hard it was to open a bra with only one hand," and "he was so aroused he nearly had my eye out!" They were well impressed. Only Miranda had the real details, which by now were old news, and she'd rather do her own practical than hear other people's theory. However, in addition to being rather bored (Ben was straight, white and a bit weedy) she was quite proud of me I think.

Obviously there hadn't been much opportunity to talk to her at the Rotary Club fiasco, so I'd arranged to meet her one lunch-time.

We didn't see a lot of one another in school anymore, and anyway she had started obsessing about her father. With the regulation birthday card and fat cheque, this time had come an invitation to France. She was beside herself with excitement about it but it felt dangerous to me. Her very intensity was unnatural. White hot but no flame. "It's the most exciting thing that's ever happened to me," she said, over and over again in a strange, somnambulist's voice. When I spoke my fear though, she just told me I was jealous.

My 'old hag' face had given me a reputation as a witch, and whereever Miranda went there were always crowds of little kids following and shouting 'Sicko' and chanting 'Marcus, Marcus,' like they were at a Wednesday match. It was bad enough trying to get around school on our own, but together it was hell. Things weren't helped by Miranda's habit of greeting her friends the French way, and then making everything a drama by insisting on holding their hands all the time. It was all right in clubs, a bit embarrassing perhaps, but in school it caused a riot.

As we sat on the great roots of the tree in the middle of the car park (technically 'out of bounds' to everyone except sixth formers) we heard 'Lezzies' shouted out of a second floor window. "That's a new one," said Miranda, cheerily. Luckily, because Byron didn't have any friends, he hadn't managed to find anyone to tell about me on the ironing board. Well, not that anyone had mentioned anyway. "So," she said, "back to our little project." I sighed and she put her arm around me. 'Lesbows' I heard from behind the changing room toilets.

"I think I might leave it a while," I said, gloomily.

"Nonsense," she replied, "come to stay at my place, and we'll get a matching pair for the night."

"What about St John? What about Byron?"

"Oh I probably won't have them by then. We'll get the 'partners in crime' from a club. Or, hang on a minute... My randy cousin! He's well experienced. We had a bit of a fling actually. He was my first snog, and he doesn't know anyone in this school, so he'd be really good." She beamed at me again.

"What's he look like?"

"A bit like Freddy Mercury, only plump." There was a pause in which I put together the image in my mind. It wasn't good.

"I can't see me getting a proper boyfriend for ages," I said at last. "I guess it better be just a one-night stand then anyway. If it all goes horribly wrong he can just disappear over the horizon. What d'you think?"

Mr Clarkson Maths came past to his car. "No Marcus? Lovers' tiff?" he chuckled.

"Et tu, Brute!" retorted Miranda inexplicably, and smiling (she fancied him). I could feel myself scowling. "I mean, where do you usually go to get hold of a bloke?"

"Well, The Limit's pretty good. Plenty of muscular older men."

"I don't think I'm up to that first time round," I said.

"Well, I could get a nice one for me, and you could have some pasty madrigal player."

"You'd have one too?"

"Well yes! What'm I supposed to do whilst you're getting deflowered all over the place?"

"Oh. Right," I said. I picked up a stick and bored a hole in the leaf mould. She was right, I couldn't really think of another option. "When, then?" I said eventually.

"What about October? You'll be well sixteen by then."

"Okay." She pulled my head towards her and kissed it as a half-full bottle of Cresta pop landed on the asphalt behind us.

"Lezers!"

"Let's go before we cause a riot."

"Right you are," she answered and, picking up our bags, we

went back up the steps toward the bell. "If we fail," she said, "there's always plan B."

"Which is what exactly?!"

"The fat cousin."

CHAPTER EIGHT

I T WAS TIME AT last for the de-flowering, but as soon as Miranda answered the door wearing her mother's kimono, I knew this time for sure that there was something fishy going on.

"You're not ready then," I said flatly as I followed her upstairs, watching her big backside jiggle under the patterned silk. She turned briefly and flashed me a wicked smile.

On reaching the landing she flung open her bedroom door and stood back to let me pass. As she did so the robe opened, showing a large, topless Miranda wearing nothing but the plastic exercise pants.

"Why are you wearing those again?" I demanded.

"I can't take them off, they stink."

"What've you got under them?"

"Nothing."

"Oh, for God's sake! You'll bloody infect yourself!"

I stomped into the room. There, standing with a hand towel round his middle was the grinning, androgynous figure of Byron Saltfisch.

"Hello," he smarmed.

Behind him was a large rocking horse, which had been moved from its place in the corner and stood, swaying slightly, in the middle of the room.

"Oh no, not again!" I said.

"We've been trying out a little experiment," said Miranda, sidling in. She stood, twisting the horse's halter rope in her hand.

Byron giggled,

"We decided we needed a volunteer," he said.

I looked from Miranda to the open bottle of baby oil on the table and back again. There was a decidedly unpleasant smell.

"No chance! Never again," I said. "You must think I'm a bloody nutter! Get ready, Miranda, or I'm going home."

"Okay, okay; don't get your knickers in a twist!"

"At least I'm bloody wearing some!"

"All right, 'don't be so hostle,'" she said in her best fake American accent. Byron snorted again.

I stared at him, memories of the ironing board and the Rotary Club bobbing queasily around my mind. "Sod that, I'm going!" I started down the stairs.

"Hey, Darling-puss?"

"What?"

She was leaning over the banister, her dark hair hanging down and now holding the kimono demurely shut at the neck.

"Come on, don't be like this. I tell you what, make us a cuppa will you, before we go?"

It had taken me long enough to psyche myself up for tonight, and I didn't want to give up now.

"Get rid of him, then!" I mouthed, gesturing viciously.

"Okay, dokey, will do," she smiled. "Byron, home!" She barked the order at him like he was a badly behaved dog.

I left them to it. That had been a bloody close escape by the look of it, and maybe this whole thing wasn't such a good idea after all.

I'd only just had time to pour the water in the pot when I heard the front door slam. In came Miranda, and I noticed she'd swapped the Oriental robe for a fetching little towelling number in powder blue.

"I see you've finally taken off the radioactive knickers," I said dryly. "You wouldn't have kept them on so long if he'd've been two years older, butch and black."

"No, quite," she replied. "Anyway, Dearie, how are we now?"

"God, you are a poser sometimes!"

She laughed, big teeth showing. "It's going to be a good night: my Mum's gone out."

"She's never in!" And it was true. That's what I liked about being with Miranda, I suppose. My parents never went out, never mind stop out the night.

"Are you all right?" she asked. "You look a bit green around the gills."

"I'm okay. I was just wondering, though. Maybe I should wait a bit, get into it gradually?"

She gave me a long look, "Not getting cold feet, are you?"

"Well, no. It's just that I've only just had my birthday. I don't feel in so much of a rush about it, now I actually am sixteen."

"'Strike while the iron's hot' is my motto, and my God is the iron hot!" She turned towards the door. "Yours might be," I muttered under my breath.

"Oh well," she said, "must get the glad-rags on, or we'll miss the bus. By the way, you look great. We'll get off with someone tonight, for sure. Toodleoo."

"And have a bath, for God's sake!" I shouted up the stairs after her. I turned back to the teapot with its hand-knitted cosy; the matching 'Let's Be Friends' mugs. Suddenly I felt very alone.

But there was no going back. It was a matter of honour now. People had been told. Louise'd been told, and Sandra.

Somewhere out there preparing for a night on the town was a lad with my name tattooed on the end of his dick. Who was he? Did he even suspect?

"Rea-dy!" called Miranda from upstairs. "Ready!" I called back.

The nerves were nothing like butterflies now. More like long, sharp fingernails dragging backwards and forwards through my guts. I was gorgeous tonight, though, and I had a packet of 20 condoms, no body hair, and my eczema was subtly dusted with tinted powder. Nothing could go wrong but I wished I could take a portable commode for the bus journey into town; or, like Dorothy, wake up in Kansas once it was all over.

"Gird your loins then, love," smiled Miranda, coming into the kitchen.

"Tad dah!" she fanfared, doing a twirl. If I'd have known what 'gird' meant, I think I would have. At that moment, my loins needed all the help they could get.

"What *are* you wearing?!"

"D'you like my veils, Dearie?"

There were three scarves, in clashing, garish colours. The one on the head was chiffon, the other two round her bust and bum were nylon and looked familiar somehow.

"Where did you get them from? "

"Granny."

"I thought so. What do'you think she'd think if she saw you in them now?!" She shrugged her shoulders and smiled, had a quick practice of one of the fancy footwork bits of the routine.

"Pass us a cuppa before we go," she said. I did.

We slurped in silence, Miranda with her large buttocks perched precariously on the edge of the breakfast barstool.

"Right, better get going before we miss the bus," she said, jumping up. I took a quick look at her, trying to see what she was really feeling. To my disappointment she looked completely normal. A flurry of activity, and we were on the street, across the road and at the bus shelter.

It was cool but not cold out tonight. Miranda had her fake fur on, and I had my Greenham Common look-alike duffle coat (my dance outfit would be more of a surprise for the bouncers when I took it off later). Most kids didn't wear coats, thinking they looked trendy without them. We weren't most kids.

"Look, fur coat and no knickers," she laughed, giving a passing car a quick flash. I stood grimly, small shivers running through me that had nothing to do with the weather. A dog came past walking its owner and sniffed my leg. For an awful moment I thought it was going to cock its own (they can smell fear apparently), but it spared me and went on its way. We didn't have to wait long, hearing the bus before we saw it.

There was a party atmosphere on board as we climbed the stairs and sat right at the top, right at the front, a girl with a mission and her coach.

I whispered, "Mission Impossible?" and managed a small smile, not lost on Miranda who fetched out her brush and started to do my hair. "Your mission, if you should choose to accept it: your first screw. Nothing impossible about that!" she laughed.

Town was buzzing as our double-decker pulled in. The streets glowed orange and everywhere there were gangs of lads with fags and girls teetering in stilettos.

At the edge of the Peace Gardens fountain (which the Council had thoughtfully put there to entertain the clubbers, glue sniffers and homeless and to provide somewhere to piss, or drown in) drunks sat comfortably watching the world go by. Occasionally, one pointed at some particularly daft club gear and you could hear laughing. Sometimes there were shouted comments: "Dracula'd like that black nail varnish!" and "I could do wi' a bit of that lace round me pants!" to the New Romantics; or "In't that cote a bit too big fe yer?" to the Northern Soulers in their long, flapping leather.

Streams of people were moving along the packed pavements, some of the lads even walking briefly in the road to overtake the clutches of girls, disabled by their uniform of high shoes and tight clothes. The crowd was divided obviously into types, each wearing different gear, going in different directions. One lot, the Northern Soulers (girls in white stilettos, boys athletic with their hands in their pockets), moved downtown towards Penny's and the derelict warehouses near the railway. Others, New Romantics, moved more in mixed groups, boys and girls with dyed-black, back-combed hair, white faces, heavy eyeliner and Pixie boots. Only in this group did male and female look a little the same. There was yet a third group, Townies who were into straight chart music. These made the most noise, the girls giggling, clutching onto each others' arms and reeling on high micro-sandals, shouting things out; their boys in ironed T shirts or shirts-and-ties, and clutching cans of lager. Amongst these, couples walked to the Cabaret clubs or Bingo Nights by the subway. These people were older, the women with long, glossy or elaborately-set hair, depending on their age; their men silent, in well ironed trousers, walking fast and low, the women safe on their arms.

"What happens if we don't find anyone suitable?" I said as we walked.

"We will. We'll attract somebody."

"No, I mean, if I don't like them, don't fancy them or

something? It doesn't have to be tonight, does it?"

"Don't be so manic! We'll find someone alright," she said over her shoulder as she strode ahead.

"Miranda, will you just wait on a minute!" I said, clutching at her wrist and turning her round to face me.

"Listen a minute, will you! If I don't fancy anyone, it's all off, right?"

"Yeah, alright," but she was looking past me at a group of West Indian lads walking easily along the pavement in front of us. It was a strange impression, but they seemed to be walking slower than everyone else, in no hurry yet covering the same ground. They called out too as they walked along, hailing other groups across the road. A couple over the other side had a ghetto-blaster on mega-loud and were walking to the deep bass. Their clothes were different too, looser, cleaner.

"Miranda!"

"Yes, Petal."

"Look, promise me you won't go in a nark if I say no, right?"

"Yes," but her eyes were still on stalks as she looked at the black lads, eyes like those of someone narrowed against the smoke slithering from a cigarette.

"Promise! We're going home alone if I say, right? Right?" I shouted, standing between her and the view. I had to give her a bit of a shake, but finally she nodded.

We were going in the same direction as the Townies, out along the streets lit with a sickly glow, from which layers of soot-blackened municipal buildings rose up, masking the sky. Here dole office mixed with sandwich bar and Christian bookshop.

"Have you ever been to a Reggae club?"

"No," she answered. There was no need to ask, "have you?"

She knew that if she hadn't tried something, I hadn't either.

"Would you like to?" I said

"No."

"Why?"

"Because I'm not black."

"Some Whites go," I said.

"Yes, I know, but I think they look stupid. Anyway, I don't like the music."

"Oh, I do. You want to be black, though."

"I know. I like black people's bodies, okay? Even fat people look all right if they're black. I hate being a pasty bloody white woman, but that doesn't mean I like Reggae, okay?"

"Okay, keep ye'r 'air on!" I said. What was she getting so worked up for?

We were in the queue by now to pass the leering bouncers, down the sweaty stairs and into the basement. This was one of the few clubs in Sheffield that didn't do just one type of music. It did do loads of chart stuff, but they had Seventies nights and weren't averse to playing the odd Donna Summer, Hot Chocolate or Randy Crawford track or even Grease or Tom Jones. We loved Motown and retro disco; anything we could do our routines to. I'd always done dance routines with friends. When I was twelvish it was the Glitter band, or ABBA in footless tights and a leotard in Ellen Davies' bedroom.

Me and Miranda though, we were special. We didn't blend. That was the idea. I did everything I possibly could to match up with nobody, whilst Miranda seemed to be in a bubble all on her own: a sort of time warp where fashions were all kaleidescoped together. Though she didn't wear trendy clothes, she managed never to look old-fashioned. Everything was too mixed up to place and her panache rendered fashion irrelevant.

Tonight she was wearing her three scarves, American Tan tights and heeled dancing shoes as usual. At the time her hair was long, dark and wiry, and she'd taken to wearing a torque thing around the top of her bare arm. "My Pagan roots," she was always telling people. I generally refused to shave my armpits due to feminist principles, so was forced to wear long sleeves.

On this occasion I was wearing my clubbing shoes: (Chinese Mao slippers in style but the Bourgeois version i.e. coloured silk and embroidery); thick black tights (I often didn't shave my legs and didn't own any sheer, either) and an amazing emerald-green-and-black mini dress that I'd found in a second-hand shop. It was tight at the bust and covered in a fetching pattern of venomous snakes.

We took to the floor where there were lots of girls in groups wearing tall heels and shuffling around their handbags. For some reason, most of the shoes and the handbags were white. That wasn't our style. Miranda went to dance classes with a passion, and she favoured trying to find a pillar or a bar to hold onto for her routine, which is very difficult to describe. It was sort of a 'kick ball change,' but side on, pulling on the object for support and leaning back where she would shake and toss her hair with one of the scarves in it. This went on at breakneck speed and seemed to go down well. She varied this move with a slower motion, whereby she would put one hand with the palm flat on her bare belly and undulate her hips round in either direction, whilst using her leg to slowly turn herself. For this movement she had a particular facial expression, narrowing her eyes, pouting out her lips and looking down at herself with her mouth slightly open. There was also a double-speed version of this one that has never, to my knowledge, been reproduced by anyone else. The scarves she picked were always in loud colours and looked stunning mixed up with her dark hair as she spun around.

My dance style was very different. I thought I'd made it up, and although I'd obviously not been able to see myself doing it, it did feel a little like the undulating dancer at the beginning of 'Tales of the Unexpected' but with a sort of Motown skipping move woven in. I had a more hip-thrashing version too but I didn't spin around.

I was a good mover but somehow we weren't as popular with the boys as we hoped. The younger lads gave us a wide berth but the older men, particularly for some reason the black men, were more interested. I put it down to the fact that I had a great arse, but Miranda reckoned it was her. Anyway, we didn't often dance with men when we were together: they seemed irrelevant, except as an audience.

Miranda went to the bar for some water. I drank alcohol a bit sometimes, but she never did, and I never bothered when I was on a dance. She crossed the dance floor with long strides, irritating the watching eyes, tossing her hair back behind her shoulder where it'd stuck on the sweat. As she leaned on the bar, one leg straight out behind her, I could see the black stretch Athletics pants, her 'heavy duty dance knicks,' under the scarf. She gestured for me to come over.

"Let's do our routine… Oh you know, the one to the Barry Manilow track…"

"I'm not asking 'im to put on Barry Manilow!"

"Yeah, okay, but we don't need the same track. We can do it to anything, any dance music."

"But we can't do it to chart stuff. You can't do it to chart."

"No, but I'll get him to change it!"

"He won't, though."

"He will," she said.

"They won't like it," I moaned.

"It'll clear the floor though. We can have some space."

"I don't really want to."

"Oh come on, it'll be brilliant!"

"But we haven't practised it enough. You've got that funny bit at the end. I've got to go backwards or something and twirl round, and I don't know what I'm doing." I was aware I was whining, but I so was worked up tonight as it was, trying to suss out a mate and everything, that I wasn't really up to a virtuoso performance.

"I'll show you. I'll lead, right; you just go where I push you."

She put down my drink and, grabbing my hand, led me to a corner of the dance floor.

"We'll have a practice, though, right?" I pleaded.

The overhead spotlight was boring into my head. I imagined it like one of those prehistoric surgical procedures where they cut holes in the skull and your headache stops.

"Okay then," she said.

She was already dancing to some sort of internal rhythm, and I could tell by her lips that she was humming,

"Okay. Yeah… I just do … this here, yeah, 'her name was Lola, she was a showgirl…' Right? No, you go round me, right? … and I reach out and grab you, and…pull you to me, yes, yeah, … and you sort of snake on the spot with your arms…up, 'dah da da de da de da'. "No, 'cause then I've got to get you and …bend you back like … this and I have to shimmy my shoulders and move you round at the same time."

The blood was weighing heavy in my skull, and by now Miranda had somehow manoeuvred us stage centre. I was starting to feel sick.

"Then you come… up, like… this, ..and I sort of…wriggle down your body, yeah? No, you go down when I come up and vice versa, keep the backs together all the time and then we finish up … like…this."

She put out her hands to me, and we braced against each other, heads back, eyes on the spinning lights, faster and faster, heads further and further back as our feet got closer and closer.

"Woooooooowa!"

My hands slurped out of her grip, and I staggered backwards. Miranda's hair was all stuck to her face and the boob scarf had gone astray revealing the squashed tops of two brown nipples.

"Hey, brill-i-ante!" called a voice.

I'd been aware of an increasing space around us, but I hadn't banked on the total clearing of the dance floor that greeted me as I finally straightened up and looked around.

"Girls, girls, that was brilliant! Don't ring us, we'll ring you. The two hottest dancers in town tonight!"

Oh no! The sarky DJ's voice was like Moses parting the waters, where a ripple of laughter wobbled on the sudden silence. Thankfully he put on another record straight away, and the sea returned.

"I need the loo," I said.

By now there was a shining ring of male faces round us, but all the girls seemed to be in a huddle in the gloom by the bar.

I made a beeline for the ladies, where even the wooden door felt slimy to the touch. Inside was that glaring white of bogs. It was quite comforting really: suddenly quiet, the smell of school dinners. I looked at my face where the eyeliner had run as usual and formed a sludge in the corner. I picked it out and resmudged the rest under the bottom lashes.

Miranda came in smiling but I didn't take any notice of her, carried on applying some cheap lip gloss which tasted like the smell of Vaseline.

"He's great, that DJ. It's good for them, having people that can dance."

"He was being sarcastic!" I said.

"Oooh, lah de dah!"

I ignored her, and she went into a cubicle. The metal arm at the top of the door unflexed, and in came a gang of girls, one by one. There was something of the Western about it, the way they come in through the swing doors, everything going silent, only the sound of the boot heels and the spurs. Most of their faces were bleached out in the overhead light, apart from the bits that still had makeup on, so the white girls looked like vampires, all red eyes and lipstick on the teeth. They had to inch nearer as more filled up the space by the door. Most seemed to be wearing glittery boob tubes. I stood back from the sink and fetched my travel brush out of the leather pouch bag (modelled on an American Indian design) which I strung round me when I was dancing.

Bending my head right down, I gave my hair a good backcombing, right to the ends. It's a strange thing, how your hair always seems greasy underneath even though the top part is dry with split ends, and even though you've just washed it. It hurts at first, but then it gets really satisfying. When I flicked my head back up it looked brilliant. Kate Bush, eat your heart out!

It was suddenly so quiet that the bolt of Miranda's cubicle opening as she came out had the same shocking effect as a loud fart in assembly. I saw her in the mirror as she hesitated for a moment when she saw them all. Every eye was on her. I didn't turn round, but in the mirror the weird light made their disembodied heads and shoulders look like a scene from the Old Masters. Miranda made it to the basins. Clearly no one fancied making the first move and they turned sideways as she passed through them.

Now we were both standing at the sink. She pumped out some soap which made an irreverent squeaking noise. I pumped some out too, and we got into washing our hands. It seemed to go on overlong, but I couldn't think how to end it. I sneaked a glance at Miranda. She was looking intently into the sink with an amused expression on her face. I kept my own eyes down, didn't want to risk meeting her eye in the mirror. She turned off her tap. I turned off mine. It was deathly quiet.

Suddenly the hand drier came on and the girl with very stiff hair who'd been leaning on it shot upright. Miranda started to hum. "You might need some body, you might need somebody too… you might need somebody too," in that Souly voice of hers, and shook some water off her hands. Some went on the throat of the small, rat-faced girl with bleached blond hair who'd come in first. She gasped. There are many distinct areas in Sheffield, and coming from the wrong one's as bad as coming from somewhere else entirely. This bog was obviously, here and now, the wrong place for two girls from Abbymoor.

"What d'ye think yah doing?" she said to Miranda's back.

There was a clever answer to this, but I didn't want to die.

"I said, what d'ye think yah doing, a' reet!"

I suddenly became fully aware of how odd Miranda must look to them. The other girls were wearing their 'camouflage' gear, as we called it, ie. whatever the current vogue was, they were in it, without a hair's difference between them. They just fitted in. But she? She was like a parrot at a pigeon's tea party.

"D'ye want a stiletto in yer face, or what?" said Ratty.

"Er, no thank you very much," I heard myself say. Looking down, there was no shortage of weapons.

"I we'nt talking to you, I wer' talking to 'er."

"What's the matter?" I asked.

"What's the maat-terr!" she took the piss out of my voice. I might have been Princess Anne to her.

"'Er there, dancing like a Huwer!"

"Oh."

"Ye fat cow!"

There was nothing more to be said. We all waited for something to happen. Miranda looked in the mirror and adjusted the scarf round her boobs. Brave move. The blonde girl addressed Miranda's reflection in the mirror again:

"Yer dancing like a lad; yer showing y'sen off you are!"

"But we're not doing any harm," I said.

"Just keep off my boyfriend, a' reet?"

"Alright," I said, "which one is he exactly?"

Miranda leant forward over the sink and bared her teeth at the mirror. She always got a bit of lipstick on the front ones.

"'As anyone gor a tissue or sommat? It really gets on me nerves, that does, lipstick on your teeth," she said in her best Sheffield, picking a bit of scum out of the corner of her lips and licking her tongue round her teeth. It seemed very quiet again suddenly.

I was aware of some movement behind me. Instinctively I hunched my shoulders, bracing for an attack. The blond looked past me, only quick, but like the one our dog gives when she wants to bite the window cleaner,

"Yeah. 'Er's sommat."

A wide girl in a black lacy top leant over me, passing a dog-eared piece of toilet paper from down her front.

"Thanks," said Miranda.

"Yer areet."

Like the bell had gone in a school yard, everyone started moving.

The blonde shoved past me to get to the sink, leaning over it to lip-liner herself, an elbow each side trying to avoid the puddles. The doors closed on a couple of cubicles; the girl who'd been leaning on the drier pulled up her leather miniskirt and started trying to feed the black top through the waist of it, while the girl next to me whipped up her skirt and started tucking her top into her tights. We wore our pants over our tights to keep them up, although it wasn't very good for cystitis. I risked using the drier. Out of the corner of my eye I saw Miranda talking to their blonde leader by the sink, passing her spray-on hair glitter. It wouldn't be any good on her, I thought with satisfaction. It looks crap on pale hair.

"That was close! Shall we go?" I hissed as Miranda crossed to the drier.

"Not yet, we'll catch the one-twenty to Abbeymoor Road. I want to get them to play some Randy Crawford. Let's go on the other dance floor."

"Is that a good idea?" I whispered, gesturing desperately at the heavies.

She shrugged, fluffed up her hair just once in the mirror and took the glitter back off her rat-faced new friend.

"Ta," smiled Miranda, flashing her best teeth at the defeated enemy as she popped it in her bag.

I held the door open as the blonde and a couple of henchwomen shoved out.

"Toodleoo!" she called after them. "Tara."

Once in the other room I sat on a step facing the dance floor.

Miranda had disappeared somewhere, and I was just watching the knees and the midriff of the world go by. Trying to look nonchalant is hard. Trying to look self-contained, attractive, nonchalant and confident is very hard. Smoking would've been handy. I think I must have been day-dreaming; my head was hanging down, and as I raised it up I found myself looking at the khaki-coloured trousers of a man standing right up close to me. He was facing me, and in one hand he carried a glass of clear liquid, whilst the other was holding open his flies. His dick was hanging limply out. Funny thing was that it was all soft and dangling. You'd've thought it would at least have been hard, that he at least would have been getting something out of the performance.

Determined to look cool, I stood up, removing my face from the direct line of fire. This brought us eye to eye. His expression was completely casual, eyes looking past me. What was he doing it for then? Before I had time to force him to answer (after all, who exactly was in the vulnerable position here?), he'd stepped back and disappeared into the gloom. He was surprisingly good-looking.

I went in search of Miranda and found her doing a complicated routine with a well-dressed black man. He didn't fit in here either. He was too up-market and too old, more like the centre-of-town glitzy clubs, where they do ties. She had cleared a space for herself as usual and had added a rather interesting new move since I'd last seen her: feet planted a shoulder's width apart, knees bent, both hands on both hips and gyrating in the middle. The scarf had slipped down and you could see her belly button and the top of the dance pants. I wish I'd had it on film, really, but a description will have to do:

For every two 360-degree turns her pelvis did in a clockwise direction, her head did two the opposite way, the long straight hair whipping round and round and settling, clinging to the sweat on her face and right shoulder as she held the pose: right hip pushed forward, right buttock thrust out, head facing to the left and looking along her stretched left arm. It was pretty mesmerising, especially as head and hips were going in different directions, and she swapped over so that her pelvis alternated, first clockwise, then anti. If you've ever wrestled with the thing whereby one arm pats your head and the other circles your stomach, you'll appreciate the expertise required.

Her partner was obviously much affected. He was managing to keep on moving, but he had ceased all pretence of keeping to the beat and was doing a slow motion version of the Travolta move with the revolving arms.

As soon as she saw me, she clicked out of it and strode over, holding her hair right back, up and off her neck with one hand, him following.

"This is my best friend, Sue," she announced, like a cat that had got the cream.

"Hi," I said coldly. "Miranda, let's go."

Standing behind me she leant across my shoulders. "This is my dearest friend," she purred in her best 'Lolita' voice. "Do you like her?"

The man smiled at me, I gave him one back; yes, he could handle Miranda,

"Are you going home, girls?" he said, in what even I had to admit was a very sexy voice. "I'd like to go with you."

"We go home together, alone," I said.

Miranda crossed the small space between him and us and rested the soft insides of both her arms on his shoulders. He was a big man, even for her. Rubbing her head against his cheek, she reached out and pulled me in too. He put one of his hands round Miranda's waist and one on me.

"D'you want to see me again, huh?" sirened Miranda.

"Ummmm.Yeesss. … Shall I see you both?" He cupped my chin in his hands, so big I felt his fingers on my earlobes; dry fingers, warm.

"Er, no, I don't think so." It came out as a pathetic squawk. "We've got to go." As I said it, I gave her bare arm a hard pinch,

"Alright!" she said. "Now!" She looked at me, just once, but enough to see.

"Here, my card," said Miranda, wriggling a small business card in under his trouser belt.

By this time I was standing back as she kissed him on the mouth, her bottom giving just a little wriggle as he put his hand on it under the scarf. He walked us to the cloakroom, his arm round Miranda, who insisted on holding my hand. Before we left he bent to kiss her again.

"Okay, see you, baby."

"Yes, call," said Miranda. I was half way up the steps.

"Sue?"

"Er, yes!"

"See you too?"

"Em, maybe." He blew me a kiss. My last vision of him is from the top of the steps. He was leaning on the stair rail, laughing at something the bouncer said.

CHAPTER NINE

HITTING THE STREET I took the cotton wool out of my ears. We walked through town to the late night bus stop without talking, me thinking about the flasher. Why pick me? Maybe he fancied me, had spotted me on the dance floor and wanted to ask me out or something but was too shy? Maybe his friends had dared him?

It was less crowded now, not quite close-down time for the clubs yet. The people that were around were in smaller groups, moving nearer the walls and looking more dishevelled. The occasional pissed clubber staggered alone, leaning onto the blackened bricks for comfort, but the drunks had gone from the Peace Gardens fountain. Even that had succumbed to the general 'has been' mood and was now no more than an unsavoury pond on which plastic bags and food cartons drifted listlessly.

It was always freezing coming out of a club, and I was glad of the Greenham duffle. Even Miranda had made a concession to the weather and fastened the top hook-and-eye of her 'fur'. We waited at the bus shelter in front of the town hall. I'd failed. More than that, I'd cramped her style. She could have been here with the black dancer now instead of me. If only I could just get it together with someone really nice and not too old. Someone who wouldn't tell all about it the next day. Someone just like Tom Booker. Bollocks!

"Pardon?" said Miranda

"Oh, nothing. Well, I was just thinking of Tom Booker. I wish I could have him."

"You can. Course you can. You can have any lad, just seduce him. I'll invite him round."

"No! I mean, I don't just want to shag him; I want to go out with him. I really like him."

"Oh." She was quiet for a while. "That's not so easy."

"Tell me about it!" I said.

The double-decker came into sight, its yellow light comforting in the dark. We climbed aboard, pulling ourselves up the spiral stairs by heaving on the greasy handrail. Our favourite seat (right up front) was occupied, so we came down again and sat on a double seat which was raised up over the wheels. When the conductor came I paid, trying to make up for it all, I suppose.

The bus rode the streets, swaying from side to side, always going double speed at night. Usually you only paid 2p, but the late bus was more expensive, not many people on, just the warmth, that safe feeling.

We hardly ever stayed at my house because my parents were always in, and even when Miranda's mother was in she never bothered with us, being always in her bedroom with Brian, her ancient lover, and trays of food. It always looked inviting, the mother's room: loads of cushions on the bed; TV and stereo in there, like in a teenager's bedroom.

"Are you pissed off with me that we didn't bring him home, Miranda?"

She looked straight ahead out of the window, diverting a snaking line of condensation with the tip of her finger.

"No," she said.

"I just didn't like him. I mean, he was probably a really nice bloke and everything, but he just wasn't suitable."

"Because he was black?"

"No. You're the one who's racially bloody obsessed! He was a man, for God's sake. He must 've been at least twenty six! I need a lad. Not a virgin, but someone a bit my own age." She hadn't answered, so I carried on.

"Anyway, we'd have had to share him; there'd be no way you were going to let me have someone like him all to myself. Go on, admit it!" I could see her round cheek bulge in a smile under the curtain of her hair, "Am I right or am I right?" I said.

"Go on then, I admit it." She took my hand and tucked my arm under her own.

It was warm on the bus; the sound, the dim light, my relief and Miranda's warmth along my left side all contributed to the blissful cocoon of security I felt as I dozed off. There was no rush; this had only been a trial run and anyway, I had got off with someone in a way, if you counted the flasher.

There were not many stops that night, and in no time the bus lurched to a halt outside Miranda's house. No lights on as usual, and I told her about the man in the khaki trousers as she fiddled with her key in the lock.

"Cheese on toast with Marmite underneath and hot chocolate. Let's have it in bed," she said.

"But Miranda, what d'ye think? What should I'uve done then? What would you 'uve done?"

"Me?"

"Yeah."

"Well, um, I'd've probably made a big thing of licking my lips or something."

"Give over!"

"Well, that's what he wanted though, wasn't it, to shock you?" She turned and looked at me for a moment.

"Yes, but you might've encouraged him or something."

"Na, blokes like that're like bullies, they can't stand it back. Call their bluff."

"Well, I didn't encourage 'im anyway."

"You did all right in the circumstances. Anyway, what're you getting your knickers in a twist for? He's gone." By now we were in, Miranda kicking off her shoes and chucking her coat down at the bottom of the stairs.

"I'm not. I'm just discussing it with you. I'm talking it over with a friend that's all; that's what they're supposed to be for, isn't it? What're you in a nark for all of a sudden, anyway?"

"I'm not. I just don't want to talk about that silly pratt anymore. He probably doesn't even like sex. What about, you do the bath, I'll get the toasties?"

I stood in the doorway for a while watching her fiddle with the food. It was clear that the subject was closed.

"Do me two, I'm starving," I said eventually.

"You're not starving, Bangladeshis are starving."

"Yeah, yeah, I know. I was the one told you, remember?"

"Yeah. Well are you doing the bath or what?"

"All right, 'keep yer air on!' "

I left her and went up to the little bathroom at the top of the stairs. Muffled from downstairs came the sound of Miranda singing softly to herself as I prepared the bathroom: putting the towel rail on; arranging the towels; lighting the scented candles. This, to me, was *her* house in a way my own home could never be mine. She was on her own so much that she knew how to cook and do basic cleaning, even how to do the laundry. Her Mum was so often away overnight at the lover's even during the week that Miranda had to get her self up and ready for school. I couldn't imagine that.

If I hadn't had my mum screaming her banshee morning call, and my dad eventually threatening to come in and rip off the bed-clothes, I know there was nothing about school that could possibly have induced me to get out of bed. Miranda, she had ambition, albeit a different ambition every couple of months, and, granted, many of them were improbable, but she always had a cunning plan. She liked school, for God's sake: loved the attention, even negative, of adults and other kids; loved the red ticks in her books, the columns of marks in the teachers' registers. She delighted in organising her life, in the little things, like packing her school bag the night before – I'd seen her laying out everything in order to go into the stripped-clean brief-case, satchel, business rucksack (whatever her current style in work-wear was) on a Sunday night. She even had control of a small budget, to buy her packed lunch and fresh stuff if her mother was away.

Me? Someone was there to control everything I did and, I realised with a shock when I pictured my own battered school bag, I didn't have pride in anything. My sandwich box was better than hers but, because I never filled it myself, it never contained what I really fancied. My house was three times the size and much more comfortable, but always inhabited. Even my big cosy room wasn't really my own. My mum had painted it for me after I'd been allowed to choose from a limited palette of colours; so different from Miranda, who took a paintbrush to hers whenever she fancied it. I was a guest in my own home; Miranda was the mistress of hers.

The bath was ready and I got in. Bliss. We liked loads of bubbles, and I loved this after clubbing, just the two of us. Miranda came in and sat on the loo. She had a nasty habit of crapping with abandon, regardless of innocent by-standers. She seemed to have no inhibitions, to lack the fear and self-consciousness of other people. A wee, okay, but that I drew the line at.

"Open the window, will you, I'm being stunk out, here!"

"Okay, okay, it's all organic."

"It may be organic, but that doesn't mean it's not stinking the place out!" She laughed and sprayed a few bursts of Tesco air freshener around. She didn't believe much in real fresh air.

She climbed back in and I washed her, careful of the big loose mole in the small of her back. We could either sit facing one another, legs apart (a bit too obstetric), or straight out, hers together on one side, mine together on the other. The second was rather squashed because of Miranda's big hips. Another problem with it that way round was that only the person at the end could lean back properly, as the other had the taps in her back. Miranda liked her hair doing and her back washing, so that meant one behind the other, like in a rowing team.

It was the most amazing thing about her that she wasn't ticklish, nowhere at all. I experimented by doing her back with loads of soap, then sweeping right up her sides and under her arms with my wet hands. I could move down and brush up as fast as I liked without her even flinching, and we'd developed a real technique. First you sponged the back, getting it really wet, letting the water trickle down. Then you rubbed the soap really hard on the sponge, so that it was full up, and squeezed it out all over the back. I liked to empty the sponge at the top and watch the foam drizzle downwards, then start in the hollow just above her bottom and move up in arc after arc, pressing hard but trying to keep one continuous movement as I moved the whole length of her back, like cleaning a window. I'd do this a couple of times, then go up her sides and under her arms, where the palms of my hands made a sucking noise as they cupped her armpits, and moved away. As I worked on her, she bent forward, one hand holding onto the tap for support, a neat 'builder's bum' showing above the water.

When it was my turn, I declined the back massage. I liked it scratched, not too lightly, not too hard. I loved the way she spread her fingers in my hair, took my skull completely in her hands and massaged with her fingers' tips; the way she washed my hair, scraping, smoothing it down, gathering it all in a bunch in her hand. I loved that feeling of being taken over, feeling my eyes going, just like a stroked cat. It's funny, but not since I was a little girl had I had anyone to touch me like that, touching to give pleasure. That is maybe the torment of that barren time between being a young child with a loved body and being somebody's lover, filled with delight inside a form coveted and fussed over. There is no one to touch older children and lonely teenagers like this. I thought of my grandmother, crippled and widowed and pulled around by doctors and care workers. I vowed that, next time she came to stay with us, I'd do her hair like she loved and give her a facial.

"A penny for your thoughts," said Miranda.

"Oh, I was just thinking of Mamgu, you know, my Welsh Grandmother?"

"Yes, she's lovely. What about her?"

"Oh, just that no one really ever does nice things like this for her."

"No. It's bad being old. I do Granny a peppermint foot bath sometimes; she's got bad circulation."

"Really! Doesn't it feel a bit awkward? "

"No, not at all, really. We like it." I could imagine that being true. They loved one another, those two. My words, even the words in my thoughts, had slowed right down to match the rhythm of Miranda's stroking hand. Every nerve in my body was concentrated on those long fingers. I closed my eyes, swaying a little from the hips and let my thoughts drift. What was the flasher doing now? What did flashers do at home? Did they have ordinary sex, or was there special flasher sex? Where were all the female flashers?

Why did he pick me?

The spell was broken. "That's enough now," I said quickly. Her hand stopped in midair as I turned to look at her,

"You all right?" she said. I nodded, "Just tired I suppose." In a flourish of, by now, foul brown bath water, I stood up. Miranda smiled and stretched out luxuriously, reaching with an expert toe to put in more hot. She disappeared under the water sending up a flurry of bubbles. I watched her dark hair spread out on the surface, thinking how unwise she was to be over her head in our bath water.

I dried myself, one foot on the closed toilet seat; dried gently even between my toes, a dusting of Magnolia talc under my breasts, arms; behind my knees and between those toes. At the last moment I patted some into my groin both sides, giving the hairs a festive look. What a theatrical touch, a proper powder puff for the talc, something only Miranda's house would have!

She heaved herself up out of the bath, water lurching crazily from end to end. Her hair was plastered to her upper body, its clinging lines accentuating the shape of her. I passed her a clean towel from the airing cupboard, which she wrapped around her head in a turban, pulling her eyes up tight in the outer corners. She stepped out, water finding ridges and channels all over her body, running faster in these. In some places, though, she was convex and smooth; here the water moved in thin, finely spread waves over her skin, like heavy rain on pale stone.

She had a spare robe for me, and we sat in them to eat in bed, still damp. The chocolate was quite cold by now but not bad after a bit of a stir, and my body felt delicious. We ate without talking, and I looked around her room, where even here she defied fashion. There was something very Brentford Nylons about the floral print of her bedspread with its precious flounces. None of my other friends would have been seen dead with one, yet she didn't care; didn't even notice. Other girls had co-ordinated bedroom suites or fitted units, but her furniture was a mis-match, family cast-offs, I suspected. On the walls, instead of the regulation pop star posters she had photos of her ancestors, all in cheap, plastic frames. The only concession to luxury was the kimono on a hook behind the door, a grubby goat skin rug, and the large silk squares she'd pinned to the ceiling. As there was only one chair by the big old desk, we always spent our time in or on the bed.

"What do you think of that bloke, though. What would you have done?"

"I couldn't have done much, really. He went off."

"No, I mean straight away. Would you have given him a mouthful or made a grab at his crotch or something? I wish I'd said some thing witty."

"What, like,' put it away the fish'll have it', or something?" she said.

"Well, yes, something like that, but not that because he might not have got it. I mean, about it looking like a maggot."

"No, but something like that."

"Yes."

"You can't think of things at the time. Not on the spur of the moment." Miranda reached over to put off the lamp. "What was he like anyway?"

"Gorgeous."

"Creep. Goodnight, Sweet Pea."

"Night."

After the usual vibrating of the bed and moaning and groaning (Miranda had recently learned to masturbate) it went quiet.

I wasn't sure whether or not I really believed in it. Well, not that I didn't believe in masturbation per se, but I wasn't convinced that Miranda was really doing it. What she was doing seemed too mundane, somehow, too regular, like scrubbing away at the bread board with a nail brush. I always pretended I went straight to sleep when she turned out the light so I didn't have to get involved, and, although I did get the feeling from the way she was heavy breathing and grinding her teeth, that she was trying a bit to keep the decibels down, to her it was only like having a crap. She was completely oblivious of most taboos, and only thinking I might be embarrassed would be making her keep a lid on it.

This night, though, it was even harder than usual to get to sleep. I'd failed. I'd got all tarted up to lose my virginity, and come back with it still attached (or 'intact' was what the Catherine Cookson novels said, didn't they?). What next? I should have asked her before she had a wank.

The occasional car headlight caught the wall through the crack in the curtain and searched aimlessly the same route across the surface. Miranda was right: it was a whole different kettle of fish to try and get a boyfriend. Did I want to lose my virginity then, or did I really just want a boyfriend? Come to think of it, the two were pretty much mutually exclusive. Any boyfriend I could hang round with and have coffees in the kitchen at home with was likely to be my age-(ish), and, let's face it, boys my age were having enough problems getting any facial hair going, let alone turning themselves into professional virgin deflowerers. Why did I have to stop being a virgin then? I didn't know, I just knew I had to. I just didn't suit being a 'Sandy'. There was no point trying to be clean cut and nice, not looking like I did, so I might as well be exciting. All the really cool girls were experienced and it made them walk differently: looser, heads up more. Once I'd done the deed I could just forget about it. I rearranged the pillow under my head.

Even when I closed my eyes I could see headlights moving again and again in the same pattern across the back of my eyes. I didn't have fags, split parents, a police record. I didn't pop pills, swear at teachers, skive school. In fact, I didn't have anything really to call my own except playing the cello and a gift (highly cultivated!) for sometimes saying the outrageous. But I did have Miranda. I needed somehow to be in the game. I just wish I hadn't told anybody I'd already done it, that would have made everything a lot easier. Anyway, I was sure I'd be able to get something sorted eventually. With or without Miranda's help, the days of boring Sue the virgin bride were numbered.

CHAPTER TEN

WHEN I WOKE THE morning after, I woke as a woman resolved. Plan A, a failure. There was only plan B left. I woke Miranda up. "Yes, what?" she said, looking like Miss Piggy as she surfaced from under the duvet. "I'm going to do it. I'm going for the Freddie Mercury option."

"Are you, Petal?" she said, vaguely.

"Remember; your gigolo cousin?"

"Oh," she said, opening an eye. "Right you are. I'll get onto it right away." So that was it, the contract was out on my virginity. No going back now.

But it turned out he didn't like me. Not that Miranda actually said in so many words, but I kept pressing her about it, and she kept trying to evade me,

"He's really busy at the moment," or "We can't, my Mum's around – she's had a tiff with Brian," and finally, "Look, shut up about him, will you? You won't fancy him!" I'd stared at her and she'd relented a bit. "We'll get someone else. I'll ask Byron."

"No way!"

"No, I don't mean to shag you... though, actually, he could..." she trailed off, thoughtfully.

"Miranda!!"

"No, right, okay. But, I mean, he could help us think of something, the male perspective and all that. He's very ingenious..."

"I've noticed," I said, sourly. There was a pause. "All right then," I sighed.

"Whatever it takes. This is getting beyond a joke."

With two of the greatest minds in Abbeymoor onto the problem, I didn't have to wait long. Within a week, Byron had found a suitable candidate, and Miranda and I had started working on the logistics. Unfortunately, her Mum was still having one of her spells living back at home, so the obvious seduction suite was out of bounds. My house was constantly policed. Byron's Dad came in and out of their flat like a Tom cat, making it difficult to arrange anything in advance, which meant we had to think of another venue.

Ashley was a new boy in my year; a very new boy, just as Byron had been the year before, but that was where any similarity between the two ended. Ashley hadn't made any friends yet. He was in the top set for most things, but you wouldn't have been able to tell from his constant, inane grin. Only Byron had befriended him, which was handy for us but, I suspected, bad news for him.

He was handsome with a wholesome, stupid face, curly fair hair like a young ram and a slim, non-descript body. He'd been told that there was an initiation ceremony for all new boys which involved showing his dick to Miranda and her friend, and then an added option of losing his virginity afterwards. Byron was a very plausible liar and, as the only other new boy himself, seemed to speak with authority. However Ashley's house wasn't any good either as he had younger brothers and sisters and his Mum was always in too. It was Miranda who came up with the idea.

"Orienteering! A tent in the woods. Go back to Nature and do earth rites and everything. It'll be brilliant, and no one'll ever know."

Ashley seemed amenable to the idea and was sworn to secrecy, and so it was that, on a chilly Saturday afternoon a few weeks later, we arrived at the clearing in the thin oak wood. For several weeks Miranda and I really had been doing orienteering, in order to leave nothing to chance on the big day. Though no one in my family could believe it at first, my little trips off in the school mini bus had become commonplace, and being asked to be dropped off at the old hunting lodge on the Moors, or picked up from the market cross in one of the local villages, no longer caused much surprise. Orienteering, or indeed any sort of intense, organised activity that involved running, was anathema to me, but it was almost, *almost* worth it for the wonderful feeling of self-satisfaction afterwards.

So it was that Mum thought nothing of dropping us off that day, not even suspicious that nobody else was there. As we crossed the stile and left the road behind, I felt shocked to think what I was about to do. Even Miranda was quiet.

As we neared the clearing, I thought I could hear the boys. The wood was grazed by sheep and almost bare of undergrowth, quite light at ground level, even though the leaves hadn't started to fall. We could hear their noise as we approached and see a red shape between the trunks. Miranda called out a greeting, but I found I had nothing to say.

Suddenly we were there, amongst the grey rocks and dry leaves, Miranda and Saltfisch lavishly embracing, Ashley and I standing on the periphery, like terrified opponents in a duel. I couldn't look at him. We'd hardly ever spoken, and I know that I at least had made an effort to avoid him since this plan had been hatched.

In addition to what we'd brought, there seemed to be a massive amount of equipment there already, including a very flimsy red tent.

"Oh, that. Ashley's dad gave it us. We told him we were doing

Duke of Edinburgh." Byron seemed proud of himself.

Miranda laughed. "Right, let's have some hot chocolate and talk about procedure," she said, flinging down my brother's rucksack.

Saltfisch fetched a carry-mat from the tent, and we sipped lukewarm liquid from plastic cups. The milk had formed a skin that seemed to catch on the corners of my mouth. As they bull-shitted Ashley with all the fabricated detail of the 'secret ritual', I looked fleetingly at his face. He was concentrating intensely, his red lips open with the effort and dribbling slightly.

He was handsome. Pretty even, and so trusting.

Miranda's mention of disinfectant brought the daydreaming up short.

"...and then they can do it afterwards too..."

"Hang on a minute, I'm not putting that stuff anywhere near me!"

She had her quizzical face on. "I mean it, Miranda, no way!"

She exchanged a raised eyebrow with Saltfisch and got to her feet, shaking out her cup with the same resolute movement my mother does on picnics.

Ashley scrambled up and was led away behind the tent by his minder, and we were left there. I got up and waited to see what would happen next.

Never did Miranda hesitate for a minute but kept on putting the plan into action, which I now realised had little to do with the version I'd been fed.

First, she whipped a nylon sausage out of the rucksack and unravelled a blue tarpaulin, smoothing it over the ground. Then she brought out a large tartan rug and arranged it on top. I stared. There was a strange horror in the way all this was so orchestrated, yet so mundane: The flask, the tartan, the little red tent...

"…and the condoms. I got a twelve pack just in case," she added, casually. Somewhere in the trees the sound of a bird. Not a song but a repetitive, percussive noise.

Miranda was busy looking for stones and putting them on the corners of the tarp even though there was no breeze. By now the light was going and with it the warmth, and I had even less desire to take my clothes off than I had had before.

"Where are you going to be? I don't want you looking – well I don't want Byron to see us."

"Well, I thought I'd stick around, in case you got into difficulty, maybe mop up the blood."

"Mop!"

She gave me a knowing look and poured some Dettol into a Tupperware box.

"We'll go in the tent. It'll be private there."

"But I thought you wanted to do it outside, 'au naturelle' – you're always banging on about it… pardon the pun," she sniggered.

But I didn't feel like laughing.

There was a cracking and swishing in the undergrowth, and then the boys' voices, or rather Byron's voice, talking excitedly. "Ready," he shouted.

"Coming, ready or not," she called back, a loud guffaw again at her own wit.

Passing behind the tent we fought our way through a couple of scrubby bushes towards the torch-light coming from a small hollow.

By now I had distinctly cold feet, and it was only the sight of Ashley's gormless, puppy face that stopped me from calling it all off.

"Right," said Byron, "you two stand here and close your eyes. Ashley's going to give you a sneak preview." I very much doubted he was going to be able to manage anything under these conditions, but by now the whole thing had a *'Lord of the Flies'* momentum that seemed irresistible. We shut our eyes and listened to Byron's counting, and I felt the warmth of Miranda's hand; she squeezed in excitement.

"...zero!" I opened my eyes and for a moment failed to focus properly. Then, through the gloom I saw the thing, shockingly white and pasty, like a blind cave fish, surprised by exploration, quivering with tension. For a moment no one moved. I looked at Ashley's face, the proud, shy smile, head angled down slightly but eyes looking up and straight at me – I couldn't let him down. As I rushed forward he looked terrified for a moment, grappling with his flies, but I grabbed his hand and pulled, dodging back through the bushes to the clearing. Happily 'Bill and Ben' had not caught up with us yet.

The 12 pack was lying on the ground by the inexplicable Paracetamol, and my hand went for it, slipped it in the pocket of my cagoule. I crossed the tarp with a few undignified steps still holding onto him – he didn't resist. As I pulled him towards the tent I glanced round to see two faces bearing down on us, gratifyingly shocked and luminous-white in the dusk light. There was some undignified fumbling as I tried to unzip the tent, then we were inside.

It felt safe, the light very red from the nylon, illuminated by the camping lamp Miranda had left on. I sat down and struggled with the zip on my cagoule. Ashley had dropped to his knees and was looking at me. I stopped wrestling for a moment, and he smiled. I'd never looked him in the eye before, in fact I'd never really seen him look up and out, head up, proud. My impression of him since he'd arrived at our school had always been a bowed head, loose Golden-retriever curls. In one fluid movement he pulled his jumper, T shirt with it, over his head. He sat back on his haunches, his eyes and mouth shining wet in the unreliable light. Suddenly I was the shy one. Having got rid of the coat, I undid my cardigan and then the front buttons of the peasant blouse underneath. He kept watching, not staring but not smiling anymore. His body was smooth and ridged. There was no fat anywhere, just light and shadows, all angular and hard.

There was a moving shadow, a sudden noise outside the tent, a suppressed giggle. "Get lost!" Ashley's voice raised, unfamiliar. He moved as he spoke, grabbing and rolling me down like a rugby ball.

For a while we didn't move. Everything seemed to vibrate – I had a vision of all my cells, all the molecules, wobbling with excitement. He smelt clean but unmistakably male. He smelt like my brother.

I found his mouth, and we kissed for ages as it got darker outside, the atmosphere in the tent seeming even more other-worldly. At first his body was still, and we lay like two sucker fish, attached only with our mouths, our bodies chastely apart. But soon he began to move up against me. I reached down and opened the tight button on his new jeans. I didn't want to see there again, but I did want to touch, and feel his weight press down hard. Soon we were all tangled up: my skirt, his trousers, our limbs, my hair getting in the way – in our mouths, in my eyes. We struggled up for air, and I turned away from him, embarrassed as I pulled off my pants, keeping the Indian cotton skirt on both out of shyness and as insulation against the sweaty nylon. Similar disrobing noises were coming from him. As I turned back I closed my eyes involuntarily – what a little virgin! But his hands, warm now, pulled me forward and down, down he pressed my hand on him, smooth and dry as talc, hot and springy, sticky at the tip.

"Condoms..."

My voice sounded drugged and muffled like a stupid porn film, but I found them by the tent flap. First the cellophane, impossibly tight! Then the individual packaging, I tore at it, then tried with my teeth but it only seemed to make it worse as it got wetter and less taut. I looked up at Ashley, but he didn't seem phased, just smiling slightly although the angle at his groin was more ninety than a hundred and eighty degrees now. Finally I got hold of the stupid thing.

Miranda and I had practised this bit on granny's rolling pin, but that rounded unforgiving wood bore little resemblance to the real thing. There was far too much give, and you couldn't get your fingers in to pull it down properly. Like a roller blind it kept flipping back up. Ashley was no help and was by now lying on his back, neck arched and groaning. I was getting into a sweat, and all the warm, urgent itch was just a memory. Two condoms later I started to cry. He sat up, an amazed look on his face,

"What's the matter?"

"Oh, nothing, obviously. What the hell do you think!" I hissed.

"Everything all right in there, Dearies?" An unwelcome voice from outside.

I noticed the groin crinkle and shrinking, a rabbit's face disappearing back into its hole. Humiliated and desperate, I made a grab for it and got going on the sawing movements I'd been told to do. 'Like sandpapering a pole' Miranda had said. Ashley had gone quiet, his torso seeming to shrink away from me, the more I did to him, the smaller, floppier and more shrunken he seemed to get. I knew it was hopeless, but I kept doing it until suddenly he yelped and pulled away. In my hand was blood.

"On the count of ten I'm coming in!" trilled Miranda. But I had blood on my hand!

Ashley was scrabbling for his clothes, his head down, face away from me. I rubbed the blood into my thigh and felt around for my own clothes. The count of ten was nearly at an end and, in the way counts do, slowed considerably towards the finish. With a huge zipping, rustling and straining noise, Miranda was with us in the tent.

"Well…?"

It had always been a test; had started out as one. It was a task, an experiment even, but for a small moment we had almost turned it into the real thing.

She was on her haunches, powerful torch in her hand, her expectant face all hollows and shadows.

"Fine," I said, "very good. Not too bad at all."

"You were very quick," she said, accusing. "And we were bloody freezing out there!"

"It takes however long it takes," I snapped, inspiration coming from somewhere. She shone her torch across the floor finding the condom packet.

"Bin bag?" she asked. Horrified I wondered for a moment whether she wanted to examine it, but Ashley patted the pocket of his jeans, "All taken care of," he said.

Byron's voice from outside, "Come on, you lot, it's bloody freezing. We've gotta go – my Dad'll be here in ten minutes. Leave the tent, I'll get it tomorrow."

There was a lot of activity coming from outside now, and with one last, sceptical look Miranda wriggled backwards out of the tent taking the torchlight with her. I didn't know what to say, but when I felt his hand on mine, the one with the blood on it, I squeezed it.

He was no idiot: in fact I think I was starting to get a bit of a crush on him.

"Come on, Love birds!" Miranda from outside – a rustling of tarpaulin, the clank of hastily chucked utensils.

I was first out of the tent, the air freezing cold now. I struggled into my cagoule and let Miranda load me up with equipment, finding a small smile on my face when I caught a whiff of discarded disinfectant.

We left the clearing first, the boys finishing the packing up, and she linked her arm in mine as we felt our way back down the path towards the road.

"Well, spill the beans" was the first thing she said. I was off my guard,

"Did it hurt a lot? Was there a lot of blood?"

I waited for a moment, my Mum's car headlights visible through the trees.

"Yes, there was a lot of blood, but, no, it didn't hurt. Actually I like him."

She laughed and was still laughing as we got into the car.

I now had a secret to keep, and I kept it from everybody. Even when Miranda found a rust-coloured stain on the orange batik throw she'd had on the floor that night and exclaimed that she'd 'keep it forever', I still didn't tell. I even thought for a while that Ashley and I would start to go out together and do it for real, but after the 'tent incident' as it came to be called, he wouldn't even have anything to do with Byron anymore.

It wasn't hard pretending to Miranda that it had been real, though. I'd read enough and had enough imagination to make up the odd cryptic sentence when required, and anyway, we had nearly got there and there was the indisputable evidence of the blood to back me up.

In the end the job was done by Ben in Miranda's squeaky bed, whilst I was staying the night at hers', and she was with her new boyfriend in his house. After the orienteering fiasco Byron seemed to have lost interest in us, and of course, as I had lied to Miranda, she thought it was a 'fait accompli'. All I had to do was give in to Ben's persistent demands and, by now, I had got used to his strange breath and dirty finger nails. He was no beautiful Jan, had no sculptured-torso like Ashley, nor Tom's drop dead smile, but at least he liked me and, as a virgin too, didn't expect too much. I'll spare you the details because the ground didn't move. Neither was there any blood to speak of.

The overriding impression was that it was clumsy, damp and strangely companionable. Probably because Miranda hadn't had a 'hand' in it, it was even mundane, and at the end of it I gathered up my clothes, leaving Ben pale and snoring, and caught the bus home.

CHAPTER ELEVEN

ALWAYS, IN MY MEMORY of that morning after, there was that sound in the background of a bus pulling away. I wondered if they'd been watching me, my parents, all the way up the drive and past the big windows. I was sure they'd be able to tell. In fact I might as well just hang a sign around my neck and be done with it. Opening the front door I heard the grandfather clock, making each second too important, taking over the house at night when the sound carried straight into our dreams. You would never be alone at night in our house.

That morning my father was in the lounge as usual playing the piano, the music carrying his presence through the house as surely as his pipe smoke did. My mother was in the dining room, which put me off guard; I wasn't expecting to see her until I'd reached the kitchen. She was bending down under the dresser doing something, so luckily she didn't see my face.

"I'm back, Mum," I said, trying to find my normal voice.

"Hello, Cariad. Nice time? Can you go and lay the table? We're having dinner early because Bethan's got a party."

"Okay, Mum." Fortunately she hadn't looked at me once, or perhaps she had looked at my feet, but I was sure they had nothing to say.

"Hello, Susie." My father coming out, filling his pipe as he walked. "How's the Bartok going?" It took me a while to register what he was talking about.

"Oh Okay. Not too bad."

"You need to get down to a bit of practice these next couple of weeks. I'll wake you at six forty-five again tomorrow."

"All right, Dad." He didn't know, I was sure of it.

Didn't I smell different even? He wouldn't have been able to smell it though anyway. He smoked too much. I went upstairs, closed my bedroom door. Through the floor I could hear my mother in the kitchen on her treadmill: back and fore, must be miles a day. Although my room felt comforting, it seemed different; sad, like we couldn't talk, didn't speak the same language anymore. Ordinary objects seemed self-conscious and unbearably poignant. The poor, battered donkey from Spain I used to love so much was suddenly pathetic in its dust on the shelf: vulnerable, dispensable.

My body didn't hurt like I thought it would, but everything felt more exposed and out of control, open like a rubber glove turned inside out, but not really sore exactly. I wanted to sit and look in a mirror, like it said in magazines you were supposed to do, explore. But I didn't have a lock on my door. I'd have to wait to smuggle a mirror into the bathroom, as Mum would be suspicious.

From then on life was not the same. It was difficult to know whether it was the deed itself, or the keeping of so big a secret, that was responsible for the way I felt towards my sister and my mum and dad afterwards. I treated them tenderly, as if I had grown up and they were still in 'Never Land' but didn't know it.

I didn't remember the actual act with either pleasure or horror, just a sort of grim acceptance, as a job well done. As far as my body was concerned, for a couple of days I was like a fresh fig turned inside out, but everything soon seemed to pull back up to normal.

The strangest effect of all was on me and Miranda. She seemed to lose interest in my sex life since I had 'lost it' in the woods. We didn't have a project anymore. She was more interested in men than she was in me, even going clubbing on her own now, without saying anything. When we did meet up she kept obsessing about her looming trip to France. In fact, there was only one really good thing about losing it (other than the fact of not having to lose it again), and that was that Ben could be relied on to pay homage, now that Miranda was no longer always there.

We went to his house a lot, as his parents were not there much. It was a rambling Victorian pile by the Botanical Gardens, and he had a suite of rooms in the attic all to himself now that his elder brother had gone off to Cambridge to read cellular something or other.

One of the rooms was his bedroom; another a bathroom, then came a junk room and his brother's room, where Ben now kept his bass guitar, amp and electronic circuit stuff. He showed me this with great pride. Apparently the wires, bulldog clips, switches and light bulbs that littered the floor were essential to the radio he was designing.

Each of the rooms had the same unwashed male smell I recognised from Huw's room, though Huw's was milder than most, since my mother went in at regular intervals to fumigate it. It look longer to choose from his amazing collection of condoms (almost a sock drawer full and all in date) than it did to have the actual sex. I suppose the extent of his collection was a sign that he had an optimistic personality. The main problem was that, because he'd taken so long to find the entrance, he'd got three quarters there in terms of excitement before he'd even put the key in the ignition, so to speak. By then I'd got really tight and tense, so there was no chance of either him hanging on, or me catching up, orgasm-wise.

After we'd done it, I would borrow a pair of his Y fronts so that mum wouldn't see any stains on my underwear, and we'd go downstairs to raid the fridge. As he walked me home at night he would reach for my hand, and there was something nice about he and I in the dark, him telling me all about black holes imploding and things. As he kissed me outside the back gate, it seemed he didn't want to go, and it suddenly struck me how much more reliable it was to have a boyfriend than a Miranda. There was no way I could compete against a man for her. At any time she could just be swept away to disappear out of my life, happy-ever-after like some lonely princess in a story.

I began to see as much of Ben as I did of Miranda. She, being in the sixth form, didn't have to come into school all the time, and I was getting busy with O levels. I knew I wasn't going to do very well, but there again, I didn't want to completely embarrass myself either. Ben lurked around school for me. He was good friends with the delicious Jan, which was a bit depressing, because the two would turn up outside my classroom, and just for a minute I'd see Jan's broad shoulders, soft hair and dreamy eyes and imagine he was mine. He was like a non sissy version of David Cassidy. He didn't seem to remember that, if it hadn't been for his bloody terrapins, I'd have got my clutches on him, instead of Ben.

Anyway I couldn't really complain because I had landed an upper sixth former who my parents actually liked. "Bright young man that, Susie. Probably go into research, given his social problems," (my father) and "Nice that you're being friendly to that poor lad Ben, Sue. His parents were awfully worried about him,"(my mum). Just because she didn't fancy him, she couldn't believe anyone else could want him. She was like Amanda Wingfield in *The Glass Menagerie*, boasting about the quality gentlemen callers of her own youth and being bemused and disappointed at the dregs I managed to get. Well she might have looked like Vivien Leigh when she was young, but as I looked more like Anne of Avonlea I couldn't afford to be so fussy. Another reason she liked him was that he always brought me right to the door (he did that so he could get a very last snog and grope!) and ate anything she put in front of him. "I'm sure his skin flare-up will calm down too, once he's done his A levels, and some young men don't fill out until their twenties," she said kindly after he'd made a rare visit in broad daylight. I didn't mind his acne much, though, as long as I wasn't eating.

To be honest, I was getting quite fond of him. For a start, I could rely on him to be pleased to see me any time. Secondly, I could go out at night safely with my own pet (though weedy!) bouncer, and lastly, I always had someone to talk to about myself. It was relaxing to slump on the floor cushions in his room while he played with his circuits, making buzzers and miniature light bulbs flash on and off.

It was such a relief not having to think of trying to get dressed up and go out and everything to try and get a boyfriend. I could relax and slob out. I had one.

Even the sex was better, though we still hadn't seemed to make any real impression on the number of condoms. The trick to sex with Ben was not actually saying or doing anything; not actually moving at all. If you did start touching him or saying or doing anything sexy, it was all over quicker than it took to hear the snap of rubber.

Miran had indirectly been the one to suggest the successful 'dead fish' routine when she was telling me about her new lover, a huge Nigerian mature student who had the same problem. It had been whilst Ben was on an intensive Oxbridge entrance crammer course for a week that I'd met Miranda in the library coffee bar, and she'd shared her wisdom.

We never let the male sex, or even sex in general, keep us from our adventures for long. She had phoned me, her voice full of that conspiratorial tone I loved so well. It promised me the unusual, the absurd or even the down-right dangerous. Travelling now to see her on the top of the double-decker, right at the front, getting a thrill from the branches scraping the windows, I tried to guess what she had in store for us.

The bus ploughed through the quiet roads of fifties detached and semis, some half-timbered, others rendered white. They had horrid mossy lawns and evergreen bushes, like some suburban nightmare, and I vowed there and then that suburbia wasn't going to happen to me. The bus passed an old grammar school, now a rough comprehensive. It still had 'Boys' and 'Girls' carved in the stone lintels of entrances in opposite corners of the building. Imagine having to go in and out of different doors according to some sexual apartheid. Sheffield Council now would have a fit! I wondered why they hadn't been down there already with a task force doing a ritual erasion.

As the bus slowed down ready to give me my weekly vertigo thrill on the downward sloping, hairpin bend, I drank a long look at the hills. From the top deck you could see right across the valley, past where the houses stopped, and to the Black Moor. In a few years time that was going to be me up there in an ancient stone farmhouse, not married but living with a man who looked like a gypsy: black curls, pale complexion, black eyes. A writer probably, and I would be a successful actress.

Actually no; the place wouldn't be in Yorkshire but Wales, and by then I'd be able to speak Welsh fluently and bring up my children, Welsh first language. All seven of them.

The top deck was rocking inexorably toward the drop where the road careered off to the right. I always held on to the safety bar at this point. I loved that moment just before the bus turned, where time seemed to stop for a fraction. I could see the driver working on the wheel when I looked down the mirror channel, and it was possible to imagine the top deck just never making it, sailing on over the park where I'd gone tobogganing once, over the bare trees and out to Buxton and away. Always at the last minute we turned, who knows how it ever stayed on the road, and pelted down the steep hill toward the main road. The journey was even better at dusk, especially in the winter. It felt so safe and warm: even the cigarette smoke was comforting.

There were street lights on in the yellow dark and the sound, that dinosaur blustering sound as the bus strained to take you, all together, somewhere.

Apparently Miranda was already revising for her mock A levels. I was never completely sure why she used to go to the library to do it. There was only her mum to bother her which was just a joke; Miranda was lucky to catch a glimpse of her. Also, it was much harder to concentrate, I thought. Not that I ever managed to concentrate very long anyway. I did all my revising propped up on the bed. But Miranda had a real routine going: get up early, have yoghurt and eggs, then on the bus to town. Once there, revise, coffee bar for lunch, or Peace Gardens with rye bread sandwiches if she was short of cash. Then revise again, home, food and work out. She was the only teenager I knew who was that sussed. As she went to the dancing school less and less, she replaced it with the gym.

The bus chuntered down the main road and on towards town, swinging into bus stops always with a scream of brakes. Then down Abbeymoor Road, with its odd mix of black stone and brick terraces set in tarmacked gardens, some with their bottom windows torn out and replaced by shop fronts. These were specialist shops: boutiques, antique, gift shops, with doors through which no one ever seemed to go in or out. There were pubs and diners; wedding shops, Uncle Sam's, where we used to go for birthdays, Pizza Hut, Tescos. As we got nearer town the mix got even odder, the terraces disappearing, replaced by big Victorian houses, in the same black stone but set much further back from the road in soggy, overgrown gardens. These all looked like squats or student houses, enticing but potentially stinking, except for those that had been bought up by the University, which could be identified by the pale grey blinds in every window and the fluorescent lights at dusk. These gave way to the sixties flats, their yellow boards set in concrete blocks, and stained, grey balconies on which washing hung from string. These overlooked the Brewery, black soot on red brick with a tall chimney. Nearly always as you passed you could smell the hops, something I hated as a child but which I grew to like. I was excited going through town, hadn't quite lost that feeling of adventure at being let out on my own, and now I had the 'clothes allowance' I could go out as much as I liked, just about.

Even town itself was the same incongruous mixture of buildings: those belonging either to a smoking, Orwelian hell, or the low, flat-roofed, concrete, glass and plastic models that were part of the post-war development. There seemed to be nothing before Victoria and not much between it and the fifties. I hated the way that everything was grey, every modern building having a pasty, sickly feel. At least the old bricks underneath all the soot were a deep, dried-blood red.

I had my own route through the centre, got off at one of two stops every time and visited the same shops. I did contemplate going in other shops, down other streets, but the compulsion of the familiar was too great. I got off at the Peace Gardens, bought my quarter of brazil nut toffee at Thornton's and walked down Fargate, past the fountains and by the beautiful Catholic church. It'd recently been cleaned and was made from a creamy yellow stone. There were high, bobbly pinnacles on the numerous false turrets; I hurried past the shop window opposite, showing statues of Mary holding up the baby, and Jesus bleeding on the cross with his mouth open and his eyes rolled back into his head. I'd never caught the shop open, but I didn't fancy being seen looking in and someone coming out and trying to convert me.

Outside the Crucible Theatre was a small square in which a group of Bagwan people sat, dressed in loose clothes, various shades of red. They were singing something slow and dreamy, their bodies floppy, their expressions happy enough. Everything was on offer in Sheffield. You could believe almost anything or indeed nothing at all; everything was up for grabs. In the same square as the theatre was the library and art gallery, a big art deco building, one of the few around. I climbed the imposing stone steps, through the heavy revolving doors to a big foyer with a grey-flecked marble floor. Huge doors led off right and left, one to the reference, the other the lending library, with lifts straight ahead. Everything was made with care, using expensive materials.

Everywhere there was heavy, gleaming wood with brass fittings; there was even brass in strips on the banisters of the stairs. I climbed up three flights and went through the big doors to the gallery, past the ivory carvings in glass cases, hating each one for representing a dead elephant, and arrived at the cafe.

There she was, on time of course, drinking elder flower presse. That was a departure; it was usually a scone and Earl Grey tea in a white pot for one this time in the afternoon; she liked her rituals. She had her back to me as I approached the glass that separated the cafe from the rest of the museum, her long hair like a cloak around her shoulders. The only time she bothered to put it up was for the gym; then it was a big pony tail, held with a towelling-elastic thing.

I tapped on the glass, but she didn't turn round although her right hand reached behind her head to gather and lay her hair in a long roll over her right shoulder. I tapped again a bit harder. She wiggled her bottom slightly on the chair and leant her head down onto her left palm. She must have heard me! I went round the side of the cafe and in through the door. She still had her head down, hair flicked over, staring intently at her book. I arrived at the table and pulled up a chair. She still hadn't looked round!

"Mi Ran daa!" I shouted." Susie!" she sounded surprised, knocking the side of her cup in the process. "Didn't you hear me knocking? Is it reinforced glass or something." She still looked clueless.

"Am I on the wrong day or something, then?"

"No. I thought you were someone else. There's a bloke been following me."

"What's new! Anyway, you obviously fancy him."

"I don't."

"You do."

"How would you know? You haven't even seen him. You haven't seen me with him."

"No, but from how you reacted when you thought he was me."

"Oh, for God's sake, you think you're psychic! I didn't even turn round. I was ignoring him actually."

"Yeah, but your bum wasn't." By this time I was sitting comfortably with the menu in my hands. I don't know why I still bothered to read it actually, I knew it all by heart. "Are you having your usual?" she asked.

"No, I'm copying you, departing from type."

"Ooooo!" she laughed. "Dangerous."

"Get lost!" I said. "Are you having anything else?"

"Tap water, please."

"I'll pay."

"It's still tap water."

"I'm going to get myself a mocha choc with fresh cream and a flake then," I called over my shoulder.

"There's been a development," she said when I got back. I waited, but she didn't go on. I nibbled on my flake. She still didn't speak.

"All right," I sighed, eventually. "Let me guess: could it possibly be the creepy, following bloke?"

"Right!"

"And?" I said,

"And… he's got a friend." I groaned.

"And…" she added, "he's not a creep."

"Oh well, that's all right then." I stirred the last dregs and gulped them down, telling myself not to bother in future as they tasted horrible. I was not rising to this one. "I've been seeing Ben again. He's gorgeous," I said.

"He's white though," she said.

"Doesn't bother me."

"Even fat people look all right with black skin."

"It's like wearing black trousers when you're fat."

"Exactly," she nodded.

"Anyway, how's your research going for the African course? What was it?"

"The School of Oriental and African studies. I want to learn Hausa. Then I'll go to Nigeria and immerse myself, maybe learn a click language."

"You've not even done your A's yet!"

"No, but I'll get in. They want some token Whites."

"It'll probably be all white," I said. "People like you obsessing with and romanticising other peoples' cultures."

She obviously wasn't too pleased. Her nose had gone red and the enlarged pores were flaming. "If you're that bothered," I added quickly, "you better check on the intake, I mean if you want to get a husband or something."

"I'd never be second wife," she said.

"Bloody hell, Miranda!" she smiled quickly to show she was only kidding. But she wasn't. "Anyway," she said, brightly, "back to Austin." I grunted.

"We're off to have dinner with them tonight."

"What's 'friend' called again, Miranda?" Miranda had started drumming some complicated rhythm under the table cloth, one hand on, the other under, the table.

"Anyway, I can't come. I'm cleaning my teeth and picking out my athlete's foot tonight, sorry."

"How is Ben, anyway?" she asked, stopping the drumming for a moment.

"All right. We're going camping at half term." She looked taken aback, I could see her hand working thoughtfully over the table under the cloth. She was completing the equation in her head: Man + woman + tent =

"Is your Mum letting you go?"

"Yes." She was calling my bluff with her eyebrows. "Well," I answered, "she thinks there's a lot of us going."

"Me?"

"No, don't be daft, she'd never believe you in a tent!"

"Oh well, just so I know. Are you nervous?"

"No," I replied, trying to hide my eyes, smiling despite it.

"You haven't! Without me!" she exclaimed.

"Shush! Of course without you."

"No, I mean, without me knowing?"

"I'm telling you now," I said.

"You know what I mean. You didn't tell me beforehand."

"Of course I didn't! What d' you want, an advance warning?"

"Yeah, yeah, yeah." She looked up at me, and I felt sorry. Like I'd forgotten to invite her to my party or something. But I hadn't forgotten.

"Anyway," I said, "back to the... Africans?"

"Of course, Africans"

"Of course," I said, "how could I think otherwise." She didn't say anything. Okay, Sheffield-born West Indians just weren't exotic enough for her anymore, but couldn't I just leave it alone? I'd punched her once in the friendship today already. "It's not really me, all this," I said. "I mean, I've got a boyfriend now." She looked away, shaking her head slightly so that her hair hung, hiding her face. She sighed, "We never seem to do things together any more."

"Well, all right then," I agreed reluctantly. "But I'm not having sex with anyone. Or eating meat, okay?" There was a pause.

"I told him you're a vegetarian," she said, refusing to meet my eye.

"Where do they live anyway? Halls?"

"No, they're doing PhDs."

"Oh Miranda! How old?"

"Erm, I'm not sure."

"Old, then." I felt grim, this was going to be another sexual fiasco of the Saltfisch ilk if I wasn't careful.

"I'm not sure," she repeated.

"Where do they live?"

"Hill flats."

"Oh Christ!"

"It'll be OK, there's two of us. They're nice. If you want, I can ask them to come and pick us up from the bus station and walk us there."

"No way!" She was looking hurt again, disappointed with me; the 'fine friend you turned out to be,' routine.

"Look," I said, "I'm going, aren't I?"

"Come on, let's go then," she bubbled, unhooking her bag from the seat back and standing up. She pulled her top down over the satin skirt and smoothed it over her tummy. She had a round tummy, very unfashionable, but I thought it was attractive on her; made her look womanly. It wasn't fat, just rounded. She didn't mind it either, especially since she'd been into African culture and going out with older men. In fact she was trying to put on weight.

"Are we going back to yours?"

"Might as well," she said. "You can phone your Mum from there if you like." We walked out through the exhibitions. It was quite sly of the library service to put the coffee bar there. You were forced to see at least some culture if you wanted some caffeine.

"How did you meet him?" I asked, as we walked through

Fargate on our way for the bus.

"In the library."

"Well yes, obviously," I said. She was smiling,

"But how? I mean, did he mistake you for a librarian or something? Did the tips of your fingers meet through the shelves as you both reached to get *The Joy of Sex* down from opposite sides of the same bookshelf, or what?"

"Much more romantic than that," she said. "He was sitting opposite me."

"Who was sitting down first?"

"He was."

"Good," I said. It meant that he was less likely to be some ancient creep haunting the library in the hope of preying on young girls.

"Listen."

"I am," I said.

"Right." We were at our stop by then. She put down her work bag and rolled up her sleeves. "OK, so he was opposite me."

"Yes."

"And I could feel him knowing I was there."

"Yeeess," I said. This was getting a bit intangible. "Go on."

"No, I could! I mean, obviously he saw me come up but it wasn't that. It was, like a heat coming off him..." I smirked. "No, listen, like a smell or something."

"Smell!"

"No, well not a smell, perhaps, but a power."

"You fancied him, that's all."

"Yes, I know, but, I mean, he's not good-looking or anything. He's quite old."

"I knew it! How old?"

"Em, thirty five ..."

"Thirty five!"

"Maybe thirty-eightish?"

"Don't tell me, the other one's his father!"

"Don't know. I've never met him."

"So how 'd'you know he's OK?" She was looking hurt again, but all I could see were visions of ancient, leering men trying to get their hands on young flesh. It felt like they were vampires; unclean. I'd always hated the thought of older men, but she didn't seem to be fussy. As long as they weren't white.

"Look..., Sue."

"I'm sorry," I said. "I'm just a bit dismayed, that's all. Anyway, how did it go from there?"

"Well, I just couldn't concentrate, I could feel this heat coming off him."

"We've done the heat bit," I complained.

"And anyway, then I could see his hand coming across the desk, and it closed around my arm, just... there." She held me tight just above the wrist, in the soft, meaty bit, looking intensely into my eyes and pressing firmly with her finger tips. "I began to feel dizzy, hypnotised."

"I know what you mean," I said. "You're cutting off the blood supply right now!" She released her grip, leaving three marks where her fingers had been.

"And?"

"It felt so big. He could meet his whole hand round my wrist."

"He's an adult man, that's all."

"I know. It makes all the difference. I don't think I could go out with boys anymore; not if this gets off the ground."

The bus swung in, and we jumped on. Miranda was unusually quiet all the way, so I sat back watching the city pass in short bursts, stop to stop, lights to lights. I put my face against the cool, sweaty glass and let the sound of the big engine rock me to a stupor like it always did, resisting the impulse to ask her about the other student, who was probably even older and more creepy.

CHAPTER TWELVE

B ACK AT HER HOUSE I made us the usual toast, this time
with a tin of tomatoes poured over it. Tinned tomatoes were
made almost decent by white sliced toast and real butter. It was
amazing to have this freedom. Again, being here made me reflect
unfavourably on my life. Miranda's was my bolt-hole. I couldn't
just go where I wanted, please myself like she could, but at least
here I was free. She was now into her second quarter hour in the
bathroom, not a good sign. I called through the bathroom door,
"I've had mine and yours's going cold!"

"Come in !" She never bolted the door, but I drew the line at
requests of 'Come and talk to me, I'm bored' when she was on the
loo. I went in. She was sitting in a bath of bubbles, only the knee
caps of her spread-eagled legs and her torso poking out of the water.
I put the loo seat down and sat on it. She was slushing the water
about vigorously, creating a Jacuzzi-effect whirlpool between her
thighs. I remembered a French film we'd seen together at the
Warehouse, which was a converted steel mill that had become
an arts centre. The place was very trendy and undiscovered, lots
of black and white films and films with subtitles. The prostitute
heroine in the film did the same thing in her antique hip bath, ten
or so times a day. The director had spent a lot of time on those
shots, creating a hypnotic, sultry, sexual ritual. I thought it was all
gratuitous at the time, but now I understood.

Miranda's need was the reverse. The douching and cleansing
wasn't to purge the men from her, as the prostitute had done;
instead Miranda was cranking herself up, easing herself from sixth-

form student to married man's young lover. I understood why he had to be an African; why British-born West Indians were no longer good enough in her eyes. To her, obsessed as she was, they were just black white people.

What had Whites done for Miranda? They'd avoided her if they were her age; obsessed on her if they were younger, following her everywhere; called her names and laughed or censored her for her voice, her clothes, her dancing, her sex. Her white father had left her; her mother was so busy with her own personal life that she didn't even see what was in front of her eyes. Miranda kept the house in reasonable order and her school reports were always good. What else did her mother need to know?

As I sat watching her then, all I knew was the deep seriousness of what she was doing. Lads were no good; I sensed that, she could have eaten them for breakfast. She wanted more. She wanted someone bigger than her in every way. She wanted someone to make her feel small. Suddenly, as if picking up on my thoughts, she stopped what she was doing and looked at me.

"You look as if you're in a film doing that," I said. She laughed and posed with two large blobs of foam on her nipples. "You're not planning on spending the night are you?"

"In what sense?" she replied.

"In the literal sense," I said. "As in... stay all night and leave me marooned there." She needed me to go with her, I knew. I wasn't quite sure what the purpose was, maybe to make sure her date didn't turn into a gang bang, or even just as escort through the rough part of town. I didn't mind, however, especially as I'd been a poor friend to her recently. I just knew I didn't want to get screwed.

"No, I've got to come home. Granny's coming round for breakfast."

"To check up on you," I said. "What're you going to give her anyway? You've got no food in."

"She'll bring something. Pancakes and maple syrup; croissant, that sort of thing." Holding onto the metal rail she heaved herself to her feet and reached down into the murky water for the soap, lathering herself enthusiastically; passing the soap from hand to hand as she reached up with one arm, then the other to clean her armpits.

"Aren't you going to shave them?" I asked. She didn't have many hairs in her armpits, not considering her dark, thick head of hair, but, as she'd already done her bikini line to nothing but an airport runway it seemed the armpits were overdue.

"Oh yes, I forgot those," she said. "Will you pass us another razor?" There were several placed head down in the glass jar on the window sill. One was rusty, another had a few bristles stuck on with dried up soap, but it looked quite sharp still. I passed it. She sat herself back down and jiggled it about in the water. I doubted whether that had been enough to soften up the old soap, but she leaned back against the shallow end of the bath and lifted up her left arm again, bending it at the elbow so that she could reach down with her fingers and pull the skin taut, stretching it in and up against the breast. As each long cut stripped a line through the hair and foam, it looked more vulnerable. Finally, when it was done and she'd rinsed it off with a jug, it was bare and pink. Though she was not bleeding, the top layer of skin had been scraped off and was raw. The tender-looking raised lumps reminded me of the skin under a man's balls; that same just-plucked, 'come and abuse me' look.

"It's a wonder I don't cut myself with this damn thing," she said, setting about the other side. "Are you having a bath?"

"No," I said. She raised a quizzical eyebrow at me. "Precautionary measure: just in case his friend wants to have sex with me, I'll be too stinky!" Putting the cap back on the razor, she heaved herself up again, leaving the bath in turmoil, water moving forward and back in a great wave, threatening to overflow. She reached for the Camay. "Not again! Come on Miranda, get going will you!" But she hadn't done her fanny. This was going to take forever. "You've done it. You must have done it to shave it. You did that hip-bath spa thing; you know, with the whirlpool of water?" But she was already standing up again and well into it, having worked the soap into a lather over her buttocks, she used the edge of her open hand to form a spatula scraping and flicking swathes of lather down into the water. They hung from her hand, dropping like saliva.

"I haven't seen you do that before," I said.

"The Romans did it," she said. "They had scrapers though. I'm going to buy one if we go to Hadrian's wall again."

"You won't go again now. That's lower sixth."

"You'll have to go for me then, when it's your turn."

I looked at her, standing there covered in foam, and she was not a modern figure. She was no model, not even totally naked, shaved and seventeen, but she would have made a good oil painting: the big hair, the long fingers; her white skin and tummy. Her bottom was two enormous pears pushed together. I remembered the letter from her father; her imminent trip. She must be so afraid. "Are you all right, luv?" she asked.

"Yep, I'm OK." I smiled a transparent smile. She was bending forward with knees slightly bent now washing her fanny. She always did it with the right hand, even though she was left-handed, reaching all the way up the front from behind and doing a sort of swing-boat motion. "It's not a good idea that," I said. "You're pushing all the bacteria up from your bum."

"I'm not."

"You are because you're dragging your hand back the other way all the time. You should keep them separate, 'front to back'." We said it together as a sort of mantra.

"I'd be so sore if I did that," I said. "You must have a fanny like sandpaper!" Soon she was back down in the bath again, generating the fearsome swirling, sluicing currents. "I'm going for a lie down before we go," I said finally.

"Bread's soggy, tomatoes're cold, orange juice's luke warm. Bye." I shut the door on her. It wasn't impossible that she'd go through the whole routine again. Was this her being nervous? She'd never have admitted it.

I closed the door to her bedroom behind me. It always smelt so good to me: an old fashioned talc and baby oil smell, a whiff of lavender. Outside, the rush hour traffic purred, comforting but far away. She had thick drapes at the window, held back by glossy rope chords suspended from brass-effect dog's claws. Although the bed was still the horrid divan with a pastel pink base, it was piled high with satin cushions, the faded floral duvet cover mostly hidden by a gold throw. Miranda's bedding went through different stages of development, but the deep blush-pink carpet, the outsize oak work table and the bed itself were always the same. I took off my skirt and climbed into bed. For my mother, duvets had not been invented yet, and I revelled in the lightness and warmth. My tights kept me warm even when I stretched my legs out to the deep dark bottom. The smell from the pillows wasn't as nice. She pretty much changed her bedding when she liked, which was not often. It smelt of old farts, which she did under the bedclothes and released after they'd warmed up, testing them with her nose, exclaiming at how pleasant and interesting one's own farts can be. I got rid of a couple of superfluous cushions and throws. One was the one she swore had my virgin blood on, which she refused to wash. I turned it over: there was a faint, rust-coloured stain, but it wasn't mine. I chucked it out onto the floor, wondering idly whether I should try and sneak it home to wash; but if it had sentimental value to her, then she might as well have it. The logistics would have been difficult anyway, "Where did you get that old thing? Why are you washing it, Sue? What's that funny stain?" Not good.

I floated into a sort of half sleep, like being in a hammock between sleep and wake. At one point the door opened and let in a slant of light and a shadowy Miranda, who rifled through some drawers in the dark and then tiptoed out. I was woken by dribble running down my cheek and onto the pillow. It was now completely dark outside, or rather, the jaundice, street-light dark of a big city. The traffic was eerily quiet for once, and there was no noise from the house itself. I had a horrible sick feeling, a dream hangover I suppose: the knowledge that I was going to die. It happened a lot when I snoozed in the daytime and woke to the dark. I lay curled up, not wanting to put my torso out into the cold and pull on the chill, sheath-like jeans. My right foot had got that tick thing again. It always happened when I was awake and trying not to get up. Bending at the ankle, beating time, manic. The door opened, "Are you awake, dear heart? It's time to go." I was actually relieved to see her. Before she had time to put on the operating-theatre, main light bulb, I switched on the bedside light. "Are you OK? You don't look very perky?"

"No, I don't feel it. I'm ageing slowly, my youth won't last long. I'm just aware of my own mortality, I suppose." She looked quizzically at me from the doorway a moment, "Too many Bronte novels and not enough happy endings. Try Jane Austen," she said.

I had to smile. "Come on, we gotta go. Things to do, places to be."

"You sound like a bloody holiday brochure," I said, but I felt better already. She could always do that to me: get to the heart of it; pull me up from wherever I'd sunk. We got dressed, and I did my black eyeliner and blusher on the apple of the cheeks. When I didn't have sex tonight, it would be because I chose not to, not because some man didn't fancy me.

We caught our second bus at the bus station in town. Sheffield always looked better in the dark. Then, its true romance came out. You could imagine struggle: *Sons and Lovers* mothers making ends meet; Catherine Cookson heroines with dirty, bare feet and big eyes.

As we lurched along the Don valley on the top deck, we could see how little industry was left. The old factories along the river were still there, all black and ghastly, but even they looked innocent in their dereliction, buddleias sticking out of their walls. There were no old trees but plenty of saplings, sickly green in colour and still wearing their plastic. Grass had been planted too, on sinister-looking mounds by the road, but it didn't look quite right. Huge billboards dominated these sparse, grassy patches. What was the point of all this advertising, because the people living in the flats behind them couldn't have had much money? There were gaps in the line of buildings flanking the road, rubble and tough plants making an uneven outline. Occasionally there were a couple of shops still open in the remnants of rows of long-gone terraces. "There be dragons," I hissed. "What?" Miranda was dreaming again, humming quietly to herself some Donna Summer song. "There be dragons," I repeated in my best Medieval yokel's accent. "Oh, yeah. You are a bourgeois little snob! Just because we've changed buses and gone out the other side."

"Gone over to the dark side," I hissed, asthmatically, but all science fiction was anathema to her.

"We're not in Kansas now, Toto," I tried again, but she elbowed me to get up and we made our way down the bus. I loved this bit, the peculiar gibbon walk you did to reach the stairs, and the skills you had to demonstrate in order not to be thrown to your death on your way down. We thanked the driver, and the doors closed on us with a swish of hydraulics. All alone.

She had her orange clogs on which clumped as she walked, drawing attention to us as we passed the rows of shops with their iron grills, at least a third of them empty and all closed up at this time of night. There seemed to be no one around at all as we turned into the complex, the paved square around which the high rises loomed darkly. There seemed to be a lot of dog shit around and paper waste shifting sinister in corners. The breeze had lifted even the heavier food cartons, which glided and scraped along the tarmac as though drawn by an invisible hand. "Come on, we're going to be late!" Was madam feeling a little tense, perchance?

Apart from the sound of rubbish moving, it was ominously quiet as we walked toward the grey mass of Hall Hill flats. It looked a bit like a multi-storey car park, only not so cheerful. As we drew nearer there were people about, but we saw only their backs disappearing around corners, or the tops of their heads as they passed overhead on covered walkways. Here too there were young trees, looking out of context, anaemic. "What floor are they on?" I said.

"Why are you whispering?" she hissed back. We walked through a deserted play area, everything new and made out of moulded plastic, a proper surface on the floor.

"That's good," I said. "Not like round the posh areas where the council doesn't bother, and you've still got that dried-blood-smelling iron equipment and the killer asphalt if you fall off." She didn't reply, but, after glancing up at the numbers, dived into the gloom of the nearest stairwell. I held my breath against the smell of urine and tried not to think about the damp lumps lurking here and there.

We climbed steadily, with every floor the view between the slats of concrete getting more spectacular. Graffiti seemed confined to the signs on each level telling us that this floor was 'Meadow Towers' as opposed to the floor below which had been 'Salmon Pastures'; the irony could not have been lost on anyone living there. Eventually Miranda came to a stop outside a door painted bright yellow. From what I could gather, each of the separate blocks had a different colour scheme. Miranda flicked her hair down and forward, leaning over so it almost touched the ground. She back-combed it maniacally with her fingers and then tossed it back over her shoulders. I was about to do the same when I noticed there was a spy hole set in the door.

Miranda tightened her wide belt and knocked hard. It opened immediately. Austin. He was a big man, though not as tall as Silvanus (or 'Silver-anus' as the fifth years called him, Miranda's previous boyfriend). He kissed Miranda on both cheeks, holding her by the shoulders, then reached out to shake my hand.

"Welcome to my home. We have made you a beautiful meal."

"Thanks," I said. I couldn't see head nor tail of his friend. He smiled at us, a wide smiled that showed even his gums. I smiled back. He didn't seem to be moving out of the way. We stood on the doorstep, Miranda and he caught in some sort of aerial glue that held their eyes fixed on one another and their smiles trapped on their faces. A wonderful smell was coming from somewhere inside. Some sort of scented fat, completely unfamiliar.

"Ah, sorry, I keep you waiting!" he said at last and stepped aside. Miranda lazed in, making sure she brushed her hip against him on the way. I passed under his arm. I suddenly knew what she meant by the heat. It wasn't that he was sweaty or anything, but he was big, his shirt stretched tightly over his torso, which was solid, like somebody's dad. Suddenly I was looking up from under his armpit into his face. I became aware of a movement to the side of me, and out of the shadows came a figure. A tiny man, shrivelled-looking, with receding hair, he looked about fifty. "Femi, this is Sue, Miranda's friend," said Austin. We nodded to one another.

"Come and meet Miranda." He turned and moved past us through the hall way. I came second with Femi behind.

Inside was a surprisingly big room with a huge window at the far end overlooking the city. Three doors led off it, one, ajar, being obviously the kitchen. The room had an unforgiving acrylic carpet in brown, and curtains sporting bright-orange, blowsy flowers on a purple background; it had obviously not been decorated since the early seventies.

Two chrome settees covered in brown corduroy dominated two of the walls (both with their backs to the view) whilst by the window stood a Formica-topped table and vinyl dining chairs with black, straight legs. Austin gestured for me to sit down. I did so next to Miranda, who ruffled her feathers in a gesture of approval. Austin went out through the kitchen door. We sat, looking at Femi and smiling and nodding our heads. Did he speak any English?

"Are you studying at the University too?" I asked, slowly.

"Indeed," he replied. "I am reading for my doctorate."

"Oh, very interesting. What in?"

"It is for Human Genetics I am studying now. To complement the others."

"Oh," I said, silenced.

Austin came in with a tray of drinks: some wonderful-looking cocktails in tall glasses with loads of ice and long spoons. I was determined to keep a clear head and took only a small sip. "What's in it?" I asked suspiciously.

"Mango, guava, orange, soda. A little crush of lime. And plenty of ice."

"I mean, which alcohol?"

"None. You are only sixteen, Miranda says?" He looked toward her for confirmation. She nodded her head. "Yes, of course," I said. "Um, your friend was telling me that he's studying Genetics; what has he been doing before?"

"He is already in charge of a small medical centre in Nigeria. It is quite an isolated site, and they want him to develop a centre for genetics across the region. Does that answer you?"

"Yes." It certainly did. They seemed a highly unlikely pair. Austin, clearly much younger; good colloquial command of English; worldly wise and obviously very good with women, and Femi? Highly intelligent, earnest and somehow desiccated, with a face like a head on a medicine-man's stick. I didn't know what to say to him in case I sounded an ignorant kid.

Both men were wearing clothes to match the seventies feel of the flat: nylon trousers and shirts in bright colours. Femi even had on one of those hyper-broad, flowery seventies ties, though he'd spoilt the look by tying it too tight. There were no pictures at all in the room, or photos. It was like a motel room, except for all the books piling out of three free-standing bookcases.

"We will eat, I think," Austin said, going out through the door.

Wordlessly, Femi rose and started laying the table from the cabinet on the fourth wall. Miranda got up to help him. She seemed a giant in comparison. "You come to the table now?" he said at last.

"Have you family in Nigeria?" I asked Femi lamely, as we three sat like Madame Tussaud's around the table.

"No, I am not married. I have many brothers and their children."

"And Austin? Is he?" I caught a glimpse of Miranda's rapier eyes, but damn it, I needed to know what she was getting herself into, so that I could pick up the pieces afterwards. *She* needed to know! "Only one wife, many children."

"Oh," I said, horrified, bending down to retrieve my napkin from the floor. It was everything I had suspected. She couldn't just play at having adventures like other girls. She had to play dangerous, go all the way all the time. What did she think she was playing at? Femi's legs were so short that only the balls of his feet touched the floor. Miranda crossed her legs sharply, only narrowly missing my head which I took to be a request to change the subject.

I could see Austin's leather-effect tan shoes coming back in from the kitchen.

"Food glorious food!" he sang, beautifully in tune, as I resurfaced with the cloth. The food looked and smelt delicious. The table was set with fox-hunting table mats on which he placed bowl after bowl of steaming concoction. I was relieved to see forks, not chopsticks; I hadn't been quite sure. "Plantain, Sue, that is what you must have first. No chicken for you." He passed me a mound of stew with rice. I was hungry. The plantain was delicious, a cross between parsnip and banana, cut into strips and fried. It was also the basis for the stew which was gorgeously sweet and spicy.

Miranda was picking at hers like a bird. "I think I'd like to borrow your toilet," she said after a couple of minutes. "You must put it back then," said Austin. They laughed.

"I'll show you," he said. It was hard to imagine anyone needing a guide in a flat this size. They were away a long time. Embarrassed, Femi and I ate on. Once or twice he looked up and smiled or, inclining his head, offered me guava chutney. "Could I have some of this, do you think?" I asked, gesturing to the stew.

"You may, of course," he said. "I didn't offer it because of the meat. You do not eat the meat."

"It's meat?"

"Indeed, fish."

"Oh I don't mind that so much. I eat fish," I said. We carried on. Although he was facing the door into the hall through which they'd gone, he didn't glance their way at all. "You need music?" he said as I copied him, scraping my plate bare with a piece of flat bread. "No, I'm fine, no worries." Miranda and Austin returned, Miranda barefoot, "Couldn't get the light switch to work, so I had to take my shoes off and get on a chair," she said in my direction by way of explanation. I deliberately took no notice.

"You want tea now?" Femi looked at Austin.

"Yes, good." This time the star-crossed lovers sat together on the settee, thighs touching. After I'd cleared the last of the dishes to the minuscule kitchen, I went to sit down on the remaining settee. "Austin's got an enormous record collection," said Miranda.

"So I heard," I said. She looked at me archly. "I mean, I am surprised because you haven't been here all that long." I tried to cover up by turning to Austin.

"It is of course possible to buy records in Nigeria," he smiled at Miranda.

"Yes I know," I said quickly. "What I meant was, they must have taken some bringing over. Heavy, all those records."

"They're only vinyl. I am a big man."

"Yes, you are," said Miranda. I grimaced.

Femi came in with the tea. Both he and Austin took it with lemon, a cinnamon stick and lots of brown sugar. Apparently, today, Miranda did too, but it was too late for me who'd been served first. I sat nursing the sickly-looking British version.

"That was a delicious meal," I said to Austin.

"Femi, he's our cook," he replied. I looked his way and he smiled deeply, proud and shy. Suddenly his whole face looked different; he must have been a handsome young man a long time ago.

"Shall we go and listen to your records now, Austin?" said Miranda in her film star voice. So that was where the record ruse came in. I studied my tea.

"Yes. Sue, do you want to come?"

"Er, no thanks, you go ahead. I'll help Femi with the washing up."

"No," he said, "you will rest on this couch." He gestured forcefully, and I sat back down. They didn't have a TV, and there weren't any pictures to pretend to study. I had to resort to feeding the toggle tie on my sweat shirt through the elasticated tunnel at the bottom. It was a job that I'd been meaning to do for ages, and I was making good headway. I was not doing so well with trying to detune my ear from activities on the record front, however. One record had been on, but it must have been a single and had long since stopped. I gathered that Austin hadn't a replay switch on his record player. There were still loud noises coming from the kitchen, possibly Femi was deliberately making more noise than was strictly necessary as a smoke screen. Just as I was about to pull the toggle through the hole, the same record started up again and Femi came in with a little crystal bowl which he put on the carpet beside me. "Ladies, they love all sweet things." I waited for a suitable feminist reply to surface, but my brain didn't oblige. He smiled encouragingly at me.

"Please, go ahead," he said, bending towards me and proffering the bowl, which I saw to be crystallised ginger. I wondered with alarm if it was meant as an aphrodisiac. "Yes, thanks. Although I haven't got so sweet a tooth actually." He bent forward earnestly. "Would you like to see my pictures?" he said. I felt myself start to prickle with sweat as I imagined exotic pornography, pictures of shrunken heads and desiccated animal parts or, even worse, metaphorical 'pictures', like Austin's records.

"Erm, I haven't got my reading glasses," I said. He looked disappointed.

"Nigeria is a fascinating place. So is Sheffield."

"Indeed," I said.

"You cannot see at all without your glasses?"

"Well, a little. Not too good."

"I would love to show you my pictures while we are waiting."

"Where are they?"

"In my bedroom." Here we go, I thought. He was very small and clearly quite sickly, but there again, could be in possession of a wiry, hidden strength. Actually, he was really quite sinewy, and it looked like he'd had a hard life, so he was probably a good fighter. My third piece of ginger stuck in my throat. "Miranda is a very friendly young woman," he said, thoughtfully.

"Yes, you're right, but she's very unusual. I'm not at all like her, not at all. Can I use your toilet?" I rose quickly to my feet, getting up and kicking the ginger over the carpet. "Sorry," I said.

"It does not matter," he said, picking up the little pieces. "You have eaten enough, ginger is good." Oh shit, I thought. It was designed to soften me up!

"I'll show you where to be," he said. "No!" I found myself shouting, remembering Miranda's return from the toilet, all shoeless and flush-faced. He looked surprised. "I know where it is, that'd be silly. I won't be long," I threw back a bit more calmly as I made it through the door. "That's another fine mess you've got me into," I said under my breath to an invisible Miranda as I went into the tiny hallway, but then that wasn't strictly fair on Miranda, as I had known the set-up beforehand. What the hell did I expect anyway? It wasn't really fair to Femi either. I shouldn't have come. This was so typical of me – bored in my own little, stifling life, I had to trail around after Miranda just to get some excitement. Then, when some came, I couldn't hack it and panicked, played safe. I was the one locked in the bathroom whilst Miranda was having fun.

The bathroom smelt of men: a little urine; mild talc; aftershave (Old Spice?) over a fungus undertow. I sat on the loo to deliberate. Walking out was not an option – not safe for me to go home alone, not safe to leave her here alone. Should I just try and play all 'jolly hockey sticks' and matey, and hope I'd put him off? Maybe show him a bit of hairy leg? There again, it was a different culture. He thought crystallised ginger was an aphrodisiac. God knows what message a piece of hirsute calf might give him. I'd vowed that the old days of 'grin and bear it' with the likes of Byron Saltfisch were over. Just lock myself in here, then? Suddenly, in a flash of genius, it came to me. Gastro-enteritis! No one from any culture, no matter how exotic their mating rituals, could stomach the thought of that.

The door didn't quite fit properly and I saw a shadow pass underneath, then again, going back the other way. He was pacing back and fore outside the door!

"Won't be a minute!" I had a quick wee, nearly worse as my innards were actually beginning to imitate the condition that was about to save me, then I did a great washing of hands. The towel was dark brown like the lino and, although it looked freshly washed, it was obviously a colour chosen to hide stains. I pushed my hair back behind my ears, splashed a bit of water on my face to smudge the mascara and show I'd been suffering, shook my hands dry and flung open the door. No one there. For a moment the front door was temptingly near, but I'd said I'd support her, so that was that.

I opened the door into the sitting room with a pained expression on my face. The record in the bedroom had changed again and my would-be seducer was sitting on the settee looking at a book. He put it down hurriedly and stood up, smiling a bit guiltily at me. I gave him a little wince of discomfort. He gestured to the other settee. I took myself over there and sat down gingerly. Full of enthusiasm, he took the seat next to me, picking up two huge photo albums on the seat in between. "My pictures," he said, producing a magnifying glass from behind his back. "I'll fix a reading light. You may be able to share them a little."

"Yes! I, mean, no," I said. "Don't bother with the light. The magnifying thing'll be great." He looked relieved. "You would like another cup of tea? You can look with them, and then I will tell you about the things you like. I don't want I breathe on you every page."

"No exactly; great," I said. He had some great photos of people and places, although, because I didn't see any shots of wildebeest, cheetah or elephant, it didn't seem much like Africa to me. Before he could come back with the tea, the two vinyl lovers came in. Miranda looked very presentable under the circumstances, although she was still without her shoes, and I noticed had an ankle chain on her left leg. Austin didn't seem to be able to wipe the smile off his face. "Oh dear, he hasn't fetched his photos out again, has he!" he groaned, showing the whites of his eyes. "Actually, they're good," I said. They sat down on the other settee, Austin picking up the book Femi had been reading and had discarded in a hurry,

"You have not been working instead of looking after Sue!" Austin said, as he came in just then with the tea. "No of course; Sue and I were talking only," Femi replied, looking furtive. "What is the book?" I asked. Austin passed it to me, 'Clinical genetics: Theory into Practice.'

"He is a work-a-holic," said Austin, smiling, pronouncing every syllable carefully. "I had to bully him to get him to give up an evening working to keep you company." His friend looked embarrassed. "No, we were chatting about Africa," I said. "I was surprised he had no pictures of the wildlife."

Austin laughed. "That is what people always think of when they think of Africa," he said.

"Most of us in Lagos have never even seen an elephant. After all, how many British people have seen otter or badger?"

"True," I said, "but an elephant is less easy to miss."

Miranda and Austin were sitting modestly apart on the settee, I don't know why they bothered with such a pretence. "Well, we'll have to go," I said,

"Thanks for the lovely food and hospitality."

"It was wonderful to be having two beautiful guests," said Austin.

Femi caught my eye and nodded at me, a little smile in the creases around his eyes. Miranda got up and walked across the room, swinging her hips in slow motion, pure *Some Like it Hot,* when Sugar walks down the railway platform.

Femi said goodbye to us in the lounge. I had a feeling he was going straight back to his book. Austin kissed Miranda on both cheeks, holding my hand again. "Thank you for bringing Miranda," he said quietly. I stood outside on the balcony to let them have a bit of peace. The sun was going down behind the city in a line of orange. As we walked away she was very quiet, linked into my arm. "Do you think Femi's a bushman" I said. "One of the pygmies, or Kalahari bushmen?" She turned to look at me, but I couldn't see her face in the gloom as she said, "With a doctorate in genetics? You are naïve."

CHAPTER THIRTEEN

USTIN LASTED A WHILE, though I never saw him again. Miranda had been more passionate about him than about anyone else since Marcus, but it was more than just this that changed things between us. Not only was I no longer Miss Hot-House Virgin, but I had a boyfriend too. So, okay, he wasn't an exotic older man, but he was my ticket out of the house and away from my parents' evil clutches. Actually, now that I was out more, I liked them a lot better. Wasn't it Mark Twain who said, something like, 'When I was seventeen I thought my father was awful. When I reached twenty I was amazed at how much he'd improved'? Well I wouldn't go that far, but I think they'd guessed I'd had sex, and it somehow made them shy with me. Instead of being interrogated about where I was going every time I prepared to leave the house, now they just asked me what time I anticipated being back. I felt a bit lost. Mum had almost given up feeding me too, which was even more alarming, saying things like, "You're growing up now. I can't be cooking all the time when you've got better fish to fry." My mother always took refuge in suggestive idioms when she didn't approve of something. It was sinister.

Whilst I was working on shifting the balance of power up the road, Miranda and Austin's affair had continued all that summer term between her lower and upper sixth years and ended badly for her in a choice.

Austin had invited her to go to Lagos as a second wife. He had been teaching her about his culture, and she was learning Hausa and reading, reading, reading, about Africa.

"No!" I said, when she told me as we sat in the park. "Don't even think about it, you must be mad!"

She'd been crying. "What will happen to me if I stay here? Loneliness, one man after another."

"Give over! You sound like Blanche Dubois."

"But Sue, we haven't got a culture; we haven't got a religion. I don't know who my family is, and they don't care about me!"

"Granny does," I said, limply.

"There's no purpose," she sobbed; even her tears were bigger, wetter, more extreme than other peoples'. "I haven't even got anyone to feel shame. No one cares enough to stop me."

"I do," I said. She hugged me, the tears giving her hair a wet dog smell.

"Do you love him?" I asked. "No, what am I saying! Look, Miranda, you'd go there and everything you'd ever known would be different. It's Africa, for God's sake! Not South Africa, even. You'd be the only white face maybe; the only bloody white woman to be second wife. How would his first wife feel, anyway?"

I could tell I was saying too much; blustering instead of going through everything slowly; driving the points home, but I never thought she would go this far. I could see her in Africa, a clear visual picture of her, as if I was remembering a large and colourful photograph. She was wearing some bright-coloured cotton wrapped around her body and face, standing behind a statuesque black woman in a market place. Miranda had a basket on her arm and a dippy expression on her face.

"They've been preparing for wife number two for a long time," she said.

"She is prepared."

"But not for someone like you!" I shouted. "Oh, Miranda, how can you even think about it!" She had a strange far away shine to her eyes, looking past me, focusing on a spot in the distance somewhere. I made her sit down on the bench. The same bench we'd sat on so many times before, her with her guitar or Socialist Worker, me with some tortured Victorian novel.

"Do you love him?" I asked quietly. I suppose, in my mind, that could be the only justification for doing anything so terribly full of risk. How could this be Romeo and Juliet though, with Romeo almost middle-aged, and openly married to someone else?

"No," she said.

"What? Don't you even love him?"

"No." We sat without speaking for a while, only the irritating tweet of nearby sparrows and the faraway drone of traffic. "He treats me well. He's tender to me when we make love; we really make love, you know. It's not like the others, he's not a boy." I could see that, but how could kindness, respect even, be good enough for a bright, attractive woman of nearly eighteen? How had she come so close to scraping the bottom of the barrel?

"But Miranda, why? You're only young. Someone will come along again and love you. Please don't go; anything could happen to you when you get there. The wife could go nuts; he could turn on you."

"He respects me."

"He does now, here, when you're on your own patch, but what about in Africa? He could learn to despise you. Please, Mand!" Now I could see a different picture. This time she was in a concrete hut with a corrugated iron roof, hair unkempt, dirty sad face, crouching over an iron cauldron suspended across a meagre fire. She was stirring the contents of the cauldron with a stick. Come to think of it now, I had probably got the image from footage of the apartheid shanty towns of Johannesburg. Certainly a well-educated, well-travelled man like Austin, whose job sponsored his study in Sheffield, would never be forced to live in such a place. But the image was so strong that I felt desperate. "Look, why don't you just go out there and see how it goes? Don't get married or anything. Just see whether or not you like the set up; see if it all works out. If it doesn't, you can come home, no harm done. For God's sake though, don't get pregnant."

Her face was dry of tears now, though still puffy and discoloured. She shook her head slowly, looking sadly at her hands, in which she twisted the frayed remains of a paper handkerchief.

"I can't do that," she said. "Austin says he could never take me to Nigeria if we weren't married; it wouldn't be respectable."

"He doesn't seem to care here," I said sourly. "Not with his wife a thousand miles out of the way." I'd tried to reason with her for another quarter of an hour or so but eventually given up in disgust, throwing, "I've had enough!" over my shoulder as I left. He was going home in a couple of weeks, and she would have to go with him then, a married woman.

I was so mad I didn't phone her for a week or so, and she wasn't in school. Eventually, though, the effort of trying to put her out of my mind was taking up so much time and energy that I caved in.

She seemed quiet and resigned. Apparently Femi had intervened somehow. He'd persuaded Austin that it was not good for Miranda's education to take her away now, and not good for him to marry her without her mother's blessing (I hadn't thought of that sensible point. She might not actually have been allowed to get married or go abroad without her mother's consent). I could imagine the dignified man saying those things in his quiet voice, so careful to get the language right. Why did she always have to be so extreme? Why did she always have to be going outside her home sphere for every answer?

I felt such relief that, when she announced on the phone she'd found God in her grief, converted to Christianity and was enrolling in a Pentecostal church, it passed me by without a moment's misgivings; yet again I was signed up to keep her company on the maiden flight of a new adventure.

I got off my bus in the middle of town by the station; Sunday morning, no one around. There was a sort of country smell in the city, like first thing in the morning or very late at night. 'And bring your cello,' she had said. No way! I wasn't quite sure what I was doing here, but it certainly was not going to involve an impromptu recital. I wasn't altogether dismayed to be there with her; being with Miranda was never dull. There was at the very least some brand new experience in addition to the crises that cropped up every now and again.

She was there under the black stone arch of the station entrance, wearing her cotton, wrap-around dress. She waved vigorously. I gave a small one back. "Hooray, at last; I thought you weren't coming!" she shouted out. Why couldn't she wait until I'd crossed the road? Why did she always have to be drawing attention to us?

"What've you been up to?" she bawled.

"What d'you mean?

She had her guitar case slung over one arm ; I wish I'd played the guitar. It looked so 'free spirit', so American road-movie, especially with long, dark hair. "We're going to be late at this rate," she shouted.

"All right! I missed the fifty."

"It's great, you'll love them. They're so friendly to you." By now I'd crossed the road and she'd taken me by the hand again. I felt a bit embarrassed but at least we weren't likely to bump into one of my other friends in a Pentecostal church.

"I wish I was black," she said, wistfully. I thought, '*Roots* has a hell of a lot to answer for.'

"How can you want to be black, for God's sake, with the history they've suffered!" But I knew what she meant: give me the abused but dignified Kunta Kinte anyday, instead of some rat-faced, raping, overseeing white-trash.

"Anyway, I thought you were going to this church for the first time; I thought I was here for moral support. What *am* I here for, exactly?" She smiled at me from around the curtain of her hair, a beatific smile, serene and very ominous coming from her. We walked on a little further without speaking, soon finding our way behind the old station.

Every building older than the sixties was black with soot. It made the new green of the leaves look even more garish. On the right behind the station were Green Hill flats, which seemed to have been architect-designed using an egg box as inspiration.

"I wouldn't want to live there, would you?" said Miranda.

"No. Anyway, what's wrong with them?" I asked. "In your opinion, that is."

"Well, they're not aesthetically pleasing, are they?"

"It's what they're like to live in that counts."

"Exactly," she said smugly.

"Well… I bet you wouldn't say no to one if you had nowhere else to go, would you?"

"Of course I wouldn't, but that's not the point. That's not the object of the discussion."

"What is 'the object of the discussion' then?"

"I'm just saying I don't like the design."

"Oh for God's sake!" I was getting puffed out by now, although

I noticed that Miranda wasn't. She went to her health and fitness club and worked out; I didn't do anything. Well, I walked in the countryside, just didn't get round to it very often. Actually it was rather unsafe walking around on your own in our area. We'd had the Panther and the Ripper round us. "Don't say 'God' all the time," she said.

"I don't."

"You do." She was getting on my nerves.

We were slogging up a hill lined with big Victorian semis, a slightly better colour than the station; obviously above the smog line in the days before the creation of smoke-free zones. It was a really poor area of Sheffield now but the houses would have been great at one time. Most of the front gardens had been concreted over or tarmacked, wheelless cars parked in the drives. "What I don't understand is, if you wanted to get into religion, why didn't you go Jewish? Everyone's Jewish in your family; you've got Jewish roots."

"But they're lapsed," she said.

"So?" I stopped to get my breath back. There was a brilliant view of the city from up here. You could see the many hills with buildings and trees on them and the occasional dense grey area of factories in the valley bottoms. "It's not bad is it?" she said.

"I'd still rather live in the country, though. Anyway, why don't you go Jewish?"

"I hate the fashions. Well, it's more the hair. I can't stand the long greasy curls." I laughed at her.

"What?" she asked. "Anyway, I've got friends here."

"Friends! Miranda, you hardly know them! How often've you been here? Twice?"

She'd started walking again. The houses were becoming detached and even more run down, the roots of huge chestnut trees buckling the pavement. "Wait on!" I jogged to catch her up, and she linked arms with me. I could never decide which was preferable; having to crook my arm like a man or be the one to wind it through. Whichever way round we did, it made me feel self-conscious, though, and perhaps a little flattered. "I told you on the phone," she said, "I was in the park feeling suicidal and playing my guitar."

"You weren't suicidal! Come off it!"

"As I was saying, I was close to despair at the loss of Austin and all my hopes and dreams when Leroy came up. He could see I was in deep spiritual pain."

"Oh yes," I muttered, cynically.

"What?"

"Nothing."

"Well, we got talking and he told me about his faith. Sue, he just told me about Jesus, about me mattering to him; me just never being alone, and it was as if I suddenly opened out. I felt like something had opened up the top of my skull and all this warmth was rushing out; all this light was rushing in. I was converted!"

"What does he look like, this 'Leroy'?" I asked, sounding suspicious, sounding just like my mum.

"Oh. Tall, muscular; very clean cut."

"I thought so."

"I know what you're thinking," she went on, "but Sue, you'll love it. I just want to share the joy of it all."

"Is he black by any chance?"

We had stopped outside a small red brick church which was covered in grime. There was no stained glass and the opaque windows were guarded by metal grills, behind which were dead leaves and the odd, sinister-looking feather. I was aware of the silence. "Not many cars up here," I said.

"People don't have a lot of money." Faintly, I could just hear singing and instruments of some kind.

"You know, I don't really think I fancy it all that much."

"Oh come on," she said and, getting hold of me by the shoulders, steered me round the side of the building. The singing was louder now and had an inspired quality. "Look, I really don't want to get converted here. I don't want to be religious all right? I'll just go for a walk and meet you back at the fort."

"What fort?"

"Your place. All right?" I had enough on my plate, trying to get through my O levels and keeping my parents on an even keel about Ben. There was enough guilt and structure in my life already. "Get on with it!" she said as she pressed down on the iron latch of the heavy door, standing right behind me and making a small gap under her arms for me to duck under. I did, and found myself in a sort of entrance hall with bare, damp-looking boards on the floor. Before us were double swing doors from behind which the sound was coming. "We're not even black!"

"You should have thought of that before we came all this way. No I'm only kidding. They won't hold that against you," she smiled.

"Why the hell not?" But she was already reaching for the handle of the right-hand door. "Oh shit!"

"Shsh!" she said. Through the open door, past the excited back of Miranda, I saw the small hall, fluorescent light flickering slightly, giving a strobe effect so that everything looked like an old movie. I shuffled in and held the door carefully, and it closed silently behind me. The singing was like nothing I'd ever heard before.

There were so many colours in the room, so much white and pink; powder blue, pale purples and lemons. Many of the women were wearing big hats or, if not actual hats, coloured headscarves or turbans. "Oh, my God, it's a wedding!"

"Don't be dull, they always dress up!" Miranda was easing herself down the aisle; a couple of the musicians at the front had noticed us and had managed to communicate a friendly greeting in the shake of a huge tambourine and the twiddled spout of a clarinet. As we moved down the centre, faces turned our way, every one smiling. No one looked shocked to see two teenage white girls, but to me the crimson carpet went on for miles.

"Oh Christ!"

"Shush," hissed Miranda. We reached the first pew at last where she planted herself right in front of the Pastor. "Shift over!" I whispered but she just kept on smiling. I shoved past her nodding to the faces that kept catching my eye and arrived at the wall. Meanwhile Miranda had fetched out a tin whistle from somewhere and was playing some sort of Irish reel. Only problem was, the pipe didn't seem to have one of the sharps in it; either that, or the worship song had a stray flat. I felt myself going red. Miranda was worse than a parent for embarrassing you. The tambourine embarked on a cadenza, and that and the repetition in the choir spelt wind-it-up time. The music finished on a long, held chord on which the tin whistle played a virtuoso flourish. People were smiling and shifting about; the Pastor shaking Miranda's hand, the air settling around us. The Pastor turned Miranda to face the audience, one hand on each shoulder. "I'd like you to meet again Miranda." There was a general murmur of greeting. "Her young friend too, Suzanne."

That wasn't strictly my name but Miranda had started calling me that to other people – she thought it sounded more romantic.

I stood up and bowed, please don't ask me why. The congregation laughed, gentle and low. "Come and join us on our witnessing Saturday week. It's good to have young people to come, we welcome all of you." Miranda came to sit beside me, and I moved up as far as I could go. She wriggled into position fitting her thigh companionably into the flesh between my hip and waist and reached for my hand. She held it in the open palm of her left, placing her right over it gently. She looked like she was trying to revive a dead starling. I could feel her taking note. Soon she was gripping my hand really hard and listening, even her thighs had tensed up. Oh no, here we go – I groaned. "Miranda, let's go. It all seems a bit personal." No answer. "Miranda, come on!" Impatiently she flicked all her hair back behind her shoulders and, leaning forward on her seat, began to clap, a hungry expression on her face. Gradually, as person after person stood up to witness, she dropped her head, wiggling her upper body slowly from the hips; it was a very bad sign. 'Ummmn's, ' yeah's' and 'ah's' were coming from the audience, and I could feel them moving behind me. I grabbed one of her still-clapping hands and, ducking under the hanging tent of hair hissed into her face, "You're getting sucked in. Come on, we've got to go!" She pushed me out of the way with the back of her hand; it was hot and damp. From under the hair I could hear weird humming. It had some resemblance to a Tina Turner song. The circumference of the circle she was making with her hips got larger and larger, and she opened her legs wide in order to drop forward more fully. Now, as she bent her body, her hair touched the ground, and I noticed that, during the upwards, backwards swing, it hit out at the smart old woman directly behind us, who, fortunately, hadn't seemed to notice (or was too polite to complain). The volume of the humming had increased enormously and moved into an unrelated minor key. I grabbed her arm and dug my nails in, "Stop it! Come on. Right, I'm going without you." I stood up, but she grabbed my skirt,

"Oh come on, come on Sue. We're finished soon, It'll be time to go."

Whole groups of people were making their way down the aisle, some hugging one another, some with their hands wide. Looking at them, there was a sense of something broken open, some shell or kernel cracked open, leaving syrup to pour out. Blissed out. I'd heard it mentioned before by Ben and his meditating buddies.

"They look drugged up. Do they take anything?"

"No way. This's what faith is."

A woman who was standing by the pastor fell back into his arms; slowly he lowered her onto the carpet where she stayed.

"Has this happened before?"

"What?"

"This mass hysteria. Has it happened before?"

"Sue, it's the Holy Spirit. They do it every Sunday."

"What! You didn't tell me!"

"It's refreshing. Relax." Things appeared to be dying down. I guess those that were going to be filled up today already had been. Suddenly Miranda got to her feet. The old lady behind us started clapping rhythmically. Oh my God! Miranda, clearly in her element, moved toward the pastor, kicking off her clogs as she went. I felt relieved in a way, the sword of Damocles I had been dreading had fallen, and nothing worse could happen now. She planted her feet deep in the carpet, a shoulders' width apart, and began to sway from hip to hip, rising up on the ball of each foot in turn. This was a fresh departure. By now even the tambourine had stopped playing, and everyone who'd been filled with the spirit (except the supine woman) was sitting on the rostra or the floor humming or singing quietly. Apart from the pastor, only Miranda was standing. He moved slightly to the left so as to see past her. She moved directly in front of him again and stepped up the swaying, which was accompanied now by a noise in her throat that sounded suspiciously like her Hausa tape and was steadily and alarmingly growing in volume; probably an attempt at 'tongues'. Several people got up and made their way back to their seats, where gradually the quiet, individual voices started to come together, and I heard a version of 'The Lord's My Shepherd' taking place, the voices splitting on the harmony, each line with a slightly different rhythm. From the back somewhere a breathy organ joined in, playing the chords slightly syncopated, as Miranda stepped up her routine.

From all around the room voices came, growing in strength. I closed my eyes. When I opened them again, she was still there, looking lost. No one was watching her. Slowly people were getting to their feet. Some held hands, their heads lowered in prayer, pastel-coloured hats tilted like plates. I felt out of place but it wasn't the colour of my skin, I just didn't believe. Even the musicians were singing now, and from somewhere a humming was coming up underneath the words. It was a sound that warmed you, made you relax, unravelled my tensed-up face. Miranda looked out of place and it wasn't just the fact that she was facing the wrong way, out on a limb at the front. It took me a while to realise that it was because she wasn't moving. Her stillness was a pivot for the eye in the warm room where every peaceful person was gently swaying: left to right, forward and back. Her head had dropped, and she was hiding her face behind her hair. Getting up, I passed along the front, trying not to draw attention to myself by walking in time to the song. I reached her and peeped in through her hair. A wet face broke out in a tiny smile, and she reached out, putting her arms around me. Some small change in the quality of the sound behind told me that people were watching and somehow approving. We broke our clinch and salsa'd back to our seats at the front.

"Here's until next week then, people," the Pastor said. He seemed not even to have raised his voice, yet it could be heard clearly. All the words had gone from the song now, and there was no organ, but the memory of the tune and the rhythm was subtly there in the low humming and formless words still coming from the congregation. No one seemed to be leading it, it just came out synchronised somehow.

"Those of us who want to witness, meet at the Peace Gardens on Saturday at eleven 'o clock. No one wants to hear preaching before then in the morning." There was a change in the rhythm for laughter. People started moving then. I waited for the organ to play us out, but nothing happened. A few people came to the front, talking to the Pastor, shaking his hand. I gathered up my stuff and made to go. Miranda grabbed my arm, "What?"

"Come on, let's go. That's probably volunteers for Saturday."

"Yes, I know," she said eagerly. "Come on."

"You must be joking! What are we going to tell them, for God's sake? I don't know what I'm talking about!"

"Speaking in tongues."

"What!"

"For starters, anyway."

"But you weren't speaking in tongues. You were doing your Hausa tape!" There was no reasoning with her when she had an idea in her head.

"I wasn't!"

"I recognised it, and the Nigerian dancing. Give over, will you!"

"But didn't you feel it? You can't have been immune!"

"What for God's sake?"

"The spirit. Holy spirit." She was looking at me, her face all blotches from the tears.

"My God, you really believe in it, don't you?"

"Don't you? Didn't you feel something? You did, I saw you singing, and looking round, your face was all shining."

"Miranda, that's only mass hysteria. Haven't you even heard of it! Anyway, whatever it was with everyone else, you weren't feeling it. You were putting on an act. I've seen that floor show of yours before."

She stomped away from me, straight for the Pastor who by now was behind the lectern gathering up some papers. I stood in the wings, holding our coats like somebody's mother. I could see her gesticulating, all teeth; him smiling slightly. But his body was only half turned her way. Twice she moved to be face on to him. Finally she gave him a quick hug and swung round, positively skipping toward me. Behind her I saw him watching us, a hint of the amused.

I dumped the various layers of clothes she'd taken off during her conversion. She linked elbows, and we set off up the aisle. A few bowed forms, gathering up children or possessions, raised their faces to smile at us. A handsome man of about twenty was holding the door open. Miranda stopped to stand at his shoulder. He was a good ten inches taller even than her and glanced at us, smiling, one eyebrow raised slightly. His shirt was brilliant white, and he seemed to have gold cuff links with a tiny gold crucifix as a tie pin.

"Hi, it's Miranda again," she cooed, putting out a white gloved hand for him to shake. "See, I did come again after all. Are you going on Saturday?"

"Yes," he replied gravely and turned to me. "I'm Leroy. Pleased to meet you."

He held open the door for me to pass, obviously a sign for us to leave. Miranda followed, nudging me out of the way as she did so. She stood propping open the door with her foot, in effect trapping him in the gap as she turned back toward the room. "I thought we might be getting there early." 'We!' I thought uncomfortably. "I'm a bit nervous, because we're new to the game." She chuckled a little. "I was hoping one of the more experienced members of the church would meet us maybe for a coffee before hand, to take us through the dos and don'ts," she purred, smiling sweetly.

"I'm sure they would," he said. "Excuse me a moment."

Miranda pressed the door open wider with her backside, and he passed through to stand by me in the vestibule.

"It's unusual for the Pastor to recommend for people to go witnessing at first. People new to the church, I mean," he said. He seemed agitated.

"Well, we're not exactly new," she said, left eyebrow raised just a little. "He said it was up to us, that we needed to think about if we were ready, if we had anything to give."

"Yes, that's his usual line I believe."

"Yes, so he said, if we were strong enough in the faith to stand some hard questions, we could go. He left it up to us." Leroy didn't reply.

"Come on, we need to go for the bus," I said.

"Where do you catch it?" he asked.

"Oh, the bus station."

"You're from the other side of town too?"

"Yes, the fifty's best for us. Oh well, must be off!" I said brusquely. He put out his hand for me to shake; it was cool and dry; it seemed older than him. He took Miranda's, and I looked away so as not to see her holding it just that bit too long, raising her eyelids to look up at him endearingly. She was so embarrassing! He was the first to turn away. I watched him as he left the vestibule, seeming to hesitate, the inner door staying open for just a moment longer than it should before swinging closed. Maybe he had stopped to talk to someone.

Miranda's face was lost again in her hair. A woman dressed in a powder blue suit came purposefully towards us. She smiled. "Leroy tells me you're thinking of witnessing with us?"

"Yes, I think my friend is," I said.

"We don't usually encourage people new to things to go out on the streets; it can be hard." She paused; neither of us replied.

"However," she continued, "I hear you're in earnest and, if the two of you stick together, it shouldn't be too traumatic. I'll meet you beforehand of course, to answer any queries you may have, and I'll stay near you all day, just in case of awkward customers. That can be my witnessing."

Miranda smiled and thanked her extravagantly, "but I think it's probably all right. We're going with Leroy."

"Oh, I'm afraid he won't be there; he's not witnessing that weekend," she said with a hint of a smile. They weren't daft then, obviously. "Let's get going," said Miranda grimly, as soon as the Good Samaritan was out of earshot.

"Killed with kindness," I muttered.

"What?"

"I said, 'That's another fine mess you've got us into'."

We pushed through the heavy outer doors and were back on the street. It seemed very quiet and still; different from before. The small church was in shadow now, the light having gone from the road, down behind the line of creepy mansions. We got to the station without talking much and took an empty fifty, sitting ourselves on the top deck. Here you could see down to the driver and get a cheap thrill from the branches bashing against the roof and windows. "Sarah calls it the masturbation bus," I said.

"You what?" Miranda's mind was elsewhere. I repeated myself.

"Sarah!"

"Yeah, what's wrong with that?"

"I don't know. I mean I…"

"…didn't think she masturbated?" I ventured. "Of course she does. Wise up, Miranda."

"No, not that, just…"

"…didn't think we'd talk about it?"

"No, not that really either. Well, yes, actually. I just couldn't imagine you two talking about it together. I didn't know you discussed things like that with anybody else."

"Oh," I said. "Well, I do." We were back on our side of town by now, not far from Miranda's.

"Did you think sex was just what *we* did, then?" I asked.

"Yes I suppose so." It was her stop. She lurched down the bus to the top of the steps, looked back at me. "Are you coming back to my place?"

"No, not today now. I'd never get home."

"I've got loads of homework anyway," she said.

"And me," I groaned, pulling a face. She blew me a kiss goodbye. Then she went down the stairs. I looked down to see her on the pavement and the bus pulled off. She always stopped and waved with both her arms until I was round the corner, as though I was off on a cruise, as if I was going away forever.

CHAPTER FOURTEEN

I WAS ONLY HALF EXPECTING the phone call to fix our 'conversion' drive and it never did come. As Leroy obviously wasn't allowed out with us, there just wasn't the same incentive. Although she claimed to have read the Old Testament 'cover to cover, over and over,' she seemed to go off the idea of being a Christian, and we never returned to the church behind the station.

We met as often as usual before her trip to France that Summer holiday. She'd stopped phoning to go clubbing for some reason, but I wasn't really bothered. The dancing drive had come mostly from her anyway. She seemed all right, just a little quiet. But then again, she couldn't really let her hair down as we were never on private territory. Her mother had nearly completed the process of unofficially moving in with the ancient lover and had gone so far as letting out two rooms of the house to a lodger, a Malaysian woman and her daughter. They were nice, according to Miranda. The girl was at the university, and they had some family in Sheffield.

I didn't know why, but Miranda no longer seemed to have friends around to her house. Granny was in and out a lot as the care-taking eyes and ears of the mother, whilst mother was 'Frying other fish' in Dronfield, but apart from her and the lodgers, Miranda never mentioned anyone else. The boyfriends seemed to have disappeared. I tried not to mention it, fearing that it might push her after Austin again. When we met at the pictures, the pool or the park I had the unfamiliar feeling of being careful with her since losing Austin and God, and in the prelude to seeing her father. There were things I didn't mention, and things, like me and Ben, that I played down. Her routine had intensified. She fitted me in between the gym, 'A' level study in the library, chores (in the absence of her mother) and what she rather ominously called 'Spiritual Study'. I had long since learned that, if you wanted to discourage anything in Miranda, you had only to feign a lack of interest in it. Most things, from crotch-less tights to missionary zeal, would then wither into insignificance. Whatever you did, you mustn't look shocked and horrified; she'd do it twice as much.

We talked in the cinema queue, the changing rooms, or over picnics, mostly about the lodgers and Miranda's looming trip to her father in France. She had met with him since that fateful letter last year, but she'd not been able to go over, some technical hitch with the stepmother apparently. He'd come here, though, and met her in London, swept her off her feet with afternoon tea at the Ritz and all the extravagant trimmings you'd expect from an absentee parent's prodigal return. She'd come back with gleaming eyes, like someone with Malaria, but I'd not been able to get much sense out of her as to what the father was actually like, only rhapsodies on the themes of Harrods food hall, the Dali exhibition and the Royal Ballet. Since then there'd been regular letters and phone calls, kept increasingly private from me, but, though I was hurt, I kept it all in perspective, feeling an overwhelming sense of relief that she had taken my advice over Austin. With him gone, she had nothing really exciting except the mounting hysteria of her impending trip to France.

It would be the longest we'd been apart, but I had Ben now, and we were going to write. As the end of term approached, she seemed to go quiet. We went into town together to get her holiday stuff, but she didn't seem excited anymore. When I questioned her, she'd said, "It's all part of trying to be grounded in myself." I didn't press her about it, but I did wonder if she had been getting involved with some guru.

Granny and I were there to wave off the National Express coach as it left for Victoria station. Granny gave her some travel slippers, "So your feet won't swell on the coach," and I gave her a lockable journal. The face looking out through the windows as the coach pulled away was smiling, a long white hand waving through the burst of exhaust fumes, but both of us were quiet as we left the bus station. As I kissed Granny goodbye, she squeezed my hand. "You've never met her father?" I shook my head. "He's a powerful man, a charismatic man. I hope he's careful." It seemed a strange thing to say.

But Miranda wasn't the only one on my mind. On one of his stints shaking buckets for the miners in the pedestrian precinct in town, Ben had met a man who'd convinced him that all worldly struggle was pointless without inner enlightenment, which turned out on further inspection to be a form of meditation taught by a Guru Maharaji from Stockport. All term, Ben had been going back and fore in his parents' battered Mini Metro, preparing himself to be 'initiated,' and all the bulldog clips, circuit boards, mini screwdrivers and condoms in the world couldn't seem to compete with this new passion. From electronics whizz-kid he seemed to have become an 80s George Harrison. I was dreading his 'A' results almost as much as I was doing my own 'O's. When I asked Huw if it was as bad as it seemed for Ben in school, he just grunted and slammed the racket even harder into the tennis ball. It wasn't a good sign, but at least I had my Miranda letters.

'…and it was both amazing and strangely matter of fact.' My letter to her was beside me on the dining room table. I liked to write with real ink on white, recycled paper; she liked expensive lilac paper with a water mark. The paper was both so thick and so lilac that it seemed to give off the scent of old lavender.

'To be more precis ach of the five techniques just worked on me straight away, first time. In the third eye one, I just felt my forehead open in the middle, the two sides unravel back; no, more a fold back, and something gently press on this centre thing that tingles,' I wrote.

'In the breathing one I just felt rich air filling me with each inhale, really tangible, and with the sound one, a rushing in my ears. I don't think I really believed it'd work, actually. They'd kept us hanging on so long, I'd gone blasé. I'd just about given up, to be honest, when we got called in and told she thought we were ready. I couldn't believe it. They took us downstairs to a converted cellar with very dim lighting and cushions. Just the one woman in there, come up from London. They look amazing, these older women. Their skin, hair and nails are all plain but sort of glowing somehow. I hope I look as good in my thirties. How's your Dad and Step Mum and the little brothers? I love the terms of endearment you get hold of for me. Particularly good are: 'Little pouch' and 'Stunted-Welsh-dwarf.'

'Do Algerians dance in night clubs?! I'm missing you, especially your ironic take on everything New Age. 'Bring back Miranda!' Don't jump into anything out there. I mean, don't do anything you can't back out of if you need to, okay? You know what you're like. (I'm sounding like my mother: "Be careful; you know what I mean.") What I mean is, don't get married or pregnant and be burned alive by an exploding oven owned by someone's mother-in-law (or is that India?)'

'School's not bad in the sixth form. Like you said, Miranda.

They mainly leave you alone if you talk nicely to them and hand in two out of three pieces of work, don't they? My father has tried to sort out a work schedule for me. I'd be better off in Holloway or maybe a Roman galley. I can't quite believe he ever worked that hard himself, despite what he says. And if he did, why he thinks he's clever, because it must be five times the hours anyone works nowadays. Maybe that's all they had to do in the days without TV.'

'Have you managed to have kinky sex with anyone, or is it banned? Since we got 'The Seeing' I haven't really got round to practising it, though Ben's at it all the time (practising I mean!). I saw Henry from your gym the other day, and he asked about you. He's gorgeous (if you like them tall, witty, high cheek bones, perfect teeth, pectoral muscles you could ski down oh, and did I mention the ten inch cock?! Tempted?) Don't hold it against him that he's not black. Don't forget your roots here in sunny Sheffield (no pun intended and there are far too many bloody brackets in this letter)! Oh and too many exclamation marks too! Sounds terrible about the woman they were stoning.

Much love anyway, love,

Sue.xxxxx'

The letters crossed the channel between us frequently. She'd stayed away for a couple of weeks into the new school year 'to improve her French' and I'd had a chance to get started in the sixth form. 'O' levels hadn't been as bad as they could have been, and I loved my own personal time table, with lies-in built in and no school uniform.

In her letters she sounded very cheery and described the life out there in fascinating detail. From France they'd gone to Algeria to see the step-mother's family. Though she herself was no longer a practising Muslim, her family still lived in a very traditional way in Algeria, and Miranda was apparently enjoying being part of the family and caring for the children whilst her father and his wife visited relatives and went sight-seeing. Miranda had never been one to sight-see as such, and she could never tell you anything factual about anywhere she'd been. On the few school trips or day's out we'd been together, she usually wandered off the beaten track and, instead of whizzing round Hampton Court, Chester Roman walls or the Industrial Hamlet, was usually to be found chatting up some teacher in a corner, or helping an old lady volunteer unpack boxes in the gift shop. One time I lost her in Peveril Castle for forty minutes, only to find her eventually performing in an archery demonstration. She was the one tied over the bull's eye with an apple on her head.

Her last letter had been a bit odd though. Apparently she'd witnessed an attack on a woman in the street. The police had been involved, and she'd been quite shaken up by it as far as I could tell. The woman had been wearing jeans, which was forbidden, and instead of the police arresting the men who'd been stoning her, they'd taken her away. What seemed to impress Miranda most about Algerian village life, though, was the cleanliness and sense of order.

After the first week her letters had been full of quite detailed descriptions of daily routine. Floor-cleansing was a favourite with her, and she'd actually told me several times about the scraping down, scouring with sand, brushing out and scrubbing with water that went on every day. I was glad she was only there for a few weeks, as she might have gone stir crazy.

There had also been several tantalising mentions of 'Cousin Omar,' who was apparently in his final year at Lille University studying Electrical Engineering but had come home on holiday.

He was old, at least thirty five, but I knew that sort of unsuitability would only inflame Miranda's interest. I wondered if it was merely coincidence that both he and Miranda were in Algeria for a holiday at the same time.

Although we'd been in touch all the time she'd been away, it was three weeks into the Autumn term, and she still hadn't called to say she was back. I couldn't leave it any longer. Where was she? Realising, with irritation, that I hadn't got a number for either her mother's new place or Granny's house, I phoned Miranda's home. Auntie answered my call, wished me good day and went to fetch her. We didn't talk long and the line seemed poor, her voice having a 'far away' quality. Apparently she'd been home a week already, which I thought was odd, but tried to explain it to myself as jet-lag or culture-shock. She said she hadn't called because she was 'sorting some things out' but, "Yes, it would be good if you could come over." So I cancelled meeting Ben on the anti-Maggie demo outside the Cutlers' Hall and went round.

It seemed ages since I'd climbed the steep steps to that front door, and there were still dandelion leaves in the cracks opening up between them. They were always there but never seemed to get any bigger. Was that natural horticultural conditions or just a sign that some half committed gardener at the house could only tolerate so much?

She must have been waiting in the hall for me, because even before I had time to knock on the glass door she had it open, slid round it and shut it behind her. Apparently it wasn't convenient: The lodgers were having a special party, and non-Muslims might find it a bit awkward. Would I like to go for a swim?

She had everything I might need ready for me in a plastic bag, including an old costume of hers that I'd used before. We went to the new pool in the centre of town. I was a crap swimmer, but at least it was preferable to meeting her at the gym. There she pumped iron like it was going out of fashion and had all the gear, favouring cut-off Lycra in loud colours. She wore the wrist and head band towelling stuff too, but unfortunately for her that wasn't available in fluorescence. I had asthma, which made me hopeless in the gym. I suppose it went with my eczema. Anyway, I never liked doing anything that made you puffed out indoors – if I was going to sweat I wanted to be out in the fresh air. One thing I did feel relieved about was the demise of the sweat pants; apparently the radiator she'd left them on at Austin's had melted a hole in them.

She looked well but thinner than before she went. As she fumbled to pay for us to get in she laughed affectedly at the attendant on the till, "Oh good grief! I'm really just not used to handling sterling yet, I've been away you see, visiting family in France and Algeria." To my great embarrassment I noticed a French accent, particularly in the way she said 'France'. Suddenly she seemed her eccentric old self.

We changed and went out to the pool. Though she had lost weight she was not too thin and looked good in her one-piece that was cut high on the leg and away at the shoulders, a cross between sporty business-like and beach babe.

It was relatively empty at this time, apart from a couple of fanatical looking lane swimmers and several elderly women who were moving up and down in the smaller pool, their head and shoulders out of the water and their hair perfectly dry. Usually Miranda surveyed the scene for talent, but today she seemed pre-occupied with trying to get her hair under a vicious looking rubber hat.

"Why the hat, Miranda?"

"Protecting my hair, of course. Chlorine's hell, you know."

"I know. Anyway, what I meant was, why the hat in particular now?"

"I just want to take care of myself that's all; honour my body." I looked quickly at her, but she hadn't even said it ironically, with an American accent or anything, like she was imitating an exercise video. I hoped she wasn't heading for some 'Cult of the body' thing. We separated: Miranda to the deep end for her maiden plunge, me to the shallow end for the gradual acclimatisation ritual. Because of the short sight, I couldn't see her in detail while she waited poised on the side. I saw only her tall, unmistakable outline bent against the huge windows, heard the deep but slick sound when she entered the water.

I was doing quite well in the free lane bit, two lengths at a time; one back, one breast and a long rest every ten. I'd lost sight of Miranda, only sometimes picking out her swimming hat when she occasionally surfaced for air in one of the far lanes, or hung over the deep end ready to dive. After a while I got fed up and went by the diving boards to wait for her. She emerged at my feet in a whoosh of water, hauling herself out directly onto the side and getting to her feet. She was head and shoulders taller than me by now, with broad shoulders and even broader hips. "Are you coming to try a dive?" she asked, squeezing my hand as she moved off. Why did she ask, she knew the answer?

As she moved up the steps to the lowest board, I could see some people by the window, but not well enough to see their faces. Above me I felt the lowest plank quiver when she took up position, pausing for a moment before entering the water with a clean, whole sound. There was a distant noise of clapping and wolf whistling. I moved away from the window and down the side of the deep end, past the rope that divided off the divers' part. Three times from each board, nothing fancy, and then go and change was her routine. "You can tell the quality of a dive by the sound it makes," she had once told me.

Her fans were knocking at the window now. By the time she reached the highest board the attendant was over there trying to get them away. It was a wonder anyone had the guts to learn to dive, with so many voyeurs. How stupid to build the baths so near the railway station and with such a bloody great window! I made my way to the changing rooms.

I was nearly dressed by the time Miranda came back. Probably because I didn't do it very often, going swimming was a shabby business for me. I had a plastic bag for my stuff, and Mum always insisted on me taking a holey old towel, since I'd once lost one in a school swimming lesson when I was twelve. I never seemed to have the right equipment and emerged at the end of a session with rat's-tail hair and eyes like a myxamatoid rabbit. True to form, however, Miranda had it sussed, planning both gym and swimming with great precision. Of her two swimming costumes, one was always dry at any given time, rolled neatly in a soft purple towel and waiting in her special draw-string swimming bag. In the said bag were a nylon purse with the correct coins for the lockers and drinks machine, and enough for a swim session and snack lunch, together with a transparent pencil case. In this pencil case she kept mini bottles of shampoo, conditioner, shower gel, a fold-away brush and a small tin of talc for between her toes and under the breasts. Most impressive of all though was the neatly folded re-sealable freezer bag for the wet costume.

I sat attempting to dry the raw athlete's-foot-infested-spaces between my toes while she sorted herself out after the swim. At least today I had one of Miranda's decent towels packed for me.

The changing rooms were starting to fill up now, as people came in their lunch hour. Most of the private cubicles were occupied, and Miranda stood and peeled off her costume, easing the floppy mass down over her buttocks. She stood naked, squeezed out the costume and hung it up to drip dry. Then she folded the towel around herself, tucking the end in with a deft twist. There was no rummaging around in the locker; everything was placed before a swim in the correct order, to be retrieved later. Never any of *her* socks in the hair-ridden sludge by the drain. She disappeared around the corner to the shower. I didn't need to see her, I knew exactly how she would do it: hair; armpits; fanny; feet. Return to hair and rinse, then apply conditioner. Whilst that is taking hold, return again to the 'fuzzy bits,' as she called them, and the feet. Total rinse. Towel twisted around the head as a turban, and return to the locker, naked. Remove towel and dry, starting at the top and working down, to finish by sitting down in clean pants, dabbing gently between the toes and applying magnolia talc. I was mesmerised. I'd forgotten to mention the clean pants and socks always waiting in the swim bag, the stale specimens popped in another freezer bag. She was my friend, and I loved her.

She was just as much of a curiosity to other women as well. For me it was the miniature lotions and potions, but what made *them* look with sideways glances at her from under their hair? I think it wasn't just the walking, sitting, bending naked that held the attention (although in Sheffield, girls and women were generally very prudish in front of one another. Miranda had had a lot of trouble with her liberated behaviour before and after school Games lessons for instance), but the ease in which she did it. As she moved about the changing room, there was something of the 'stiletto in the toilets' feel about it. Last on her list was the hair. In went the ten pence, and she brushed and brushed as the machine spat out its meagre air.

"Food, Miranda?" I held open the heavy door as she flung the swim bag over her shoulder. She smiled, "How did you guess?"

We ordered from the counter and went to sit down in the best seats, which had a view both of the pool and of the street outside. She did look different after her holiday, but it was hard to pin-point why. Maybe more definition to her face, perhaps. Less puppy fat? The clothes were different too; a wholesome gypsy look, with a clean, brilliant-white cheese-cloth shirt, all wide sleeves and embroidery, and a full skirt. "Go on, then. How did it go?"

She fetched out her photos. I'd seen a couple of snaps of her father before, but he hadn't looked as young as this. My parents had been old having me, nearly forty having my sister. Here, though, was a man not even forty now, a blondish Charles Bronson. With him in the pictures were assorted horses, cars, two matching sons and a beautiful woman. "She's Algerian," Miranda kept saying, rather obviously. Eventually we got to one where Miranda was in the scene. Her father had his arms around her and her step-mother, and she had her hands on the twins' shoulders. One had a Dachshund, one a cat in their arms. "It looks very posed," I grumbled. "It was. We were at Grandmere's Summer house." I rolled my eyes.

The food arrived: over-baked potatoes in their jackets with tuna and the mandatory dead piece of lettuce and slice of tomato. I even knew how she would prepare this food for herself, removing as she always did the tuna, putting all the butter in and replacing the fish, squeezing both sides together hard and leaving for a few minutes.

She told me of family gatherings and parties and trips to the beach; of huge meals and lace table-cloths, and always there was what her father said, what he wore, what he kept on promising for her. There were so many plans, "…and so we'll go to Algeria again at Easter, and I'll look after the children." She was back to her old self, the eyes glistening, hands articulating ten to the dozen. Out tumbled the words-: "after 'A's, Papa says… and then we'll… Papa says I'm just like Aunt Cecile." It was almost more than I could stand.

I told her about Ben and the guru but her face had that over-polite expression, and I knew she wasn't listening. We talked about school and the teachers for a while, then I went to get us a couple of coffees. When I came back there were two lads sitting at our table chatting her up. She was turning it on full blast, telling some tale about visiting family at the end of her summer holidays from the Royal Ballet. She was being groomed as a soloist.

"Tha looks a bit big hefty fer a ballet dancer," the good-looking one said.

"Oh yes quite, but fashions are changing you know. You don't have to look like a fairy anymore."

"Oh aye," he said. He smiled at me. "There's a friend then, is there. How do." He shook my hand and got partially to his feet. I was blown-over.

"You're not from Sheffield then?" I asked. "Can ye're it, then!" He laughed. I nodded. "Me dad's gor a farm out on t' moors." He turned back to Miranda who was giving it her all: wiggling in her seat, fluttering the arms around to illustrate her words, opening her eyes wide to show the whites, which were white even after a swim, because she also carried some soothing eye drops in her post-swim kit. She told him more and more fantastic tales. Apparently her father was an Italian count, Vittorio Vertuni D'Albinoni no less. As the tale got more and more animated, Mark sat back in his chair and crossed his arms across his big chest. I had a feeling he was enjoying her immensely. "Oh aye," he said from time to time, giving me a quick grin. He reminded me a bit of Tom Booker.

His friend Michael seemed less interested in her or, more like it, knowing my luck, realised that Mark had bagged the best already and he'd have to put up with me. He pulled his chair over to mine and started giving it the twenty questions. However I wasn't in the mood. I might have answered Mark but I just couldn't be bothered with some skinny runt who looked like he'd been fed by a deficient placenta. I felt thoroughly pissed off. The only good thing about it was that I now knew Miranda was back to normal with a vengeance.

"Right, I'm off." I scraped the chair back and stood up. Mark was just telling Miranda how he'd seen her diving. How they'd been walking past and he'd seen the people watching and gone to investigate. "Wi could ge' together if you wan. I cou' teach yer a few mor o them dives." Strangely, though, she didn't give him her card. Meanwhile slimy Michael had dropped into step with me. Just before we got to the swing doors, I stopped and looked right at him. "No I can't dive, and I bet you can't either. In fact it's a good bet you can't even swim, and no I'm not interested. To be honest, I'm a lesbian."

I exited, so angry that my feet had got me across the dual carriageway and onto the traffic island before Miranda'd had a chance to catch me up. "I see you're back to your old tricks, then," I snapped at her.

"Delicious wasn't he!" She crooned.

Obviously I didn't need to worry about her anymore. We saw one another now and again in our old haunts, but I had enough on my plate with Ben, who'd had to stay back a year to re-take his As. Huw had gone to Cardiff to do medicine, and the house seemed very quiet without him. My parents now had a dangerous amount of time and energy on their hands to bug me and my sister, me especially. Ben's failing had put the wind up them. My mother had stopped trying to 'put meat on his bones,' and my father had stopped asking his opinion about quantum physics. He'd let me down too in a way. When I first went out with him, I'd thought he was an eccentric genius, but now he was just an eccentric flop, and what is endearing in a genius is just pathetic in a failure.

Anyway it wasn't as if anything better was on the horizon. Tom Booker had gone to do training as a prelude to joining the Royal Engineers and, although Jan was still around, having chosen to work with a vet prior to taking the course at university, he was still in cloud-cuckoo-land as far as girls were concerned.

Miranda, however, seemed strangely content with doing her routine and getting on with school stuff. Granny went around most nights to do her tea or just for a cuppa, and Miranda was doing a lot with the lodger and her daughter. She'd latched herself onto the woman, substitute mother I suppose, and I'd seen them out and about a couple of times, the woman all covered up and Miranda demurely dressed as if butter wouldn't melt.

There were other friends too for both of us, though we made a point of never meeting one another's. When she was there I didn't really do a lot with them (I suppose for the same reason you can't see the moon in the day time) but I wasn't going to wait and twiddle my thumbs for her. She went down-market for her other female friends in my opinion, picking real squares. I suppose she had all her adventures with men, or me, so she only picked those other girls as a bit of relaxing light relief. This was a good time for us however. The calm before the storm.

CHAPTER FIFTEEN

I T WAS ONLY A few weeks before Miranda was due to go back to Algeria for Easter that I got a terrible phone call. Her Granny was dead.

Miranda's mother was the one to tell me and the fact that she was back home at all painted a bleak picture of how Miranda was coping. Granny had always been the foundation of Miranda's life. It was Granny who taught Miranda how to cook. She was always on Miranda's side; always ready to put her own life on hold for a few hours and listen to Miranda; to help her. This was a disaster.

I was asked to go and stay with her for a few days whilst her mother arranged the funeral. She herself would then move back in, to keep her daughter company for the few weeks before Miranda went to Algeria.

I told Mum, and she gave me a lift down that evening with my small case of clothes and school things. Mrs Gee the lodger opened the door to us, and my mother kissed me goodbye, putting an envelope into my hands to give to the family. The woman led me upstairs to Miranda's bedroom, as if I didn't know perfectly well where to go. She was small, with a lovely make-up-free face framed by the clean, pale-blue scarf she wore carefully folded and pinned to hide her hair. But things were disturbingly different. The house smelt clean and somehow empty. I hadn't realised until then just how long it had been since I was last here. It must have been before the Summer holidays, and now it was nearly Spring half term.

Lots of the mother's stuff had gone but her room was still full, only now full of Mrs Gee's things. It looked like the Ashram in Manchester, I realised with surprise, only this room was furnished with old things rather than new and seemed less self conscious. It was the sense of order and of an almost commercial cleanliness that reminded me of the Ashram, and the quiet. In our house someone was always pacing in the kitchen, playing instruments, listening to records or the TV or radio, shouting at someone else.

As she opened the door of Miranda's room, I felt the lodger was the boss; a calm, Malaysian, Muslim Mrs Danvers. That must make Miranda Rebecca or the new Mrs De Winter. Which? I was pondering this to myself as the door closed behind me and my eyes adjusted to the dim light of her room. She was sitting up in bed, a white shawl around her shoulders and her long hair spread over the pillows. Her face looked very white as did the long hands, which she had folded over the bed clothes. She or someone else had composed her into a tableau of grief, and it was highly effective. You could almost detect the TB spores hanging in the air.

"Hello, Petal. It's freezing in here!" I started cheerily.

She smiled wanly and shifted in the bed, breaking the gloomy spell a little.

"She's gone. My Granny's gone." I climbed onto the bed and hugged her rather awkwardly. Again I had that strange feeling of everything having been choreographed, but then I suppose I'd never really met death before. Never really had to react to grief.

"Can I open the curtains, Miranda?" She nodded.

Everything felt instantly better in the real light. I sat by her and held her hand, but even that gesture seemed affected. In the end I climbed in with her, nicked a couple of her pillows and snuggled up.

"Her heart just gave up. It was heart failure."

"I know. Your mum told my mum."

"Poor Granny."

She started to cry, huge tears like the ones in 'Alice in Wonderland' moving down her face. I tucked my arm through hers, and we just sat there for a while. Her crying made very little noise.

The door opened, and in came Mrs Gee with a tray. On it were tea things, Granny's best service presented on a clean napkin with home made butterfly buns. We tucked in, and I was glad to see she hadn't lost her delight in cake. Whilst we ate, the woman moved around Miranda's room noiselessly, her small feet partially hidden beneath the long, batik skirt. She put things in order on the work table and Miranda let her; usually she was so touchy about people controlling her things. She removed the newly-laundered kimono and hung it in the wardrobe out of the way, crossing to the bed with the blue towelling robe, which she placed neatly on a chair within Miranda's reach. Lastly she began to re-arrange the bed clothes around us. This was too much for me and, as we'd nearly finished anyway, I gave her the tray to take instead.

"Thanks, we've finished. That was delicious."

"Thankyou, Auntie Gee," said Miranda. The woman smiled and for a moment put the back of her hand to Miranda's cheek. She murmured something and left, closing the door behind her.

"What was that?"

"A blessing," replied Miranda. "Where do they go, the dead ones? Where has Granny gone?"

"Who knows. There probably is a God. There again, though, it is quite comforting to think of just dissolving and being part of the trees and the soil." She looked at me strangely. "Well, I mean, from an environmentalist's point of view, nothing gets wasted." I shut up, suddenly aware that no one wants to talk hypothetically about the after life when someone they love has just died.

She started to lose tears again. They didn't seem to be pushed out like in a sob. There was something much more passive about it. They oozed out, gathering mass at the corners by her nose and then, dragged down by their own sheer weight, moved down her face. Some comfort I was being.

"The Angel Gabriel will come down and rip her soul out through her throat. It'll be so painful. Oh poor Granny!"

What on earth was she talking about? "Where did you get that from?"

"It's in the Qur'an. Auntie was telling me about it this morning."

"But Granny wasn't a Muslim; she was a lapsed Jew!"

"I know, I know." That only seemed to make her worse. I felt at sea. What did I know about it? It was only that I didn't see the point in getting all upset about somebody else's religion if you had your own, equally all-absorbing, home-grown one. Some people would pay an arm and a leg to be born a Jew, and Miranda was looking everywhere but under her nose for some scheme, some explanation for her life.

It was a very long few days. I went to school from her house, sleeping with her at night, whilst during the day she was ministered to by Auntie. Auntie's daughter wasn't there, being on a field course somewhere. I wondered how that worked out vis-a-vis chaperones. Anyway, that wasn't my business. Miranda's mother was rushing around like a blue-arsed fly in the way everyone had to after a death, and Miranda was giving it the Emily Dickinson treatment. I couldn't wait to get home to Nationwide and my father practising Chopin.

Even ordering Chinese takeaway was a problem in the 'grief house'. I didn't eat meat, or fish either now; Auntie and Miranda wouldn't eat pork (apparently it was unclean) and Jean the mother didn't like vegetables. Jean slammed about the house, and Auntie crept around in her thick, white ankle socks. Jean made extravagant dinners using every possible pan and utensil; had huge, long baths that soaked the carpet; filled the house with steam and drained the hot water tank. Mrs Gee abluted quietly before praying five times a day, and produced exquisite meals using only a red pepper and a pineapple.

Jean was sleeping in the spare room, and when the ancient lover came round they retired in there, being careful not to leave the door ajar. As the funeral approached, things became more and more tense. So tense in fact that I called in at home after school on the fourth night for some normality.

My mother's questions were remarkably restrained, for her. I think she was probably too surprised to be *compos mentis*. After all, I had spent the whole of my teenage-hood trying to get away from my own life and into Miranda's. It had begun to occur to me that they were treating Miranda all wrong. Her distress seemed to expand when they paid it attention, like one of those Chinese paper birds in water. In my opinion they should have re-homed Auntie Gee and talked a bit about Jean's feelings. She was officially the chief mourner; it was her mother after all. Miranda's grief seemed to me to be just a huge monster that got fat on sympathy.

The funeral came and went. My mother attended, and I sat with her. Miranda had insisted on a proper veil for the service, modelled no doubt on pictures of Jackie Kennedy. The church was packed and a lot of the old faces were ones I recognised from the Rotary club. As I looked at the small coffin I said goodbye to the lovely old person who'd picked up so many pieces.

I tried to be attentive without being fussy with Miranda over the next couple of weeks. She came back to school, but had surprisingly few tales to recount; usually she couldn't wait to tell a good story. But we had both changed. 'Us' had changed. I felt impatient with Ben and me. Impatient with Miranda's crying eyes and soul searching, and frustrated with myself. I was tied in knots and stuck in a school where I wasn't doing very well for nearly another two years. As the time approached for Miranda to go, I felt more and more deadened. I think Jean was pleased, though, as she could finally sneak back to Brian without feeling guilty and start to mourn her own mother properly. Auntie Gee's daughter was back, and together they were going to look out for everything while everyone else was away.

This time her mum and Brian drove her to the coach station. It was tender to see Miranda when she was with her mum and being cared for. She seemed to drop the airs and graces and just be a normal screwed-up teenager.

I hoped the going away would be good for her. Particularly being away from things that reminded her of Granny and, for some reason I couldn't quite explain, from Mrs Gee.

There were no letters this time, despite the fact that she had extended her stay beyond the Easter holidays 'to improve her French' again. That's what Mrs Gee had said when I'd phoned, after failing to see Miranda in school at the beginning of term. Eventually she did come back and rang me, her voice sounding odd. I put it down to too much travelling and attention from her Dad. It was agreed I'd call round after lessons the next day, as she had been ill and was not back at school yet.

She opened the door to me wearing an antique skirt of her mother's. On her head was a navy chiffon scarf with glittering silver thread sewn into it, the same one she used around her boobs for clubs. She'd lost even more weight, and wasn't wearing makeup. We didn't embrace, though her face was full of smiling and, as I passed her to go in, she smelt different.

I stood feeling a bit aimless in the narrow hallway, not knowing whether to go up to her room or the kitchen, but she held open the front room door. Again I passed her; again the strange, perfume-less, clean smell. Like a pavement after rain. This was a truly old fashioned 'parlour'. Not that the furniture was particularly old; more its function, it being always out of bounds. The very fact of being ushered in there was a bit unnerving. A big lace cloth covered the table. There was a gleaming Christmas cactus and a large, framed photograph of Granny. The settee was pink velveteen with lace antimacassars which matched those on the table. In a polished, marble-effect mantle piece a coal-effect fire gathered dust. She gestured for me to sit, and so I perched, being too short to lean back comfortably on the settee.

"I don't think we've been in here since the quartet days," I said.

"No."

"Why now, then?"

"It's nice for guests," she said.

"Give over!"

"Tea? Coffee, or lemonade?" she asked. "It's home-made."

"Is it? How do you make it?"

"Fresh lemons, water, lots of sugar."

"Wow, it's like a Western or something, 'Good ol' southe'n hospitality!" She smiled.

"Did you want some?"

"Yes Ma'am, I sure do!"

I knew I was being a prat, but I just wanted to break the ice. It was formal, like my parent's front room, but more aloof. In ours my Dad was 'holed up' with his piano, radiogram and archaeology books, putting his pipe-smoke-scent trail on everything. She returned with two long glasses filled with crushed ice, sugar-rimmed and each placed on a doily. She was obviously very proud of herself. I tasted mine. "It's delicious, Miranda. Will you tell me how to make it?"

"I'll write out the recipe for you."

"Where's your mum?"

"Still in Dronfield"

I wasn't used to us suffering these huge pauses. "Um, how are the A's going?"

"Fine," she said. "How are yours?"

"Fine. I'm enjoying them, actually."

"Good," she said. I couldn't believe this. At any moment she's going to start giggling and everything'll be all right; she'll be back to her old self.

"Miranda, have you ever seen the film, *The Stepford Wives*?"

"No." She didn't watch much TV.

"Why?"

"Oh, nothing," I said. If it had been colder, we could have filled the space with the murmur of gas and watched the fire through the lemonade in our glasses. But then we probably wouldn't have been drinking lemonade. "Why the scarf?" She didn't answer straight away. I sipped my drink, looked up, asked her again with my eyes. "It's in lieu of a chador," she said quietly. The word did sound familiar, but not enough to conjure up a picture. I waited. "I'm a Muslim."

This did register. The initial, momentary reaction was fear, unanchored in anything definite such as fear for her, me or our friendship, but it was soon blown away by a sense of the ridiculous. It was the black church all over again. "Don't be daft!" I guffawed, but she wasn't smiling. "You can't be a Muslim, you're a Jew for God's sake!" I waited for an answer. "It's not something you can just do, wake up one morning, "Hey I'm a Muslim!" Still nothing. She had on her a beautiful smile. This was the 'Born again' routine; I waited. She turned in the big chair to face me, putting her glass down carefully on a cork mat.

"I am a Muslim. You are not born a Muslim. It's a way you learn. I will learn to follow the path of Islam." Was it my imagination, or was she talking weird, like she'd learned English as a foreign language?

"But what about your life?" She smiled at me, one that said I was being naive. I wasn't used to being so lost. My mind felt so dense with arguments that I was unable to tease any free. A sort of mental constipation.

"But why?" I asked, at last. "I mean, when?"

"While I was away. I knew it was the right thing to do."

"But you said in your letters, you said when you wrote last time, you'd seen that woman in jeans being stoned." She nodded and waited, it was a sort of 'and...?' expression.

"I mean, you can't countenance that. Surely?"

She arranged her head scarf, tucking in a tuft of hair that had come free and which looked sleeker than normal, lying flat, less dry.

"Violence obviously is hard to understand, particularly for a Westerner."

"But you said the police did nothing to help her. They didn't do anything to the men. You were shocked."

"I didn't understand then."

"But they arrested *her!*"

"For her own safety." I looked hard at her, trying to see if she really meant it. She was looking at me with a patient amusement: it seemed she did.

I had the strange feeling of talking to walls again. Talking to a pure white wall, made of something inert, some perfect marble. Somewhere in the wall would be a door, however camouflaged, behind which she was standing and could hear me, if only I could find the right words.

Her skin was good, better than I'd seen it in a long time. The open pores round her nose were clean and had shrunk right down. "Is that Omar making you do this?" She looked shocked at that.

"No."

I looked at her now with that same sceptical face she'd used on me when I'd told her I was getting the 'Seeing' from the Manchester guru. She capitulated.

"Look, Sue, it's a good thing that's happened to me. I'm happy."

"Yes but in a repressed, drug-induced way." She looked horrified, and I said quickly,

"I don't mean literally, I mean drugged with religion."

"I feel free," she said quietly, a sort of Madonna smile coming out of her face, a soft moonlit glow, as if from a light shining behind the skin itself. "I feel really free, as if all the struggling and suffering, all the moithering about is over."

Into the still room traffic noises came, muffled but oddly reassuring through the heavy lace curtains, effective in the way they filtered both light and sound. It was clear I wasn't going to argue her out of being a Muslim for the time being. I was even a bit afraid she would argue me over with her. Was trying to dissuade her the right thing anyway? I knew woefully little about it, but felt distrustful of people who convert dramatically to other people's religions or cultures. She was like a lobotomy patient, suddenly placid when all her life she'd been restless and dynamic. I was afraid to remind her of what was lost for fear she'd start raving at me.

Some liberal voice whispered I was being an ignorant, supercilious Western git, imposing my value system on another culture. I told it to fuck off. We seemed locked in stalemate. I didn't quite know what to do with my face, but there again, I couldn't look down at my hands forever. These heavy philosophical discussions weren't what we did together anyway. My other friend, Sarah and I, we were the ones to really chew the fat. She was an obsessive amateur psychologist, and we'd sit talking for hours whilst she demolished jars of peanut butter and chocolate spread, and I worked my way through the filched Cadbury's family bars from her dad's collection. Miranda and I just didn't do this. We went out together; cooked together; went dancing; walked in the park. We talked yes, but not this heavy stuff. Mostly we relived our adventures.

"Come on, then, show me the book." She mumbled again. This time it sounded like a prayer. "What is it you keep saying?" She went a little red in the face. "Incha' Allah, God be praised."

"Why God be praised? Why be praised now, in particular?" I asked. She hesitated a moment.

"Don't go trying to convert me, please," I said. "Remember what happened at the born-again church, Miranda!" She looked at me quickly, I don't know what made me say, "You are still called Miranda?" She didn't answer. "You've not gone and changed your name!"

"Fatima," she said. She was by the door by now, her toes clenching in the deep carpet like they always did, managing to find their way through the hideous white fishnets she was inexplicably wearing. I rolled my eyes ceiling-ward and followed her into the hall and up the stairs. She even seemed to be moving differently: holding the upper part of her body rigid, moving only her legs, as if someone had put a vice around her hips and pelvis. We went into her room. It smelled different and was extremely tidy. "What does your mother think of it all?"

"She doesn't know everything. She's not too happy with me eating vegetarian…"

"Veggie! I didn't know."

"Well, I can't have Pork. It's unclean, and it's everywhere. Gelatine, everywhere, even in yoghurts."

"Ugh!"

"She's banned the headscarf too, but I've got to wear it because of Brian. Only with your family can you really relax." As she was talking, she was wriggling about in her blouse, trying to get some sort of undershirt off without taking off her top.

"What are you doing that for?" I asked.

"I'm too hot."

"No, I mean fiddling about under your shirt?"

"It's immodest."

"But it's only me!" I waited for an answer, but none came.

Her desk was completely empty apart from a Qur'an, bound in red plastic with intricate gold lettering. I picked it up. Inside the paper was delicate, the inner leaf like tracing paper. Inside the front cover in neat, bold handwriting was the inscription, "To Fatima. May you grow with Allah. Auntie."

"Fatima?"

"Auntie Gee," she said. "She found my name. She's my mentor now."

"Are you going to have an arranged marriage?" I said, suddenly. She laughed. "People are obsessed with Muslims and sex! Muslims don't understand it. It's all rubbish."

"What is?"

"That women are abused in Islam! Women are respected, we're safe. Even divorce. You just say, 'I divorce you' three times; it's as simple as that."

"And that's good?"

"What's the point being together if you're not right? Why should Allah want that?"

"What about the multiple-wives syndrome?"

"Oh, that old chestnut! The same questions all the time. They warned me." I put the book down and sat on the bed, which released a comforting, familiar, dirty-fur smell.

"I'm only trying to play devil's advocate."

"Exactly," she said.

"I mean, six months ago you came runner up in the erotic dancing competition at Isobella's, wearing nothing but your 'Amazon woman' nippleless bra, a chiffon scarf and Granny's silver 'come dancing' sandals." She laughed.

"More than one wife's not really recommended, but in some circumstances it's better to save a marriage or save sin by marrying another wife."

"Like…?"

"Like, say, if a man's very highly sexed or if the wife can't have children."

"Oh come onnnn…!" I cried, exasperated.

"Or, say, to save a widow or an ageing spinster…"

"…from being without a man perhaps? What a disaster!"

"Well," she said, "in many societies it would be."

"Yeah well; marrying them and having sex with them's not the way – those countries want a welfare state or something."

"Only men that are relatively well off can afford to do it."

"Yes, great. Sharing your husband with another woman, brilliant! 'Where've you been the last six nights?' 'Down the hall will the new one, Dear.' Not on your life!"

"No," she said, smiling at my out-burst. "It has to be equal. Equal money and he has to visit them all. That's why it's not recommended in most cases. Most men wouldn't be able to cope." She had sat down on the bed next to me by this time and had absent-mindedly picked up my hand and was holding it in hers. It was more reassuring than she could know. "You know, in Britain after the first world war, there were not enough men to go round?"

"Yeee-s," I said, guardedly.

"Well it helps then too." I must have looked dim. "It helps share men around when there's been a war."

"Was this Qur'an written by a man by any chance?" I asked. She did smile at that.

"Another thing is, they're good at charity."

"Who, now?"

"Muslims," she said. "It's not just left piecemeal to the individual. You give away a set percentage. It's high."

"How much?"

"I don't know exactly. Ten percent?"

"That's loads!" I'd obviously got a bit of a one-sided view of Islam. Although I'd been sitting on the edge of the bed for a while and wasn't very comfortable, I didn't feel I could just sprawl back, and anyway, pulling away from her hand might have made her go all tight and formal again. The doorbell went. Miranda scrambled for her scarf.

"That'll probably be Ben," I said, standing up. "Shall I let him in?"

"Do. Take him into the front room." It was usually her bedroom that we ended up in, but that was obviously out of bounds to men now. She came down the stairs after me and stood whilst I opened the door. He bent down to give me a hug and then turned to Miranda, whose hair was mostly covered by the navy scarf, though she still had that same evil glint in her eye. She backed off, uttering a high pitched, "'Aiyee, don't touch!" I didn't invite him in. "Why the head scarf?" he asked.

"Ah ha!" she said, "forbidden fruit." He looked mystified.

"I've gotta go," I said, giving her a quick peck on the cheek, from which she backed off. I shoved my arms into my coat.

"Let's go," I said, planting myself in the doorway. "Bye, Fatima."

"Bye, Precious," she said and mumbled another prayer, different this time.

"Fatima?" Ben mouthed at me as I reached for his hand and we negotiated the steep steps. "It's a long story," I whispered back. On the pavement I turned back and waved. She was still standing there fiddling with her headscarf, watching after us, her lips moving.

CHAPTER SIXTEEN

BEN WAS STILL COMMITTED to meditation. He'd given up cigarettes, and his personal hygiene had improved. Astrology was a turn-on for him too (certainly since he'd discovered that his family were cosmically aligned, in fact that he himself was something very special; some really unusual congruence, like a messiah figure) but he was open minded on the question of God. I wasn't sure about the astrology, and losing my two closest people to mumbo jumbo made me back off from any whiff of religion now. I'd stopped meditating myself, because I realised it was only the chemical reaction from the hyperventilating that was really having the effect.

Miranda had gone. Religion had taken hold of her, and I hadn't done anything to stop it. It was too late. I realised it had crept up on her gradually. At first it had seemed okay, made her quite cheerful after losing Austin and Granny, but then she exchanged the Pentecostals for Islam. It had started of course with 'Auntie'. She talked calmly to Miranda, gave her the Qur'an to read, took notice of her. More and more I remembered getting together and Miranda talking about them, about things in the Qur'an, about what 'Auntie' had said, how everything about Islam was just common sense, there for the safety of people, there to help guide people to respect one another; and the disturbing thing for me was that she had a point.

At first I had tried to shake her up: "Well what about the women then, covering their faces, that's not fair, men don't have to do that."

"Well it doesn't actually say that in the Qur'an. All it says is that women should 'pull their headgear over their bosoms'."

"But why shouldn't men do it?"

"They do have to."

"Give over!" I'd shouted.

"But they do. Except when they're working in the fields, they have to dress modestly too."

"Oh. Right. Well, why can't women drive cars in Saudi Arabia, then?"

"Saudi Arabia is extreme. They're just interpreting Islam how it suits them."

"Miranda, you're sounding like one of them!"

"If you mean a Muslim, I wouldn't be ashamed to."

"But it's against your culture; it's against your own religion."

"What religion! I've told you: my mum's a lapsed Jew and my father's a sinning Catholic."

"But what about self-determination, what about socialism, 'religion as the opium...', that sort of thing?"

"No man is an island." (She had always been able to outquote me).

"But Miranda, do you want to be a clone?"

She laughed, "There's no one less like clones than the Muslims I've met. Honestly, they're the happiest people I know, really kind to each other and really calm."

"I know but, Miranda, you don't fit in! How'd you stay faithful?"

"Well, Auntie was saying that's why it's all going so wrong over here. Men can do what they like, dumping women. That's not allowed in Islam."

"Yes but you'd have to do what your husband said. Think

about it, it'd be awful."

"But he'd respect me. He'd never ask me to do anything that wasn't for my own good. Anyway you can divorce. All you have to say is 'I divorce you' three times. I told you before."

"Well you're back to square one then, aren't you; broken families!"

"No. Your family stand by you. There's a strict code. It's safer for women. Men know how to behave."

The arguments went on and on. I'd even taken to reading the Qur'an myself in order to improve my ammunition base, but had suddenly left off in fright after catching myself coming out with little 'ums' of agreement.

Since the second trip to Algeria she had taken to murmuring blessings, and occasionally, when we passed someone on the street, she'd exchange a greeting in Arabic. It was frustrating. Not so much that what she was getting into seemed evil, but just that it was changing her. I didn't want to insult her by slagging it off all the time; anyway she nearly always had a disarmingly practical answer, like the health issue with the pork and the shellfish thing, but it was like it wasn't her speaking. Another thing that was strange was the things she adopted and the things she hadn't yet taken up. She completely changed her diet and took to covering her hair, yet she still couldn't resist a flirt.

Ben was with us at her house one night. She insisted on wearing a scarf but it was worn so loosely she had to keep shoving it back on. I didn't get it, it seemed to draw attention to her hair rather than rendering her immune as a sex object. "I haven't got any knickers on," she laughed to me in a stage whisper. "I've got these tights, crotchless fishnets," she fiddled with them all evening, giggling and smiling at the bemused Ben.

I didn't get it, and when I brought up the inconsistency between what seemed a vital tenet i.e. no flirting outside marriage, and what seemed a peripheral practice, i.e. wear something on your head, she said, "I'm young in this; I can't get everything right at once; incha' Allah I will grow in faith."

Not even disapproval from her mum was a problem, as her mentors urged her to believe that 'Your mum will come to respect you and maybe follow, given time.'

Granny was dead; Austin gone; her mother gone back to Brian, and there was no one to save her but me. It was exhausting, and I was not winning. We didn't lose touch, but it wasn't the same anymore. She had got incredibly modest about being undressed in front of other women, so there was no more sleeping over, massages, hair dos, and of course there was no more dancing or diving in a public place. One thing we did make a success of, though, was the Arabic dancing. We used to go up to her room and put on the cyclic, aimless music and shimmy. There was the bust dance, where you shivered your shoulders as fast as possible, and the sinewy pelvic rotations, which I was particularly good at and could do both clockwise and anti-clockwise, changing direction without missing a beat. My best step, though, was the buttock vibration, one where you had to turn slowly using the ball of one foot to move whilst the other provided a pivot, and at the same time you furiously waggled your buttocks. Miranda said I was faster than anyone she'd seen, even in Algeria.

Each time we met, though, the conversations got heavier. We went round in circles, and any point I did score against Islam just backfired with a bitter taste as I hurt my friend. I did force myself to see her and vice a versa, but there was no fun to be had any more. So many subjects were too sensitive to touch upon, whilst with others it was like conversing with a text-book. And then we lost touch altogether.

She'd done her 'A' levels that Summer and was going to France for a year to study French before going to university. She said she missed Algeria terribly; she 'longed for it' in fact. She mentioned nothing more about the woman being stoned in the street but waxed lyrical about the architecture and house-keeping practices. There were beautiful walled gardens with fountains. No horrible, dusty soft furnishing. Everything wiped clean "and the "…brushing, brushing all the time. Sluicing it all down with pails of water, really sweet water from the well." It did sound refreshingly no nonsense, but I wondered if it just seemed so great because she had been so hot all the time. According to her, everything British was bad, and everything French, and particularly Algerian and Muslim, was great.

Myself, Jean, Brian, Ben and her friend from school (the fat girl who played the flute) were the only non Muslims at the party Auntie Gee threw for her the Sunday before Miranda went away. She'd been seeing a lot of the fat flautist recently, probably trying to convert her too.

This time, when she left, I had nothing to give her. Though she'd be staying at her father's house near Toulouse initially, she was going to move up to Lille to do some English teaching next term, to help fund the degree from a French University which she was hoping to start the following year. It wasn't lost on me that the handsome relation was studying there too. I just felt tired of the whole thing. How did I know if Islam was right or wrong anyway? All I knew is that I had lost her, the person she used to be, as surely as if she had been abducted by aliens.

Anyway I was busy too. It was my turn to do A levels this year, and I was useless at studying. I was great the first time round, quick as anything with the theories, in the class discussions, but revision literally sent me to sleep. The only way I could make myself revise was to do it somewhere odd like the garden or my bed, anywhere that didn't smack of study. Sometimes I would just go to sleep, waking up half an hour later, more sometimes. I wasn't going to do very well. With Miranda gone, things were looking bleak and empty for me. My sister had turned into a genius like Huw, so it was apparently going to be me that society would have to depend on if it wanted the shelves stacking in Tescos. That Autumn I did see a little of analytical Sarah and the delectable Jan, but it was just a wind-up really.

I thought of Miranda a lot over the next months. There was a slight sense of relief when she went away; relief from the intensity of being friends with her, but mostly her going this time made my life just seem so bland. Even Ben had gone away, though I realised that might be an advantage: things might spice up again between us in the holidays, instead of being all comfortable and boring.

I remembered her in love that first time with Marcus. They'd been inseparable, sauntering along the corridors oblivious to the evil glances of the teachers and the herd of little kids following them and calling them the 'loony lovebirds'. That had been the beginning of me feeling protective towards Miranda, I suppose. Although the ostentatious 'feeling up' of each other all the time was embarrassing even to me, I didn't like people being picked on. It wasn't that she didn't care what people thought exactly; just that she was usually oblivious. Sometimes, though, the venom would hit her. Then she'd find me, weeping and praising me, 'her only true friend, her real friend, the one who'd never betray her'. That was one way of making a person loyal. Tell them all the time that you love them and how loyal they are. Make even a moment's disloyal thought burn them in the acid guilt.

But I never did betray her. Not when she was wearing the three scarves to go dancing, nor later with the chador around her hair.

So I joined the trampoline and Drama club in school. Suddenly I was hot property. The pale faced, ginger freak apparently had a gift on stage. I'd never had the dainty, fairy face I'd craved, or the curvaceous body, but apparently my large features (eyes, mouth and nose); big statement thick auburn hair that formed natural ringlets, as well as muscular legs and bum, made me look 'shit hot from a distance'. I had arrived! That year I played Abigail Williams, 'I have known her!,' and Hero in *Much Ado*: 'Don't give that rotten orange to your friend.' I played Juliet, and chief whore in, *Oh What a lovely War*. I didn't have much time for long phone calls to Ben in Birmingham or careful letters to Lille, even if I'd had her address.

Then, in June, in my final year at school, came the letter from France. She was married and pregnant (the right way round, like Granny always used to tell her!) having married quietly in Calais. She was telling me, and had told her mum, but not her father. Since he'd not bothered to come to Granny's funeral, slowly all the lustre had rubbed off his image. Even his wife was *persona non grata* in the eyes of Miranda and her new friends: a lapsed Muslim was much worse than someone who'd never had the chance. Really damned.

I was glad she hadn't told me before she did it since I wouldn't have known how to stop her. I wouldn't even have known whether I should. I wrote back, sending a card, as she'd included an address this time and she invited me to stay in their flat in Lille. Ben was back home over the summer, and there was no point sitting around waiting for my crappy A level results, so we hitched to France.

Ben had really improved his looks whilst he was away. His skin had cleared a lot, and he'd taken up swimming and cycling. The one expanding his top half and the other streamlining the bottom bit. For the first time it crossed my mind that maybe someone else would try to get her claws into him at University, which gave me an unpleasant feeling in the gut, but I appreciated him more because of it.

Once on the ferry he paraded around the deck in impossibly short shorts with his shirt off, whilst I scratched at my eczema and tried not to be sick. I had no idea where we were going, but my beau had a map and had done a similar thing all the way to Amsterdam the year before (I hadn't been allowed to go then, because I wasn't eighteen and was still worth saving from pre-marital sex, or so my parents had thought!). It was even easier to hitch in France than it had been in Britain, though the conversation was not as lively, obviously. You seemed to get offered food more often too. In Britain, we only got offered food by lorry drivers, or once by an insane ex-Nottinghamshire miner driving the Robin Reliant he'd bought with his redundancy money.

Anyway, we were nearly there. She was going to meet us from the underground in Lille, and I was nervous. What was the husband going to be like? Some seedy old bloke with a teenage wife, the cat that's got the cream? And how was it that, if they were so hot on 'the family,' they hadn't even had her mum to the wedding? I imagined her new life all the way through France. Miranda a devoted wife; Miranda the loving mother. I felt a strange stab of envy.

We got off the tube and waited. The architecture was huge; a flyover just in front of us, and beyond that, flats. It seemed there were no people who lived in houses in Lille. Around the station exit was waste ground with the same familiar weeds, the odd buddleia but no butterflies; well, perhaps a lonely cabbage white. I saw a figure leave the little road under the flyover and pick its way over the rubble. It was her, looking down at her feet, trying not to fall. She didn't look pregnant; in fact she seemed smaller. As she came nearer she looked up and smiled. I waved. Her headgear was on properly this time, down over her hair, crossed under the chin and tied securely in a knot at the back. Its pale lemon was picked up in the A-line skirt that went nearly down to her ankles, and she had a strange check shirt with a high collar which, despite the heat, had every fastener done up. It buttoned to the side and had a feel of *Little House on the Prairie* about it. She held my hand and kissed me, and then held Ben's for a moment. She had lost a lot of weight, but she looked pretty, and I couldn't take my eyes off her on the journey back. She was like a woman on the telly, in Beirut perhaps; a spokeswoman for the PLO, big mouth moving, cloth tied tight around the neck. As a frame draws the eye to a picture, so I found myself mesmerised by her scarf-dressed face; no make-up made it naked, personal. I was like a peeping Tom, drinking her all in, watching how the heavy ring hung off her long finger. She'd put clear nail varnish on; I wondered if it was allowed.

"...so I had to go into hospital for a few weeks." I heard her say to Ben.

"What? What's wrong with you?" I asked.

"Nothing, not now. I'm fine now. I had kidney problems after cystitis." Looking down, I saw her feet in the familiar clogs, but she was wearing tights with them, pretty bloody impossible to walk in polished wood clogs without bare feet. Then I registered the fish nets. "Miranda, they're not THE ones are they?" She looked a bit dim for a minute and then started to laugh, "For God's sake, isn't it a bit unhygienic? Anyway isn't it against Muslim law or something?"

"The prophet didn't say anything about women's underwear. Anyway nobody knows, except you."

"Except me, exactly!"

"Anyway, the doctor said I should get plenty of fresh air and not wear anything too tight and restrictive."

"Yeah, but I bet he didn't tell you to go round in crotchless tights!"

"She, actually. It's not as if I'm going to get pregnant from bus seats or anything, is it?" She laughed again, the same, flamboyant, un-English laugh that she'd been doing all her life.

"It wasn't you I was worried about. It's the health of the civilian population of Northern France."

"What about the soldiers?"

I had to admit it, she was on form, married woman or not. I felt relieved. She reached for my hand and held it in both of hers, rested the three hands on her knee.

The bus seemed to be going round in circles, all of Lille looking like all the rest of Lille. Everything seemed to be concrete. Flats, even the roads had that colour and texture.

Finally Miranda released my hand and started to adjust her scarf and pull her cuffs down to cover her wrists. Sure enough the bus slowed down and pulled in at a deserted square, where I supposed there were shops during the day, but where window after window was grilled up now. No one seemed to be about. We shouldered our bags and got off. I remembered a 'merci beaucoup' for the driver. The bus pulled off, and as we stood, I registered the ominous feel of the place. It was dead quiet, something that always makes me nervous in a city. It never seems like an innocent silence, always more of a tense hiatus, a narrow window in which something unpleasant quietly gathers strength.

"It's not very picturesque, Miranda."

"No, I suppose not, but Omar gets reduced housing because of his job."

"Yes. What does he do again?"

"He's a Physics teacher for the moment."

"Oh yes." Our voices and feet made such a noise in that place. As we crossed the square, it was a relief to see two dark men coming toward us. Miranda looked down and mumbled the Arabic greeting, with which they nodded briefly to her and passed on. "Do you know them?" I asked.

"Fellow Muslims."

"How do you know? They might not be."

"They will have been born Muslims. That is the right way to greet people."

We went through a dank underpass and emerged in another, almost identical, square, except for the sudden addition of some dusty French trees and a lot more people, "Here we are, Chez Nous," she called over her shoulder.

At the far end of the square stood another block of flats, about ten storeys high; on the balconies people were flying their washing. "I didn't know you lived in a flat!"

"Oh it's very convenient, beautiful and clean. Hygienic, really. Marble floors everywhere. You just hose it down."

"Oh God, not the cleansing thing again! It's not exactly hot here. I mean it's only Northern France. We're not in Tunisia now."

"We never were." Even Ben laughed at her joke.

"I meant Algeria," I said cuttingly.

She stopped and pointed upwards, "Look, there's Omar." There was a figure standing on a low balcony watching us.

Although I couldn't see very well, it seemed significant that he wasn't waving.

The flats developed detail as we approached, and the evening sun dropped behind them, out of our eyes. What had been mainly shadow became distinct, and I could see people on their balconies and even dark figures moving inside the French windows of some of the lower ones. The sound we'd been hearing was growing, and as we walked forward it too developed definition, became people's voices, the sound of televisions, even a dog's bark. Nearly everyone I saw seemed to be Algerian, although there were quite a few white women. Not all of the dark women were wearing scarves, but many of the white women were. Those who passed near us were greeted by Miranda in Arabic. Inside, we chose the stairs. Ben liked to get his exercise whenever possible, and the rucksacks weren't particularly heavy. Everything was made of concrete, like stone and brick had never been invented, but the ugliness was broken by a foot-deep band of pale turquoise tiles set in the walls at chest height, which caught the light coming through the grills at either end of the corridors. "It must be freezing in the winter, Miranda!"

"No worse than the street. At least there's some shelter."

"I suppose so, but it's a bit glum."

"We're here m' dears," she said, approaching a pale yellow door which stood ajar. The sound of the television could be heard here, the same as from almost every doorway we'd passed on the way up. Blocks of flats always reminded me of a sinister version of Blyton's *Magic Faraway Tree*, always got me wondering what strange, warped creature lived behind the multi-coloured doors. We found ourselves in a narrow hallway with lino underfoot and two doors, straight on and left. Straight on I'm sure was Omar and the telly and the view, such as it was, from the balcony; she took the left into another, bigger hallway, from which led four doors. Two of these were open. "The bathroom and toilet," said Miranda rather obviously, "and your room. It's a single bed I'm afraid" (and it didn't even have an external window) "my bedroom, and…" she reached past me for the door handle "…the lounge and kitchen." As we were both still carrying our rucksacks, I wasn't sure why we'd come the convoluted way. The kitchen had different, more friendly lino, a free-standing cooker, sink, side and two cupboards, one high, one low. It just seemed like a rented apartment, holiday accommodation.

"How long've you been living here, Miranda?"

"Ten months, thereabouts. It's Omar's flat. He's been here since he started work at the school part-time, a couple of years now." The television noise was loud in here, but I couldn't see the lounge. It went round the corner of the L shape.

"Where's Omar?"

"He's here … Omar!" (something in French and an answer). I peeped round the corner of the cooker, to see him come in from the balcony. He was nice looking; dark curly hair ; white, even teeth. Very small by Miranda's standards, but not as bad as I'd feared: no beard, no fez, no long house-coat thing. He came forward and shook my hand, holding it for a little too long (or was that my imagination?) and holding my gaze.

"Welcome to my house, Miranda's friends." He'd turned to Ben and proffered the hand. Ben said later that he'd felt his handshake with Omar was a bit long and intense too, so that probably meant he wasn't after me personally, it was just an Algerian custom, or a French thing.

We stood there for a couple of seconds smiling stupidly at one another. I still had my rucksack on, but Ben had managed to jettison his somewhere. Omar said something in French to

Miranda, and she grabbed the rucksack off me. "Come on, folks, sit down, you must be tired out. D'you want some tea? I brought loads back with me last time I was over."

"Don't they have tea here then?"

"Yes, of course, but nothing tastes the same as Typhoo."

"What are you, a shareholder or something?" By now she had us sitting down with the telly turned down. Omar was sitting back in the big chair opposite the set and smiling, whilst Miranda flitted back and forth laying up a large table at the far end of the living room.

"Can I help with anything, Miranda?" Ben said, anxious I suppose to get out of the mutual grinning circle.

"No, non, no, Miranda will dou iet!" Omar looked quite perturbed. I wondered if it was a man thing.

"Shall I help you lay the table, then?" I offered.

"No no, Babe, you're a visitor. There're strict rules, Muslim hospitality."

"Oh, yeah."

"We wait on you for three days, anything is yours. After that, it's as though you live here, and you can do things for yourself."

"Sounds a nice idea," Ben grinned.

"Have you a good treep?"

"Yes, thank you Omar, very straightforward."

"I'm teaching Omar English; he's teaching me Arabic. He speaks three languages," Miranda said brightly.

"Are you teaching Miranda Algerian as well?"

"No, she has no need of iet. She will learn to read the Qur'an in Arabic for her."

"Incha' Allah," murmured Miranda.

Food was ready, a lovely couscous with cooked aubergine and

raw tomatoes, roasted sesame seeds and fresh flat parsley mixed in. "You have this meat? Fatima, you call iet?"

"Stew."

"Stiew," he repeated.

"Lamb stew."

"It is good. Halal meat for you?"

"Um, no thank you Omar, I don't eat meat. Thanks very much."

"I'd forgotten that," said Miranda. "Sorry, Petal."

"That's okay, no need for you to be sorry. That's my problem."

"The animals, they are to be eaten." Omar had a typically French way of gesticulating with his cutlery when he talked, which made everything he said hard to disagree with. All the time the television played on in the background, just loud enough so that you couldn't, but were never-the-less straining to, hear it through the conversation. Miranda cleared away the dishes and padded back and forth. Omar broke the curfew. "We have a festival tomorrow, a very special day for us. You can come with us in the car of a friend to the festival… Fatima?" he called in French to her as she passed into the kitchen, listening for an answer. "Yes, then, we will go. Ben will follow with me and enjoy."

"What is it exactly?" I asked her.

"Well, it's Aid Al-fitr. A special outing in a way, with Mosque in the morning…"

"Are we allowed in, then?"

"Yes, of course…"

"Great, I've always wanted to know what goes on."

"… and then there's food afterwards in a local park."

"Like a Sunday school picnic then, I suppose. Great." Miranda brought in a hot, hand-made lemon meringue pie, my favourite. Omar excused himself and left the table, asking Ben if he'd like to join him watching the match. "This food, I do not much like the sweet things. You like, Ben?"

"Well not really over much, but I do like this pie. I've never really had it home-made before. It looks delicious."

"Miranda is good wife, very good."

"I think I'll probably just stay here for a while and see if I get lucky with the second helpings." Omar shrugged for answer and settled into his chair in front of the box.

It had always amazed me how she could do things like cooking and making clothes. I'd been to the same school as her, and my mother had been Miranda's Domestic Science teacher, but I hadn't seemed to pick up very much at all. Okay, I hadn't been very interested, but then you'd think some of it would have rubbed off, by osmosis or something.

"This thing tomorrow, Miranda, do we have to wear anything special? I mean, do I have to wear a chador or something?"

"No, it's accepted you're not a Muslim. Just cover your hair as a sign of respect, that's all."

"Yes, of course. It'll be great, really exciting."

"Yeah," said Ben. "Really exciting." Miranda got up and started clearing the table. As she passed his chair, Omar looked up. "Du cafe?"

"Oui." He didn't seem to be stirring himself at all, and this hospitality bit was making me feel uncomfortable, so I got up to take a couple of dishes through. "Fatima!" As she came through from the kitchen, he laid it on in French with a lot of gesturing toward us. I sat down but Ben was already halfway to the kitchen with the remains of the pie. Miranda snatched the bowl off him and rushed it into the kitchen as though it were about to explode "Sit down, for goodness sake will you, Ben. You're a GUEST. It's only for a couple of days... Please," she begged.

"Okay, anything you say, okay. It's just it gets a bit hard sitting here like a dunce, watching you run yourself into the ground."

"I'm fine!"

We sat opposite one another at the table whilst Miranda cleared up the remaining things. Finally it was all done, except for the crashing of Miranda washing up in the kitchen; Omar turned up the television. "You want the match now, Ben? Come and with me, enjoy." Off he went, looking rather reluctant, I have to say. I went in to Miranda.

"Don't you take your scarf off in the house, M'anda?"

"Usually, yes, but not with visitors. Well, male visitors not in the immediate family."

"Does Omar have family here at all, or are they all back home?"

"They're in Algeria, yes."

"That's a shame, really, isn't it. With the baby you could do with some help I suppose. Are you going back to the University?"

"Yes, well, I hope so. Anyhow, you must be joking! They're illiterate. Well his mother is anyway, and they can't speak French."

"Yes, but they'd be fond of the baby and some help to you. Anyway, the whole argument's academic. They're not here."

"Thank God!" I looked at her quickly to see if she noticed she'd sworn, but I couldn't tell. She was drying the dishes, putting them away and bleaching round the sideboards. "You're conscientious! D'you do it after every meal now?"

"Of course I do, don't you?"

"Well no. As a matter of fact I don't believe in too much bleaching and chemicals and stuff:

A/ because things get immune to it and

B/ because it's so bad for the environment."

"Me doing this isn't bad for the environment."

"Well no, but the whole manufacturing process, and when the stuff gets flushed into the rivers and the sea it is."

"But it's not going to the rivers or the sea. It's on my sideboard!"

"Yes I know. But in general, if you were to put it down the toilet or something."

"You're not saying we shouldn't be bleaching the toilet are you!"

"No, I'm not. I mean just to keep it to a minimum that's all. You could buy the biodegradable stuff of course."

"Not in France, you can't. Anyway I've got too much to do to start worrying about things like that." I was secretly enjoying the fact that she was arguing with me, like in the old days. She might be modelling herself on the Madonna or Mother Theresa with the tea towel on her head, but she was still a pain in the arse.

"You can't afford not to buy Green products. Nobody can. Chuck away a plastic bottle or a wasted battery, and the world lives with it for the next millennium!"

"Oh … for goodness sake, gloom and doom or what!"

"Can you please make more quiet in there; we cannot hear the voices!" came a voice from the other room.

"Sorry, Omar, we're nearly done!" I shouted in. "Miranda, come on, let's get packed or unpacked or something in the other room."

"Okay. I'm so glad you've come, love; I'm so glad to see you."

She put her arm round me. She was as big as Ben, I'd forgotten.

We went into her room and shut the door. Straight away she pulled off her head scarf and shook out her hair, giving her scalp a good scratch. "That's better! It gets really itchy, like taking your bra off at night. Speaking of which, look at what Omar bought me." She whipped up her loose check shirt. Underneath was an amazing black lace construction with no nipples; each fitted neatly through its hole. "I've got the knickers to match."

"Perish the thought. And before you ask, I don't want a demonstration, thanks!"

"Coward! Anyway, I haven't got them on. They got dirty."

"I'm sure… My God, you've got an enormous bust!"

"Great isn't it: the only perk of being pregnant."

"How is it that you've got these sexy things anyway?" I was so pleased to see that she seemed to have forgotten her prudishness too.

"What d'you mean?"

"Well, I mean… how is it you're allowed sexy things to wear. Isn't it immoral or something?"

"My husband buys it for me."

"No, I mean against your religion."

"No of course not. I'm married. Sue, anything goes between husband and wife. It's not like Christianity, Jesus lying between you or something sick like that."

"Oh, that's all right then!" I mocked.

There were some clothes in a blue laundry basket by the bed. She fetched them out one at a time, shook them, pulled them straight, flattening the larger garments along the front of her body and then folding them on her lap and putting them in a pile to one side of her. It made me feel strange, someone just a little older than me folding and touching a grown man's clothes. I'd never washed for a man. Actually, I'd never even washed for myself. I felt mesmerised, seeing her handle his shirts, following the line of his trouser crease with her fingers. "He takes pictures of me. I'm really into it, actually."

"What, porn ones?"

"Yeah, it's great fun. Don't you do it?"

"No! How on earth do you get them processed?"

"There's a friend of Omar's, he does it for us."

"He SEES you? How can you stand it?"

"He doesn't, it's all automatic."

"You must be joking! Anyone could get hold of them!"

"He's a friend of Omar's; he's a Muslim for goodness sake."

"My God, Miranda, you are naive sometimes!"

"Look, just let it alone, will you?" Suddenly she was shouting. "It's bad enough as it is!" She reached for her scarf that she'd thrown down on the bed. "Excuse me will you, you're sitting on my headgear."

"I'm sorry."

"'S all right. It's not creased."

"I mean I'm sorry about going on. It's none of my business." Miranda was twisting up her hair in an elastic band. Her hair was different from how I'd remembered, not 'fly away' any more. I passed her scarf.

"Will you scratch my back?" she said, spreading the scarf over her head and twisting it at the throat before bringing it round to make a knot at the back. I nodded.

She smiled, manoeuvred down the bed and tucked her legs up under her. For a moment she waited and so did I. How could I scratch her back through the shirt ? "Shall I pull your blouse up,

Miranda?"

"No, leave it, better not." I rubbed her back through the cloth and we chatted about things we'd done back in Sheffield for a long time, enough for me to have my turn. "Do my hair instead?" I asked.

She fetched her bristle brush for me. "Spot the nits," I joked.

"There aren't any."

"No, I mean mine," I said. She laughed, brushing and brushing until the pain of the scabbing on knots turned into delight, till my hair turned oily as she pulled and pulled my head back, gathering the hair in one, long hand -so delicious I could hardly keep my eyes open. There was a knock at the door ... Omar ... some French. Miranda jumped up to open it. I gave my scalp a ruffle, tried to look normal, he smiled.

"Come on, Ma Cherie," Miranda said, taking my hand as he turned and went down the corridor. "Omar wants his bed."

She still treated me as if the age gap made a difference, but I was glad of it. That divide between us was the least important now. I wanted to get to bed quickly to think, talk about things with Ben, smell his Englishness all night. We were the first in bed, and I could hear Miranda for ages afterwards padding backwards and forwards across the corridor. We couldn't completely close the door to our cubby-hole, because the bed was in the way and the door onto the lounge area was nothing but reinforced cardboard, so you could hear everything going on in the flat.

Several times during the night I woke up, sweaty and half suffocated in our cupboard with no air conditioning and no windows. I'd had the choice of near the wall or the edge, which was a bit of a Hobson's choice between being crushed or kicked out all night. I'd chosen the wall, as otherwise, being the smallest partner, I was bound to end up clinging to the side of the bed, if not actually on the floor. The walls were as inadequate as the doors though. I could hear every squeeze of wee, even though I was trying not to.

In the middle of the night I heard the weirdest noise: hacking up; rinsing, gurgling, gargling; both Miranda and Omar spitting loudly into the sink and sloshing water into the toilet. I looked at Ben's fluorescent wrist watch.

"Wassa matter?"

"Nothing , go back to sleep." He did and the sluicing finished. It was about three in the morning.

CHAPTER SEVENTEEN

I WOKE TO THE SAME sound a few hours later but at least it was light by then, the day of the big trip. Miranda was cooking, that old faithful Jewish recipe we used to live on at her house, Matzos, bashed up and fried in beaten egg with sugar on top. I think it was suitable at special times of the year, because it was unleavened or something, and most of Miranda's relatives were Jewish. I felt like I'd spent the night having the skin peeled off me, with a horrible head and dehydrated mouth to go with it. I think it's the worst I've felt in the morning without being hung over, but of course there'd be no hangovers on this holiday.

Finally I got myself a turn in the bathroom which was the only room in the house that looked as if it belonged to someone. Miranda hadn't made much imprint on the bedroom; it still had the regulation furniture and bachelor black, red, white and grey striped duvet cover, but she had made her impression on this room all right. It was still damp from Omar's shower, and there were some of Miranda's long hairs stuck to the side of the bath. They always used to get everywhere, especially in food and in the bath sponge. Here too were the little glass jars filled with decanted products (when did she ever get time to do that!) but they weren't dusty and sticky like her mother's at home. The tops were on all the bottles and jars, with a shallow wicker basket brimful of miniatures, all sorts of tantalising French products and even a few with Arabic writing. A hessian bag hung from the medicine cabinet doorknob with a paint brush, plastic gloves and some henna. What really stumped me was the beech wood creation that looked like a single roller skate and was perched on the side of the bath. It was wet so had obviously been either recently used, or had fallen in. By the toilet were two full jugs of water, obviously something to do with the sluicing down business of last night.

"Sue, are you all right in there? Not sick or anything?" Ben.

"I'm okay. Just trying to wake myself up a bit."

"Well come on, we're all waiting for you at the table. Omar wants to get going."

"Okay, I'll be there now." When I came out Miranda was standing there, and there was no sign of Ben.

"You haven't used the water."

"Er, no. What's it there for, anyway?"

"Well, to wash with."

"Well yes, obviously. Start again: why's it so important?"

"Think about it: with loo roll all you do is just move it around a bit."

"Ugh."

"Exactly."

"Yes, but with water surely you just end up getting it on your hands. That's worse in a way. I know you could wash them, but it'd be hard getting rid of the smell."

"Sue, you use both! Paper first, then a good rinse."

"Ah. That makes sense actually; yeah, it really does! Ugh, I can't believe all we do is scrape it around with the paper!"

"It's like a lot of things in Islam."

Irritated, caught out again, I tried to change the subject. "What were you doing last night anyway. I mean, why all the hosing down in the middle of the night? Is it prayers or something?"

"Well yes, but a husband and wife must always wash before and after sex and be always clean in the eyes of Allah."

"Ah... right..." I was wary of committing myself on this one, just in case I ended up praising Islam by accident.

"You mean you don't wash before and after?" she asked.

"Well um, before sex yes; usually, I suppose, but not after as a rule."

"You lie in your own dirt?"

"I suppose. The way you used to!"

"Yes, I know. I didn't think about it, but I couldn't stand to be so filthy now."

The more I thought about it, the more I could see they had a point about the washing thing.

"To be honest with you, I think you've converted me with the washing business," I said reluctantly.

Omar's voice got us out of the corridor, "We will be having a lift. We can not be late, many people waiting on us."

"For," said Miranda, as I took my place, and she poured our coffee, "you wait FOR someone, Omar."

"Yes, of course, my thanks." The Matzos were delicious as always, Omar putting Lea and Perrins on his. "I thought you were supposed to have hot chocolate and croissant for breakfast in France?"

"Yeah, in text books," laughed Miranda. "Are you disappointed, then?"

"Yes, a bit, I like things as they should be. I like things to be a bit different if I go abroad."

"Soppy thing."

"We ready now? You go now to make the hair, Fatima,..." he gestured dismissively in my direction.

"What, me?" I asked.

"... and clothes. This is not the thing." He pushed his chair back and left the table, a man obviously accustomed to making statements without awaiting a reply.

"What's the matter with them? I thought I was okay, if I could borrow a head scarf. They're long, these, nearly down to my knees, look," I pointed at my baggy culottes, which came down to just below the knee.

"No. Too much leg: it's disrespectful. Have you got anything else?"

"Well, the skirt I wore last night, but it's heaving."

"Never mind. No one'll notice what you're wearing anyway." Given the obvious tension just raised by what I was and wasn't wearing, I thought I wouldn't point out the discrepancies in logic there. Omar came in again as we were clearing up; he didn't seem to notice the guests had stepped out of line on the 'three days' rule. "Where is Fatima, please?"

"I thought you'd have passed her," I said. He looked perturbed. "Well, she went to get a scarf for me; didn't you see her in the corridor?"

"You can not wear these things." He wasn't looking at me but at Ben now.

"What?" said Ben

"The short trousers are showing leg tops, very high."

"Oh, sorry. I've only got shorts. I thought men were allowed to do anything."

"They must have respect. You change."

"I'm sorry, Omar but I haven't got anything else. I haven't got any trousers. 'Pantalon'." Omar frowned. I had to admit Ben did go in for incredibly short shorts these days. Someone had once told him he had good legs, and they were always out, from March through to October.

"You must wear my trousers."

"Omar, they won't fit him!"

"Or you must not go."

"Well I don't mind not going." Ben was looking hopeful at this suggestion.

"What's this?" Miranda's face appeared, peeping round the doorframe and clutching an armful of large scarves. I suppressed a snort at the memories they conjured up. "He must not hurt the people in these trousers. They must come out," threatened Omar.

"But Omar's won't fit him, no way." I got my oar in too.

"Ah," said Miranda. For a couple of seconds everybody stayed in position. We seemed to be in stalemate. Suddenly, "I know," she cried.

"What?" I asked.

"Omar…" she began, saying something to him in rapid French. "Mais, oui," he replied at last, visibly relieved. "I go now."

He left the flat for ten minutes or so, returning with a pair of light trousers with a drawstring waist. They fitted perfectly and eventually we were all decent. Miranda was wearing the same skirt as yesterday with the same shirt design, only this one was Brownish gingham. It didn't suit her. The head scarf was the same pale yellow as her skirt, and she seemed to have the same tights too. I wondered again whether they were the crotchless ones and, if so, if she'd put on any knickers. I hoped it wouldn't be windy. My head scarf was a lovely dark pink chiffon one that Miranda had draped fetchingly over my hair, though bits were straying out everywhere, and it was transparent anyway. However, according to her, I didn't need to be totally covered as I wasn't a Muslim myself; all I needed to do was to show respect, which sounded reasonable to me.

We went around the back of the flats to the garages where there was already a large gathering of people and an array of unlikely-looking vehicles. Some of the cars were full already, and I noticed were all being driven by men. "Why aren't the women driving? Auntie used to drive. Muslim women are allowed to drive usually, aren't they?"

"Of course, but everyone's doubling up," she whispered. "It wouldn't be right to sit next to or talk to a man not your husband or a very close relative."

"Right."

Omar came over to us, taking Ben by the arm. "You come with me; we have a lift."

"Can't I go with Sue?"

"No, come, your lift iz here." Ben departed with a hang-dog look. Then it was our turn. A massive blond woman with her headgear loosely strapped on was gesturing us over. "Sylvie!" smiled Miranda and took me by the arm. They kissed and chatted in French. There were already two women in the back seat looking very serious. "Who's going?" I asked Miranda, nodding to Sylvie.

"All of us."

"What, Sylvie as well?"

"Yes, of course." (Why 'of course'?) I shrugged my shoulders and shoved in; Miranda squeezed in beside me, and Sylvie put herself in the front seat.

"Who's driving?" I asked.

"Sylvie's husband."

"Ah. Well at least the women'll be able to have a few beers. Ah, whoops; no, maybe not!" Without looking round at us in the back at all, Sylvie's rather gorgeous, curly, muscley husband climbed in and started up the engine.

"Sylvie?" I said, loudly. "SSh!" hissed Miranda." Don't talk front to back."

"Oh." Why not? I wondered, but I suppose I knew. As we pulled out of the car park, Ben's car pulled out alongside us, and I saw his grinning face in the back of his all-male car. Did they not trust him with the women, or not trust the women with him, more like? He waved. I was about to wave back when I saw Omar bat his hand down. Ben looked so surprised.

We sped off in front. Ben's whole-food, meditation world-view was taking a bashing this holiday. I watched Lille go past greyly, listening to Miranda chatting to the other two women in French and at one point accepting a boiled sweet from the one with glasses. We were obviously leaving the suburbs behind. The architecture got more varied, more French, to my mind, but with a faint Flemish twist, and shops, squares and the occasional fountain appeared. We turned in before a gloomy building looking a bit like a Methodist chapel. We braked suddenly. I remembered that from before about France, never coming to a controlled stop, always bailing out with a screech somewhere.

A couple of the cars were there before us, whilst the others skidded to a halt in succession around us.

In the square were lots of other people, dressed formally like us. I saw Ben's car pull up and he got out, Omar holding his arm firmly like he was going to faint or make a grab for one of the women. I was starting to feel nervous and was glad when the separate huddles of people started drifting toward the double doors.

Inside we had to take off our shoes, and I suddenly realised there were no men around. We'd got left with the children obviously, and I suppose logically, as who else has nipples to latch them on to? Despite the shoeless feet it wasn't smelly, and we went into a huge room covered in deep carpeting. Towards the front were all the men and older boys; we were behind an ornately carved fence at the back of the mosque. The women and children settled themselves down. Miranda had her eyes closed and was murmuring something, prayers I suppose, so I tried it too, well, closed my eyes anyway. It was such a relief after the strain of looking.

The mosque sounded, smelt and felt so different from a church. There were no cold echoes; sound was muffled by the carpet, and it was warm too, in a way that an old church never is, even in Summer. It was packed, and I imagined so many more people could be crammed into a building without seating than onto even the most tightly packed pews. It all smelt different too: wood, heat, humans, bodies not coats; no stone, no damp. I was coming to the conclusion that much of what passes as cultural differences between people is just a result of adapting to different environments and climate. When I opened my eyes after this revelation, whatever was happening at the front was lost on me. I was too far away to see and the children were too distracting. I wondered later whether that was why the Muslim man is supposed to be the wife's spiritual guide. Women can't have much of a clue about what's going on in these circumstances.

The women didn't seem to be taking much notice anyway. Some had brought cushions, others just sat on the rich carpet cross-legged or with their feet tucked up underneath them, chatting quietly. The children were good, none of that terrible wriggling I used to be accused of in church, and they seemed to be allowed to play, doing so amazingly quietly. I noticed a couple of babies on the breast too, nothing overt but all very relaxed; not something I'd ever seen or could conceive of happening in church. Maybe this was the plus side of being segregated. It didn't seem to go on long either, which was not what religious ceremonies traditionally meant for me. The only thing I couldn't hack was not being with the men. Having them cordoned off like that only made me want them more, and I found myself virtually salivating at the bars for a glimpse of the forbidden fruit.

Ben was in there somewhere, and it rankled. Why did his hanging genitals entitle him to be there at the front, with access to all sorts of secret knowledge? How powerful and insidious, the self-perpetuating message, once received: women at the back, men at the front. I could feel myself getting quite militant. It was a strange feeling, and I wasn't enjoying it.

Even though we had been at the back, the men left first and gathered outside by the cars. The light and noise once we got outside was a shock to me, like coming out of a cinema matinee, and I felt odd, bruised. I caught myself pulling my headgear tighter, trying to pull it over the bare patch at my throat. I felt very exposed. Suddenly I knew what Miranda meant about feeling more comfortable covered. I wish I'd got more organised with the safety gear.

Back in the cars. This time I was in the middle of ours, which was a pain, as the women kept trying to include me in the conversation. I had a hunch that the French of the one with the glasses was not too good, and their English certainly wasn't, being about on a par with my French. We headed back out of town, but this time there was a happier atmosphere in the car with Miranda laughing more (God knows what at), and the husband and wife team in the front inexplicably talking too. We drove in convoy into a huge park with an avenue of horse chestnuts on each side of the road. Sylvie's husband pulled the car onto the grass and stopped. "Just sit there a minute," whispered Miranda as I grabbed the handle to get out. "I can't wait to get out of here," I said. I could do with a really good scream or something."

"Ssh."

I caught the husband's eye in the mirror. I would have grinned or pulled a face but something stopped me. All the men were piling out of the cars, unpacking vast amounts of supplies. Some of the stuff they were leaving in the clearing, but other bits, furniture and boxes of food, were going round behind the bushes to my right.

"What's behind there?" I asked Miranda.

"Don't know," she shrugged. It was quite good having English in France. I'd noticed that, especially if we spoke fast and put on strong Sheffield accents, we had a secret code going.

Our driver had disappeared with some deck chairs from the boot but returned to open the doors for us. "Where's Ben and Omar?"

"I don't know. Here somewhere I'm sure," she replied.

All the women were carrying something and going behind the bushes. Miranda seemed intent on following. "What *is* behind there?"

"Must be where they're preparing food," she answered.

Most of the men were sitting in clutches beside their cars. Some had deck chairs, but most were on blankets. I followed Miranda through the gap in the trees. There were all the women, delving into boxes, sitting on blankets surrounded by children, milling around a huge portable table laying out food. Although they were all covered (no skin at all, apart from hands and face), there were so many colours and designs. This wasn't Iran. You didn't have to wear black or poke a single eye out of a tiny meshed slit. Most even had on high heels, some with white socks but others with tights or stockings – pop socks maybe, if they didn't have any taste. Though some women had pastel-coloured creations with matching head gear, many were wearing baggy Western clothes like Miranda's, some in rich colours. One tall woman had on a black lace headdress over a chiffon dress in royal blue. For good measure she'd put on a pair of trousers underneath and what looked like her husband's maroon wool jacket over the top. She must have been baking, and although no one could have accused her of being immodestly dressed, she reminded me more of a drag club than a convent. The clothes looked so incongruous in a public park in France.

"Shall we help, Miranda?"

"You stay here, love, in the shade. Have a bit of a rest."

"I'm not the pregnant one. You have a break." But her face was already set with a strange smile, her gaze focused on the large, colourful carpet in the centre of the clearing; the plastic bags and baskets were laid out prior to the contents being spread on the tables. I was just in the way.

Soon there were no men in the clearing. Some of the uncovered food must still have been a little warm, because the smell was delicious. I hoped someone had made that sultana-and-coconut-rice thing.

It was titillating to watch for their bodies through the clothes. In the light, hot breeze sometimes the clothes bulged out, showing a patch of chunky or slim calf, sometimes winding the clothes round the body so I could see their whole woman's shape for a moment.

It seemed to be Miranda's job to decant the food from various dishes onto paper plates. I didn't see the point of this really. Why didn't everyone just serve themselves? But as Miranda and a couple of other women had amassed about twenty of these, it soon became clear: five of the older women were going out to the car park in order to serve the men. They returned again and again, and Miranda and her colleagues kept on serving. It's bloody going to run out! The stupid women are then going to feed the children, who won't care a damn if the mother's fed or not, and that'll be it, sod us. I imagined Ben with his stupid grin living it up with Omar and the rest, and I wondered how it was that Muslim women didn't hate their men. I couldn't stand it anymore. Going to the table, the worst was confirmed, sod all left. What would they do now if I pulled off my scarf and ran next door? I could show them my arm pits, dance round the blankets with my arms in the air and pull up my skirt, the skirt that I'd tied round my boobs to act like a dress. 'Horror of horrors, a leg!' Quick, die of shame.

"Sue … d'you want some food?" Miranda asked.

"Eh? Yeah, of course, I'm bloody starving!" The little that was left was being devoured by the hoards of children, aided and abetted by their stupid mothers. "There won't be any left! Why's it that women always come last? They made the stuff!"

"Keep yer air on, there's plenty more"

"Oh yeah!" But even as she spoke, various women were riffling in the bags again. I helped Miranda pile the empty dishes back into the baskets. Women came up to the table with clean china bowls and began loading them with more food from the baskets. By now the children were drifting off to play on the grass or amongst the trees, the older girls fetching out books or braiding each other's hair. Someone gave me a porcelain plate with a knife and fork neatly folded in a cloth napkin. I began to relax. "Can I take my head gear off from around my bosoms now?"

"Not here."

"Why not, there's no men?"

"Well, one might come round the corner; you don't know. It's better to be safe than sorry."

"A stitch in time saves nine," I said flippantly.

"What?"

"Ah nothing; sod it. It'll stop me from getting sunburned anyway." The food was great, even for a vegetarian. The only thing missing, an ice cold bottle of Budweiser, but at least I knew the men weren't having one either. I ate until I couldn't stuff anymore in and copied some of the women around me, lying back on the lovely cushions and planting slices of halva to melt on my tongue. There was something special about being with only women. I couldn't have cared less whether I was showing a double chin as I lay there.

I heard the thin sound of a portable radio coming from the other side of the trees, and a couple of women got up and started their dancing, a bit like belly dancing but in the baggy gear not giving the same effect at all. After a minute or so Miranda followed suit, and I knew I'd be hauled up next. Sure enough, "Come on, Petal, show them your Arab dancing." So I gave them the Sheffield version.

Several of the little kids started copying us, going round in a circle on the spot with their arms in the air. But it was no good. Where was my audience? Where were the salivating eyes? In a nutshell, where were the men? Miranda's performance was wearing a bit thin too, and I guessed it was the same for her. "I'm going to find Ben," I said at last.

"You can't!"

"Don't be daft."

"Well, he's with the other men. You'll disturb them."

"Look, I'll just poke my head around the bushes and catch his eye, all right? I mean, I won't do the Can-Can or anything." She didn't answer me, just stood there looking droopy and disappointed. "I won't be long, okay? I won't do anything stupid, insult anybody or anything." She had her own friends there anyway. Why did I always have to be there going through things with her all the time?

I peeped into the car park, making sure the scarf was intact. I didn't want to inflame anyone. Couldn't see him anywhere. I went around the front of the cars, trying to lie a bit low and peeped round the back of one of the furthest: there he was lying on the grass, hands behind his head, cloud gazing. Most of the men sitting round him were smoking, and it looked like a couple were playing chess. I couldn't see how I was going to catch his eye. It seemed I was crouched behind the car for ages, when I caught sight of myself in the window, skulking there. What the hell was I doing, ashamed to show my face in France? I tied a firm knot in the scarf and went straight toward him. Someone turned the radio down and a couple of the reclining males sat up in alarm. "Ben," I called.

He shot upright.

"Come on, let's have a walk somewhere. Well, around the park."

"Yeah, great. Right, I'll just find Omar."

"No need, leave 'im be." I was getting some bad looks.

"Oh, okay. How'll he know where I've gone, though?"

"For God's sake what does it matter. Is he his brother's keeper or what!"

"What?"

"Oh, never mind. We came to Lille on our own. We can blummin well find our way back to the flat if we need to." By now he was on his feet. I took his arm and we made a quick getaway.

Immediately I felt better. Large trees spread in front of us, the grass cut underneath them. Through these the road continued through the park and in the distance I could see the wire of a tennis court and the structures of a children's playground. "I wonder if there's a lake 'round here?"

"Must be, I imagine," Ben replied. We walked hand in hand through the trees toward the tennis courts, leaving the sounds of the Muslim party behind us. I kept finding myself sneaking glances at him, thinking sexy thoughts. I'd never thought about sex so much in my life as I had staying with Muslims. I suppose it'd wear off after a while, but this segregation business just wound me up. I let my scarf fall provocatively from my head, but he didn't seem to notice. "I could just get you under those trees and eat you up like a freeze pop."

"You what!"

"You are gorgeous, ummm." I sucked on his earlobe as he laughed.

"D'you think we could find a quiet corner and have a sesh?" I whispered into the hot nape of his neck. He looked very pleased with himself. "Are you ovulating or something?"

"Why don't you look and see?" By now we were up by the tennis courts where there were a bunch of topless men playing football. I stood enjoying the show. Most were dark skinned, and men's bodies always look better when they're moving, everything on show, sweated up. Most of them had curly black hair, my favourite.

"That's Omar, isn't it?"

I lifted my hand up to shield my face against the sun and yes, the bastard! Stripped to the waist he was in goal, hands on his hips, thumbs down the back of his trousers somewhere. "The bloody hypocrite!" He saw us, looked really pissed off, gestured for us to get away from the mesh.

Grabbing Ben by the hand, I picked up my clogs and ran, looking behind me to see if he was following. I felt like a boarding school runaway in a Blyton novel. But he hadn't followed us. "What'r we running for?" Ben panted as we ground to a halt. I reached up on tip toe and gave him a snog, and he wrapped both arms round me and bent down over me, pushing me off my feet. I keeled over on the leaves with him on top, his arms either side of me like he was doing press ups. I grabbed him down on me and kissed him deep again. There's something so satisfying about being underneath a man. Heavy, warm, comforting even.

"I don't usually do this in public," he slurred, coming up for air.

"Not my style either, as a rule." We weren't being followed and, after embarrassing some passing dog walkers we sat up, eventually settling on our fronts, propped on our elbows. I was bent at the knees, wiggling my toes in pleasure, and I suppose my long dress/ skirt would have flopped down a bit to show the famous calves, but it was hardly a crime. Then I saw from Ben's expression that something was seriously the matter, and that something was coming towards me from behind. Omar. His dark eyes were very bright, his curly hair and face glistening from the exertions of the match, I supposed. He looked quite dishy. "What do you do here? Huh? Put down your clothes!"

"What's the problem? It's a park. We're in France for God's sake. Cool it."

"You are my guests. You shame me."

"Heck, Omar, don't get so worked up! There aren't any Muslims round here anyway. No one's going to see me," I argued. But he looked so distraught, veins all up on his temples disappearing viciously into his hairline. "Ben, say something will you," I hissed. Ben looked confused. "For God's sake just reassure him or something, will you!"

"Um, it's okay Omar, nobody's looking," he said, lamely. We remained there for a minute or so, Ben studying Omar's feet; me with my legs pulled up under my skirt and my chin on my knees, Omar rubbing and squeezing the back of his neck again and again with his fingers like he had a headache. "Ok, Omar, we're coming back now anyway. I'll put the head gear on, of course, I don't want to insult anyone."

"No, we don't" said Ben.

"I just needed a bit of a break." Omar looked relieved and put out his palm to shake hands with a bemused Ben.

As we retraced our steps he put his arm round Ben's shoulders and I followed behind, making sure everything was well tucked in.

When we arrived it was back to the apartheid again, Omar actually accompanying me to the women's quarters behind the bushes and handing me over to the care of a middle-aged Western woman Muslim. Of Miranda there was no sight. I went to sit by the remains of the food and picked despondently at some sweet coconut balls that were left. Someone came up and gave me coffee. She didn't seem to speak much French, so we sign-languaged to one another about the hot weather for a bit. It seemed that it would soon be time to leave. Some of the women were starting to gather up food and children and moving slowly back behind the bushes to the cars. I got up and meandered over there myself. Suddenly I saw Miranda in the middle of a group of women, sitting behind some overgrown rosemary. I went over.

They were rapt in conversation and nobody really noticed me when I sat down slightly behind and to the side of Miranda. There was plenty of laughter and smiling going on. As I watched, one woman brought her baby out from under her robes and passed it to Miranda, who held it so tenderly, the woman next to her adjusting the baby's head ever so slightly on her arm. As she looked down at the child, who was grimacing weirdly and rolling, opening and closing its eyes like a mad person, I saw an expression on her face I'd never seen before: a funny smile; a drugged smile almost like a Madonna in a painting, smug, self satisfied and dozy with contentment. It seemed as though all the features of her face were smoothed out, and glowed. Another woman was gesturing animatedly with her hands, and there was more laughing. Someone leaned over and put her hand on Miranda's bump under the baby, seeming to try it for size and shape. I felt a real voyeur. Suddenly one of them noticed me and said something, and Miranda turned to me and smiled broadly.

"Oh come and see him, Sue, he's gorgeous. Little Rashid! Oh, I hope I have a baby boy." I shuffled forward a little to show willing and put my finger out for the baby to hold. He closed his tiny red fingers around it. He was quite sweet, really.

"Why's he making those weird faces? I said in an aside to my friend.

"Oh, it's only wind," she said. The baby had blotches on his face and some yellowy scurf on his forehead and in his hair. "What's that?" I pointed.

Miranda said something to the mother and got an answer. Apparently they all had it. You had to rub olive oil into it and peel it off. Yuck! The mother reached for him back, and a couple of the women got up to go.

In the meantime activity had intensified behind us. Apparently it was time to strike camp. Miranda kissed me on the cheek, and I helped her up. Several of the women came to her and held her hands or gently touched her bump. I wondered if it was some sort of pre-birth good luck ceremony. "They're wishing me well and praying for a safe delivery," she said, as we walked back. "I may not see some of them again before the birth, but they'll be praying for me."

"There's no need. You're in the twentieth century now, you know!"

"I know, but bad things can still happen. Anyway, some of these women weren't born here. They've seen and heard about births going wrong."

"I suppose so," I conceded, reluctantly, "I hadn't thought of that." I felt a fool.

There were lots of little convoys forming, women clearing up and bringing things to the edge of the car park, whilst the men did the actual packing into the cars, too technical for women, I suppose. Soon everyone was in their respective cars and we set off.

I was on the outside this time, and put my head back to rest on the back of the seat, and closed my eyes. I really didn't feel like talking my lame French or anyone else's lame English. The leaves of the trees overhanging the road played shadow patterns on my eyelids, switching on and off the sunlight as Miranda and the other two women talked quietly. After a while I opened my eyes to see the town of Lille again, occasionally pedestrians staring into the cars as we went slowly through the worst traffic. I found myself averting my eyes, hunching further into the seating. Soon we were going fast through the grey suburbs, past dry municipal fountains and empty concrete squares. It was very hot still, but I'd been asked to close my window again. I expect because of the rude comments they suffered sometimes as Muslims. We turned in behind the flats and pulled up in front of the garages.

"We're here," said Miranda, somewhat obviously.

All the front passengers got out, all the men-only cars were unloaded as us women waited, and then Sylvie's husband came round to open our door. Miranda linked arms with me. I smiled a wan good bye to the others, and we went to our apartment.

CHAPTER EIGHTEEN

ONCE IN THROUGH THE red door I pulled off my scarf. Omar looked round as he reached to put on the telly and smiled. "You enjoy the fest-i-vel?"

"Good," said Ben.

"Interesting. I'm really glad I went. I wanted to know what went on," I answered.

"I am happy." Omar sat himself down. Miranda was in the kitchen doing the coffee.

"Can I have a tea, Miranda?" I called to her as I went out through the long gauze curtains to the balcony, where the same people as last night seemed to be walking in, out and around the complex. Fast food cartons played tag in corners. French TV jingles came from every open window.

I sat on the plastic chair out there, watching clouds slowly forming in the baby-blue sky. Footsteps, bare feet on lino. I turned round to see Omar with a cup of coffee for me. He sat down and pulled up his chair to face mine. "You are Miranda best friend." It was not a question.

"Yes, she's mine too."

"That is good. You are making her happy." He took my hand, holding it as though he were about to put a wedding ring on my finger, brushing back and forth across the top of it with his thumb. I was too surprised at being touched by him to move. "You come and stay with us when you want. You come perhaps when the baby is born."

"I think she's planning on having it in Britain anyway," I said.

"Yes, but soon after, we will come here."

"Right, well, I will if I can, but I start at Bristol University in October, if I get the grades."

"Ah, yes, Oct-oberrr." I extracted my hand and scratched my scalp as he pulled the chair closer. "You do not shave your legs."

"Sorry?"

"French ladies, they shave their legs. Many Muslim women. It is all of it coming off. Some women not. I like it."

"It's a nice evening, isn't it? Even the concrete looks quite picturesque in this light, quite pink and...cute even," I blustered. He didn't answer.

Through the curtains Ben was sitting somewhere, and Miranda was working away in the kitchen. I looked down at my legs, followed those eyes that were assessing me in an objective way, not unadmiring, like a stockman appraising a good heifer. I remembered the pornography: how did that fit with today, with all the scarves and mannerisms and angst? He put his other hand lightly on my bare knee, his long middle finger fitting into the warm hollow behind. I held my breath, hardly believing what was happening. He was chatting up his wife's best friend, and him a Muslim, for God's sake! Even an ordinary, non-religious bloke in Britain would know better than to do that, and this was who she was married to and would never be able to leave behind. I didn't know if she could even have custody of the child if there was a divorce. Roughly, I scraped my chair back and stood up. "I'm going to find Miranda." He looked surprised at my sudden 'spleen' – I was rude to walk out on him like that, but I didn't care – hypocritical bastard!

As I passed the telly, a woman wearing nothing but a body stocking was dancing seductively, surrounded by yoghurt pots which revolved around her like juggling balls. Ben was transfixed. Miranda was wrestling with the stove. Her headgear had slipped and strands of hair were stuck to the side of her face. Three saucepans were bubbling steam. She hugged me as I appeared in the doorway, and I could feel the lump through her clothes, surprisingly hard, bony even. She pulled back and started stirring noodles round in one of the saucepans. "You must be boiling! Look, you're all sweaty."

"I'm okay," she replied quietly. She'd kicked her shoes off, and a big toe was poking out of one of the holes in her tights. It looked raw, exposed like some dug-up bulb, so much more shocking than all the bits of her she'd ever shown before she was a Muslim. It was that strange shift of reality again. I wanted to take her away, rip off the stupid blouse and say 'spin on this' to the husband … If only she'd asked me to; if only that was what she wanted. But I just wasn't sure. This was her world, and our magic didn't work here. I certainly couldn't share the creepy leg-stroking with her – she was married to him, for God's sake!

"I want to go home." I hadn't meant to say it. She looked up, a bit of the red pasta sauce smeared on her chin. "I'm homesick, Miranda. I just don't feel right here. I think it must be hard to be a Muslim outside a Muslim country. Easy to get corrupted." That was the closest I was going to get to telling her about the seedy husband.

I was expecting her to try and persuade me to stay, but she didn't. Turning down the saucepans, she took my hand, and we went into her bedroom closing the door. "I want you to see something," she murmured.

From the bottom drawer of her wardrobe she pulled out several large cellophane envelopes and put them on the bed. She sat down on the edge of the mattress and started to tease open the sellotape.

Outfit after tiny outfit came out of the bags. It would be nearly winter of course when the baby was born, and she'd knitted the most exquisite things, all matching. There were tiny dresses with pants, mittens and hats to match; knitted trousers with matching jumpers and cardigans; a little knitted sleeping bag with press-stud fastenings; booties in every possible colour and two shawls; one soft white wool, crocheted; the other primary-coloured patchwork. "How do you know it's a girl, Miranda? Is it a girl?"

"I don't; little lass. I don't really mind. Omar wants a son."

Picking up the booties, I held them to my face. It made me ache: that smell, the feel of them, never been washed. She reached under the bed and pulled out a big bundle, something wrapped in a white sheet. She undid the safety pins holding it closed. There, on the carpet was the most beautiful Moses basket dressed in white broderie-anglais.

"Did you make this too?"

"Yes; well I dressed it myself. I can't wait," she said. There were tears in her voice. From under the satin quilt she fetched thing after tiny thing: towels with hoods, talcum powder, little plastic pants; a rattle with pink elephants; a dummy and finally a mini brush and comb set. It was that that did for me, I think. I found tears on my face and a sense of such desolation, a physical, hollow feeling in the gut. I could *see* the feeling, dry and brown, as though I were a rusty gourd.

Miranda put her arm round my shoulders and I stretched mine as far as they would go around her middle. She held me against her brushed cotton shirt and rocked me for what seemed ages, to and fro, practising for her child. "I've got everything I ever wanted." I felt her lips breathe into my hair as she held me against the bump, amongst all the irresistible props of motherhood.

So we stayed on, though after the festival and the leg-stroking incident I didn't feel comfortable with Omar. It would have been better perhaps if I had told Ben about it, but I couldn't – don't know why.

We shopped and wandered around the town; cooked and talked about old times. Omar was only there in the evenings, but he seemed tolerant and generous to us, bringing home something for us women every night: roses, chocolates, a piece of lace. Every night he returned with a British newspaper for Ben. But I felt as if we were just treading water, as if the real business of Miranda's life was beyond me, as though she was looking past me, over my shoulder at the future. I could never compete with Omar and, certainly, when the child arrived, never, never with him or her.

I was sleeping badly: the box room was airless, Ben sweating, the regular ablutions woke us again and again, and whenever I closed my eyes scenes from the day seemed to haunt me. I'd thought it was okay, the old woolly liberal idea that people were all the same when you got to know them, that Omar would turn out to be just like Ben, like me, like any other Westerner. But it wasn't true. Different cultures made people different, and he was almost a different generation too. In fact it was he who had told me that most women he knew in Algeria were married by eighteen. At thirty five that made Omar almost a father figure to me. We didn't share a language properly, so there was nothing to shine a light on the dark of each other.

Everything he'd known as a boy, a young man, was unknown to me. Just being French would have been far away enough, but to filter that through Algeria and Islam was taking him beyond my reach. And if he believed in Islam, as it seemed he did, how must he see me?

I was no different from a whore.

My bare legs, my arm pits, showing even my arms, was nakedness to him. To look at my hair was forbidden, as though he were staring at a bare cunt over his supper table. How could I have been so naïve as to stay, and how could she not see? As we struggled to dress in the tiny room some weeks after our arrival I was terribly aware of myself. All I had to wear was brief or tight. Miranda was making breakfast. She looked tired, caught me looking at her. "I was awake a lot," she said.

"Me too. It was hot and you two kept sluicing. Do you have to do that every night?"

"No. Only after sex." I smiled. She was always making me re-invent my impressions about pregnancy!

"Oh, right. Are there a set number of times to ablute, then, after sex?"

"No, just once."

"Yes, but you were…" my voice trailed off in shock, and she smiled wanly. I got a knife and helped her chop some mango. We were quiet for a while.

"Miranda, I never know what to wear," I said at last.

"Anything," she said. "We're going to Ypres; you've never been to Belgium."

"No, I mean in the house, with Omar here."

"Oh, whatever. You're not a Muslim. He wouldn't want to force it on you."

I must have looked sceptical. She continued, "The festival was special."

The door opened and Ben came in wearing a pair of the micro shorts again. Miranda looked away. I would mention it to him when we were alone.

"Looks nice," he said, peering at the food. "Where's Omar?"

"He went to get an English newspaper for you."

"That's nice of him," said Ben. "Which one?"

"Who knows? Probably one with lots of football." They laughed.

We carried the food through and set the table. The front door opened, closed. I rolled my sleeves down to cover my arms. The top was light cotton, tight and low at the front, but it was the only thing I had that covered my arms, except for my coat and an alpaca cardigan. The dilemma'd been: bra and cleavage, or nipples showing and no cleavage. I hadn't been able to decide on the lesser of two evils but had picked the no bra option in the end, as it didn't look so much as if I was trying to impress. I'd be alright as long as it wasn't chilly.

Omar didn't look tired. His tanned face was shining, and it was only the hair, thinning slightly, that gave a sense of his age. He smiled at me as he sat at the table, inclining his head a little, I did the same. Desmond Morris' *Manwatching* had been a present from Ben, and apparently you signalled good manners and a willingness to co-operate with a stranger by echoing their body language. It was usually the case for the submissive partner to mimic the actions of the dominant. I kept smiling. "Penny for your thoughts?" said Miranda.

"Oh nothing really," I answered. "Just wondering what Belgium'll be like."

"Belgium as Germany but Holland too, only no black faces," Omar said, thrusting the paper at Ben. "Here's for you."

"Thanks," Ben smiled.

The meal continued pleasantly enough, me trying to keep my eyes down so as not to 'eye-ball' Omar. Miranda's friend had said looking them (Muslim men that is) in the eye was rude.

It seemed it was all right for us to help with things, now that we had been here so long, and that made it feel easier. We cleared away together and went our separate ways, making ready to go out.

Today the area outside the flats was almost empty. Graffiti, sometimes in French, sometimes in Arabic, was splashed across the corrugated iron of the garage doors. Omar's and Miranda's door opened easily; the metal arm looked new and had been greased. Inside was an Aladdin's cave: all the tools and gadgets well-presented, everything in its place. After years of living with her scatty mother, Miranda had finally found someone as ordered as she was.

We climbed in, the men in front again, but this time there was some chatting front to back and exchange of merchandise: the vast packed lunch Miranda had brought to the front, and travel sweets and gum from the glove compartment to the back. We chatted in English, Omar sometimes joining in, though mostly he flicked between stations, humming along or drumming on the steering wheel.

Lille passed by outside, the streets filled with colour and variety: Arab, Algerian, North African, mixed with Northern and Southern French; bar tabac, Halal butcher, mosque, nightclub. Everywhere were advertisement hoardings; the noise of car horns; street signs and lights suspended over the road. Beyond the city the land was quite flat and seemed dusty and haphazard; the smaller villages hardly inhabited, only sometimes a scraggy dog, a teenager on a moped, a fat woman with a basket on her arm. Most of the houses fronting the main road had their shutters down, and those that didn't had heavy lace curtains.

"Belgium is near. It is there," Omar pointed.

"Just over the river; you don't know you've crossed over, really. Suddenly you're there," Miranda said. But I knew.

Straightaway it looked different. The houses looked German or Dutch, no peeling paint on stucco walls; no quaint, faded, ornamental urns filled with dead flowers. It was immediately a different country. Here the flat fields did not look dusty and scrubby but were manicured within an inch of their lives. There seemed little in terms of field demarcation: hedge, fence, wall. Maybe, as in the Fens, they were divided at ground level by ditches invisible from a speeding car. Everywhere I looked was green and carefully cultivated, and there were many more people in the fields than on the French side. I could almost taste the smell of manure, it was so strong. We began to see cemeteries and I was shocked at their frequency, amazed by the immaculate rows of blazing white stone seeming to ripple in the strong sunlight.

In the small towns we passed through beyond the border, there was no litter that I could see and few hoardings, even fewer neon lights. The whole country, to me, passing through as a stranger for the first time, seemed under control. As if everyone had agreed to be neat, efficient and minimalist. It had gone quiet in the car while we enjoyed our own thoughts and observations.

Omar had switched to Belgian radio, and the language provided a perfect soundtrack. As I listened I could hear nothing at all of French in it. It sounded Germano/Dutch to my amateur's ears. It was a flat language like English, like the Belgian countryside itself, and seemed full of space between words, of 'G's and 'U's and many suspiciously English-sounding words with odd endings.

"When we are out, you English must to speak English. They do not like it, the French language."

"Really!" I said. "Why, Omar?"

"Of course it is the big economy."

"The thing is," said Miranda, "France's bigger and more influential. They're afraid of being swamped."

"Ah, like Welsh," I said

"Well, yes, I suppose. To them, English is an international trade language, not the big bully living next door. Less of a threat."

"I bet it'll be English that wins out in the end, though," Ben said.

"Of course," Omar replied.

Signs for Ypres were coming thick and fast. On each side of the road Flanders stretched out flat and green. I had read descriptions of the three major battles of Ypres; the deliberate razing of the Cloth Hall; the Last Post at the Mennen Gate.

"Omar served in the Algerian army for a while," Miranda said. "They all did National Service."

"I don't believe in war," Ben said. "I don't believe a peaceful solution can be found through violence." I kept silent. Thinking about the First World War, indeed reading or thinking about any war made me aware, simultaneously and disturbingly, both of war's complete destruction of human decency, and of its inevitability. War seemed such a human phenomenon, as natural as the kissing of a baby's hair.

"You would believe if it come to you," Omar said grimly, taking him literally. In the mirror I studied his face, carefully and perhaps for the first time.

It was a big face. His whole head, his whole frame, was built on a different scale from Ben's. Although only about five foot nine to Ben's six one, he must have weighed at least two stone more. Every feature was big, luxurious even: the mouth, nose, forehead. His eyes were dark; not brown, but almost black, with long lashes. The brows were thick but sleek and rode low over the eyes, making him look severe.

The skin of his muscular face was slightly pitted with scarring. I wondered with a shock if they had still suffered small pox in Algeria when he was young? When would it have been, 1950s?

The date itself came as a shock. How could I be sitting in the car with Miranda's husband of thirty five years of age? Talking to him as an equal (well, in theory at least!). I thought of how we must all three seem to him: like big kids playing at being grown up. With a shudder that was part disgust, part excitement, I thought about him and Miranda together. He'd picked a child bride! To be fair, he was from a different country, and maybe people grew up faster there. A young wife was the done thing. Why her, though? Why (given he had a good job; spoke excellent French apparently, serviceable English and was quite attractive) had he picked a badly-connected (her family weren't even Muslim), recently converted English girl whose virginity was long gone? Surely that sort of thing would really matter to a Muslim man seeking a wife?

I had asked Miranda when she'd first written about her marriage, but the reply hadn't held water for me: 'marriage in Islam was an institution for the mutual comfort and benefit of the man, woman and their children, and he was happy to rescue her from her bleak, lost past and reform her,' she'd said. Certainly, Miranda admitted that she hadn't known him well enough to love him before they got married. I couldn't imagine her even considering marrying someone without the prospect of lust. Even born-again, fanatical Muslim Miranda would have some memory of her real priorities in life.

"Money on your thoughts," said Omar, catching my eye in the mirror. I laughed and looked away, annoyed by my blushing.

"I've read up a lot about it," I replied, gesturing to the scenery.

"It's actually so like I imagined it to be."

We were approaching Ypres now. There were no sprawling suburbs; instead the farmland went right up to the town, like pictures of Medieval walled towns. Even in the town centre itself, it was unnaturally clean. I had expected, from having dwelt on picture after picture of mud and ruination, a brand new settlement: no sign of the previous decimated town surviving in the defiant reconstruction of the place after the First World War. The streets were quaint and cobbled; lined with mature trees and mellow, three-storey houses. It was this that made me realise just how long ago nineteen eighteen had been.

As we followed the single-lane traffic through the middle of the place, I saw the Cloth Hall itself and the church beyond. It was only its magnificence, really, that gave it away as a reproduction. Its lines were clean and unworn, its colours sharp, just like the original must have been when new.

Ben wound down his window, and the car was filled with the sounds and smells of Ypres. Faintly (or did I imagine it?), I could smell the rich manure. Unlike Lille, there wasn't an underlying 'continuo' of car horns. The frequent cyclists moved between cars that seemed used to them, treated them with a tolerance unknown in France.

To me the street names looked like Dutch or German. To the eye, as well as the ear, there was very little of French in the language.

"Do they speak French?" I asked Miranda.

"Oh yes! Almost everybody, fluently. They just don't like to."

Omar brought us to a stop before what looked like the remains of a bridge across the road. "Town end," he said, but I could still see buildings carrying on beyond.

"These are remnants of the old town walls," Miranda said.

"There were a few parts still standing after the war."

We got out, and I was surprised to see Omar disappear into what seemed like a pub.

"Omar doesn't drink, does he?" Ben asked.

"Of course not, it's haram." Ben looked clueless,

"Forbidden," I said. Miranda smiled.

Omar appeared out of the building and crossed the road towards us.

"We go in," he said, as he opened the driver's door and put his sunglasses back in the glove compartment.

We crossed the road and into the bar, which was dominated by a large television mounted on the wall. Miranda and I were the only women apart from the landlady, and both she in her headscarf and Omar attracted some unashamed curiosity. The ageing landlord smiled at us, and we followed him into a small courtyard filled with flowers in tubs and basket. On one side was a small brick building; he opened the door with a key. I was first in line, and he gestured for me to pass, holding open the heavy black drape that covered the entrance. For a moment I felt fear twist in my gut, but I went in and waited in the damp gloom as one by one the others followed.

Immediately there was the sound of a machine gun, men shouting and muffled explosions which grew louder. As the explosions seemed to get nearer, so a man's screams increased. I felt water from the shock of the unexpected sound irritating my eyes. Miranda's fingers were digging into my arm, and Ben had pressed himself against me. The lighting seemed to be linked to the sound track and white and red flashes burst in tune with the mortars. Suddenly it all went quiet apart from the sound of a single man moaning, and another sobbing piteously for help.

"This is horrendous!" whispered Miranda. I moved reluctantly forward and against the wall to let Omar through. He took Miranda's hand, she took mine. Ben followed up close to me. As we turned the corner in the narrow corridor, we saw a small room set out behind glass. It was a dug-out, complete with mannequins dressed in British uniform, bunks, a stove. One soldier was cleaning his bayonet; another writing a letter. The sound track started up again, no less horrible, and I caught myself waiting with dread for the beginning of the screams. I wanted to scream back, stop them. Then the sobbing, the begging for help. It must have been torture to hear the injured calling from out beyond the wire and not be able to help or even silence them, the cries getting increasingly desperate, then weaker and weaker. We moved on, everyone silent, ears poised, waiting with dread for the guns to start again. But this time the sound of men singing, all the British army favourites. Ben started singing along quietly, and the tension lifted, Miranda letting go of my hand, Ben stopping to peer into a head height display case full of the stuffed bodies of giant rats. A label told us that these 'super rats' were just a fraction of those shot and trapped in the trenches, which had fed by gorging themselves on the bodies of the dead. In the next case were photos of the rats' colleagues committing vicious acts of bad taste. Two were fighting over a human arm; one suckled what seemed like scores of young in the muzzle of a toppled gun; yet another looked out from the eye socket of a partially rotted human face.

"Oh, no, I can't stand this!" Miranda said, grimly. "It's not good for the baby, me seeing this." She spoke to Omar in French, turned back to us. "I'm going out," she said. "See you outside." They left us in the gloom, quiet for the moment. "How're you doing?" Ben asked.

"Not too bad. How're you?"

"Okay." He slipped his hand around my waist, and I turned and gave him a snog. We hadn't been managing to be very close for a few days. It seemed rude in front of Omar, and at night the room was so small and stuffy, the bed narrow, and every sound we knew could be heard through the walls. Anyway, I hadn't really felt like it. Maybe, I wondered idly, was Miranda in her pregnancy giving off some hormone that was suppressing my own sex drive and fertility? Rather like in a wolf pack, where only the Alpha female can mate?

The guns started again. "Oh no!" Ben said. It was actually getting worse, just waiting for the screaming to start. The only thing helping at all was the thought that at least it was an actor. We reached a display of weaponry, and Omar joined us again. "I put her on the chair. She is good now." I nodded my understanding.

We had reached a corridor with walls hung from floor to ceiling with photographs of the war. They were set out carefully to tell a story. Early photos had been taken in Britain and showed clutches of young men smiling at the camera, still in civilian clothes. Then in uniform on parade, marching through towns whose streets were lined with people waving flags, both men and women in hats. A newspaper cutting showed Kitchener's army recruits loaded with equipment about to board a troop-carrier for France. Then came pictures of guns, rest billets behind the lines, columns of troops and supplies being moved up by mule train to the front.

There were photos of trenches, the earlier ones showing dugouts and duckboards and aerial photographs of the two fronts running parallel to one another. They were castellated from the air, following the convention of building at right angles, to protect one section of the trench from another if there was an enemy bombing raid, and to make them easier to seal off and defend in the event of an enemy breakthrough.

As we moved along the corridor the photographs became more gruesome. Now scenes were cleverly contrasted into before-and-after shots. Here we saw Ypres and Thiepval; Bony and Amiens. Woods, appearing in all their black and white mystery, disappeared to become skeletons of themselves, like the sunken stumps of ancient forests long buried in peat. Here too were long shots of trenches filled with recent dead, duckboards across a mud wasteland; the stiff legs of horse corpses could occasionally be seen, almost comical. Now we were seeing pictures of trenches filled with the crumpled, deflated bodies of the long dead and ground's eye views of No Man's Land, scattered with the lumps and humps and bits of fallen men. Almost at the end of the corridor, before pictures of the armistice signing and celebrations in Paris, were two strips of wall left totally blank. In one, a recess had been cut with a table, chair and lamp. On the table was a huge photo album. Writing in Flemish, English, German and French warned that visitors may be 'disturbed by the pictures of the injured and the dead'. "No thanks," Ben said, "count me out. I'm going to keep Miranda company. Coming Sue?"

I shook my head. I did feel dread, but I wanted to know as well, like when you can't help yourself looking at roadkill as you pass. I had lost a Great Uncle on the Western front and had been doing a lot of reading about it. He died on the Somme, near Lempire, his body never recovered, and I felt I had come so far, I wanted to look the horror in the face, not turn away. I went into the little booth and sat on the chair facing away from the corridor, pulled up to the table,

"Have you seen them...?" I asked Omar,

"I watched the other time. I do not see again."

"No, quite," I said and opened the book.

Again it started, quite innocuous at first: photographs in field dressing stations, rows of blinded men coming in; men on stretchers with burned faces; seas of men on crutches, amputees waiting to board ships home. But then the camera got closer to the battle and showed wounds before they had been dressed. Case after case of gangrene and trench foot; men missing eyes; the tops of their heads; parts of their faces.

I could feel myself getting dizzy and hot. Turning over the page, I saw a close shot of a young soldier, his genitals all shot away. The room started to lurch and swing. Omar took the folder off me and put it down on the floor. I felt sick and ashamed of myself. Ashamed for looking; ashamed for being so pathetic as not to be able to look. Men and medics had lived it; I couldn't even look at black and white photos of it. I thought of the guns we'd seen in the cases, the photographs of the big Howitzers and the trench mortars. It was obscene. Even to conceive of building them, knowing they were designed to smash men.

"The bloody guns," I said, and to my shame, started to sob. Omar crouched in front of me, his head level with my belly,

"It is shock. They have bomb, how you say..?" I knew his gesture.

"Hand grenade?" I said. "Yes. They are much badder for men. Men, they die in the big bombs. Small bombs take a leg, the eyes. My friend, he has not eyes."

"Did you have to fight, Omar? Miranda said there was conscription in Algeria when you were young."

"Yes, I fight." I looked at him, a question. He nodded. "I kill someone."

"No!"

"Il faux, me or that one dies." As my face cooled, he told me about his time as a young man in Algeria. Independence hadn't been that far away, and there was trouble between the 'progressive,' westernising factions and the more fundamental Islamic groups.

He spoke to me in a mixture of English and French, his man's voice filling the small room. Several times during his story the tape had started up, followed through and ended with the desperate pleading of the injured man. Omar told me it was easy to attack, even to kill, in the army. It is just set up for that, a whole world with different rules. It is the coming back and going between the two that is hard. He had left Algeria because he was no longer sure which side was right, which was wrong, and to live there you had to take a side.

"I am coming a Muslim again in France, but a French one. That is why I take Fatima for my wife. She is a good Muslim wife but also from Europe. She knows what it is to choose Islam. And," he smiled and stood up, stretched his arms behind his head, pushing his torso out, "she is very young and beautiful." I felt myself going red. Why did he make me so bashful?!

I got to my feet suddenly, and for a moment we were squashed into the cubby hole face to face. I couldn't move without pressing myself against him. He reached past me and moved the chair and desk back, his arm muscles bulging under his T shirt, his face only millimetres from my right cheek, I could smell him.

But I moved too fast, before he'd made space for me to get out, and speared my thigh on the metal-tipped corner of the table. I cried out, to the sound of guns and shouting, as the tape started up again.

"It bleed, the leg?" he said.

I shook my head, but to my embarrassment tears were stinging my eyes for the second time that day. We were still squashed between the table, chair and the wall and, as I bent to rub my thigh, he put his hands gently under my armpits and lifted me onto the table top. To him I weighed nothing. I could not look at my leg properly without lifting the skirt right up, so I fingered the spot carefully through the material. He looked on for a minute, then lifted my skirt, put his hand over mine on the deep bruise and pressed down hard.

We stayed like that for a while, until the dying men's sobs had ended. Having no fluent language in common is a sort of freedom, like not having to talk in a loud club. I kept my head down, looking into my lap, afraid perhaps to raise it and find his man's face so near. Though I had got a bit of a tan over the summer, my red-head's skin was so white in contrast to his hand. I had always loved to look at Ben and me together: large and small; hard and soft; hairy and smooth, but Ben was as different from Omar as I from him. Omar's hand was that of a man, large and shapely with muscle. A thin scar ran along the top of it, in line with where his life line would cross his palm underneath. In contrast to the darkness of his skin, the nails were pale and clean, hair growing between each joint on his fingers.

"Good?" he said at last, I nodded.

He stood back, and I came out into the corridor, shaking down my skirt and fluffing up my hair that was probably now plastered to my head. In one sense nothing improper had happened: my best friend's husband and myself had stayed behind in a war museum open to the paying public to look at a rare exhibit. I had to remember he had not sought to be alone with me. Ben had suddenly walked out, leaving us on our own, and Omar had not abandoned me to the hideous sights I insisted on seeing, but had stayed to keep me company.

I'd come over faint, he'd talked to me to get my mind off it. I'd got up, and he'd been trying to move the furniture out of the way of the exit when I'd panicked and tried to bolt, injuring my thigh in the process. Even then there had been no gratuitous examining of the leg. All he'd done was lift me onto the table so that we could establish how badly I'd hurt myself. Probably he'd had some medical training in the army too, and thought I might pass out, for real this time. So why was I making such a big deal? Why was my heart pounding, my blood hot as melted lead?

As I walked I could still feel his hand on the bruise, as vividly as if it was still on me now. He opened the external door and light shot in, obscene. He laughed as he held the door open for me, shielded his eyes with his other hand.

I saw Miranda and Ben sitting at a table in the sun and hobbled over. Ben was having a beer and Miranda 'Citron Presse.' I briefly described the album, my reaction and the leg incident.

"I'm glad I didn't see it," Ben said. "What would you like to drink, Omar? Sue?"

We talked in English about the war. No one seemed to see anything wrong, but I couldn't remember how to be normal. How long did I usually spend looking at a speaker's face? How often to blink or nod agreement. I couldn't seem to get my tone of voice quite right, either; it sounded brittle to me; over bright, false.

The sun was warm, and we left the pub to walk around Ypres. On the street we divided by sex: like adult couples, I thought to myself. On the few occasions when we'd gone out with Ben's friends, we'd been all together in a small gang on the street; or lovers, girl draped around boy, lurching along the pavement. I remembered going out with my parents and their friends, and the women had walked together chattering, the men behind talking and smoking, hands in their pockets.

Miranda walked slowly because of her pregnancy. Under the baggy clothes and scarf it would have been difficult for a stranger to tell her age. Up ahead, Omar and Ben walked, incongruous. They looked more like a young father and his gangly son. I wondered what on earth they could have found to talk about in Frenglish.

We sauntered in the sun. The streets were filled mostly with plain, well-dressed Belgian-speaking people, but we heard French, English and possibly German and Dutch too. I wasn't sure. We bought an ice cream, calling the men back to have one. Omar insisted on paying, and we ate them on a bench in the square overlooking the Cloth Hall. Even the choice of ice cream seemed to mark us out as different generations. Miranda had a plain strawberry, myself a black cherry with puree sauce and chocolate pieces; Ben a chocolate fudge sundae buried in all manner of confectionary detritus and Omar plain chocolate. Where Ben snuffled his down like a kid, managing to cover his mouth with it and drop a smear down his T shirt, Omar ate his systematically, cleaning around the melting edges with his tongue and taking pieces of hard ice cream from the top with his teeth. When we'd finished, he rose to take Ben to see the Cloth Hall exhibition, and I stayed with Miranda on the bench in the sun. I lay back with my eyes closed, face open to the sun's light, and let my mind drift. Again and again it returned me to the small room off the dark corridor. I could feel his hands in the hollow under my arms, feel him lifting me as though I'd been a child. I must have been so light to him. Each time I returned to the two figures, the man and the girl, I became more convinced that on any terms, in any culture, something powerful had happened. A grown man, somebody else'd husband, had put his hands on me. Most important of all, how I'd loved it.

"How's your leg, sweet meat?" said Miranda. I sat up quickly, taking my hand off my thigh where it had been lying comforting the bruise that was surely forming there.

CHAPTER NINETEEN

THE DRIVE HOME SEEMED quicker, as it always does. It seemed to be the companionable silence of old friends, all things at rest for the moment. Miranda sat quietly and still, her eyes most often closed, face searching out the sun's warmth through the glass. Sometimes she squeezed my hand. She'd been holding it ever since we'd passed out of Ypres under the sober beauty of the Mennen Gate's arch, crawling with names. Sometimes her cat's eyes opened, and she smiled, a small movement of the face but one that expressed a contentment so deep it seemed almost a spiritual thing. I sat back and watched Omar: the back of his head with the tight black curls, a natural sheen on them like wax; the hairs on his forearm as it appeared and disappeared from my line of sight ; the way the muscle worked underneath, the long sinews moving when he flexed and relaxed his hands against the wheel.

As long as I could remember how to behave normally everything would be all right. Miranda was second only to my mother in her ability to second guess me, root out and probe any anomalies in my behaviour. It was Tom Booker all over again. When he'd been around, I'd been on duty all the time, unable to concentrate on anything but him, and he'd dominated, for me, any room he was in. Three weeks ago this man had been nothing to me except a gate-crasher on my relationship with Miranda.

How had it come to this?

It was nearly dark when we got back to the flat. Miranda seemed tired, and I think must have said something to Omar; it was he who took over in the kitchen when we got back. Ben was in there helping him, and I was the spare part. Miranda hummed in the bathroom, steam coming out into the flat when she moved to and fro preparing a gargantuan hydro-therapy session. I walked out onto the veranda again. Veranda was perhaps not the right name for the stained concrete slab bounded by rusting cast iron that jutted out from the living room.

The night was buzzing. Strange how the poorer the area, the more life out in the streets. Miranda had made an attempt at livening up this space with some geraniums in pots, but the effect was spoilt by the fact that she'd left them to die. The soil had shrunk from the side of the pots; all but the growing tip had become brown and dry, and spiders had made their webs between the leaves.

This was a bad trip. What had I come to do? Kick-start things with Ben; rescue Miranda from a life of servitude and ideological repression (pure Marcus-speak I know; funny that his political patois had lasted me all these years); try and find some of the enthusiasm I'd had in the Golden Age when we were still in school, and Miranda and I were having our adventures. But Miranda was okay here, happy even. Well, at least more contented than me in my life; Ben was no more enchanting on French soil than he had been at home; I still felt dowdy and unsatisfied, and to top it all I was developing a crush on the husband. Now, going back to face my A level results and all the so called 'choices', the clearing system, all the boring courses at mediocre universities, seemed even worse since I'd put some distance between myself and home.

There was movement behind me and Miranda was suddenly in the doorway wearing her old silk kimono, her hair covered for modesty with a bath towel and looking 'normal' for the first time since we'd got here.

"Here you are, Petal," she said in her lovely voice; "de'you want to come and talk to me in the bath?"

"I'm not allowed. It's immodest or something, isn't it?"

She laughed. "No. Where did you get that idea from?"

"From you. You started taking your bra off under your clothes and everything."

"Oh, that. I was over zealous, like any new convert. Come on, we haven't had a proper chat since you got here."

I felt better as soon as we'd gone inside and shut the doors on the dark sky. The flat smelt of food, unfamiliar but delicious.

She'd worked her magic in the bathroom with the scented candles, and it was almost like old times as I sat on the toilet with the seat down. She shrugged off the robe and climbed carefully into the bath. This was the first pregnant woman I'd ever seen properly. Though the bump itself was not very large (she was a big woman and had nearly three months to go) what surprised me was all the other changes to the body I'd known so well. She seemed pregnant everywhere. Her bottom, her thighs, even the tops of her arms were bigger, seeming even a little mottled, fine blue veins showing up just under the surface. Across her hands, raised veins were visible and her breasts were enormous. Even the nipples were enlarged, their sparse circumference of hair seemed to have thickened and now a fine line of hair ran down her belly too, disappearing into her dark triangle. I was transfixed. She laughed,

"You look horrified! It's only a pregnant woman."

"I know but what a change! Everywhere!"

"They don't tell you this," she said as she lowered herself gingerly into the foaming water. "I suppose that's why you get pregnant when you're young, it's so much of a strain on the body."

She settled herself deep into the water, her two raised knees, bump and breasts sticking out like footage of the Loch Ness monster. Through the thin door we could hear the radio sound and the clash of cooking.

"Are you happy?" I said, suddenly. She chuckled. "I mean, do you think you've done the right thing?"

She sat up and started moving the water around, palms like paddles sending it clockwise around the island of her body.

"What do you think?" she asked. I thought for a moment.

"Yes," I said. "I came here to try and save you, but I don't feel the same anymore. You seem different. I don't know how, but like, it's like everything's over."

"It's only just beginning," she said archly, looking at me.

"Yes I know. I mean, I know what you mean, about the baby and your life with Omar and everything. I was meaning all the struggling. You know, trying to get into my family; trying to find the love of your life; going to the church and everything."

"You're not expressing yourself very well," she said, running some more hot water and settling herself down. "But I know what you mean. I've got plans now, the baby, Omar, study at the university. I know how it's going to be. I've got friends here, they know how to behave and support you. When my dad left my mum, she was all on her own trying to look after me. Only Granny was around. Here this wouldn't happen. There are rules; people know what's right and wrong."

I wanted to argue back. What about the freedom she'd left behind? Wearing what she liked; dating whom she liked. But even as the argument formed in my mind, I could see it was hollow. Fashion was a hard master, like the Qur'an, and what was the freedom to go out with and sleep with different men except the ability to be hurt and left, over and over again in Miranda's case, or, in my own, to be stuck in a relationship going nowhere?

"What about fun though, what about friends?" My words came out sounding strident even to myself. She smiled as she dipped her head under the bath water, holding it there for a few seconds.

"We have both," she answered, as she resurfaced. "Plenty of fun, many friends. People like us, Westernised Muslims; people that've been around a bit. People who have chosen Islam; that's important. We do things; there's always some festival going on, someone celebrating something: Aid Al-Fitr; Eid Al-Adha. You can go and talk to the Imam if things get tough. Anywhere you go in the world, you can just turn up at the local mosque, and they'll help you."

"I bet that's the same with all the major religions, though." But even as I said it, I was thinking of the sad sham of Christmas and Easter. She was getting really quite convincing. Was I going to convert too then? What was to stop me?

"I never did ask you, Miranda." I said, passing her the towel as she carefully stepped over the rim of the bath, "What finally did convert you in the end?"

"Well…" she thought for a moment. "I think in the end I just gave in. I was unhappy, if you remember. Granny had just died, and I kept thinking, 'Where is she?' No one seemed able to say. People said, "Some people believe this/some people believe that". It all sounded so woolly and relative. I wanted to know. I wanted someone who was sure."

"And there was Auntie," I said. My voice sounded bitter. "Just in the right place at the right time."

"Well, you see," she said ignoring me," Auntie was there. She seemed so quietly confident, so organized. She looked after her daughter so well, and there were people around her all the time, supporting her, coming to her for advice. When Granny died she knew what to do. She had answers and a proper process –"

"Ah!" I gloated, "you always were a sucker for certainty and discipline."

"She knew how to mourn properly and what to do. My mum was clueless."

"Years and years of people trying to undo organized religion, and now you'll do anything to get it back!"

"Sometimes you need it. Anyway, I just felt myself slipping into it, like a warm bath." She gestured and grinned. "It felt so peaceful; coming home."

"But you could have picked any religion! I bet your Mum's family, I bet Judaism's got all those procedures for coping with a crisis."

"Perhaps," she said, finishing her dressing and flexing her exquisite toes individually, sprinkling powder between them. "Probably even my father's Roman Catholics could have helped me, but they weren't there." She shrugged. "Islam was." She prepared her hair and put on her scarf, tucking in all the stray bits. I had a wee. She mumbled something in Arabic.

"What?" I said.

"Oh, piss on Iblis," she laughed. I was clueless.

"The Devil, Iblis. He lives in filthy places. You can piss on him on purpose."

I looked at her quizzically as she finished her hair, but I couldn't tell if she really believed it or not.

We sat down to food together: Haloumi cheese grilled and served with apricots, almonds and couscous.

"The food is not the food of Algeria; it is French, Algeria." Omar made a wobbling motion with his hands, I laughed. It was yet another example of the cultural melting pot.

"It's still delicious, though." He smiled at me, his teeth

amazingly white. You could tell he hadn't grown up on a Western kid's diet.

Ben and Omar chatted a little in their respective patois, but Miranda had gone quiet and was looking tired again, and I felt too down really to be talking. We helped clear away, and then I took myself off to bed in the airless box room.

We left them a few days later. Even Ben seemed subdued. "D'you think she'll ever come back?" He'd asked that last night, as we'd lain squashed together in the single bed in the stuffy room. I hadn't answered. All the structures of her life were in place: she had status as a mother and a wife; security with Omar, and the degree course in French she was determined to keep on with; friends in the other Muslims and an explanation of how to live, how to die. She even had a rule book, for God's sake! Why then was I being such a wet weekend. Was it just jealousy? Jealousy that I wasn't any longer so important to her? Jealousy of what she had perhaps? I nuzzled up to Ben's thin chest, pretended I was asleep and thought of my future.

I could see it like a straight dirt road across the prairie – mile after mile. My crap 'A' levels would get me on some stupid course, and I'd end up working in personnel somewhere. Perhaps Ben would come back after he left university, and we'd buy a little house in Steeler's Bar. Maybe he'd find someone else. Whatever I did from now on, I knew it would never be extreme: that I could never be daring without Miranda. As I drifted off to sleep, that same feeling I'd had in her bed the evening before the two Nigerians crept up on me again – the best is past.

The next day my face was still a bit puffy and blotchy from the tears the night before, but while we had breakfast I explained it away as sadness about leaving. Miranda looked tearful too, but we didn't really have a chance to talk.

As we loaded our stuff into the car she turned to me and hugged me tightly. "I wish you could come here and live with us, Sue. You could look after the baby. Actually you could be an English assistant in a school. Omar could get you a job, I'm sure he could!" I'd hugged her back. "I'd look stupid as a gooseberry."

"You're like a sister to me," she said. But she had no idea what having a sister was. It wasn't intense and painful like this – it was just normal, comfortable. If I was saying goodbye to Bethan or Huw, I'd be cheerful, give them a big hug and look forward to seeing them in a few month's time when my nephew or niece arrived.

"You could always be second wife!" Ben laughed. For a long moment nobody else seemed to move, to breathe, but Ben was oblivious.

"Could you really share a husband?" I whispered to her once the engine had started, and we were on our way.

"We have already, in a sense," she said, smiling slightly. She looked at me quizzically only for a moment, shrugged slightly. I realized with relief that she was talking about our adventures with Byron.

Sometimes we talked on the journey, there being none of the strict 'front to back' rules between us four anymore. I caught Omar's eye in the mirror looking at me from time to time, thinking perhaps what a baby I was.

We checked in and took our leave. Miranda held us; Omar held our hands. He didn't seem to mind that she was hugging Ben.

As the ferry pulled away, we stood on deck, looking down at

the car parked far below on the harbour wall. Ben was waving vigorously, looking forward to going home and seeing his Votee friends again, no doubt.

I saw Miranda bend down and climb slowly into the car; probably she could still have seen me, but her face behind the wind screen was lost in shadow. For a while I watched as the little car took her away; waved and waved until she was finally out of sight.

It was the end of July, and I was eighteen that year, but nothing felt like I had imagined. Instead of relief at being home, I felt only wooden, deadened. Everything seemed a big effort, as though I was suffering some terrible, bone-deep fatigue, yet on another level I was manic, unable to sleep, not much appetite and constantly on edge. I seemed immune to the music I usually liked; ordinary household noises seemed to jar horribly: a radio on in the morning was all too much; the buzz of Dad's shaver. I felt like somehow I'd lost a layer of protective skin, both raw and jaded at the same time.

Mum and Dad had been pleased to see me home, but somehow the going away with my boyfriend for those weeks, obviously having regular sex, had made them realise they couldn't control me, and they were different. Now I told them what I would be doing rather than asking them, but ironically the transition had made me more considerate of keeping them up late worrying, and anyway there wasn't really anywhere I wanted to go anymore.

Ben seemed totally unaffected. He whizzed around catching up with his friends, who were mostly home from studying like him. He was meditating constantly, as though making up for lost time. I had a job in a Pizza outlet, which was OK except for the fact that the same pop sound track went round in a loop all day. Huw was off somewhere in South America on a volunteering adventure trip, and 'Bethan-the-Good' was now my parents' flavour of the month. She was obscenely like Huw, sporty, effortlessly academic and well-balanced: strange how I couldn't hate them.

July had passed me by. Sometimes I did my Miranda trick and went visiting her in my head. It was odd the way that, in her new world, I couldn't really imagine anything I hadn't actually seen. All I could do was re-play scenes and people, lingering on those that fascinated me. I often dreamt of Lille. Always it was dusk; often there was a journey, but sometimes it was the museum.

Occasionally I got a thick, fragrant envelope from her, which kept me going for days, and I waited for my results.

At the beginning of August, Miranda phoned. Her voice had the trace of an accent. At the sound of it my body seemed to come to life: heart thumping inside my chest, insides chaotic as a swooping kite. I could hear Omar in the background talking quietly to her as she spoke to me, the meaning of her words sinking in somehow, although I didn't seem to be able to hear them individually. Her letters had never really said she was lonely or she missed me, and even now I caught my breath when she said his name; she claimed it was Omar's idea, that he wanted me there, felt someone close should be with her as the baby approached.

I put the phone down slowly and sank onto the bed in my parents' room. I'd been helping Mum change the duvet, a new-fangled idea she'd only just adopted and which she found extraordinarily difficult to manage. She looked at me expectantly, and I realised how little I must have been saying on the phone, standing with my mouth hanging open probably. I went through it with her, found myself saying I could even afford to give up my crappy job, because they'd pay my fare, and all board and lodging was free of course. Obviously Ben wasn't invited, but that was good practice for another year away from one another. She could go and get my results for me and, as the baby was due in September, I'd definitely be back in time to go to any place the school's Head of Sixth Form would have managed to beg me into.

She bought it.

I felt literally feverish making the preparations to go, my old life like toy land-out-of-scale and artificial, too small for me now.

This time they came to fetch me from the ferry. Everything in Lille was the same, but I wasn't. It didn't take me long to settle in to the routine with them. Without Ben, my Britishness, my non-Muslim nature, was overrun and it was easy to settle. I had a role too. Even the constant prayer routine didn't seem awkward any more. Whilst they went off somewhere quiet with their little carpets, I took time out too, getting into the habit of closing my eyes and meditating quietly, or writing in my diary.

The days developed a strange quality. It was like a half-dream at the end of that Summer, still hot, but everything full-blown, waiting. It was still green, but a dark, exhausted green and, although the leaves had not changed colour, they moved in the wind on their branches with a dry sound. At the very end of Summer I began to search with dread for that subtle cold at the beginning and end of the day.

We had more than three weeks to go. Everything was ready, and Miranda was calm and looking forward to the birth. It suited her sense of drama. Omar was quiet. He went out a lot, and I wondered what a man who wasn't allowed to drink, gamble or be with women did so often from home. I had become a handmaid. I served the great, swollen belly, anointing it with smelly lanoline and massaging the feet that would puff up slightly in the evening. Miranda said how glad she was that she was pregnant young and she'd managed to escape all the horrible complications such as varicose veins. Secretly though, when she said those things, I thought to myself, 'This is only the first. You'll swell like this every year until you're too old, or until he's sick of you.'

She was big and well, her hair unusually glossy, and her young skin clear for the first time. I watched her move around the flat doing her chores and wondered what she was thinking, but I couldn't ask those things anymore. Our conversations when we were alone relied heavily on reminiscence, but they were a strangely edited version of events. Miranda had made it clear how uncomfortable she felt with references to our more raunchy adventures, although sometimes I caught her out in a sly, secret smile at something I said that reminded her.

It was hot and still, and I was always tired. It was not me carrying around a baby, I know, but I was disturbed away from home, my sleep shallow and full of vivid dreams still punctuated by the often twice-nightly ablutions of the lovers. My cupboard was airless and crowded, even though Ben was long gone. I was starting to pick up a lot of what they said now, language forming in my brain like a stirred pond clearing. It was as though I could at last *hear* French. Before, I couldn't; it was on the wrong frequency. At first, occasional words and phrases had stood out, like rocks below the surface in a pool; then more and more, strings of them, held up suddenly and frustratingly by whole minutes I couldn't understand. I had found the French dial in my ear, but I could still just switch it off if they were talking of something that didn't interest me. It was great the way I could make French either just background noise or tune in to it and understand. With English I couldn't do that. The path between hearing and comprehending was so clear, I couldn't choose not to receive its messages.

I worried for the baby under the nightly onslaughts, but Miranda had said, "It's fine. It's good for my muscles and my heart and lungs. Anyway, it's important for my husband not to turn away. I might be injured by the birth and be a long time coming to his bed."

"Give over, Miranda! You sound like Goody Proctor," I'd said. Sometimes she talked funny, as though she were a ventriloquist's dummy.

"What do you mean? Say it in your own words!" I'd say.

"Okay. I just like it," she'd said, simply. I wanted to ask how it was possible, I mean, the logistics of it during pregnancy, but I couldn't now she was a Muslim. Anyway, a marriage was not something you could ask about. It was a secret box with a closed lid, out of which came muffled sounds.

Sometimes in the middle of the night I wondered why I was still here. Wasn't it unhealthy, this three-some: Earth Goddess, Impregnator and Nun? What was I doing in my windowless box-room, unwittingly eaves-dropping on a relationship that seemed bigger than the sum of the two people in it. Well, initially, it was unwitting, but, worryingly, it was starting to become something I anticipated, even stayed awake for. Maybe I was undergoing some chemical/hormonal castration, my body kept down by the dominant female's more powerful drives and scent; forced to be drone to the queen bee. Yet, though I was behaving like the maiden aunt, something strange was happening to my body. If Miranda's hormones were supposed to be dominating mine, they weren't doing a very good job. My sexuality was monstrous. Celibacy, and my proximity to pregnancy, were turning me into a frustrated nymphomaniac. Every night I wanked myself to sleep, sometimes doing it more than once. I'd learned to do it never more than three times, as I got too wound up and ended up awake all night, tormented by the electric itch that, scratched once too often, was insatiable. Often I woke in the night to the sound of sluicing and found a hand on a nipple, the nipple sore where I'd been pulling on it. Sometimes the only way I could sleep was to wrap my legs around one of the hard French bolsters and pull it up high and tight. It comforted me.

Most days I spent with Miranda in the house. She didn't go out much but seemed content. Omar didn't like me to go out on my own, but I often went shopping with him after work, or sometimes met him at lunchtime so that we could shop together, me buying some intimate purchase for Miranda or special things for the baby. Why Omar couldn't have done it I don't know. Apparently Islam wasn't precious about men buying that sort of thing if they needed to, but I wasn't going to argue; it got me out of the house and gave me and Omar some time to ourselves.

Just like my French, his English was improving fast. For some reason, he was improving faster than me. When we walked together I felt proud. He walked well and, although there was nothing striking or statuesque about him, he had a confidence and independence that made his muscular body attractive. I thought it was probably his army training that made him so comfortable in himself.

Although I always dressed modestly now (I just felt more comfortable that way), I didn't look like a Muslim and, apart from those in the local shops, people in the town treated us as an ordinary couple. It excited me to think they thought I was his lover when we loaded up the car with shopping, or caught a coffee in a bar at lunchtime. They probably thought we were a passionate couple, the English girl and her Algerian lover. Me all white arms and red hair, him dark and fit; a sexy, young girl and an older man. Sometimes we met people who knew us, and Omar'd stop and talk whilst I'd nod, joining in if I could and it was appropriate, or just keeping quiet. I made sure not to eyeball Muslims, as it embarrassed them. I'd learned too to give the Islamic greeting. Somehow Omar could spot a fellow Muslim anywhere, even though they weren't obviously non-French or wearing special clothes.

We talked and there was no awkwardness now. It helped, I think, that one or the other of us was always talking in our second language. The contact was more naïve, I suppose, more convoluted and not so direct. He was funny too, often doing silly things to make me laugh when we'd run out of ways of understanding one another. I'd told him about not stepping on the cracks on the pavement, and he liked to do a funny walk, half bounding, half mincing ballet steps to make me giggle when no one else was watching. I was teaching him his cardinal numbers, and he'd put the limes or peaches in a bag with an exaggerated mime, getting the numbers wrong on purpose and putting on a Stan Laurel face, scratching his head and raising his eyebrows.

I often didn't want to go back to the still flat, found myself going home along the bare walkways of stained cement feeling guilty towards my friend, but what we did together never seemed to bother Omar. He was always cheery, kicking open the door with his foot when he was carrying something heavy and calling out, "Bonjour, ma cherie". Often it was quite late by the time we got back, and Miranda was asleep in the gathering dusk. He'd put down the bags and cross quietly to her and kiss her, sometimes the palm of his hand lingered on her belly. It was a gesture shocking to see, more intimate even than sex, and it seemed to stab at me.

CHAPTER TWENTY

BRITAIN SEEMED FURTHER AND further away. I wrote to Mum and Dad once a week. It was an old-fashioned thing to do, but I liked the discipline of it, and after the first couple of weeks I tried to sit down on the same day every week. They were highly edited letters of course featuring food and weather, but definitely playing down Islam and pregnancy. I think my parents thought both were catching, maybe they were. I tried to start each week positively, getting up when Omar did, giving Miranda her cuppa in bed and then going out to post the letter to England. Sometimes I'd walk Omar to the bus stop, wait with him until it came, then spend the morning on my own, exploring. I didn't want him to be aware of everything I was doing. There were nearly always some errands to do in the local shops and reasons to meet Omar at lunch time or after work, if something was needed from the town centre.

Occasionally I met Sylvie, Miranda's large blonde friend from the Muslim feast all those months ago. She was French and, although superficially at least in the same situation as Miranda, i.e. a Western woman married to a Muslim, her attitude couldn't have been more different. Her English was virtually non-existent, so we did the best we could with my weird French, which I'd largely learned from Omar. She only did the Islam thing when she was with her husband, his family and friends. She cooked Halal and dressed modestly, but Miranda said she wasn't a Muslim herself. She just loved her husband and had a respect for his beliefs and didn't want to hurt him. "Does he know she doesn't believe and meets her friends and shows her hair to men in their houses?" I'd asked, after having gone round with her to a pamper party at her friend's house one afternoon. "Oh yes. He knows all about how she feels. He knew when he married her." According to Miranda, Islam was very tolerant in not forcing itself on other people. It seemed like a 'pick and mix' situation to me, though. If they really believed, why weren't they like Christians, desperate to try and save the souls of the people they loved? If Sylvie didn't believe it, how could she go along with it as she did? Anyway, I didn't have enough French to cross-question her, and Miranda seemed reluctant to, so I just had to keep guessing. She was fun though; she made me feel normal, holding dresses up to me and forcing me into the hairdressers and beauty parlour where she held my hand and laughed as I had my first underarm and bikini-line wax. She reminded me of how Miranda used to be.

"But what's the point? Who'll ever see it? It'll all have grown back by the time I go back to England, and I can't show it off here."

She'd just shrugged her shoulders and smiled. She asked me once, on one of our excursions, if I missed Ben. I was about to say yes, of course, acting automatically, but something about the way she was looking at me made me hesitate. She had stopped walking and waited for me to speak. "Actually, no. I don't very much," I'd said.

"Hum," she said. "He is a boy only. He is a baby. Leave in England."

I felt tears at my eyes when she'd said that. Shock I suppose. But then it was only one woman's opinion, and what did she know anyway? But it had affected me so immediately and so much that, over the next few days I realised it was true. In fact, I had left him already.

It was hot all the time. Not the clean, bleached white I thought of when I'd thought of France, but a wet, British heat, the air made almost palpable, sitting low on you and hanging around like an odour. Miranda had finished work now for the maternity leave, and she hardly went out. Instead women friends called often during the day to chat and drink coffee or black tea. Sometimes they brought things for the baby or soaked Miranda's puffy feet in evil-smelling saucepans. I suppose I was jealous, of the way she enjoyed seeing them, listening greedily to their stories of men, babies and Algeria. Jealous too of their attention to her. I didn't have a husband to discuss; most of all didn't have a baby lurking powerful beneath my heart to interest them.

Me? I just served up food. I did a good fresh mint tea with loads of sugar. Miranda had renamed me Martha, a joke that wasn't terribly funny, but I was happy to call her Mary. Although I hadn't seen her actually drying any feet with her hair, I wouldn't have put it past her!

Sometimes Miranda's friends tried to be kind and include me, but they had no English and their second-language French, particularly when they were all talking and laughing at once, was completely beyond me. I felt like a servant girl. Some of the women were beautifully dressed underneath their outer clothes and would take off their head gear in our flat, looking suddenly marvellously exotic. The effect was stunning, and I realised with a shock how powerful it must be for a woman's husband to know he was the only man to see her like that. Okay, it didn't work quite so well here in France, where loads of French women spoiled the 'forbidden fruit' effect by hanging out of their clothes at every opportunity, and every advert had someone topless or in a thong.

My favourite times were when the women brought food and put on a record and we did our 'Arab' dancing (as Miranda and I called it). I suppose to the unpractised eye it was like belly dancing but it was great fun, and we had a good laugh when I showed off our dance routines from the clubbing times.

It was at one of these informal 'soirees' that I met 'A' and 'B', the two wives of a recently arrived Algerian, Salah. It was clear right from the beginning who was number one and who was the number two wife. Unlike what I would have expected, number two was older but always seemed to hang back, deferring to 'A' who took care of her in a casual way, as if she were her big sister. 'B' had a newborn with her, which she kept in a sort of sling underneath her top garment, its little head poking out for air, and she went away to breastfeed in private. I understood nothing of what she said. She had no French as yet and apparently she spoke a particular dialect that even some of the Algerian women didn't understand much. She covered her hair even in front of us.

'A' chatted away, her legs tucked up under her on the sofa. She had light skin and almost tawny eyes and hair. Miranda said she was Algerian but she could have been Kurdish in looks. She always arrived to these dos with bought food from the supermarket, and although the etiquette was to bring your own plates and utensils to save your host on the washing up, she always served up straight from the packet.

Like Sylvie, she gravitated towards Miranda, and they sat and laughed and stuffed their faces. She was always first up for the dancing, often grabbing a partner from one of the women and wafting imaginary veils around seductively. She was full of laughing and always solicitous to 'B', making sure she had food and taking the tiny baby off her so she had a chance to eat.

I couldn't wait to meet the man, imagining him as an unsavoury old bloke who 'A' had been only too pleased to pass on to 'B' for the weekly servicing.

"No," Miranda'd said later. "He's nice. Quiet, a real gentleman, I'd say."

"But how can they stand it! How on earth can you bear to share a man?"

"Sometimes it's just the best thing to do," she'd said, driving me nuts again with her self-satisfied, beatific smile. "I think she was a distant relative, a widow I think. Apparently she was in dire straits, and they took her in. Sue it's nothing new or weird. Loads of cultures do it: look at Jacob and Leah in the Bible."

"I bet they did," I'd muttered, ignoring her. "And I suppose he just had to get her pregnant! What a big sacrifice that must've been for him! Oh poor sod; two wives to fiddle with!"

She'd looked at me, not shocked or angry but, annoyingly, almost resigned. Like she was used to me disappointing her. As though she was tired of me but she just had to put up with it. It drove me frenzied. "I mean, what about the logistics of it! Does he do alternate nights; or three nights on and a day of rest? What?"

"Why don't you just mind your own business," she said. I was pleased. At last I'd got to her, broken through this stupefied calm. Was it just pregnancy hormones, or was she completely duped by her religion?

"You always have some bloody pat answer," I shouted. "You're so self-satisfied and sure of yourself all the sodding time. You drive me nuts. One day the world's going to come down on your stupid head, and it'll serve you right."

"Go away," she said. "Just go away and leave us alone, will you? You're just a kid. What are you still here for anyway?"

That had hurt. Didn't she want me, then? Hadn't she wanted me? Why *was* I still here?

The women had left, we'd had a fight, and Miranda had gone to the bedroom to lie down. I washed up and sat, flicking through the channels, wanting Omar to come home and feeling a thought forming quietly, one that I didn't want to look at straight on, a plan to go home.

The rest of that evening had passed quietly, with Miranda friendly but distant. There was a time we wouldn't have been able to stand nursing hurt like that for more than a couple of hours, but things had changed. I was a drawbridge for her, I suppose, over which she could go to get back to a lost world, and in a way she was that for me too, but going the other way. That bridge was drawing up now, and it seemed neither of us was doing any running to get through to the other before it was up completely.

The next morning I set off to do the, by now, daily forage for supplies. I'd left her in bed nursing a bad back, and took my mood, not exactly of misery, more a certain deadness, on the bus to the hyper-marche with me.

I had been waiting for Omar to collect me in the car for nearly thirty minutes, and he obviously wasn't coming. The bags of shopping weren't too heavy, but the package with the bouncy chair in it was bulky. Why they had to have such a chair and get it before the baby was even born I didn't know. It had been big Sylvie's idea, 'Oh it was essential! Oh no, the baby would never let itself be put down and left for you to do things around the flat if you didn't have one.' She was a great lover of lifestyle magazines, a wonderful source of the most up-to-date old-wives tales, but why people took any notice of her baby-care advice was beyond me. She wasn't even a mother.

As I crossed the square to the bus stop, the grubby swimming pool tiles of the stagnant fountain, the crisped up leaves draped with small feathers, the fluff and rubbish that rattled along the concrete in the bitter, dry wind, all seemed so sordid, and I felt tired in every part of myself. Tears seemed so close to the surface these days. I'd missed the usual greeting this morning. Miranda's daily wake up call, 'Rise and shine, my precious,' piercing through the thin walls of the apartment, I had been finding harder and harder to get up for. That 'Glass Menagerie – rise and shine': not just the words themselves, but that determined jollity in the tone, and perhaps too, the familiar, washed-out kimono hanging behind the door.

The bus was late and too full for me to sit. I hung onto the suspended, cock-like creation in the aisle, the packages held tight between my knees, and watched bland, town-centre Lille turn into sordid, suburban Lille. I didn't switch on the French switch, and all their talk was harmless background to the voice which had begun when I crossed the square from the cafe and kept repeating itself: 'Go. Go now. Go home.' As the baby got nearer, paradoxically, it felt that my time was running out. The English voice had a real authority, and suddenly, here on the lurching bus, I felt for the first time a stabbing need to be home in my parents' house again.

I got off and walked the few hundred yards through the underpass and across the grey square to the flats. Sounds were coming from nearly every door; many were open, and there were children playing in the corridors and on the stairs. As I approached our door, though, it seemed unnaturally quiet. Thinking about it, I supposed it was rare for the TV or radio not to be on. Loaded down and irritable with the bags, I didn't bother trying to find my key but knocked instead. No answer. I knocked again harder. Swearing then, I put them down and started searching for the key.

Once inside, the door slammed shut, the bags dumped, it was even more uncanny. There was an unmistakable aura of emptiness. It was creepy and I realised, as I moved from room to room calling, that I'd never been in the flat alone before. There were no signs of why they weren't there. No note anywhere.

I knew where to find Miranda's 'baby case,' as we called it, since I'd been helping to fill it for the hospital, but that wasn't missing. With frustration I realised I didn't have Sylvie's number. There must have been some medical emergency. I didn't have the hospital number either. I needed to phone and find out what had happened. Thank God my French had improved! My stomach had begun to wobble, and I made my way to the bathroom, rushed down my trousers and breathed a sigh of relief. Only then did I notice the thick, bright blood, still wet on the inner rim of the toilet.

The phone rang, but I was in no position to answer it. I struggled to finish but the ringing stopped, leaving the air still vibrating. It seemed now even more silent. I flushed the toilet but the blood remained, garish, demanding. It was hers, I knew.

I moved through the flat. Dusk had come, paradoxically defining the silhouette and magnifying the bulk of each piece of furniture. I sat by the phone, a pointless move but it made me feel better. How long I sat there I don't know, but it grew dark around me. From somewhere I remembered Lucy Snow in *Villette,* a novel I'd never liked. It was dense with the narrator's voice and desperately slow-moving, but that night it came back to me. It was something to do with the situation: events were happening to the people around her; they were part of the very structure of their world, yet Lucy was alone, trapped inside the school, feeling a stranger. Perhaps it was this terrible imbalance between the weight of feeling I was carrying and my inactivity, my insignificance here.

I felt like I knew what no one my age should ever feel, that the best was past, that there was nothing for me. Not that there was horror or pain or loneliness, nothing as substantial as that, just a nothing, a no one. I was a dried-up maiden aunt, tolerated by all those who were in the action.

The door opened. For a moment it was only the outline I saw against the weak hall light. The shadow said my name, and I ran to it, selfconscious, as though I were Scarlet O' Hara, and flung my arms around his neck. Though he wasn't tall, the bulk of his chest made me have to reach for him, lifted me for a moment off my feet, and he held me. How can I tell you what it was? He felt to me so familiar, fitted to my arms, as if I'd been waiting for him all my life. He released his hold on me and I gradually slid down his body. When I reached the floor with my toes I had the feeling of wanting to keep going and fall to a heap on the ground. Somehow he must have had a sense of it. He reached under my armpits and supported me, saying something low in French which I didn't understand. Time, what was time then as we stood in that doorway? I looked into his face and drank there. His back was to the light, and I couldn't see his eyes or expression, but he would have seen me clearly. I feasted instead on the shape of him, the angle of his jaw and cheek, the slope and breadth of his neck and shoulders.

A noise behind us made him nudge me forward with his knee, and he kicked shut the door. Gently then he set me down, as you would a wobbly child, the hands lingering a while under my arms. He went to sit on the settee, neither of us reached for the light. I was suddenly aware of myself and of the display I'd just made to him. It could be blamed on panic: being young, in someone else's country, being worried about my friend although in truth I had forgotten to think about her. I sat alone on an easy chair facing him.

There had been bleeding, he told me, but both were all right, the baby's heartbeat strong. She was to stay in hospital and rest for a few days while they monitored it all. Maybe the placenta was low? In which case it'd be a caesarean, I remembered, from all that reading we'd done together. Then she'd be in hospital a long time, really need help when she came out.

As if he'd been reading my thoughts he began again. He would phone Sylvie. I could go there. It wasn't right for us to be alone in the house, it would compromise me, he tried to explain. How right he was to know we needed a chaperone. The listlessness seemed to creep up on me again while I watched him take the phone and talk animatedly to whomever, I suppose it was Sylvie's Algerian husband. It wasn't French they were speaking. Talking in French I'd noticed always necessitated a certain amount of hand gesture, but Algerian even more so. The movements were different, though, being smoother, involving more opening and closing of the hand, 'cat-stroking' I thought of it. He put the phone down.

"No luck?" I asked in French. He shook his head. "Sylvie is not here for some days."

"We have to have a chaperone?"

"Mais bien sur," he said, but he didn't seem surprised at my question; in fact he was smiling slightly.

I thought again how I liked men this age, their bodies properly grown and powerful, but young enough still to look boyish when they smiled. I heard myself sigh. He frowned. "You want food? We eat, perhaps?" I nodded and went to put on the light. But tonight was full of surprises. He gestured for me to sit down, and I did, in the seat he'd just left. It was still warm, and I burrowed into it, trying to hide my gluttony towards him and everything he touched. He cooked for us, seeming easier in front of me, physically less formal than usual. I'd seldom seen him in the kitchen before, even to wash up or clear away, but there was nothing of the vague or clueless about him. His movements were deft, and he obviously knew just where to find everything he needed and what to do with it all. Outside the long windows the sky was very dark, the navy-black dark of first night, before stars or moon have come to mitigate it. At last I thought of her, Miranda, alone and perhaps thinking of me.

"Shall we see her tonight?" I asked ...

"No, she rests tonight. Tomorrow we go." He stopped for a moment and looked at me. "Sylvie is away. We must send you somewhere for tonight. For the other nights. Have you friends in the other women, perhaps one of the other women?"

"Not really. I suppose it might me good for me to go to A&B. There's their new baby. I could pick up some hints."

He frowned slightly and continued chopping some vegetable. Why had I suggested them? The three of us, the husband and the new baby, interesting.

"You don't seem very keen," I said. That drugged up, luxurious feeling I'd had in his arms had receded, and I was feeling a bit more normal. "Don't you like Salah, then? I asked.

"I don't know him. I don't really understand their ways. They are from a different part"

"D'you mean the plural marriage?" He was silent. Perhaps I'd gone too far.

"Who it is doesn't matter, but you must go. It is bad for us." I watched him bending to prepare the food, some of the dark, waxy curls entwined with grey.

I was playing a dangerous game, I thought suddenly, but the knowledge gave me a stab in the gut that was more thrill than fear.

"I phone Salah now, after the meal," he said. It was no use me arguing I was one of the family now. We both knew the truth, and if I carried on behaving so overtly, I was in danger of being chucked out and sent back to England, not even being allowed to stay and help with the baby when Miranda did come back. Something I suddenly didn't want.

I excused myself and went into the bathroom. It seemed silly to lock the door with only the two of us. Anyway, it was wishful thinking.

I looked at myself in the mirror for a long time. The eczema had come back with a vengeance, but I'd somehow got over the habit of picking it. It was at times like these that it had come in handy, like some kids razor at their wrists or others smoked, I suppose. I looked at every part of my face in turn, in order. The nose, though not small, was straight and shapely. The chin and jaw curved and angled like a woman's should be. Cheek bones quite high, a lovely sweep from the temple to the cheek. My forehead was clear and broad, the neck long and the lips, though not full, carved and defined as though with an artificial liner. There was even a slight upward curl at the corners. But the eyes were the best. I realised, for the first time, I had one of those faces that seemed to grow into itself. I'd never been a pretty little girl or a Lolita, but now some sense of shape was beginning to win through. I assessed the eyes, as though they belonged to someone else. Long eyes, proper almond-shaped eyes, dark grey with a hint of blue, of green. I'd been so lucky in the genetics lottery too; instead of the pale lashes, I'd got dark ones with my auburn hair.

"And today we have naming of parts." Each was lovely, but

together, I thought, they just don't do it. Like Frankenstein's monster, I was a collection of separate perfections that just didn't work together.

"Food, Susie." I loved him call my name. Was I mad! I knew what it was to have a crush. It was inevitable really. Miranda and I had always shared sex; she meant sex for me. She'd even loaned the boyfriend/cousin to me, or at least intended to. So here I was, trapped in a goldfish bowl, like a fish out of water, like a cold fish (I almost laughed). Up front for the first time with a real man and stuck in the middle of a passionate new marriage. Of course I had a crush on him! He was everything that was mysterious, everything unfamiliar and fascinating. This was a hothouse, with me having trapped myself in a strange country where I didn't even speak the language very well, let alone have the faintest clue how to behave in front of Muslim Algerians. Everywhere I went with them the modesty customs made me think of sex, sex, sex. Every time they separated us from the men, I lusted after them. Every glimpse of virtuous Muslim ankle had more clout than 'Emmanuelle in Soho' for this impressionable English girl. I laughed. I was living in a fantasy land, my own live movie, with myself as the tortured heroine and the hormones thick as amniotic fluid.

A slight tap on the door, time enough to turn on the water fast and pretend I was rinsing my hands,

"You okay, Susie?"

"Fine. Out now."

He was only a crush, and he was Miranda's husband. I didn't have to have everything that was hers! Anyway he was a religious man and though all this plural marriage business was titillating, and I was obviously developing an unhealthy interest, once away from here I'd be all right and have great tales to tell that'd keep me popular at parties for years to come.

Our table was set with food, and we sat at right angles to one another so, mercifully, it wasn't necessary to look him in the eye.

I loved the way he ate; loved the way he rested one bare forearm along the table top as he used fork, spoon.

"I'll give Salah a ring after food,' he said.

Yes, that would be best, I knew.

It felt so strange to be alone with Omar. I was sensitive of where he was every moment, as though some charged wire connected us. I packed a small case of Miranda's with my stuff, and we left the flat, me feeling like a child being packed off to her grandparents for safe keeping. We walked the short journey to their apartment, the night sounds of the street mixing with the more localised sensations: smells of cooking, shouting, television, music; as we passed an open window, an opening door. He carried my case as though it weighed nothing, as I had carried the small vanity case that held my ballet shoes so many years ago.

They lived on the ground floor of one of the older blocks, newer immigrants I supposed getting the worse deal, but there was more privacy to be had right at the bottom or the top. Only other people on three sides.

'A' answered the door. She seemed to occupy a 'front of house' role in the family: she was 'stranger-liaison' officer. We went inside the flat, which smelt very strong, though not unpleasant. It was cool, again an advantage of being at the bottom perhaps. Salah and Omar shook hands, well, not in the British sense, it was more a firm holding of hands whilst 'A' took my case and smiled for me to follow her to the bedroom. Mine was the box room again, the exact parallel of the one I had in Omar's flat. There was evidence of it having been hastily vacated in the pile of dirty bed linen outside the door; a full bin on the threshold. As I stood in the doorway, she quickly scooped some male grooming products from the small chest of drawers. This was interesting. Each of them must have their own room then. Did he go creeping about in the middle of the night, the women waiting (with anticipation, or trepidation?) to see if it was their turn? Or was there a rota stuck to the fridge?

CHAPTER TWENTY-ONE

THE PHONE CALL CAME in the middle of the night. 'A' answered it. I heard her voice murmuring in the passage way, and I knew immediately. I'd only been partially asleep, 'shallow grave' sleep my mum called it, in their house where I was alert to every noise, waiting to hear how they arranged this thing between themselves. There had been no night-time sluicing, and I would have heard, being next to the bathroom again.

She tapped lightly on the door, but I was already up and getting dressed. "I'll make you coffee," she whispered. Her French was excellent. Miranda'd said she'd been to university and everything, was really quite Westernised. So what had made her marry her devout husband and agree to a plural marriage?

There was no time to drink the coffee. The flats were silent. All the day shift asleep, the night shift at work. All the babies between feeds, all the cats put out and all the dogs in bed (not that there were many dogs around this area, Muslims didn't like them).

This was an adventure for us; well for me. Omar's face was closed as we hurried down the corridors and stairs, avoiding the lifts because they were noisy and also, perhaps, because we wanted to keep busy, keep moving.

We took the car, saying little. It was almost as if we were a normal couple; no one would have known that we weren't husband and wife. Scenes were playing and playing on my mind, Westerns mostly, where women under patch-work quilts screamed and screamed, their men helpless at the foot of the bed, miserably twisting their Stetsons in their hands while the tumble-weed rolled about in the storm outside.

Scenes in Elizabethan mansions where old crones shook their heads and boiled endless water. The Doctor arriving on his horse, asking the handsome, rugged father, "Save the mother or the child?" Pale, beautiful, haemorrhaging women, their long dark hair matted with sweat, lying in white linen sheets. All these lucky women in the greatest drama of their lives. Strange, but not once on that journey to the hospital did I see a vision of a woman, healthy and strong, crouching down and heaving out a baby, or even see a birth trolley surrounded by leaning figures masked in green.

And still we had not really spoken, even after parking the car and entering the hospital foyer. He took my arm and led me down strange corridors lit by neon. For a moment I didn't understand that we weren't going to the ward but the birthing suite. We didn't pass anyone in all the hundreds of yards of corridors. Surely there was some nearer car park we'd just missed?

Eventually we went through some double doors and into the delivery wing. At last some sound, someone. "Fatima ...?" he asked of the nurse in the doorway. She smiled, rather serenely I felt in the circumstances, and gestured for us to follow her. We could see bright lights and hear noises behind a glass door. Omar hesitated, but the nurse held it open for us, seemed insistent; we went inside.

There were three people; one was Miranda, smiling wanly from a narrow bed. I hung back as Omar went to her and held her hand. A shadow crossed her face, and she clenched her teeth, arching her back slightly, then, as quickly as it had come, the shadow passed. For a moment, a long, long moment, they were together, he leaning over her, masking her face, her neck stretched up and back, she listening to him. Then he turned and gestured for me to come. Again came the grimace and attention of pain upon her, and she screwed up her face in a gargoyle's smile and turned away. He took my hand and closed it in a fist around Miranda's arm, hovering over her until the convulsion passed. Then, with a slow kiss for his wife, he left us as they had planned.

What was so unexpected for me were the times of absolute calm between the contractions. In these, increasingly close together, she would be talking perfectly normally, tired but normal; then the pain would come again and she'd turn away, disappear from everything. As they got stronger and more frequent, I felt more and more useless and hopeless. Omar was not going to be there. Though it was the trendy thing for fathers to do now, it still wasn't the Muslim way. I admired him for it. I wished there was something to get me out of there, out of that hot room, where time had gone warped and strange; out of someone else's melodrama. I knew now more than ever that I was the spare part. That crawling, eating thing that is jealousy was festering like a physical, squirming sensation in the gut. It was so strong I could even recognize it as I felt it. But what was I jealous of? Take your pick. Her and the huge thing that was happening to her; the kid who would be so loved, so feted (how could I ever compete for her attention again?); him and her making this thing together?

Miranda's groans had turned to roars now, and she was crouching on her knees on the trolley most of the time, gripping onto the bars at one end. The nightdress/birth-robe had come loose and gaped open at the back but nobody seemed to care. The midwives (and there had been two shifts since I'd been there) seemed to be leaving most of it to me: the little sips of water, the cold flannels – where was the boiled water? I tried to avoid going near her for long as she grabbed me, sometimes by the hips, sometimes hauling on my arms, clenching down.

For some reason the pain was in her back as well, and a male nurse who'd happened to wander in – surely against all protocol for a Muslim birth? – showed me how to grind into the hollow of her back with my fist. I did so, again and again, and she grunted for more and harder, so hard that I thought I would injure her, so hard it hurt me. It went on and on all day. Someone brought me a cup of tea. At last someone suggested I go and get a sandwich.

The father's room was empty of Omar, and I found a sandwich, more tea – my kingdom for a proper cup of British tea at a time like this, for God's sake! – and some sickly French chocolate. All chocolate bars here seemed to have children in mind. Where were the adult addicts of France? People busied themselves in the hospital foyer, while I sat at a small metal table and ate. No one knew of course what I was going through, had still to face. I had lost nearly a day of my life in that white room.

With dread I girded my loins and retraced my steps. Still no proud father-to-be in the waiting room. Before I opened the door to go in, I hesitated, took some breaths. All seemed quiet.

The scene that greeted me was quite different from the one I'd left half an hour before. Miranda was down, breathing heavily like a lassoed steer, a figure bending between her open legs, arm invisible, masked face angled away from her, the better to concentrate on what it was feeling. The midwife ushered me in with a gesture. The man's voice was talking quietly, keeping up a steady commentary, but it was too quiet, too muffled and too French for me to make it out.

Taking me aside the midwife filled me in, slowly in French.

"The baby, wrong way. Big baby. Still not open. Will be a long time. Everything is alright but she has had a 'pethedine' for the long wait. She will be calmer, not so tired when the pushing comes." Yes, and a relief from the constant baying for you too, I thought.

As a contraction hit her Miranda writhed and groaned, and the Doctor pulled his arm away, holding the gloved hand up at eye level. I was surprised to see no blood on it. He eased down his mask with his gowned arm and somehow managed to communicate to me via mime that he would shake my English hand if only he didn't have Miranda's vaginal secretion on it. I gestured back that I thought it was oh so amusing, and that he was to consider his hand as good as shaken anyway. He then spoke cheerfully and vigorously with the midwife and left.

I tiptoed towards the head end. Her face was turned away and her damp hair was sticking to her. She looked very white and tired lying there, and suddenly the birth picture seemed at last to be familiar. I gently moved her hair away from her face; she opened her eyes and managed a weak, Jane Seymour smile.

"Okay, Love?" I said. She nodded.

The midwife came, and together we tried to prop her up on her pillows. I put the straw from a carton of fruit juice against her lips, and she sucked on it a little, but it was a different woman now the drug was working. I stood back. At last here was the picture I'd expected to see: a pale woman, exhausted, hair spread like a mermaid's on the pillow of a white bed. No flesh was showing; the gown was closed from the front. Only her long calves poked out the bottom.

The contractions seemed to be coming every couple of minutes, but she only groaned to herself, her face a distortion. She was locked away in the pain now. I held her hand willingly, but she no longer squeezed on it. Instead I could feel her body clench in the waves of pain, her fingers opening straight and taut, like she was being electrocuted.

It was growing dark beyond the window when they came again to examine her, hardly finding time between her contractions. They looked pleased; the midwife turned to me, "Come, we get her up and push."

"Already?"

"Yes, she is there now, she must do eet."

We heaved her up and onto all fours, but she didn't seem to want to push. I whispered to her in English what the midwife had just said, and she seemed to understand, I think the pethedine was wearing off, but still no pushing.

The woman got her down off the bed, and we slowly walked her around, now the contractions began to change. She went heavy between us, seeming to sink down, her face going red, not a grimace like before but something more conscious and striving.

"Good. Good girl!" said the midwife, and we leaned her against the bed, where she bent over, the gown hanging open now, one of only two ties having come loose whilst she was tossing and turning on the bed.

Her legs splayed, her huge bottom taut and quivering by turns, she strained and pushed in a half-standing position, the midwife occasionally bending down to peer between her legs.

It was grown dark outside, and I felt insane, like nothing could ever be the same again. Miranda's teeth were clenched, and a growling noise, so regular and repetitive it seemed mechanical, came from her body. She was straining down in what I recognized was a gesture of supreme constipation. At one point the midwife tried to move her to lie on the bed, but she seemed so unreasonably distressed to be on her back that we let her crouch up again, this time on all fours. The midwife manoeuvred her so that her back end was facing away from the bedstead, and I watched as the hole bulged and strained, again and again.

"It's stuck! It's not coming out, for Christ's sake do something!" I felt beside myself, but the midwife didn't seem unduly concerned. At one point the same Doctor put his head round the door, but the midwife gestured him away, quite complacent. Once she even pushed against the bulge with a flattened, gloved palm, as if to push the baby in, not urge it out at all, and I wanted to scream under the flickering fluorescent lights. Miranda seemed to be tiring, though, holding onto the bars of the bed-head again, even the sound effects mercifully weakened.

"I think Madam's tiring. It is a big little one, who doesn't want to come out does he? Come on, do me a few nice good big pushes."

But it didn't seem to be working. The bulge wasn't even coming out as far as it had done. I pictured a baby on the end of a rubber spring, dipping down and bonging back up.

"Right then, I think we've all had enough. Let's give this baby some help."

"What do you mean."

"A little cut; help him out."

For the first time I felt faint. I went to sit by the head. Suddenly there were three or four staff in the room, arranging Miranda and laying out equipment on a trolley that had suddenly appeared. I could tell there would be a lot of blood from the number of green cloths that were being laid under her buttocks.

"Why me?" I thought. How the hell did I get myself into this! Couldn't I think of anything better to do with my holidays? Presumably there was an injection for the pain; presumably the horribly stretched skin was cut and parted like an unripe apple under a sharp knife. I didn't see, but Miranda made no special noise. There was only activity, the staff talking and suddenly a sea-change of atmosphere (was it the tone of the voices or some specific sound). The word, "baby" entered the room. There was no sound of a slap, wail or cry, but I was watching Miranda's face when they brought the bloody bundle towards her, and on it was an expression I've never seen. She held her baby, placed there gently by an unfamiliar nurse like it was a precious egg, and I watched. There was still a lot of activity around her back end, the Doctor being by now down there too, but she didn't seem concerned.

The midwife asked me to go and tell the father and fetch him in whilst she 'finished off'. I left Miranda, who did not even glance up once. After everything I'd done!

He was there, leaning against the back wall, facing the door as I opened it. He seemed to know and smiled. I must have crossed the room quick. Suddenly I was in his arms and up against that chest I'd looked at for so long, the chest that was a little like Oliver Reed's, and crying. Sobbing would be more accurate, keening would be the most honest of all. He just held me, even though his baby was waiting (was it a boy or girl? I hadn't taken it in). Eventually I shuddered to a stop, and he moved away from me and to the door. I didn't follow. Why should I have needed to? I had his grateful face; the condescending/indulgent faces of the staff; Miranda's tired, Madonna face, already and forever in my mind's eye.

I sat on a vinyl chair, exhausted as if it had been me who'd given birth, but without any of the high, without any of the credit. It seemed a long time, sitting there, and I'd dozed off, dimly aware of unhurried activity passing and re-passing beyond the heavy door. Eventually it opened, and Omar stood there, his hand outstretched.

He held me as we found the lift, thanking me, his hand on

my skinny ribs, just underneath my breast. "You have been so wonderful for Fatima." As the lift doors opened and we walked through the ward corridors where she'd been moved to recover, he moved away slightly with every step so that, as we reached the doorway of her room, we were again apart.

She was sitting up in bed eating toast and drinking tea as if nothing had happened. Somehow she'd managed to charm a nurse into making her a cup of proper, English tea. Her hair was arranged carefully over the pillow, the way she liked it to be, and apart from looking a little white, she was beautiful.

With a shock I realised I hadn't really met the baby, didn't even know whether it was a boy or girl.

"The baby?" I heard myself say. Omar fetched it from a plastic fish tank at the bottom of the bed,

"Our son," he said, holding the child high by its bottom and its head like Kunta Kinte's dad in *Roots*. There is something so powerful about a man holding a young baby. He looks so big, so masculine and the child's feeble grace is brought into relief too: 'The lion lies down with the lamb'. He handed the tight bundle to me, all wrapped up in a white, brushed-cotton sheet, and I held my arms in the position a woman is supposed to do, holding his head in the crook of my arm. But I felt nothing. He was heavy, and, though sleeping, full of movement like a cat in a bag. I bent over him, and the smell was like nothing I'd ever smelt before. There were no metaphors, no similes to be found. I picked him up under the arm pits and put him on my shoulder where the hot smell seemed to intensify, coming particularly from the furry hollow at the base of his skull. I looked up and caught Miranda's eye. She was wearing that same maddening Madonna smile again; as if she owned him, but she didn't. No one owns another human being, not even a mother. If he was to be taken away right now, he would never know her, and if he never knew it had been done, never miss her. I didn't believe any of this sacred mother crap.

He snuffled and stirred on my shoulder, and gingerly I sat down on the bed. She put out her long arms for him, and I gave him over to her where he lay, tucked in under the breast. He looked quite small on her, yet it seemed impossible to imagine him being folded and scrunched up in the birth canal only an hour before.

None of us was saying anything.

"Have you fed him yet?" I asked, suddenly.

"Oh yes, in the delivery room. He's a good little feeder."

"What about the naming?"

"We'll do that later. He'll have his head shaved of his baby hair, have it weighed and the money given to charity."

"Oh yes, I remember."

Though it was still night, there was quite a bit of activity in the corridor beyond our room. I saw several women pass, one woman bent double, like an old lady with osteoporosis of the spine, hand pressed cradling her loose abdomen. I must have looked a bit horrified, because Miranda said in a stage whisper,

"Caesarean. Sylvie told me you can tell what sort of birth the women have by the way they move afterwards. Caesarean's are bent over, hardly breathing and trying to hold it all in with their hands. They can't stand up because they feel it'll rip their stitches, apparently, and the episiotomy girls like me sort of shuffle along, trying not to open their legs too wide and carrying their cushions with them."

"Did it hurt very much, the episiotomy?"

"No, actually. I don't know why, but I don't really remember it being done or the stitches. It hurts now, though, and I'm dreading having a wee."

I shuddered. Miranda yawned, and I saw a look of concern pass across Omar's face.

"We will go now, my darling."

"No, don't go, there's no need."

"You must rest."

"Aren't you going to phone people, tell them the news?"

"It's too late, my love. I'll tell everyone in the morning."

"What time is it then?"

"Nearly half three."

She looked incredulous and laughed, "Doesn't time fly when you're enjoying yourself!"

I kissed her and she patted my back with her free hand; then I kissed the sleeping cheek of her little boy, so cool, plump and clammy. I left them to say goodbye together.

The nurses were chatting away in the nurses' station. Though by now Miranda and Omar's familiar voices in French were no challenge to me (in fact, for long periods of time I would have difficulty saying whether things had been in English or French), strangers speaking, particularly if there was background noise or I was tired, were still hard to understand. I stood like a spare part, but eventually Omar came out to me. He smiled quietly, and we walked away, every footstep making me feel better.

In the lift I studied the wooden button of his shirt, looked at the dark hair escaping at the collar, promising so much. I felt him looking at me too, as we walked the last few corridors on the ground floor. I could hardly move myself forward, had to think about every step, and stood by the double doors waiting for him to bring the car around, swaying like a dying tulip.

I got in next to him. "I don't want to go back to Salah. I

want to stay with you." So bald a statement; nothing hidden, but I suppose, after what I'd seen over the last 24 hours, there was nothing to lose.

"It is too late for us to go there now. We go home."

He drove slowly, for him, and I let my head rest on his sleeve, my hands holding around his arm. I knew I was like a love-sick woman in a B movie, but everything he did made me feel like a cliché. I had no excuses: I knew he was someone else's and a Muslim; I knew it was wrong, but knew it somewhere so insignificant, in such a small and silent place, that I didn't care.

We picked up takeaway, Persian, Moroccan, I don't remember. I watched him through the steamy window of the shop, not too smitten not to be aware of how each movement of his fascinated me; not too far gone to realise the idiocy of my sitting there waiting for him to come out again, so proud to pretend he was mine.

We parked, not bothering to put the car away. Who cared if some right-wing 'whities' graffittied it. His first son had just been born, and I cared for nothing. We walked across the empty square towards our block. He held me again on his left, his hand under my heart, and I could feel him all the length of my right side. He'd changed towards me, would never have risked our reputation, his dignity in public before. We took the stairs to make no noise in the silence. He unlocked the door, we entered, and as I stood there in the semi-dark he put on his music, that special pipe, weaving figures of eight in the air...

CHAPTER TWENTY-TWO

THAT NEXT DAY THE noise of the hospital hurt me. Omar had guided me gently through the corridors, his hand on the soft skin above my elbow. "Tell me how to do this!" I was pleading inside, but I said nothing.

Miranda looked tired, her long hair untidy on the pillow. I kissed her, and she asked questions; what had we eaten; had I slept well? I answered, then went to lean over the baby. He was asleep, his big feet flexed against the cot sides. Omar looked at him and chuckled.

They spoke together in French. Omar fetched a chair for me and placed it behind my legs; I sat. Though I looked and looked, I could see nothing different in him towards Miranda, no sign of awkwardness or guilt. The only difference was the way he looked right at me now, as though he was fond. A tender look, a knowing half-smile. Was he remembering how I'd begged for him? I wanted him now; wanted to sit on his knee, legs each side of him, my arms around his back under his arms; to grind and grind on him.

He asked me in French if I wanted a cool drink, and I nodded.

He left us then. Miranda gestured for me, and I went to sit on her bed. She reached out her arm, and soon I was cuddled into her. Who was comforting whom? Surely she must know, and surely. I hardly dared to look the thought in the face. If she did know, she must mind! Didn't I reek of her husband?

The getting her ready; the journey, both passed in a fog, myself and the baby sitting in the back seat. I looked at her head, at his, as they sat together in the front. Once outside the flat, she made him put down the car seat. Slowly she bent down and undid the sleeping baby, bringing him up to nestle gently into her shoulder blade. I noticed how she didn't hold him to her shoulder as other mothers did, but lower, as if worried he would see something behind her that he shouldn't. Omar kissed her; kissed the baby on his fluffy head and opened the door to the flat. Light poured into the dingy corridor, and we shuffled inside, each negotiating the narrow hallway carefully with the luggage we were carrying.

Miranda sat down on the settee, the baby beside her, and carefully Omar reached down and took off her headgear. I could not bear to watch.

He put on the record, the same undulating pipe music from before and went to make tea. Miranda put out her hand to me, and, reluctantly, I went to sit beside them. Now the baby was lying on his back, snuggled into the crook of her arm. He was a big, strong child, but next to her he seemed small.

"It's so wonderful to be home with you all," she said. I wanted to cry. Two days ago they had been a couple, well, two very different people, man and woman married together. I had been a visitor. Miranda and I had been a couple from so long before; Omar and I had been together in both loving Miranda, being needed by her. Now everything was different. Miranda and Omar shared a being who had not and could never have anything to do with me: one triangle.

This child would be everything to her in a way I could only faintly understand. Omar shared the child, therefore he shared her in a way I never could.

And Omar and me? That was a bruise I couldn't even look at.

Would I ever be able to touch it?

"What's the matter, love?" she asked.

"I want to go home."

"Oh, no, not yet! There's nothing to go back for. Stay here for a few weeks 'til I get used to the baby. Take a year out. Stay until Christmas; come and live with us, even."

I looked through to the kitchen, involuntarily, just quick, but Miranda was astute,

"Omar won't mind. He grew up in a household with all sorts of women around, an extended family. He'll have to go back to work after the weekend and it'll be good for me to have company. We could go shopping together, the mosque. It's good for women to be with other women."

"No," I said, "it wouldn't work out."

"It would. Listen… Omar!" she called through.

"Mais certainement…" he replied.

"It'd be too complicated. It wouldn't work out, and you're never going to convert me to being religious, so don't even try!" She looked surprised, and the baby stirred lightly in her arms.

"What have you got to go back for? You could learn French and teach English here. You'd be way in demand. They probably wouldn't even bother that you're not qualified, if you went to a private language school. Think about it; don't just go."

"Stop trying to control me!" I shouted, ashamed as Omar came in with the tea; handed it to me making none of the careful effort he used to do not to touch even my hand.

They were both looking at me earnestly. In him no trace of guilt; in her no suspicion or pain. "I need the loo," I said. I closed and locked the door and sat on the floor hugging my knees with my arms. I sobbed, coughed and out of me gulped moisture, him, soaking into my pants. For a moment my chest was so tight with shock I could hardly breathe. I could be pregnant! A spasm of fear shivered through me that betrayed me at last in a tingle of delight. But then I wasn't his wife! How could he square this with his religion? How could I have him when he belonged to Miranda? How could he come and fetch me and our baby home from the hospital like this? But, oh, the thought of him coming to me again and again; squeezing my massive milky breasts, sucking on them! I moaned out loud and quickly shoved a hand over my mouth. I pinched my nipples hard between my fingers like he'd done: hard, so they hurt; so hard that I'd cried out, but not for him to stop. It had only been the once; pregnancy probably wouldn't happen. Anyway, even if he'd have me; even if Miranda'd accept me as second wife, how could I ever share him?

I sat, head resting on my knees for a long time in a sort of doze, woken at last by the sound of feet in the passageway, making their way to the bedroom. I washed my hands, flushed the loo and opened the door.

"Hello, Petal. We're just on our way for a feed. Come and keep me company."

I followed her into the room. The bed was unmade, and she put the baby on the duvet while she propped up the cushions. She moved slowly and with exaggerated care and I remembered her episiotomy with a shudder. I was still bruised and tender between the legs from her husband. How much greater must her pain be?

She settled herself against the cushions, and I passed her the baby, holding him underneath his neck and bottom. He was top heavy and lolled dangerously, the navy eyes looking at me and past me at the same time.

She had undone her blouse, and I saw, as if for the first time, her huge breast. She smiled. "Feel it" she said, gesturing. I lowered the baby into her arms and reached out my hand, gently prodding the hard, mottled skin. She took my hand in hers and put it around the breast. It was hot and taut, so full it almost throbbed. I moved away and sat on the end of the bed.

"Look," she said and squeezed. Out of the centre a thin jet of pale liquid. It went so far! She laughed and, lifting the baby, turned him towards her. His head nodded crazily, butting at her, and he made little wailing sounds for a moment, then was still. I could see the muscles of his jaw working.

She settled back on the pillows.

We talked about my life: options, possibilities. All the time my eyes were drawn to the child feeding, the breast. Soon he slowed, and his head sunk backwards on her arm, the eyes closed, the thin milk dribbling from the corner of his mouth. She put him down and pulled up the flap of her bra, positioning a pad there. As we talked, more quietly now so as not to wake her sleeping son, she picked up one of the pillows from the other side of the bed, picked fluff from the brushed cotton as we spoke. For a moment she was silent, suspended mid-sentence, as she picked up a long red hair, looked puzzled. Then another. She held it up to the window to examine it with her long-sighted eyes. Then she looked at me...

I heard Omar call. Heard his footsteps in the corridor, a tap on wood, "I come in?"

"Oui," said Miranda.

She looked again at the hair and let it go, dropping her hand over the side of the bed and lightly rubbing her thumb and two fingers together.

My back was to the door, my eyes cast down in shock, so if there was a look that passed between them I didn't see it. I felt the mattress dip as he sat on the bed beside me, took my hand, a gesture that should have stopped my heart.

"How are you?"

He spoke gently in French. I daren't look up. "All right," I said.

"You will stay?" he asked. "Help with the baby; be with Fatima? A woman needs other women after a baby?" I nodded, smiled as well as I could manage and nodded from behind my hair. "Fatima does not have her mother or anyone from England. She does not have my mother. You want this, Fatima?"

The baby stirred, making small sucking noises in his sleep. Still I could not look up, could not speak. Every muscle was concentrated upon holding myself away from his body which called me, pulled on me.

She reached for my other hand and I was in a motionless tug of war. Her hand, dry and cool, held firm. His was hot, had folded mine up in a fist.

Perhaps lightning passed between them in the space above my head; perhaps there was the growl of thunder as the mechanism of my life groaned a little, rollers and cogs slowly beginning to move; but, as I held my breath, no sound entered the small, metal window from the street below.

I willed it. Silently, the words a mantra, "Say yes, yes!"

It was a maddening tableau that lasted, oh, so long.

"You must change your name," she said, at last. "Perhaps…"

I looked up then at Omar, saw a slight frown cross his face.

"…Rachel," she said, and though my own nails, digging into my palms as he squeezed his closed fist down on my knuckles hurt me, I never said.

"Rachel, yes, in the Old Book, yes," his face opened in recognition. He laughed.

I felt the charge fly at last across, from one pillar to the other, and as the arch was found between them, triumphant, I raised my head.

AUTHOR BIOGRAPHY

This is Jane Blank's first novel though she has had work published in several genres. Poems have appeared in *Planet, Poetry Wales* etc; many anthologies from different publishers, and *The Observer Magazine*. In 2003 she had a solo collection, *Naked Playing the Cello* published by specialist poetry press The Collective.

More recently she has had autobiographical writing published by Honno in their award-winning collection *Laughing, not Laughing,* and 'flash fiction' stories last year in a collection edited by the University of Glamorgan.

Other publication includes reviews and articles in various magazines, from *New Welsh Review* to the *Communications Network Journal,* whilst her work has been discussed in *Poetry Quarterly Review, The Big Issue, The Western Mail* and *The Independent,* amongst others.

She lives in South Wales, teaching English and Drama in a Welsh Language secondary school and freelancing in theatre and as a tutor, running courses on Shakespeare, creative writing and literature. She is currently working for The Hill College in Abergavenny.

She enjoys walking her dog on the hills, playing her cello and drinking in the pub with friends.

REVIEWS

'Irrepressible Susie and irresistible Miranda are the oddest couple in school, unrelenting in their quest for the good things in life – music, dancing, laughs, and especially boys. It is typically weird when Susie and Miranda graduate from boys to men and both become involved with the gorgeous French-Algerian Omar. This is the funniest, sexiest novel I've read in a long time. It is also a serious, truthful book about how strange we are when we're growing up.'

Norman Schwenk

'I have known Jane and her work for many years, watching her poetry grow in stature and confidence. She is a natural born writer. Now, with this first novel, she is taking another step forward. Leaning lightly on her experience, her world-view and her uncompromising commitment to telling the truth, she will not put a foot wrong.'

Ann Drysdale

REVIEWS OF PREVIOUS WORK

From a review of the anthology *Private People*. 'Best for me was Jane Blank's (poem): A sassy, expressionist piece that left the rest for dead.'
Steve Davies, for *PQR Magazine*

On the anthology, *Of Sawn Grain*: 'I like particularly the quirky eroticism of 'Fly On The Wall' by Jane Blank.
Ifor Thomas, for *The New Welsh Review*

On Jane's first solo collection, *Naked Playing the Cello,* critic for The Welsh Arts Council: 'Deep and even violent emotions are projected onto the external world … brilliantly handled …there is a distinct poetic sensibility at work here. It is one of the most exciting typescripts I have read…'

Also on Jane's collection, 'This is live poetry; provocative, sensual, aware: it is strong and it is moving.'
Chris Torrance

We publish a wide range of contemporary fiction and books of Welsh interest. For a full list of books in print, why not order our new, free Catalogue? Or alternatively you may surf into our website:

www.ylolfa.com

where you may order books on-line.

TALYBONT CEREDIGION CYMRU SY24 5AP
email ylolfa@ylolfa.com
website www.ylolfa.com
tel 01970 832 304
fax 832 782